Eliza and the Alchemist

Eliza
and the
Alchemist

Carlos Lacámara

Eliza and the Alchemist
Published by Fixed Mark Productions, Inc

Copyright © 2023 by Carlos Lacámara. All rights reserved.

No part of this book may be reproduced in any form or by any mechanical means, including information storage and retrieval systems without permission in writing from the publisher/author, except by a reviewer
who may quote passages in a review.

All images, logos, quotes, and trademarks included in this book are subject to use according to trademark and copyright laws of the United States of America.

ISBN: 979-8-9867427-0-0

Fantasy / Humorous

Cover and interior design by Hudson Valley Book Design,
Copyright owned by Carlos Lacámara

This is a work of fiction. Names, characters, businesses, places, events and incidents are either the products of the author's imagination or used in a fictitious manner. Any resemblance to actual persons, living or dead,
or actual events is purely coincidental.

All rights reserved by Carlos Lacámara and Fixed Mark Productions, Inc
Printed in the United States of America.

With full knowledge and understanding, they offered up their own children, and those who had no children would buy little ones from poor people and cut their throats as if they were so many lambs or young birds; meanwhile the mother stood by without a tear or moan; but should she utter a single moan or let fall a single tear, she had to forfeit the money, and her child was sacrificed nevertheless; and the whole area before the statue was filled with a loud noise of flutes and drums so that the wailing should not reach the ears of the people.
—Plutarch, 110 AD

Living off borrowed time, the clock tick faster.
—MF Doom, 2005 AD

To my father, who taught me to love books and silent movies. And my mother, who taught me the power of unconditional love.

PROLOGUE

WHEN JAIME SAW THE GUN pointed at his face, he thought, *Not again.*

And thinking that really bummed him out 'cause having a big-ass revolver shoved in his face should be a once-in-a-lifetime thing, not a stroll down memory lane. It was all Angel's fault. Jaime should have kicked his ass a long time ago. He'd have done it now, except Angel was on the ground with his brains splattered all over the alley.

Sandy had been right. It was time for a change. Jaime'd been hanging out with Angel since kindergarten, and sure, they'd had some good times and lots of girls and tattoos and shit, but none of that mattered much when he was looking down the barrel of a gun. He was still gangbanging at twenty-three, and he didn't even have a wife or kids, none he was allowed to talk to anyway. Worst of all, he still lived with his mom.

When Sandy had asked him how he envisioned his future, Jaime had no answer, mostly because he didn't know what "envisioned" meant, but also because he always got dizzy when he talked to Sandy. She'd pull her chair up real close, not like the other parole officers who stayed behind their desks writing shit. No, Sandy would look him in the eye like she could really see him and—this was the weird part—she liked what she saw. Jaime certainly liked what *he* saw. Sandy had big blue eyes and these little freckles on her nose, and she didn't wear any stupid lipstick and stuff. She was honest and nice, and she smelled real fresh, like a forest or something. Sandy would have told him to stay away from Angel.

"Twenty thousand *each* in one hour," Angel had said.

"Who we gotta kill?" Jaime had joked, 'cause no way they could make twenty big ones so fast.

"Chango," Angel had said.

Jaime's gut hurt. He didn't want to kill nobody. He just wanted to kick back with a couple six-packs and play some video games, but Angel had reminded him of all the bad stuff Chango had done. Chango was a badass Filero 13 gangbanger. He'd killed one of Jaime's homeboys and shot up his mom's house a couple times, but stuff like that happened all the time in his neighborhood. Jaime didn't take it personally.

"I ain't seen Chango around lately," he'd complained. "Maybe he stopped banging."

"Once a Filero always a Filero," Angel had said.

Jaime couldn't argue with that. Nobody betrayed their homeys; it just didn't happen. Angel had laid out some coke, and the more wasted Jaime got, the more sense Angel made. Someone *had* to bring Chango to justice. Why not them? And, why not get a reward for it, like in the old west, dead or alive, you know?

While Angel talked, Jaime's stomach hurt real bad. Jaime's stomach always hurt before trouble. It was like the violence was a monster in his gut trying to get out. The hurting only stopped after Jaime kicked some ass.

Still, for all the gangbanging Jaime'd done, all the drugs and the fighting, he'd never killed anyone. Everyone figured Jaime'd wasted lots of dudes 'cause he was so big and tatted up, but he hadn't, and he was kind of proud of that. They could lock him up for lots of shit but not for murder, and Jaime wanted to keep it that way.

"I'll do it, 'mano," Angel said. "You don't gotta do nothing but drive."

❧ ☙

Jaime didn't watch Angel do it, but he'd heard it. Angel had texted Chango to meet him in the park. Jaime didn't know how he got Chango's number or what he'd said, and he didn't want to know. All Jaime cared about while he drove down the 10 Freeway that night was his car. Jaime had this teal green '65 Chevy Impala with a lime green interior, which he'd fixed up real nice, and now it had a pinche dead guy in the trunk. Angel had brought some trash bags, but that didn't stop the stink.

"That's our exit, pendejo!" Angel shouted.

Jaime pulled off the freeway onto Boyle Avenue.

"Where we taking him?" Jaime asked.

"To the buyer," Angel had replied.

"Why would anyone want to buy Chango?"

"He didn't ask for Chango *specifically*. He just seemed like a good choice. You know, kill two birds type shit."

"Who is this dude? Why does he want a dead body?"

Angel ignored Jaime and pointed his finger out the window like it was a gun. "Boom, white motherfuckers!" he shouted.

They had just passed this new restaurant called Spoor Gastric Bistro Pub. Jaime had no idea what any of those words meant, but the place was packed with white people eating, drinking, and laughing. Angel hated gabachos coming into the barrio with their art galleries and expensive stores they called "shoppes" and restaurants with names that don't tell you what kind of food they've got inside. Jaime didn't have an opinion on the subject, so he made a mental note to ask Sandy what he should think about it.

Jaime belched.

"Jesus, dude," Angel groaned, waving his hand to blow away the smell.

"Sorry," Jaime said as he pulled a bottle of antacids out of the glove compartment. He flipped it open with his thumb and poured a bunch of tablets into his mouth.

"How can you eat that shit?"

"My stomach hurts."

"Your stomach always hurts."

Jaime belched again.

East Los Angeles was quiet this time of night. It looked like one of them tourist postcards with the downtown lights shining behind all the dark buildings. They drove past their old school, which didn't bring back many good memories, and by El Gordo's house. He was dead—drive-by last year. And Miss Sanchez' house. Jaime loved Miss Sanchez. She used to give him lemonade and pan dulce when he was a kid. She was old back then. She must have been like a thousand now. He loved her house, too. It was old fashioned with white walls and a red-tile roof. Best of all, it didn't have any bars on the windows like all the other houses. No one was going to mess with Miss Sanchez, not in his barrio. Jaime had this recurring memory from when he was real little of playing tag at Miss Sanchez' house with a little girl, must have been her granddaughter or something. Could have been a dream.

"Watch-alé," Angel growled and jerked his head toward six gangbangers drinking beer on the corner. Jaime slowed down to check out their tats. "Eight Street." Angel flipped the safety off his rocket. Jaime pulled up close. They weren't going to shoot them or nothing. That would have been too much mayhem, even for Angel, but they still had to drive by real slow and give them a hard look. It was just the right thing to do. Jaime recognized one of the gangbangers and smiled. The gangbanger smiled back.

"What the fuck you doin', vato?" Angel asked, all angry and shit.

"It's Luis. He was in Mrs. Greenberg's art class," Jaime explained.

"Fuck, man. Now you ruined it. Dale gas. Go."

Jaime drove away.

After crossing the Fourth Street bridge, Jaime turned into a dark street behind a row of warehouses. The Chevy's V-8 throbbed as they cruised down the alley. A fluorescent light flickered on the walls, making the graffiti dance around like a cartoon, not a good cartoon like *Beauty and the Beast*, but like one of those old black-and-white ones that Jaime's grandfather used to watch with cows singing scratchy old songs and smiling like they were fucking insane. Those cartoons scared the hell out Jaime.

"Stop," commanded Angel.

Jaime hit the brakes. There was a man standing in front of the car. He was wearing a black suit and tie, and a *vest*. Dude looked like an undertaker or something, a *Badass* undertaker. Jaime grabbed his gun.

"Chill, homey," Angel said as he stepped out of the car. When Jaime got out, the Badass undertaker dude was gone. Jaime spun around and found him standing behind the car. This guy was slippery.

"Open the trunk," ordered Angel.

"*You* open the trunk," Jaime shot back.

"You got the keys, bro," Angel explained, never taking his eyes off Badass Undertaker Dude.

Jaime grunted and pulled the keys out of the ignition. He gave Badass Undertaker Dude his hardest look as he strutted to the back of the car. He couldn't see the dude's eyes 'cause it was so dark, which made Jaime nervous, so he pulled up his T-shirt to show off his gun. Dude didn't flinch. Even though he was like a foot taller than the dude, Jaime waited for him to step aside before he popped the trunk.

The dude pulled out a little flashlight and shined it down on Chango, who looked like a baby all curled up dead like that. It made Jaime kind of sad.

Then Chango coughed.

"He's not dead," Badass Undertaker Dude said in this low, cool voice.

"Shit." Angel pulled out his pistol and jammed it into Chango's mouth.

"Not in my car, 'mano!"

"A murdered cadaver is of no use to me," said Badass Undertaker Dude.

"Why not?"

"Unless he was killed in self-defense."

"He was."

"Good night, gentlemen." Badass Undertaker Dude turned to leave, but before he'd taken two steps, Angel had pulled his gun. The dude stopped at the sound of the pistol cocking.

"We want our money," Angel said in his super-chill killing voice.

Jaime fumbled to get his gun out, too, so when Badass Undertaker Dude turned around, he had two rockets in his face. The dude sighed like he was bored. "Very well," he said. This guy was way too cool. Jaime belched. His gut was telling him to waste the dude right now.

The dude set his bag on the ground and used his foot to slide it over to Angel. Jaime looked down at the bag. When he looked back up, he saw blood and brains shoot out the back of Angel's head. When he turned back to Badass Undertaker Dude, he was staring into the barrel of the biggest revolver he'd ever seen in his life.

Not again.

Book I:

To Have Loved

Chapter One

Eliza stared into the lizard's cold, angry eyes and thought, *Don't judge me.*

She looked away from the framed photograph of a Galapagos iguana hanging above the fireplace and turned to Ryan, who sat at the other end of the couch talking about dieting or something. This was their third date, and Ryan had not tried to sleep with her yet. She had agreed to go to his apartment after dinner for a glass of wine, which she knew meant sex.

"We waste one third of our food in the west while seven hundred and fifty million people in other places don't have enough to eat," Ryan explained thrusting his index finger in the air. "One out of six children in underdeveloped nations are underweight and..."

He's good-looking, thought Eliza. *Not good-looking exactly.* Eliza put great stock in language. She liked to find the perfect word for every human experience. *Magnificent.* That was the word. With his blue eyes, mop of blonde hair, and casual linen attire, Ryan looked like he had stepped off the cover of *GQ* magazine. *And he's not stupid.* Eliza knew that labeling extremely attractive people as stupid was a form of prejudice, but it was her favorite form of prejudice, and she hated to give it up.

"I just think no child should have to go without soap."

"Yes." Eliza nodded emphatically as if she'd been paying attention. "Children need soap. We all do, really, except maybe Eskimos."

"Eskimos?"

"Yeah, I thought with all the snow— No, I guess they need soap, too."

"They do, and they don't like the term 'Eskimo.' They prefer Innuit or First Peoples."

"Right. Sorry."

"Native communities suffer from all kinds of preventable diseases since the destruction of their traditional lifestyle…"

He likes Eskimos. That's nice. I mean, somebody has to, and he has an amazing apartment for a college student. She noted how the muted earth tones of the furniture drew focus to the brilliant wildlife photography lining the walls. *Maybe he's gay.* Eliza pictured Ryan as her gay best friend. They would discuss art and politics and movies all night long, and then go shopping the next day and make fun of poorly dressed people. *That would be so much fun.* But Ryan wasn't gay. He was straight and nice, and unlike her high school English teacher who spurned her passionate overtures because he was afraid of "getting arrested," Ryan was age appropriate. He was exactly the kind of boyfriend any woman would want. Tonight would seal the deal, and Eliza would finally have sex. She hadn't told Ryan that she'd never done it before. She didn't know any other nineteen-year-old virgins, and she didn't want him to think she had weird emotional issues, which she did, of course. Who didn't?

"Mostly they need clean water."

"Yes. Innuits need water," Eliza jumped in.

Ryan gave her a pained smile. "I'm talking too much, aren't I?"

"No, no," she assured him.

"It's just… I've lived a privileged life, and I feel it's my responsibility to help those less fortunate than me."

He's a much better person than I am, she thought to herself, but to him she said, "I feel the same way."

He brushed against her as he reached for the wine bottle. She flinched and chastised herself for it. *Relax.* He refilled their glasses and gave her an inviting smile as he took a leisurely sip.

She gulped down half her glass.

"So Braunmuller's a pro-slavery Nazi bigot?" he commented with a twinkle in his eye.

"Huh?" Eliza asked, taken off guard. Then she remembered. "In class?"

"Yeah."

"I didn't say he was a pro-slavery Nazi bigot," Eliza replied, relieved by the distraction. "I said he was *like* a pro-slavery Nazi bigot."

"I don't think he appreciated the difference," he quipped.

"That's his problem." Eliza shrugged, downing the rest of her wine. "*Taming of the Shrew* is not a feminist play about how men should be ashamed of mistreating women. No matter how much we all love Shakespeare, he wrote a play that says women should be broken like horses to make good wives. I'm sorry. That's what it says, and no amount of wishful thinking or mental gymnastics is ever going to change that. It's not like Shakespeare can rewrite it. He's been dead for five hundred years, and that's my point. Shakespeare was a product of his time. Morality was different back then."

Ryan knitted his brow playfully. "And that makes Braunmuller like a Nazi how?"

"Because when he reinvents *Taming of the Shrew*, he's rewriting history to fit his personal ideology, just like Southern whites did when they said the Civil War wasn't really about slavery, and the Nazis did with all their master race crap. Braunmuller should know better. He's a UCLA professor for Christ's sake. I didn't want to make a scene, but somebody had to set him straight."

"You stand up for yourself. I love that. Like when you sent back the crystal cake tonight."

"That was my own fault for ordering a Chinese desert."

Ryan had taken her to Spoor Gastric Bistro Pub, a trendy new joint that looked like a cross between a loading dock and a slaughterhouse. The food was good, but the waitress had annoyed her with her long-winded descriptions of every dish, and her condescending compliments of every choice Eliza made, and the way her hair looked so great—dyed blue-black and half of it shaved. Eliza wished she could shave off her own mop of curly brown hair and get a cool cut like that, but it would upset her father, and he had enough stress in his life right now. More than anything, Eliza hated how the waitress fawned over Ryan, laughing at his jokes, marveling at his culinary sagacity. Occasionally, she winked at Eliza to let her know how lucky she was. She wasn't the only one. Several women shot her lascivious grins, a male couple flashed her a thumbs-up, and an older woman in a business suit silently mouthed, "Wow." Eliza felt like she'd stumbled into some weird tribal cult that wanted to sacrifice her to their love god.

The love god put his hand on her leg.

Stay cool. She shot the iguana a dirty look. *Shut up.*

Eliza looked down at Ryan's hand. He had long, delicate fingers. *Thank God,* she thought. Eliza didn't like thin hands on a man, and she took comfort knowing that Ryan had at least one flaw. He leaned closer. She faced him. His sharp blue eyes radiated a ferocious desire that cut short her breath. Her vision narrowed. Her stomach turned. She commanded herself to calm down. *You want this*, she told herself. Today, Eliza's life would change forever. On this night, she would leave the vagaries of childhood behind and become a confident, actualized adult. She could not ask for a better guide through this rite of passage. Ryan was gorgeous, smart, kind, and of all the women he could have had—and he could have almost any—he had chosen her. Eliza should have felt flattered.

But she didn't. While Ryan's heart burned with ardor, Eliza's contained only fear and—most of all—envy. She wanted to feel the same passion Ryan did. She wanted to so badly.

But, she didn't.

It's his long fingers, she told herself, but if she hadn't chosen his hands, she would have invented some other flaw. The truth was, Ryan was young and available, and that scared the hell out of Eliza. It made her feel like Giles Corey in *The Crucible* getting slowly crushed to death with stones.

Eliza longed to have a healthy relationship, but she had no idea what one looked like. Her mother had divorced her father when Eliza was seven years old. She then dragged her to Tucson, where her mother met Michael, a fun-loving cowboy who broke her heart, compelling them to move to Massachusetts where she married Kevin, a nice man whom she divorced within the year. She met Stewart in Charlotte, Brad in Tampa, and Emilio in Portland. Her mother had reunited briefly with Michael, the cowboy, in Tucson, and then she settled down with Walter in Seattle before leaving him for a boat builder in Port Townsend. Her mother's misadventures taught Eliza that there were only two kinds of relationships—boring or tragic, and by far, boring was the worst.

Eliza found boys her own age, no matter how beautiful, depressingly dull.

Ryan moved closer. *Here we go.* His breath smelled of mint and wine. *Not bad.* He pressed his lips to hers. They kissed. He tightened his embrace. She felt his heart pound and his breath quicken.

She closed her eyes and willed herself to feel something. *Come on. You can do this. He's not a bad kisser. His lips are soft and sweet like... crystal cake. I should have had the flan. Why can't the Chinese make a good dessert? They've had thousands of years to work on it, and the rest of their foods so great. I wonder if it's biological. Someone should do a study. I bet—*

He broke the kiss. "You're so beautiful," he whispered.

"You, too," she replied sincerely.

He glared at her with hungry eyes and leaned in to kiss her again. She turned her head to the side and giggled.

"Is something wrong?" he asked.

"No, no, no," she laughed. She stood up and grabbed her purse. "No," she continued, still laughing. Her last word to him before she stepped out of his apartment and shut the door was "No." Then she burst into tears.

I'm going to die alone.

Chapter Two

Eliza emerged from the parking structure to join the army of students dressed in shorts, T-shirts, sneakers, and flip-flops, marching to class with their noses buried in their phones. Eliza gazed up at the purple jacaranda trees glimmering in the cool morning light. It was spring quarter. The air smelled of jasmine and sunscreen, a combination that filled her with vague longing. She veered off the foot bridge that crossed the UCLA sculpture garden to pay respect to *Standing Woman*, a statue of a confident zaftig female that made Eliza feel proud to be a woman. She rubbed *Standing Woman's* belly for luck, like she had done on the first day of every quarter, and moved on.

Eliza planned her summer while she marched beneath Bunche Hall—commonly known as the Waffle Building—toward her first class on South Campus. Her father would send her to Paris if she begged just right, or maybe Venice. She'd always wanted to see the canals, but despite her daydreaming, Eliza knew that she would end up in England again. Eliza loved all things British. She longed to spend her days in Oxford, reading great works of literature by a roaring fire while eating cucumber sandwiches with the crust trimmed off. She would socialize with urbane intellectuals, perhaps have an affair with a great writer or, even better, a British earl like Lord Grantham on the television show, *Downton Abbey*.

When Eliza had first admitted that she found the portly, middle-aged patriarch attractive, her classmates snickered with disbelief, but one girl stuck up for her. "Eliza's not hung up on body type. She's not shallow like the rest of us," to which Eliza replied, "Sure, I am. Old and stocky's the body type I like. I'm every bit as shallow as you."

Reveling in her idiosyncrasies, Eliza imagined herself accidentally wandering into a private drawing room one day and finding Lord Grantham, dressed in an elegantly casual tweed jacket. She would apologize for the intrusion and ask for directions, and he would gallantly offer to accompany her. They would talk and laugh, and even though he was already married, he would succumb to Eliza's charms. After all, Elizabeth McGovern was old, and she wasn't a very good actress. She and Lord Grantham would spend the summer fox hunting—without killing a fox, of course—going to polo matches, and making passionate love. And then, come fall, Eliza would have to leave, and their goodbye would be gloriously heartbreaking. He would take her in his big, strong arms and—

"What the fuck?" Eliza cursed.

Some idiot bumped into her. "Sorry, I tripped on that crack," the student said, pointing behind him.

Eliza didn't bother to look. She knew there was no crack. Ethan was just a moron. "What are you doing here?" she asked with an exasperated huff.

"We have class together," Ethan said, straightening his glasses.

"What class?"

"Cultural and Intellectual History of the Fourteenth Century."

Eliza frowned and resumed walking. "Since when do you care about culture?"

"I needed some extra units, and you said you were going to take the class, so I thought it would be fun," he said as he tightened his backpack straps. He picked up his pace to match hers.

Eliza groaned, not because Ethan showered her with unwanted

attention—she couldn't blame him for that—but because he had ketchup stains splattered across his T-shirt after she had repeatedly told him that women didn't want to have sex with slobs.

"My mother says a good woman doesn't care about appearances," Ethan had argued.

"Your mother's a liar," Eliza had retorted.

Ethan lived in Eliza's apartment building. One day, she noted that he wore different color socks. "Are you color blind?" she'd teased. When he guilelessly replied yes, Eliza realized that the kid had no clue that she was mocking him, which made her feel like an ass, so she decided to help him. She had regretted the decision ever since. Ethan proved incapable of changing, and no matter how badly she treated him—and she could be quite cruel at times—he followed her everywhere like a lost puppy dog. Eliza would have cut him loose long ago if not for two reasons: First of all, he was the only human being in the world who had read *the Lord of the Rings* as many times as she had. Second, she enjoyed being mean to him.

Unfortunately, her forbearance now meant that she had to sit with Ethan in a class that she had signed up for on a whim. She already had enough units. She just wanted something easy like yoga or folk art or whatever, when "The Cultural and Intellectual History of the Fourteenth Century" had caught her eye. "That looks like fun," the little girl's voice inside her head had said.

The little girl was Eliza's imaginary childhood friend. She had never lived in one place long enough to develop lasting friendships. Fortunately, she had the little girl. She went wherever Eliza went, always ready to have a tea party, jump on the bed, or gossip long into the night. Even now, Eliza attributed her sillier impulses to her imaginary friend, or "inner child" to quote her mother's irritating therapist. Normally, the girl wanted to eat ice cream or watch *Toy Story 2* for the twelfth time. This time, she wanted to learn about the fourteenth century, which was totally absurd, but Eliza was a fan of absurdity, so here she was.

"I got the new season of *Doctor Who*," Ethan announced. "It's so cool they made the Doctor a woman."

"Yuck," Eliza sneered.

"What?"

"I like David Tennant. He's sexy."

"But it's a real breakthrough for women. I mean…"

Eliza stopped listening, mostly because she wasn't interested, but also because she saw a strange man walking toward her. He had black hair, and he wore a black suit and tie and… a vest. *Who wears a vest in L.A.?* And, he carried an old black valise. *Is he looking at me?* She looked behind her. There was no one there. When she turned back, the man was almost upon her. His green eyes glittered with the pitiless conviction of a gladiator entering the arena. Eliza stifled the urge to run, dropped her backpack, and planted her feet. If this guy wanted a fight, he'd get one. On he came, closer and closer until, at the last moment, he swept past her. Eliza spun around, but the man just kept walking. She exhaled with relief, then sniffed. The man's scent lingered. He smelled like the retro barber shop where she'd bought her father a gift certificate once—he never used it. She watched the mysterious man disappear into Royce Hall.

"You dropped your backpack," Ethan said, holding it out to her.

She snatched it back. *What was that guy's problem? Was he messing with me, or am I crazy? How old was he? Forty? Forty-five?* He looked like some old-time movie star, Errol Flynn or Cary Grant, only meaner.

"I like Wonder Woman, too," Ethan continued. "Of course, it doesn't hurt that she's attractive, but why can't attractive women be heroes, too. I mean—"

"Do you know anyone who wears a *vest*?" asked Eliza.

༅ ༅

Ethan sat beside Eliza explaining how Davros created the Daleks during the thousand-year war between the Kaleds and the

Thals, and how they mutated and became Doctor Who's greatest enemy.

Eliza, already quite familiar with the Dalek origin story, ignored Ethan and focused on the chalkboard where someone had written in bold letters, "No Computers. No Phones. Pen and Paper Only."

"Got any paper?" she asked Ethan, interrupting his critique of the Daleks' plan to exterminate humanity through the use of time travel technology.

Ethan tore several sheets of paper out of his notebook and passed them to her. "To achieve their ends, the Daleks must first destroy the Time Lords…" he resumed.

Eliza looked around. The lecture hall was packed. Since when do so many people care about a history class?

The doors burst open, and the man in the black suit and vest swept in. Eliza perked up. *The plot thickens.*

Without acknowledging the class, the man set his valise on a table, unbuckled the straps, and pulled out a small stack of papers and an old kitchen timer. He gave the timer one big crank and placed it on the table, facing him. He turned to the class and raised an eyebrow as if he found the mere presence of students somewhat distasteful.

"Cui opus est permission formae?" he asked in a deep voice.

No one responded. The mysterious man scanned his young audience with disdain and repeated more forcefully, "Permission formae. Qui desiderat?"

A brave young man in the front row ventured, "We don't understand."

The man shot him a menacing look then shook his head. "Worse every year, old man," he mumbled to himself then sighed. "Who needs a permission to enroll slip?"

A slip of paper? Half the room raised their hands. The man pointed to the stack on his desk. "There. When my eyes mist," he proceeded without pause. "And my hearing ceases, and my nose grows cold, and my tongue folds back, and my lips blacken, and my mouth grimaces, and my hair falls out, and my body stiffens, and my heart grows cold, all too late. All too late when my corpse is at the gate."

He stopped and stared at nothing in silence.

Eliza whispered to Ethan, "Who is this guy?"

Ethan replied too loudly, "Oliver Crowley."

Crowley shot Ethan a look that made him slink down into his chair.

"It began with a fever," Crowley continued. "Followed by black swellings in the armpits and groin that grew to the size of eggs or small apples. The growths oozed blood and puss. The stench was unbearable. Internal bleeding spread the boils over the entire body, causing agonizing pain until, mercifully, the victim died."

It's not British, Eliza decided, trying to figure out Crowley's accent. But it's... what's the right word? Forced? No. Deliberate. That's it. And a tad archaic.

"They tried to cure the plague with aromatherapy, leeches, and prayers. They rubbed their sores with live chickens, bathed in urine, killed Jews, some even sacrificed children to the gods of their pagan ancestors. All to no avail. Death showed no mercy, and half of the world perished."

He's too handsome, Eliza lamented. But on the plus side, he's creepy.

"Of course, people in the middle ages had no idea that they lived in the middle of anything. They thought they lived at the end of time. They believed God would soon destroy the world and send them to heaven or, more likely, cast them into the lake of eternal fire. People grew fatalistic and cynical. They lost faith in kings and churches, in life itself. They knew that all they could rely upon, the only thing that would never fail them, was death. The cultural and intellectual life of the late middle ages revolved around death."

An eager student raised her hand and asked, "What about chivalry? And courtly love like in the time of King Arthur? Weren't they big in the middle ages, too?"

"Chivalry was no more than a justification for mass slaughter, and what was the essential theme of courtly love? Chastity. Love went unconsummated, producing no progeny, no future, no hope. Medieval romance ennobled loss and despair."

I like him, Eliza decided.

"Fourteenth-century man sang, danced, and prayed to Death. She ruled supreme."

The enthusiastic student's hand shot up again. This girl was starting to get on Eliza's nerves. It wasn't just that she was cheerful—an attitude Eliza always found suspect. She looked familiar. *Where have I seen her before?* Then it came back to her. That girl had been dancing on a pool table in her underwear at the only frat party Eliza had ever—or would ever—attend.

☙ ❧

Some guy in her Post-War British Drama class had invited her. *What was his name? Jason? Justin? Jackson? Who cares? Something-N.* He seemed like a nice guy, and Eliza thought she should sample different facets of the college experience.

She thought wrong.

When Eliza saw the mob of students spilling out of the two-story, Spanish-style fraternity house, shouting over a pounding bass rhythm that made her eyeballs hurt, she realized two things—she needn't have spent an hour picking out the perfect summer dress since everyone was wearing shorts and tank tops, and she was leaving.

To her misfortune, Something-N yelled to her from a balcony, and Eliza made the mistaking of looking.

"Go around back!" he shouted.

Eliza's instincts told her to run, but she didn't want to look like a coward, even in front of some guy she barely knew, so she girded her loins and waded into the sea of partygoers. She regretted her decision instantly as the human riptide swept her into a whirlpool of flesh, elbows, and sweat. She could barely move or breathe. Her face burned; her heart pounded. Someone stepped on her foot. Some guy burped in her face. She was about to scream when a hand yanked her onto an empty patch of grass.

"Wanna beer?" Something-N yelled through the noise.

Eliza tottered. Something-N straightened her up.

"Looks like you already got started. Come on."

Before she could catch her breath, Something-N dragged her off through a maze of tiki torches and students drinking from red plastic cups until they reached a group of shirtless young men standing around a large metal keg.

"Two beers!" Something-N commanded.

"At once, Me Lord!" shouted one drunk shirtless dude. While he filled plastic cups, another drunk shirtless dude leered at Eliza and ran his hand over his taught belly. "Wanna rub my sixer?"

She ignored him and reached for a cup of beer, but the bartending shirtless dude held it back. "First, you must say, 'Oh great God of Beer, I worship thee.'"

"No," Eliza stated flatly and snatched the drink from his hand.

Something-N led her away from the keg and yelled, "You look nice!"

"Bath-room!" she shouted back.

Something-N's lips moved, and he pointed to the house. Eliza handed him her beer and marched off. She did not plan to return for it.

Her shoes squished on the frat house's wet, sticky floor as she carefully wound her way through undulating fissures in the crowd. Despite her caution, she took a wrong turn and found her path blocked by a pair of bare woman's legs. She looked up to see her future classmate dancing, stripped down to her underwear on a pool table.

As Eliza searched for a new breach in the mob, a guy wearing a bed sheet hopped onto the pool table with a bottle of hot sauce and yelled, "Dude!" to some idiot who joined him atop the table. "You and me, bro!" shouted Bed Sheet Guy, and he gulped down half the bottle of hot sauce. His idiot buddy drank the other half, and together they vomited on the crowd. Stupid underwear girl squealed with delight as people screamed and fled.

Eliza took advantage of a gap created by the showering barf to dash for the front door, but something yanked her head back. She turned and saw some guy chewing on her hair. Eliza punched him in the face and ran.

A half hour later, Eliza sat in her car eating a Double-Double from In-N-Out Burger. She had parked in a quiet, secluded part of campus. She didn't even turn on the radio. She just listened to herself chew and let ketchup and tears drip onto her ruined dress.

She finished the burger, sucked down the last drops of her chocolate milkshake and went to start the car when she heard piano music playing softly, somewhere. She scanned the dimly lit campus and spotted a man in a suit escorting a stylishly dressed woman down a tree-lined path. They looked so serene that Eliza got out of her car and followed them. The music grew clearer. Cole Porter. *Anything Goes.* Eliza watched the couple enter the Faculty Center, a sleek redwood and glass building that looked like it belonged at a ski resort rather than the campus of a public university. She saw soft light coming from the back. She wound her way along a brick wall until she reached a wrought iron gate. Inside the patio, mature men and women clustered under Japanese lanterns, sipping wine and chatting. They listened and laughed, enjoying one another's company with an elegant ease that Eliza had not seen since her father took her to the opera as a child. She watched a distinguished-looking professor speaking to one woman while stealing glances at another. She saw a woman squeeze a man's arm as she walked by and several other people exchanging furtive smiles across the patio.

Eliza's heart ached. She pressed her forehead against the cold iron bars and sighed wistfully. *This,* she thought, *is sexy.*

"Isn't Death a man? I mean, traditionally?" Annoying Underwear Girl asked the professor.

"Death is a woman," he replied.

"Doesn't the female symbolize life and birth? I mean, as a metaphor—?"

"Death is a woman," Crowley repeated in a stern voice that brooked no dissent. "Beware the metaphor. We Homo sapiens use metaphors to condense reality into familiar images to make us feel less idiotic. We have personalized reality to such an extent that we now believe truth has no value if it does not teach us something about ourselves. As if truth cares about us, as if the laws of nature exist merely to guide us to some great epiphany that will enable us to live happily ever after. Alas, metaphors do not reveal the meaning of life because…" He looked straight into Eliza's eyes. "…life has no meaning."

Eliza flushed.

"This desire for meaning, albeit a natural one—it almost certainly helped us evolve from dirty, savage monkeys into dirty, savage humans—leads us astray, especially in regard to history. Suppress it. This is a class about how people thought and behaved in the 1300s, not about how you wished they behaved or about how their behavior personally affects you. Fourteenth-century Europeans did not care about your opinions, and neither do I. In this class, I will speak, and you will remember what I say, or not, as the mood suits you. All I ask is that you do not rewrite history to conform to your personal agendas. Despots have done that from time immemorial, and I find it annoying."

Eliza's heart beat faster. She looked at the professor's hands. He had square, manly hands, the hands of a steel worker or a cowboy, yet he wore a suit and tie and… a *vest*.

Warmth pooled in Eliza's pelvis.

DING! Crowley's timer sounded while he had been describing three ways to defend oneself against an armored horseman. "First of all, have a light breakfast that morning. You want to remain nimble footed during battle. Secondly, avoid letting the horseman's spear pierce your skin. I cannot over-emphasize the importance of this point. And thirdly, and most importantly, you must always—" *DING!*

Crowley terminated his treatise mid-sentence. Ignoring the class's disappointed moan, he stuffed his timer into his bag and pointed to the stack of papers on his desk. "Permission formae," he declared and strode out of the hall.

"Where do you want to eat today?" Ethan asked.

Eliza didn't answer. Her mind was on Crowley. *Who is this guy?*

Apparently, Eliza wasn't the first person to ask this question. She had just finished reading an article in the *Daily Bruin* from May 2005, entitled "Who is Oliver Crowley?" *I was hoping you'd tell me,* she thought as she scrolled through reader's comments. "I've never seen him out of class," one student wrote. "He has no email, phone number, or address," wrote another. "He's dreamy," observed a third.

"He only teaches one class a year, usually in the spring, on all sorts of subjects, like history, literature, folklore, art, science," Eliza informed Ethan, who sat opposite her at Kerckhoff Coffee House eating a sandwich he'd brought from home. Kerckhoff was Eliza's favorite building on campus. While other UCLA landmarks like Royce Hall and Powell Library were built in an ornate Romanesque style, Kerckhoff was pure Tudor Gothic. Its arches, spires, and stained-glass windows reminded her of Oxford or, better yet, Hogwarts. If the students wore uniforms and spoke with British accents, the place would be perfect.

She took a sip from her double-shot soy latte and continued, "If you believe the comments, Crowley's a French, Romanian,

Cherokee shaman who beats his wife and plays cello at a downtown bistro when he's not spying for the Kremlin."

"Really?" Ethan said with his mouthful of sandwich.

"Closed," Eliza commanded.

Ethan shut his mouth and swallowed. It frustrated Eliza that Ethan, who was smart enough to do her math homework for her, couldn't remember the basic rules of etiquette. She constantly had to remind him to wash his face, blow his nose, tie his shoes. She'd already given up on his facial hair. Ethan's pathetic attempts to shave left splotches of sandy fuzz and bloody pimples strewn across his face.

"Oliver Crowley is a mystery," Eliza concluded with a gleam in her eye.

"He's a jerk," Ethan commented.

"You're a jerk," she lashed back.

Ethan recoiled as if Eliza had slapped him across the face. He sullenly rubbed his cheek and stared down at the table. They ate in silence for a while until Ethan ventured, "Do you want to watch *Doctor Who* tonight?"

"Yes," Eliza replied as she reread the article.

Chapter Three

Jaime feels sick to his stomach. He can hear the audience talking. He peeks through the red stage curtain. *Puta madre.* There are hundreds of them. He should have rehearsed his speech. "Ladies and Gentlemen…" No. That's lame. "Órale, vatos!" Do these people even know what a vato is? He'd have to explain it. "A vato is…" Wait. What the hell *is* a vato? Is it like saying dude? "Hey, dudes?" That sucks.

"You're on, Mr. Santos."

Jaime gasps. He barely has time to nod to Vice Principal Hernandez before the curtain opens, and a spotlight blasts him in the face. The theater grows quiet. Jaime squints through the glare. How'd so many people get so quiet so fast? He clears his throat.

"Ladies and Gentlemen. I…" He stops. He knows his speech. He just needs to relax. The words'll come. They're on the tip of his tongue. Jaime wipes sweat off his face. His stomach is killing him.

"Ladies and Gentlemen… hello."

Somebody laughs. Jaime spots his stepfather, Vince, sitting in the back row with that ugly smile of his. Jaime's gut tightens.

He's eight years old, coming home from school. Vince's Chevy Nova is in the driveway, with that stupid bumper sticker. "IF YOU'RE GOING TO RIDE MY ASS, AT LEAST PULL MY HAIR," and rosary beads are hanging from the rearview mirror. Jaime hates those beads. Vince is always going on about God and sin and the Lakers. He quotes Jesus and basketball stats while he punches Jaime. "I come not to bring peace, but to bring a sword." *BAM!* "Magic Johnson was the all-time leader in average assists per game. Eleven..." *BAM!* "Point..." *BAM!* "Two!" *BAM! THUMP! BAM!*

Jaime wishes Vince hadn't come today. He looks around for a friendly face, for Sandy, but he only sees angry people. There's his fifth-grade teacher, Mrs. McCloud, with her long, wrinkly neck and crooked teeth and his grandfather, sticking out his chin all dignified and stuff. Paiyaso and Spider are sitting up front. He'd beat the shit out of both those cholos a few years back. They can't be happy to be here. And, Rita's here, all smiling and happy. She looks good. Last time he saw her, she was all puffy and blue and... *Should I tell her she's dead? No. That would only bum her out.*

Jaime'd better nail this speech.

Vice Principal Hernandez hands him a script. *Thank you, Jesus!* He clears his throat and looks at the paper. "Ladies and Gentlemen, I... I mean..." He can't focus. The harder he stares at the words, the more they swim around the page like fish in a lake.

Vince laughs.

Jaime looks down. He'd pee his pants if he had any. He's totally naked. *What the fuck's going on? Where am I?* Then he remembers the gun in face.

Oh, hell.

Chapter Four

Eliza awoke like she always did, with a gasp.

She was late. No, wait. It was Tuesday. She didn't have any classes Tuesday morning. She just had to outline her essay on James Joyce's *Ulysses*. That wouldn't take long. She would defend her decision to not read the book with two arguments: First, she refused to support another canonical white-male narrative instead of works by diverse writers like Ta-Nehisi Coates or Junot Diaz. Second, and most important, a handful of brave scholars had already read *Ulysses*, and for her to slog through all that gobbledygook would only demean their noble sacrifice. She would never, for example, disregard the achievements of medical researchers and create her own smallpox vaccine, or make her own wings to fly across the country. That would be stupid, but not as stupid as reading James Joyce.

Eliza sat up, rubbed the sleep from her eyes, and focused on her poster of the 1977 horror film *The Sentinel*. Christine Raines' mediocre acting, along with the director's jarring zoom shots and awkward framing, lent the film a delightful cinema verité eeriness. She adored the climax when all the white-eyed demons, including Christine Raines' boyfriend, Chris Sarandon—perhaps the creepiest actor of all time—came after her, and she had to become the Sentinel and guard the gates of hell for all eternity. Eliza quietly mouthed the movie's tag line, "She was young. She was beautiful. She was next." It made Eliza happy.

She glanced at the other posters in her bedroom: *Rear Window, Double Indemnity, Audrey Rose,* and one of Benedict Cumberbatch gazing at her with those liquid blue eyes of his. She rarely looked at Benedict's poster. It made her anxious, like smelling French pastries through the window of a closed bakery.

She had reserved one entire wall for her father's movies in case he ever visited her: *Hard Steel; Hot Lead; Flames of Fire 1, 2, 3, and 4;* and *Jack Cox.* They were all successful action thrillers. Eliza hadn't put up a poster of her father's best movie, *The Long Road Home,* because it had done badly in the box office. Mentioning the film upset him, and the poor man had enough stress in his life.

She scanned the clothes strewn about her room and realized she had nothing clean to wear, so she laid back down to formulate a new plan of attack in her campaign to conquer Professor Crowley.

For the past eight weeks, Eliza had tried to solve the mystery that was Oliver Crowley, hitting dead end after dead end.

"He doesn't have an email," the middle-aged faculty administration assistant had said without looking up from her computer.

"Phone number?"

"Nope. See him during office hours."

"Where's his office?"

"I don't know."

"How can I contact him?"

"Leave a note."

"And you'll give it to him?"

"No."

"Why not?"

"I have no idea where he is."

"Then why should I leave a note?"

"You shouldn't."

"Do you have a supervisor?"

The assistant finally looked Eliza in the eye and said, "Sweetheart, Oliver Crowley teaches one class a year. He has for as long as anyone can remember. For your own good, do not bother him."

"Why?"

"I don't know. I was just told to say that."

The office assistant's evasions had only fueled Eliza's curiosity. *I love mysteries*, said the little girl's voice in her head. She studied Crowley closely. He followed the same routine after every class. When his timer rang, he marched out of the lecture hall, turned left at the door, walked twenty-three feet—she had measured it—then turned right down another hallway and disappeared. He didn't vanish in a puff of smoke like the witch in *The Wizard of Oz*. He just entered the crowded corridor and never reemerged. Eliza repeatedly checked every door along the way but found only empty classrooms.

Her failure as a detective was only surpassed by her failure as a woman. Eliza had tried to get Crowley's attention with flirtatious glances, witty remarks, sexy outfits, exemplary schoolwork, fawning, and praising. Seductions that flustered lesser professors had no effect on this man, which, of course, was one of the reasons she had fallen in love with him. Eliza knew that the University of California forbade professors from having romantic relationships with students *while* the student attended their class, but UCLA was on the quarter system. Crowley's class only lasted ten weeks. She didn't have to worry about starting a relationship too soon. She feared not starting one at all. Only two weeks remained before finals. Eliza had to move fast, especially after the previous day's humiliation.

She had come to class wearing short shorts so Crowley could see her new tattoo—a snake winding up her calf like Hermes' staff that he had described the week before. It was only a temporary tattoo, but she would have made it permanent had Crowley asked her to. Throughout the lecture, she crossed and recrossed her legs, but of course, Crowley paid no attention. No matter, she had a secret weapon. When Crowley's timer went off, she raced up to him.

"Professor Crowley?" Eliza said with a warm, casual smile. "Oliver." She lightly laid her hand on his arm. "Can I call you Oliver?" He responded with cold silence. She removed her hand. "Professor. Here."

Eliza dug into her backpack and pulled out an old, five-pointed brass star.

"I thought you'd like this."

Crowley reluctantly took hold of the object and gave it a disinterested perusal.

"It's from the 1920 silent film *The Golem*. It was based on that legend you talked about last week with the rabbi using a magical star to bring a clay monster to life? My father is a well-known film producer—so was my grandfather and my great-grandfather—and he's given me all sorts of memorabilia."

Crowley turned the star over, revealing strange symbols stamped on the back.

"I think that's an ancient Hebrew curse," Eliza ventured.

"It's Chinese," Crowley replied evenly.

"Oh?"

"Made in China."

"Oh," Eliza said, hiding her disappointment. "I didn't know the Chinese made film props back in the 1920s."

"They didn't."

Crowley plopped the star into the side pouch of his valise, which Eliza sadly noted was full of other gift trinkets. "Miss," he said with a cursory nod and marched out of the room.

☙ ❧

Eliza lay on her bed, perfecting her new battle plan. She forced herself to look at Benedict Cumberbatch. "How do I let Oliver know that I'd be a good friend, and more importantly, that I can keep a secret? I have to break the ice. That golem star might have worked if it wasn't fake." Eliza inhaled sharply as the solution popped into her head. She knew where to get something real, something Oliver Crowley could not ignore. "If this were an old movie, I'd laugh like a villain right now," she confided to Benedict. Eliza jumped out of bed and began sniffing T-shirts to find one that wasn't too musky.

◈ ◈

That afternoon, Eliza grabbed an empty backpack, hopped in her huge Ford SUV—which her father had bought her because it was the largest and, he reasoned, the safest car available—and drove to her father's house.

Eliza had been accepted to Bryn Mawr, Cornell, and Princeton, all of which she had applied to in part because of their collegiate gothic architecture, but she chose UCLA so she could live in the same city as her father for the first time since she was six years old. The campus was less than a mile from his house in Bel Air, and in no time, Eliza drove the SUV through the iron gates of his property and up to the main building.

Eliza had said "Yuck," the first time she saw the concrete and steel monstrosity her father called home, and she had said, "Yuck" ever since.

"Yuck," said Eliza.

She hopped out of her truck, trotted up to the front door—also made of steel—punched in a key code, and slipped inside quietly. Normally, she would have called out to her father, but he was out of town working on some mystery project, which fit her plans perfectly. She had come to commit a crime, and she didn't want to run into anyone, especially her new stepmother, Aurora, who was only four years older than Eliza and insufferable.

Eliza looked around, saw no one, and continued into the house. She walked beneath a twisted iron chandelier, which looked like a tribute to industrialized mass slaughter, and up a steel staircase to the living room. Of all the ugly rooms in her father's ugly house, Eliza hated this one most. Her stepmother had painted it fluorescent green and furnished it with a pink velvet couch that belonged in a nineteenth-century bordello, a yellow polka-dotted coffee table, a cowhide chair with a bull-horn backrest, and several misshapen mounds of leather that Eliza assumed were chairs but looked more like giant fungi sprouting from the floor. Eliza's stepmother had boasted, "It's Goop's new Sludge Collection. It's organic and made by Mexicans *in* America."

Eliza kept her eyes glued to the floor as she made her way through the nauseating room and almost bumped into the last person in the world she wanted to see, ever.

Aurora.

The ludicrously beautiful young woman was bent over an end table arranging a set of ceramic dwarf figurines. With her legs straight and her back arched, she looked like she was posing for a beer ad.

Eliza had always thought that women like Aurora did not really exist. She assumed they were caricatures created by men to belittle underprivileged women who had to use their sexuality to survive in a patriarchal world. Eliza was wrong. Aurora was real, and she was dumb as a sled track. At first, Eliza had attempted to engage her new stepmother in meaningful conversation, to make a connection, to find even one redeeming quality. She failed. Aurora was awful. The woman had obviously married her father for his money. Eventually, she would leave him financially and emotionally drained, and Eliza could do nothing except hate her, which she did with remorseless abandon.

Eliza tried to sneak past her stepmother, but Aurora spun around and squealed, "Eliza!" in a grating whine that conveyed both joy and pity, before flinging her arms around Eliza. Eliza recoiled at the stench of Aurora's potent perfume that reeked of bananas and cherries.

"Hey," she mumbled, holding her breath. Eliza patted her stepmother's back to terminate the hug, but Aurora only squeezed harder.

"It's so good to see you," she sing-songed.

Eliza squirmed out of her grip. "Okay," she panted, trying to catch her breath. "I don't want to bother you. Go back to your dwarves."

"They're sprites, silly! That's Lilly Sprite and Lamo Sprite and Charmo Sprite—"

"Great," Eliza interrupted. "I just have to get something out of my room real quick."

"You're not going to see your father?" Aurora asked with an astonished pout.

Eliza's stomach twisted. "Daddy's home?"

"He *does* live here," she squawked, making a stupid face to assure Eliza that she was joking. "He's in his office doing whatever it is he does."

"Working on his movie, I imagine," Eliza replied, not hiding her annoyance.

"I hope not. His movies are so bad. I'm kidding!" She chuckled then admitted, "I don't watch movies. They're too long."

"Why'd you marry a film producer if you don't like movies?"

"He's great in bed."

Eliza scrunched her face to squeeze the image out of her head.

"Bubelah," crooned a male voice.

Eliza turned to see her father standing on the landing. As far as Eliza knew, Jerry Horowitz had never gone to temple in his life, but he loved to spout Yiddish. It used to drive her mother crazy. "I converted for the putz. Now he won't let me forget." Eliza, on the other hand, thought it was cool that her father spoke a dead language.

"Pumpkin!" Aurora squealed as she scampered to Jerry and kissed the top of his balding head. "Eliza's here!"

"I see that," Jerry replied with an indulging smile.

"You guys want a cocktail?"

"It's ten in the morning, honey."

"Mind if I have one?"

"Trip the light fantastic," he said.

Aurora laughed in a series of staccato snorts reminiscent of a goose with a head cold. "I don't know what that means!" she hooted, then gave Jerry another kiss on the head and sashayed down the stairs.

Jerry sighed and turned back to Eliza. "Bubelah."

Eliza hugged him. He felt smaller than she remembered. "Are you all right?" she asked like she always did, and as always, Jerry replied, "Same as yesterday," which was true. Her father loomed so large in Eliza's memory, that she repeatedly forgot he stood just shy of five feet six inches.

She stepped back to take in his outfit. Jerry Horowitz was one of the highest-grossing producers in Hollywood, and he dressed the part. Today he wore a white linen sport coat over a red Givenchy T-shirt, meticulously frayed Dolce and Gabbana blue jeans, and yellow suede tennis shoes. "I want to look like I just threw something on and accidentally look great," he would say, but there was nothing accidental about it. Her father fretted over every detail of his outfit.

Since she was a child, Eliza had spent hours in his cavernous walk-in closet helping him pick out tennis shoes from his floor-to-ceiling rotating shoe rack, debating which graphic T-shirt would best suit the tone of an upcoming meeting. Eliza appreciated her father's effort to look cool, but she treasured the little foibles that showed he wasn't. Jerry tucked in his T-shirts, dry-cleaned his blue jeans, and kept a scented handkerchief in his front pocket, which he would offer Eliza when she needed to blow her nose, then refold it and place it back in his pocket. As far as Eliza knew, her father was the last man on earth who still followed that gallant, if unhygienic, custom.

"Nice shoes," Eliza said.

Jerry glanced down at his Maison Margiela trainers. "I don't know," he worried. "They're too comfortable."

"Shoes can't be too comfortable."

"Yes, they can," her father stated emphatically, glaring at her with his intense grey eyes veiled by drooping eyelids—a combination of family traits that made Eliza feel as if he could see the darkest sins of her soul, yet forgive them.

Eliza doubted he would forgive what she planned to do today.

"I just came by to get—"

"I have a surprise for you," he interrupted and marched off to his office.

Eliza cursed quietly and followed him.

❧ ✍

In contrast to his self-consciously hip wardrobe, Jerry Horowitz' office was a tribute to arcane masculinity. It had wood-paneled walls, leather chairs, and a wood-burning fireplace with giant bull horns over the mantle. He kept a horde of mounted birds, rodents, and monkeys posed dramatically throughout the room. Jerry loved animals. He just found dead ones easier to care for.

On an easel behind his desk, he displayed a first edition of *Death in the Afternoon* signed by Ernest Hemingway. "Hemingway was a man's man," her father had insisted. Jerry Horowitz revered all things manly. He never shed a tear over a lost pet or a girlfriend, but mention the Spartan's last stand at Thermopile or the charge of the Light Brigade, and he'd blubber like a baby. "Such sacrifice!" he would cry. "True greatness demands sacrifice!"

Unsurprisingly, Jerry Horowitz loved bullfighting. He would proclaim that, "*Matador* in Spanish means *killer*! You go to a bullfight to witness death, to be horrified, moved, and cleansed by the experience."

To which Eliza would retort, "Oh, Daddy. You've never seen a bullfight in your life," which was true. As far as Eliza knew, Jerry

Horowitz had only been "cleansed" by the make-believe death he watched in his private screening room.

Despite wielding great power in the film industry, Jerry Horowitz was, at his core, a shy, disarmingly insecure man. He shunned the spotlight that followed him incessantly. He hated crowds, yet repeatedly found himself surrounded by the public.

"People are animals," he would tell Eliza when she was little.

"I like animals," Eliza would reply.

"Not noble animals, like a lion or an eagle. They're dirty scavengers that will devour you the first chance they get. Especially, boys. Boys only want one thing from you. Stay away from boys."

Fortunately, he hadn't mentioned fully grown men.

Jerry's favorite movie was *Blood and Sand*, not the tolerable version with Tyrone Power, but the scratchy silent one with Rudolf Valentino. Her father screened it for her when she was seven years old, and for some reason the old melodrama about a doomed bullfighter terrified her. Eliza had watched *Nostradamus, The Bride of Frankenstein*, and *The Mummy* without batting an eye, but when that black-and-white bull gored Valentino, she screamed until her father had to stop the film.

"You're behaving like a child," he had barked. It was the first time in her life that she had made her father angry. The memory of it still filled her with shame. Eliza loved horror movies, haunted houses, and ghost stories. When something frightened her, she faced it head on and learned everything she could about it. She researched vampires, zombies, late night televangelists, serial killers, bees, toothless old people, and eventually those things stopped scaring her; but the more she learned about bullfighting, the more it frightened her. She watched gruesome footage of bulls thrusting their horns into matador's bellies and necks. She told herself that those fools deserved to suffer for torturing innocent animals, but the images still haunted her. She had recurring nightmares of horned beasts chasing her through narrow streets. The dreams didn't stop until her father agreed to never mention bullfighting in her presence.

Jerry clicked a button on his antique intercom. "Bring Eliza's present."

"My birthday's not for two weeks, Daddy."

A gaunt, middle-aged woman skittered into the room carrying a long white dress.

"Oh, it's so beautiful!" Eliza crooned, then added as an afterthought, "Hi, Margarita."

"Hello, Little Lamb," Margarita replied in her sullen, accented English.

"I love it!" Eliza exclaimed with an extra pinch of enthusiasm to compensate for Margarita's relentless despondency. Margarita Del Rio had been her father's personal assistant since time immemorial. She took calls, read scripts, managed schedules, fed her father's live pets, and dusted his dead ones. She also raised a family of her own and played scratch golf.

"You like it?" her father asked with a wide-eyed grimace.

Jerry always bought Eliza a dress for her birthday. Before college, she only saw him one week a year. She lived for those trips to Los Angeles where her father took her to film studios, introduced her to movie stars like Harrison Ford, Tom Cruise, and Benedict Cumberbatch; the latter of which triggered a three-month Cumberbatch binge that culminated with the purchase of her magnificent poster. Best of all, her father watched classic movies with her, which she loved. Every visit was crowned with a birthday dinner at The Ivy. The restaurant's flowery pastel seats and wicker ceiling fans made Eliza feel like a Southern Belle at a spring cotillion. She would wear her new dress, and her father would don an elegant suit and tie. They would comport themselves with exaggerated elegance while ordering their customary fried chicken birthday meal. When the chicken would arrive, they'd abandoned all modesty and rip the bird apart like savages. This was their private little game, a rare moment of childish abandon for both father and daughter. Birthday dinner at The Ivy was one of the few things that Eliza could depend on, and she treasured it—until last year when her father brought Aurora.

Eliza shook her head to purge the memory.

"I love it," she replied. "It's so elegant and... white."

"You're going to be a woman!"

"I'm going to be twenty."

"In the old country, a girl became a woman at twenty."

"I thought it was thirteen."

"No."

"What about the Bat Mitzva?"

"Bat Mitzva, Schmat Mitzva," Jerry scoffed.

"Can't argue with that."

"Try it on!" he commanded and strode toward the door.

"I can't. I have to—" she complained, but Jerry had already left the room. "Damn it," she grumbled then shot Margarita an apologetic smile.

Moments later, Eliza studied herself in a full-length mirror. The dress hugged her upper body and hips and flared at the bottom, spilling onto the floor. She ran her fingers across the floral embroidery on the sheer netted neckline. Jerry's head popped up behind her in the mirror.

"Perfect," he said.

"It is long," Margarita sighed glumly.

I look more like a bride than a birthday girl, thought Eliza. *But if I hem it real short, put on some high-heeled sandals, Oliver might like it.*

Her father took her hand. She was surprised to see tears in his eyes. "This will be..." he started, cleared his throat, and continued, "momentous."

Eliza choked back her shame. Her father had given her a precious gift, and she wanted to chop it up to seduce a man. *It wouldn't work on Oliver anyway.* No, she wouldn't despoil her father's gift. She would just stick to her original plan and rob him.

"Thank you, Daddy. I love it. Now, if you'll excuse me, I have to—Margarita, what are you doing?" The woman had dropped to her knees and started fiddling with the bottom of the dress.

"Hold still, please," Margarita commanded as she plucked some straight pins from her sleeve. *Who keeps pins on their sleeves?*

Eliza tapped her foot impatiently as Margarita marked the hem. "No tapping, please."

Jesus Christ.

Jerry followed Margarita's progress closely. "Not too high."

Eliza needed an excuse to get away from these people. She searched the room for ideas. *Fireplace, dead animals, bull horns...* She looked out the window into the backyard where a marble rotunda in the shape of an ancient Greek temple towered over the sprawling estate. Eliza never asked her father why he had built such an archaic structure that clashed so dramatically with his house because she feared that he might take it down. Tacky as it was, she preferred it to the brutalist architecture of the rest of his house.

She looked away from the rotunda to the swimming pool where Aurora chatted with the pool boy. Her stepmother looked amazing in her bikini as she slinked closer to the young man, who looked pretty good himself in shorts and a tank top. Eliza had not seen him before, which didn't surprise her. Every time she came to her father's house, they had a new pool boy. She watched Aurora lay her hand on the guy's chest. *Interesting.*

"He's very handsome," Eliza declared innocently.

Jerry followed her gaze out the window. His jaw stiffened. "Not now," he growled under his breath and stomped out the door.

Eliza smiled. *Trouble in paradise.* She glanced down at Margarita methodically hemming her dress. "Thank you!" Eliza shouted as she yanked off the dress, grabbed her backpack, and dashed out of the office.

Margarita gathered up the gown and rushed after her. "I have more pins."

Eliza raced down the landing. "Gotta get something from my room," she shouted as she dashed inside and slammed the door behind her.

Margarita shrieked.

Shit. Eliza opened the door to see Margarita holding her nose.

"I'm so sorry! Are you all right?"

Margarita shrugged stoically, tilting back her head to keep blood from dripping down her chin.

"You should get some ice," Eliza suggested.

"No. The bleeding will stop sometime. Or it will not," Margarita sighed morosely as she walked into the room. "What did you want in here, Little Lamb?"

Eliza wanted nothing from her old bedroom. She had lied to divert attention from her true objective, and now she had to come up with another lie to back up her first one. She took inventory of the room she had lived in for only one week a year—a canopy bed piled high with stuffed animals; green velvet curtains just like the ones Scarlett O'Hara had made a dress out of in *Gone with the Wind*; posters of *The Wizard of Oz*, *Charlie and the Chocolate Factory*, and *101 Dalmatians*, films that she loved as a child because they all scared her. She slid open the closet that held every dress her father had ever bought her. She had never taken any of them home. She feared that her mother would mock them the way she mocked her father. Running her fingers along the gowns, arranged neatly by year, Eliza traveled back in time to a little puffed sleeved dress with a Peter Pan collar.

"Can you believe that I fit into this once?" she asked Margarita who stood by the bed sticking a wad of tissue paper up her nose.

"Yes," she remarked in a nasal drone. "I put a bow in your hair that year."

Eliza remembered the huge yellow bow. It had kept drooping over her face until her father plucked it off her head during dinner. The next year Margarita had wanted to give Eliza two bows, which she'd adamantly refused. Margarita had always fretted and fussed over her like she fretted over everything in her father's world. During Eliza's yearly visits, Margarita woke her up every morning, minded her all day, and put her to bed at night with bizarre stories about gods and goddesses and monsters, which put Margarita to sleep instantly but kept Eliza up for hours. Eliza thought it odd that, despite their long history, she never felt any affection for the woman, which probably said more about Eliza's selfishness than Margarita's worth.

Eliza didn't have time to worry about her relationship with her father's assistant right now. The woman hindered her plans. She had to go.

"How are your kids?" Eliza asked, vamping.

"Terrible," Margarita replied wearily.

"Oh, no."

"Oh, yes. They are terrible people."

"I always liked Isabel," Eliza ventured.

"Isabel is a criminal."

"No."

"Yes. I do not lie about this. Isabel steals things like spoons and children. When I am not working for your father, I am returning children to their mothers. Isabel should be hanged. I would do it myself, but my heart is too soft."

Eliza cocked her ear. "What was that?"

"What?" asked Margarita.

"Nothing. I just thought I heard Daddy yell something."

Margarita sprang to attention and bolted out of the room.

That was easy. Finally alone, Eliza darted into an adjoining bathroom, locked one door and ran out the other, through a room with a treadmill and rowing machine that no one ever used, and out onto the landing. She scooted against the wall so that no one on the bottom floor could see her and stopped at a metal door with a push button lock. She punched in the code she had learned as a child by disobeying her father's command to cover her eyes, opened the door, and ran down a circular staircase to the basement. She punched in another code, which she had cracked easily years ago—0624, her birthday—and entered a pitch-black room. She clapped her hands and lights sprang to life, illuminating a large library.

Eliza paused to take in the floor-to-ceiling shelves crammed with books. Her father had collected a trove of rare volumes, which he permitted Eliza to see only in his presence and only inside this room. Eliza attributed her love of literature to her father's forbidden library. The more he denied her access to his precious books, the more she wanted to read them.

Many nights, during her yearly visits, Eliza would sneak into his library and read first editions of *Wuthering Heights*, *Frankenstein*, and, during puberty, *Lady Chatterley's Lover*. Sometimes she had to duck behind a shelf when her father entered the room unexpectedly. One night, while spying on him from behind stacks of books, she saw where he hid his greatest treasure.

Eliza stepped into the library but stopped when she spotted a small black bubble protruding from the ceiling. A camera. *Damn!* Her father had installed a video surveillance system. *Had it always been there?* No. She had inspected every inch of this room as a child. She would have noticed an ominous black eye looming overhead. The camera had already seen her. *New plan*.

She sauntered to the shelf below the camera, casually pretending to search for a book. She looked up as if something on the top shelf had caught her attention. She dragged over a ladder, climbed up and pulled out a book. She arched her eyebrows to show the camera that she found the subject matter incredibly interesting. *Don't overact*, she admonished herself. She relaxed her face and set the book atop the shelf so that it blocked the camera lens.

Eliza raced down the ladder and ran to the back wall of the library. She counted bookcases from left to right, *one, two, three*, then shelves from top to bottom, *one, two, three, four*. She searched for... *The Siege of Carthage*. She pulled out the book, reached into the empty space on the shelf, and found a button on the back panel. She paused. *What if there's an alarm?* She decided to take her chances and pressed the button. A section of the bookshelf popped open like a door, disclosing a small recess in the wall. Eliza reached inside and pulled out a heavy book.

The oxidized copper-inlaid cover crackled as she opened it, revealing a picture of a king and queen embracing, hand painted in brilliant tempera and gold leaf. Eliza had examined this medieval illuminated manuscript many times through the years, and it always intrigued and frustrated her. It featured wonderfully bizarre illustrations of dragons perched astride the earth, half bird–half dog creatures barking at a tree upon a hill, a crucified snake, complex astrological charts, and tiny men called homunculi growing inside horse bellies. Though it was written in English, Eliza couldn't understand it. What did "That which is dry doth not enter nor tinge" mean? Or, "The sun is animal because he receiveth three constrictions, white and red"? Today, Eliza didn't care what the old book meant. She only cared what it might get her.

Oliver Crowley's attention.

When Margarita burst back into the bedroom, she found Eliza sitting on the bed hugging a stuffed rabbit. She smiled up at Margarita. "It's Raymond."

"That is Edgar," Margarita corrected her. "Your father said he did not call for me."

"Sorry," Eliza chirped with a shrug and scampered out of the room.

Suppressing a triumphant smile, Eliza carried her loaded backpack toward the front door.

Aurora intercepted her. "You're not leaving so soon?"

"Yeah. Where's your handsome pool boy?"

"He's gone," she pouted.

"I guess good help is hard to find." Eliza smirked.

"We'll get a new one tomorrow," Aurora chortled nasally, and stepped closer to Eliza. *Too close.* The woman had no concept of personal space.

"Do you exfoliate?" she asked with a scrunch of her nose.

Eliza backed away. "Incessantly."

Jerry stomped up. "Back to class?"

"Yeah, Daddy. Busy, busy," Eliza gave her father a kiss on the cheek and made her escape.

Chapter Five

Professor Crowley sang in a surprisingly clear tenor voice, "Bullock starteth, buck farteth. May ye sing cuckoo! Cuckoo, cuckoo! Well, singest thou cuckoo! Nay, cease thou never now!

"Music like that," he declared when he finished, "made medieval man long for death. Mercifully, death was never far away."

Eliza drew hearts in her notebook.

"While rulers, doctors, and songwriters failed the medieval populace, there was a secret society of scholars that offered hope—the alchemists."

Annoying Underwear Girl spoke up. "Weren't they trying to turn lead into gold?"

Read the book, idiot, Eliza thought and smirked to herself. But to her surprise, Crowley gave Annoying Underwear Girl his full attention.

"Alchemists attempted to distil matter and, more importantly, consciousness to its purest essence."

Eliza sketched a knife plunging into one of the hearts she'd drawn.

"Gold, the sun, the Phoenix, were symbols of the alchemical transmutation that created the elixir of life, sometimes referred to as the magnum opus, which would conquer death. Modern chemistry learned a great deal from alchemy, but it rejected alchemy's most crucial element—consciousness."

Eliza kept one hand on her backpack while Crowley spoke. She had come to class armed for battle in a "no-makeup makeup" look, which ironically took twice as long to apply as regular makeup, and she was wearing an invitingly low-cut top. Ethan sat beside her sneaking pained glances at her bosom.

"The alchemist's psychic communion with material elements helped transform them and himself—"

"Or *her*self," Ethan corrected.

"Shut up, Ethan," Eliza hissed.

"Or themselves," Ethan murmured, looking down at his desk.

"—Into something sublime," Crowley continued. "Ultimately leading him to the source of all existence, the secret of life."

A student interjected, "Isn't God the source of all existence?"

Jesus Christ, Eliza thought. *Let the man speak!*

"No," Crowley replied.

"Then what is?" asked the student.

"It's rather obvious, isn't it?" Crowley paused. The room grew quiet. "The secret of life is—"

DING! rang Crowley's timer, and he began packing his valise.

Students moaned with disappointment. Ethan stood up. "I'm starving. I—"

Eliza knocked him down as she rushed to the front of the lecture hall, but Crowley strode out the door before she could reach him. Dropping all pretense of propriety (and propriety was always pretense for Eliza), she ran after him, plowing through throngs of students like a football running back. By the time she burst out of the room, Crowley had almost reached the end of the corridor. In seconds, he would turn the corner and disappear.

"Professor Crowley!" she yelled.

He ignored her.

"Amica mea!"

Crowley stopped and glanced around with a look of horror.

Eliza had been practicing her Latin in preparation for their first date. Crowley's confusion gave her time to reach him. "Sorry," she panted. "I just... I wanted to show you this."

"Good Lord," he sighed.

"Just look. Please."

She held out the book. Crowley took it warily. He froze. His eyes widened as he cautiously ran his fingers over the cover. He opened the book and inhaled sharply.

"Where did you get this?"

"It's a family heirloom. My great-grandfather brought it from Russia."

Crowley carefully turned a page, revealing etchings of dragons battling in a sea of flames and a lion holding the moon and the sun. "Vellum, block leather binding, eighth, ninth century," he mumbled to himself.

"It's really old," Eliza piped in.

"Could it be, old man?" he murmured.

He calls himself Old Man, Eliza thought, thoroughly charmed.

"I thought you'd like to look at it."

Crowley snapped out of his reverie and gave Eliza a brilliant smile. "I would. Thank you."

Eliza flushed. She dropped her chin and gazed up at him from beneath her eyelashes. "I'm glad you like it," she purred.

Crowley glared at her intently.

Eliza held her breath and leaned closer, lost in his fiery eyes that sparkled green and gold beneath the fluorescent lights and seemed to cut through her as if... she wasn't there.

Crowley abruptly strode off with his face buried in the book. Eliza scrambled after him. "My great-great-grandfather was a rabbi," she said, casually strolling beside Crowley as if they'd been close friends for ages. "When his son, my great-grandfather, came to America, he brought this book with him. I've spent a lot of time studying it. I'd love to discuss it—"

Someone knocked into her. Ethan. She shot him a murderous look then turned back to Crowley. He was gone.

"What the fuck?" Eliza shouted. Students in the hallway backed away from her. She pointed at a young man with shaved temples and a bushy beard, "You! Beardy! Where did Crowley go?"

"My name's not Beardy," he whined.

Eliza flipped him off and grabbed a small Asian girl by her sweater. "Where's Crowley?" she demanded.

"Get off me!" the girl yelled and pushed Eliza away.

"No one leaves this hallway until I get some answers!" Eliza hollered. Everyone quickly left the hallway except Ethan. "He went in there," Ethan said pointing to a door.

Eliza yanked it open and found an empty classroom. "There's no one here," she snarled.

Ethan shrugged with a pout. Eliza huffed and walked inside. She stomped down the rows of modular desks until she reached a projection screen at the head of the room. She turned back the way she'd come and finally saw it. Inside an alcove, invisible from the entrance… a door.

"Aha!" she cried.

Eliza yanked it open and found a stairwell. She rushed down the steps and reached the bottom floor in time to see Crowley disappear into another room.

"Professor!" She ran over and noted a faded plaque that read, "CROWLEY." *His office!* She knocked. "Professor Crowley?" No response. "Professor?" She tried the doorknob. It was locked. Eliza gritted her teeth. "Professor Crowley, that book belongs to my father. It's very valuable. We could look at it together, but I can't let it out of my sight."

Crowley did not respond.

Eliza beat on the door. "Professor!" Nothing. "Professor! Open the door right now!"

Okay. Calm down. Don't panic. He's a professor at the University of California. He's not going to steal a book. Eliza did, but he wouldn't. He could lose his job. Unless he denies it. Then it would be he said, she said, and nobody would ever believe her, especially since she's a common book thief. No. University professors don't do things like that. He's not like Professor Chen Peiquan of Leesburg, Florida, who got fired, then stabbed a bunch of students with a vegetable knife. Who kills people with a vegetable knife? What is a "vegetable" knife? Can it cut meat? Of course, it can. Students are made of meat. *Stop! Get a grip, woman!*

She took a deep breath. "Very well," she declared loudly, doing her best impression of a mature person. "You leave me no choice but to call the authorities." She pulled out her phone. "I am telephoning the Campus Police right now." She began to dial then stopped to reevaluate the wisdom of calling the police over a book that *she* had stolen in the first place. Eliza's self-righteous anger evaporated. She slid down the wall, pulled her knees to her chest and sat beside Crowley's office.

Two hours later, Eliza lay curled up on the floor, sleeping. She woke with a gasp and checked her watch. *Could he have gotten out?* No, she would have woken up. He must still be in there. She stood up, stretched her sore muscles and knocked on the door. She tried the doorknob. Still locked. She sank back to the ground, dropped her forehead onto her knees, and pictured her father's face in the courtroom when they convicted her of aggravated book theft. He wouldn't rage at her like her mother did when she spilled diet soda on her white rug. He'd just glare at her with cold, disappointed eyes like he had when she threw a tantrum at Nate 'n Al's Deli, and he declared, "This bores me," and left the restaurant. Her father always expected her to behave like an adult, which she tried her best to do because nothing scared Eliza more than the memory of her father's emotionless face at that restaurant when she was six years old—not even bulls.

※ ※

The late afternoon sun hurt her eyes as she plodded down Bruin Walk. Gravity seemed to grow stronger with each step she took, as if the earth wanted to suck her down into its fiery bowels. She trudged through crowds of students in colorful shorts and flip-flops, hauling backpacks by both straps. Eliza didn't care that styles had changed. *Two straps are dumb.* She slogged beneath banners announcing, CAREER WEEK and EARTH DAY, past placards promoting Phi Beta Kappa, Middle East Peace, and Salsa dancing. A starry-eyed couple passed her, giggling and cooing. *Lovers are stupid.* She trudged past a group of activists entreating people to, "Save the Glaciers." *Stupid glaciers,* she thought. She saw a gardener placidly hoeing a flowerbed. *Stupid flowers.*

Eliza trekked past Pauley Pavilion and the tennis courts until she reached her apartment at the Gayley Towers. Stepping inside, she found her priggish roommate, Tammy Wong, sitting at the kitchen table, wearing noise-cancelling headphones, lost in her laptop.

Because her father had money, Eliza could afford an off-campus apartment, but because her father distrusted college boys, he insisted that she have a female roommate. Jerry had interviewed each potential student and picked prim, studious Tammy Wong. It turned out to be a horrible decision. Tammy and Eliza had nothing in common. Tammy was well-behaved, dependable, and cleanly. Eliza left dirty dishes in the sink, clothes strewn all over the living room, and she never, ever cleaned a toilet. Every interaction with Tammy involved an excessively polite critique of Eliza's hygiene followed by a plaintive request for Eliza to do something that she had no intention of doing.

Tammy glanced up at Eliza when she entered, adjusted her glasses, and continued typing.

"Got any weed?" Eliza asked.

Tammy couldn't hear through her headphones.

Eliza shook her head in disgust, ambled into the kitchen, and opened the refrigerator.

"I had to throw away your yogurt. It was moldy," Tammy yelled, overcompensating for her headphones.

Eliza shut the refrigerator.

"What *I* do," Tammy continued, "is use a marker to write the expiration dates of all my perishables before I put them into the refrigerator, that way—"

Tammy stopped mid-sentence and looked up, her face frozen with terror. Eliza noted that the lamp hanging over the table swayed gently. Tammy had thrown off her headphones, leapt off her chair, and crouched down beside the couch before Eliza felt the room shake. Eliza had never experienced a big earthquake like the ones in the movies where entire cities crumbled to the ground, but she really wanted to. She thought humanity needed a good disaster to cull the herd and relieve traffic on the 405. Unfortunately, this tremor was too weak to get her hopes up.

"What are you doing?" Eliza asked.

"The triangle of safety," Tammy declared with her face tucked between her legs.

"The what?"

"If the ceiling falls, the rafters will hit the sofa arm and the floor leaving me in a triangle of safety."

"So you'll be buried alive," Eliza snorted.

"At least I'll be alive," Tammy shouted, still crouched.

Eliza groaned and slogged into her bedroom. She pulled her stashbox out from beneath her bed, grabbed a pipe, and scraped resin off the bowl with a nail file. She fired it up, inhaled deeply, and coughed up a cloud of rank smoke. Then she lay back on her bed and gazed at her poster of *The Sentinel*. She focused on the pretty star with all the white-eyed ghouls clawing at her.

Some people have all the fun, she thought before she curled into the fetal position and closed her eyes.

☙ ❦

Two days later, Eliza marched through the sculpture garden like a soldier ready for battle. She wore a black top, black jeans, and black boots. She wished she could have cropped her hair, but no matter. She felt tough enough as she barreled past clusters of students who stopped fiddling with their phones to let her pass. She didn't even rub *Standing Woman*'s belly for luck. Today, Eliza *was* Standing Woman.

Eliza had spent the previous day staking out Crowley's office and sending threatening emails to the Dean, all to no avail. But Crowley had class today. Today, he couldn't hide. Today, she would confront him before her peers, and she would not cower or beg. No! She would demand her book *and* an apology. Oliver Crowley would soon see that Eliza Horowitz was no frightened little girl. She was a woman. A strong, smart, erotic woman who could take him to heights of ecstasy that— *Stop that!* She was there for her book. Nothing more.

"Nothing more, nothing more, nothing more..." she quietly chanted as she entered Royce Hall, stomped through the musty old hallways, and up to a gaggle of students gathered outside Crowley's class. She squeezed past them to the door and found a note: Class Canceled.

Eliza screamed as she tore the note to pieces. She ran down the hall and down the stairs to Crowley's office where she rattled the handle. She stepped back and crashed her shoulder against the door. "Ow."

Eliza was waiting for Ethan when he emerged from Franz Hall. She seized him by both of his stupid backpack straps and shoved him up against a wall.

"Your father's a janitor here, right?" she asked.

"My *mother* is the Dean of Engineering and Applied Science," Ethan replied.

"Whatever. I need a key to Crowley's office."

"What?"

"Crowley took my father's book. I've waited outside his office for two days. He went in, but he never came out."

"Call the police."

"No! They'll tell my father. He can't find out I took his book."

"My mom doesn't have keys for every room at UCLA."

"She knows where to get them."

"I can't ask my mom to help me break into a professor's office. It's unethical. It's—"

Eliza grabbed Ethan, gave him a big kiss, then she shoved him away. "I am not interested in you. I just need that key."

"Uh huh," Ethan replied in a blissful stupor.

"Get it."

"Okay," Ethan sighed and staggered away.

Chapter Six

Ethan didn't go to his next class. He rarely went to any of his classes, and nobody cared. He always got A's, and his presence tended to put people on edge. Ethan didn't mind. He had a job to do that required his full attention. He called it, "Operation True Heart." It involved following Eliza and devising clever ways to "accidentally" bump into her. It was exhausting work that rarely reaped a reward.

Until today.

Eliza kissed him. He didn't kiss her. *She* kissed *him*. It was, by far, the most momentous two seconds of his entire life. Ethan had seen thousands of love stories in movies and television, but he never took them seriously. Filmmakers exaggerated violence and heroism, why not love? But, like an unbeliever graced by a vision of God Himself, Ethan had seen the light. It was all true. People really did fall madly in love. They did kiss passionately. They really would sweep everything off a table to make love to each other. Ethan would certainly knock everything off his desk, even his *Star Wars* action figures, to lie on top of Eliza and… Ethan shook his head. He had to keep his wits about him. Eliza had sent him on a quest to prove his love. He would not fail her.

Ethan walked straight into his mother's office without waiting for her secretary, Todd, to announce him. He didn't care how important people thought she was. When he wanted to see his mom, he saw his mom.

Ethan found her sitting behind her desk speaking with two men in suits. She wore a sharp business suit that complemented her short salt-and-pepper hair and angular features. She would have seemed intimidating had she not decorated her entire office with family pictures, most of them chronicling Ethan's childhood through a series of rollercoaster rides.

"Ethee!" she chirped.

Ethan hated when she called him that.

She gestured to the two men sitting before her. "This is Chancellor Dickinson and Mayor Garcetti. Gentlemen, this is my son, Ethan."

"I need to talk to you," Ethan declared, ignoring common courtesy.

The two men looked to his mother, nonplussed. She smiled apologetically, "It'll just be a minute. Todd can make you cappuccinos."

The two men mumbled their assent and left the room.

"Can I have a master key to the school?" Ethan asked.

"What?"

"There's a book I need in an office in Boelter Hall, and no one can find the key."

"Honey, I'm not a janitor. I don't have keys to all the buildings."

"But you can get them."

"I don't know if I—"

"Please," Ethan whined.

"I'm sorry, Ethee. I just can't."

Ethan took a deep breath. "Okay. I'll tell you the truth..." Ethan paused for effect.

"Please do," frowned his mother.

"Me and my buddies are working on a new app, and the master computer's locked in this room"—Ethan knew that a nonsensical term like "master computer" would impress his tech-challenged mother—"and we want to get in there at night so we can—"

"You have *buddies*?" beamed his mother.

"Sure," Ethan lied with a casual shrug.

"Who are they? What are their names? When can I meet them? Can I take you all out to dinner?"

"Sure, but can I get the key first?"

"Of course!" his mother exclaimed as she typed deftly on her cell phone. "I just asked Todd to find your key, and I made you a dental appointment."

"Mom," whined Ethan.

"And please answer when I text you."

"I do."

She picked up her phone and put it back down quickly. Ethan's phone buzzed in his pocket.

"Who's texting you?"

"You are, mom. I'm not an idiot."

"Why don't you look?"

Ethan sighed, looked at his phone and saw a half-dozen hearts. He hit a button and put his phone away. His mother's phone buzzed. She looked at it and smiled. "Thumbs up," she cried and held out her arms. Ethan rolled his eyes, walked behind her desk and leaned over so that she could kiss him on the cheek.

"Could you please tell the mayor to come back in?" she asked as he fled her office.

Chapter Seven

Vince's Chevy Nova is in the driveway again. Why doesn't Jaime's stepfather ever go anywhere? Jaime could run away, but Vince's homeboys would find him and drag him back like they always did. Vince is old-school gangster with friends all over the barrio. Jaime doesn't know how so many people could like a pendejo like Vince. Maybe they know something Jaime doesn't. Maybe Vince is actually a good guy, and he only beats the shit out of Jaime to make Jaime less of a moron. Maybe Jaime's real father would have kicked his ass, too, if he hadn't died. Otherwise, why wouldn't Jaime's mother protect him?

Jaime knows he's stupid. In fifth grade, Mrs. McCloud told him he was lazy. Maybe he was, but who the hell wants to do what they can't do? Like reading. Jaime would listen to Sofia Rocha read *Harry Potter* out loud in class, and it was like magic. Sofia was the same age as him, but she read great. Jaime couldn't put the letters in the right order for them to make any sense. It pissed him off to hear Sofia read so good, but he loved *Harry Potter*. It was the only book he ever read in his life. Or, you know, *heard* read.

Jaime decides not to go home. He doesn't care if he deserves a beating. He doesn't want one, so he runs away. *Why not fly?* He flaps his arms, and *Órale!* He starts rising up off the ground. It's slow going 'cause he's a big guy, but he waves his arms real hard and up he goes, higher and higher. Then a hand grabs him by the leg and throws him back to the ground. Vince. He stands over Jaime, with this big smile so you can see all the gold in his teeth, and it's like he's saying, *I know what you're gonna do before you do it 'cause I'm in your head, moron.* Jaime wishes Vince would get out of his head, and that his stomach would stop hurting.

Vince snorts up a gob and spits. "What was the all-time greatest Lakers team?"

"Nineteen seventy-one, seventy-two," Jaime answers quick as he can.

"Three top players?"

"Wilt Chamberlain, Jerry West, Elgin Baylor."

Vince backhands Jaime across the face.

"That was right!" Jaime squeals.

"I know."

"Then why'd you hit me?"

"God told me to," Vince pulls his arm back. Jaime covers his face and waits for the next punch, just like he's done all his life.

Just like he'll keep doing for forever and ever.

Chapter Eight

"If the series of vectors converges absolutely—infinity over sigma over $k=0$, double vertical uk is less than infinity—calculate the convergences using the Cauchy-Schwarz Inequality." Tammy hummed the latest Jonas Brothers song while she scribbled the formula on a pad of graph paper.

She adjusted her glasses and resumed reading, "According to this theory, all alternate possible histories and futures are real, each representing an alternate universe." Tammy grunted. *A parallel universe?* She didn't think so. Sure, the theory offered an elegant mathematical solution to the unified field theory, but theoretical mathematics and reality were two very different things. *And thank God*, she thought. She hated when people corrupted a pristine theoretical formula with a practical application. It felt like plucking an angel from heaven and putting her to work in a coal mine. Why couldn't people just revel in the abstract beauty of thought, free from the depravity of this ugly world? A tear welled in Tammy's eye as she savored the sweet fragility of beauty.

She sighed wistfully and continued reading, "According to the Copenhagen Interpretation devised in 1925—" A flash of color caught her eye. She looked over her laptop and saw a pink sock stuffed under the couch. *Eliza!* Tammy yanked off her headphones, walked over and picked up the sock with two fingers. *Yuck.*

Tammy committed herself to being a good roommate. She always paid her bills on time and cleaned up after herself. *A girl who leaves garbage is garbage*, her mother's voice echoed in her mind. Tammy left the kitchen spotless after she used it, even when most of the mess belonged to Eliza. She had written out a very fair schedule of vacuuming, dusting, and bathroom chores, which Eliza totally ignored. Tammy often heard her roommate laughing on the phone while Tammy scrubbed the toilet on her hands and knees. "Wasted time is a wasted life," her mother would say.

Sometimes Eliza would go out wearing a skimpy dress and heels. *Men don't marry whores.* Tammy's mother hadn't allowed her to date in high school, which made her sad at the time, but she appreciated it now. "Boys might have fun with a slut," her mother had said, "but they only marry hard-working, respectable girls that they can trust to raise their children." Not that Tammy was perfect; she had sensual desires like any other girl, but she kept them in check. She knew that one day she would meet a wonderful man—looks, age, and race didn't matter, *as long as he's not Black, Mexican, Indian, or Filipino*, and they would start a beautiful family together. The fantasy filled Tammy with joy.

"Ow!" She had subconsciously dug her fingernails into her palm. Tammy wiped the blood off on her pants and sighed. One more bad habit to fix. *You have so many.*

Tammy left Eliza's sock folded neatly on the coffee table and walked back to her laptop. Someone knocked on the door. Tammy froze. People didn't normally come to the apartment unannounced. Another knock. Tammy rifled through her backpack and pulled out a cannister of mace. With her finger poised over the button, she looked through the peephole and saw nothing but a blurry kaleidoscope of color. She squeezed her eyes shut and looked again. The colors sharpened into definable shapes. Flowers. *The devil always brings a gift.* Tammy secured the safety chain, cracked the door open and gasped.

The most beautiful man she had ever seen in her life stood on her doorstep, holding a bouquet of flowers. Sunlight cast a halo over his golden hair and reflected off the door onto his piercing blue eyes. He smiled, revealing a set of brilliant white teeth.

"Hi," said he.

Tammy frantically shut the door, ripped off her glasses, unfastened the chain, and pulled it open.

"Hi," she squeaked.

"Is Eliza here?"

Tammy recoiled as if he had thrust his hand into her chest and squashed her heart. She smiled stiffly and shook her head.

"Could you give these to her please?" he asked with an apologetic smile. "Tell her they're from Ryan."

Tammy grinned harder. "Of course."

His eyes sparkled. "Thank you."

Tammy slipped her glasses back on to watch the shapely young man saunter away. She remained motionless, holding the flowers, her face frozen in a fierce smile that made her cheeks ache. She noticed a note in the bouquet. Tammy could not read the note without violating her own deeply held standards of right and wrong.

"Dear Eliza," the note read. "I had a wonderful time the other night. We can take it as slowly as you like. Very fondly, Ryan."

Tammy took a deep breath, and still smiling, she closed the door, walked to the kitchen, opened the cupboard beneath the sink, and crammed the flowers into the garbage.

Chapter Nine

Eliza paced in front of Crowley's office until Ethan ran up with the key. "If you knew what I had to do to get this..." he panted. Eliza jammed the key into the lock and opened the door. She gave Ethan a big smile and pocketed the key.

"Thank you."

Ethan beamed. "You're welcome. I had to get through three levels of security. Fortunately, I know taekwondo, so I—" Eliza entered Crowley's office and shut the door in Ethan's face.

Inside the room, Eliza recoiled. She had expected Crowley to have a strange, even macabre private sanctum, but nothing could have prepared her for the horror she found.

Crowley's office was... just an office. It had an institutional metal desk and a rolling chair, a metal filing cabinet, a metal bookshelf with some boxes of paperclips and staples on top of it. A faded poster of a cartoon man leaning back with one leg extended that read, KEEP ON TRUCKIN hung on a bulletin board. This wasn't the sanctuary of an enigmatic iconoclast. It was a civil servant's office.

Something inside Eliza died. "Ethan, come in here," she grumbled. She walked back to the door. It was locked. *What the hell?* "Ethan!" She banged on the door. No response.

Then *BABOOM!* An earthquake. *Okay, this one's a biggie.* What had her stupid roommate said? *Quadrangle of—?* She stumbled back against a wall. It swung open, and she fell backward out of the room and off the edge of the world.

Time slowed as Eliza fell. She watched with detached curiosity as her hand shot out on its own and grabbed hold of a railing that she hadn't seen. *That's cool*, she thought a nanosecond before time sped up to normal. She was hanging by one hand over a steep flight of metal stairs that led down into a black abyss.

Eliza gasped and pulled herself away from the precipice. She stood atop a small landing illuminated by a weak lightbulb overhead. She spun back to the door. There was no handle. Eliza pushed. It wouldn't budge. She kicked it and tried to pry it open with her fingers. Nothing. She searched for a keyhole, an alarm, anything. Still nothing. She pulled out her cell phone. No service. Eliza clenched her jaw and swallowed her fear. *Calm down. Focus. Assess the situation one fact at a time. Fact one, you can't get out the way you got in.*

She wailed and pounded on the door.

She stopped and inhaled slowly. Okay... Fact number two. She was trapped at the top of a metal staircase that descended into utter darkness.

"Jesus Christ, help me! My mother's Catholic! She just converted to marry my dad!"

Okay. She cleared that up just in case a supreme being existed and He preferred Catholics. So... Fact number three: She had to walk down the stairs.

"Nooooo!" she shrieked.

Eliza ping-ponged between reason and madness until she grew too exhausted to scream. "Okay," she whispered hoarsely.

Eliza switched on her phone's flashlight, took a deep breath, and lowered her foot onto the first step. The clang of her boot heel striking metal echoed through the stairwell. She froze. She made a mental note to wear sneakers the next time she broke into a man's office. She took another step. *Clang!* Damn it! She panicked and ran. *Clang, clang, clang, thud!* Her feet hit bottom. She was standing on a cement floor. She shined her phone light in a circle around her but saw nothing.

It's an adventure, she told herself. A mystery like Sherlock Holmes. What would Benedict Cumberbatch do? Benedict would tell Watson to eliminate the impossible and whatever was left, no matter how improbable, must be true. Okay, Benedict, there was a secret door in Oliver's revolting office and… That was as far as Eliza got. She was no Sherlock Holmes.

CRACK! A light snapped on in the distance. It came from the far end of a long tunnel. *Light means people. People can help me… or murder me. Shut up!*

"Hello!" she called into the tunnel. She held her breath and listened. She heard nothing but water dripping, somewhere, and the pounding of her own heart. *Okay, okay. Here we go.* She stepped into the passageway and heard a soft splash. *Just a little water.* She took another step. *Splash.* She clenched her jaw. *Splash.* She whispered, "It was the schooner Hesperus"—reciting *The Wreck of the Hesperus* always calmed her down—"that sailed the wintry sea"—*Splash*—"and the skipper had taken his little daughter"—*Splash*—"to bear him company. Blue were her eyes—" *Splash splash.* She stopped. Had she heard a second footstep? She listened intently. Silence. "Blue were her eyes as the fairy-flax," she continued. "Her cheeks like the dawn—" *Splash!* That one came from behind her. She spun around.

A silhouetted figure stood at the tunnel's entrance.

Eliza ran, splashing wildly through the shaft until she emerged into a large, well-lit chamber. She searched for a way out. To her left, she saw the entrance to a much larger tunnel; same thing to her right. She walked forward and almost fell into a dark trench with train tracks. On the opposite wall, she read the word Westwood written in tile.

She was in a subway station. *There's no subway under UCLA. Is there?* The response to her question came as a low rumble. The sound grew louder until a light appeared in one of the tunnels.

Eliza stepped back as a train roared into the station and screeched to a stop before her.

Eliza had ridden the Los Angeles Metro many times. This was no Metro train. It looked more like a relic from some dystopian Disneyland. It was red. Or rather, it had once been red. Now, it was more of an orange-brown rust. It had three cars made of steel plates bolted together, and beneath the windows, Eliza made out faded yellow words, PACIFIC ELECTRIC. The train's interior lights sprang on and its doors slid open. Eliza hesitated. She looked back the way she'd come. She didn't want to meet whoever was lurking down there, so she took a deep breath and stepped onto the train. The doors slammed shut and, with a wrenching scrape of metal, the train started moving.

Shit.

The subway train picked up speed until it raced down the track. Eliza spread her legs to keep her balance and pulled out her phone. Still no signal. The train car veered sharply, knocking her against a window. *The back of the train's the safest place in a crash.* She didn't know if that was really true, but it made sense. Of course, nothing had made any sense since she'd entered Crowley's office.

Eliza made her way to the last car, sat on the floor and hugged her knees. *Please don't crash,* she prayed to the god of Catholics or Jews or atheists or whomever. As she sat juddering on the floor, she took in her surroundings. The train car had worn leather seats, cracked linoleum floors and crumbly old ads above the windows. One ad showed a baby shaving with a Gillette Safety Razor. Babe Ruth drank a *Rock Cola* in another, and in yet another, a doctor smoked a cigarette and assured his patients that "20,679 physicians say Luckies are less irritating!"

Maybe I went back in time? No, she reasoned. First of all, the subway would have looked newer back then. Secondly, Eliza was pretty sure that the past had people in it, and she was definitely alone. And finally, it was a stupid idea.

Eliza looked out the window. Pitch black. *A normal subway would have reached a stop by now,* she thought. *This must be an express. Yes, it's an express train to hell—* She shook her head. *Breathe.* If these were her last few seconds on earth, she should savor them, take in every detail. She had already inspected the train car, so she decided to think about the people she loved. She imagined her father's face when he learned that she had died. She pictured tears welling in his eyes until he let loose a wail of grief so terrible and pure that God Himself would bow His head with sorrow.

That'll be sweet.

Her mother would curse Eliza for making her suffer and lament having given birth to such a selfish child. *Okay,* Eliza conceded. *She would also be devastated—not "devastated."* That wasn't the right word. *Desolate?* No. *Blue.* That was it. Her mother would be blue. Eliza grunted her dissatisfaction. She had spent her entire life trying to manage her mother's moods. Dying in a runaway train would at least free her of that responsibility. Eliza didn't want to think about her right now.

Professor Crowley, on the other hand... Professor Crowley would blame himself for her death and cry like Heathcliff in *Wuthering Heights,* or like people did in *The Long Road Home*— her father's film about an old Jewish woman, played by Meg Ryan, who only had a couple of weeks to live, so she took a train back to her old neighborhood in Brooklyn, where she met this cool black guy, played by Eddie Murphy, who apparently had not died in the 1980s like Eliza had assumed. The point was, it was a good movie, but hardly anyone had seen it, so her father stuck to making big-budget action films.

BAM! The cars knocked into each other as the train rounded a curve too quickly. "*Oh, God, please don't let me die, please God, please...*

Eliza knew that God always showed up during times of trouble, like when you're drunk in the gutter or hunkering in a foxhole. He never came when you were having cocktails with a charming gentleman. If God was ever going to call on Eliza, it would be now. And sure enough, God came, and in a deep comforting voice, He said, "Eliza. You are insane."

"Of course!" she shouted with a smile. This was just some kind of psychotic episode. She was probably lying on the sidewalk somewhere, drooling. *What a relief.* Now someone could stick her in a hospital, give her some drugs, and life would return to normal. *Thank you, God!*

BAM! The train hit another curve. "Thanks for nothing, God."

Apparently, God had grown less touchy since the time of Moses because He showed Eliza mercy and slowed the train to a stop. She jumped out, spun around, and kicked the subway.

"Fuck you!"

The train doors closed. Eliza looked around. A sign told her that she was at the Eighth Street Station, but which Eighth Street, downtown or Santa Monica? It didn't matter. She spotted an EXIT sign. *That* was all that mattered. She marched through a wooden turnstile and up a set of metal stairs until she reached a solid cement wall.

"Oh, come on!" she yelled.

She raced back down the stairs and spotted an old freight elevator. It had a folding metal gate that allowed her to see into the shaft. She doubted that such an old contraption still worked. She pressed a button, which produced a loud *thud* followed by the grinding of cables and pullies. An elevator car descended and stopped before her. She pulled open the gate and poked her head inside. She definitely did not want to get stuck in an underground elevator where no one could hear her scream. She had to find another way out.

All the station lights went out, leaving only one light inside the elevator.

"Goddammit!"

Elevators are fun, said the little girl's voice in her head.

"No, they're not!" she shouted back, but she got in anyway and hit the button. It thudded and the gears grinded, and up she went. Eliza assumed that she would pass floor after floor like in a normal building. She shouldn't have. She was deep underground, so the elevator groaned upward through a long concrete shaft. If it stopped now, she would never get out. Sweat trickled down her back. All she could do was stare at the concrete wall and hope that the rusted old contraption kept moving.

A large solid steel door gradually descended before her, and the elevator jostled to a stop. The steel door had a handle. Eliza grabbed it and pushed down. It didn't budge. She pushed again, straining with all her might. Nothing. She held on to the side of the elevator, climbed atop the handle and jumped up and down until she slipped and fell back into the car. The handle wouldn't move, but she had to keep trying. She stood and grabbed it again. This time, she pulled up instead of down, and the steel door slid open easily.

"Whatever," she growled.

She stepped off the elevator into a warehouse packed with wooden crates and steel drums. The place reeked of rotten eggs. Eliza covered her nose and walked toward a light coming from the far end of the room.

Chapter Ten

Jaime squeezes his eyes shut, waiting for Vince to hit him again, but he doesn't. Jaime peeks through his hands and sees Vince looking at something behind Jaime.

"Who the fuck are *you*," Vince demands. Jaime turns around and sees Badass Undertaker Dude standing in the driveway of his old house. *Puta madre. How'd he get here?* Jaime curls up into a ball.

"Hey, fuckhead," Vince says. "I asked you a question."

Badass Undertaker Dude pulls out his crazy-big gun, shoots Vince in the face, and Vince blows up like an M-80! Out of the smoke comes this black, slimy worm with tons of little legs and a face like a creepy old man.

"Id nocet multus," the worm says and crawls away.

Jaime doesn't know whether to scream or laugh, so he does both.

The dude lowers his gun and looks around like something smells bad. "Dreary, but I've seen worse," he says. Then he steps up to Jaime and asks, "Can you see me?"

Jaime trembles. Tears run down his cheeks. He nods weakly.

"Good," says the dude and reaches out his hand. Jaime wants to run or fight, but he can't move. Badass Undertaker Dude touches his chest.

And the world ends.

Chapter Eleven

Eliza thought that she had entered some old factory. The cavernous space had brick walls, scuffed plank floors and grimy, metal-framed windows all bathed in flickering firelight from a cylindrical furnace in the middle of the room. *This would make a great condo.* Beside the oven sat a long table full of beakers, test tubes, and a twisted copper contraption that looked like a moonshiner's still. To her right, she saw a small kitchen tucked beneath a steel loft loaded with boxes. A tall black curtain screened off the other end of the room. She didn't see a door, so she figured the exit had to be behind the drapes.

Eliza tried her phone. Finally, she had a signal. She checked her GPS. She was downtown. She stepped to the curtain and peeked inside.

A lifeless white face glared back at her.

Eliza jerked the curtains closed. *What was that? A ghost? That would be cool.*

She cracked open the curtain again. The face belonged to a porcelain baby doll. She snapped the curtain shut. Dolls were much scarier than ghosts. She had to get out of there before it wormed its way into her nightmares.

She heard someone say, "Dreary, but I've seen worse."

Oliver?

She peeked inside once more, and there, before the doll, sat Oliver Crowley cross-legged on a rug, still wearing a tie and vest, gazing into a black mirror by candlelight. His eyes looked unfocused in the murky glass. She closed the curtain once more to call the police, then stopped. *What is he doing?* Once more, she peeked inside. Crowley sat in a chapel of sorts. Engravings similar to the ones in her book hung on the walls—stars, moons, and comets, a King and Queen embracing, snakes and lions devouring one another. Above the mirror, a dazzling sun gazed down on him with placid eyes. Crowley did not move.

Is he meditating? Did he take that subway here? He must have. Why? He's crazy. I knew it. He's too cool to be sane. What childhood trauma drove him to this? I hope he doesn't start masturbating. I have to get out of here. No! I need my book. I can't let him get away with—

Crowley stood.

Eliza leapt back and ran behind a table. She crouched down and listened. She heard nothing, so she peeked over the table. Crowley remained behind the curtains.

Then she realized that she had hidden behind a gurney not a table, and there was something on it. She refocused her eyes and saw the profile of a man's face inches from hers. He had a shaved head with a tattooed scorpion curling along his temple and jaw. His skin was grey, his eyes were milky white, and he smelled like pickles.

This guy was dead.

Eliza bit her knuckles like a silent movie star to stifle a scream, just as Crowley burst out from behind the curtain and strode toward her. She dropped to the floor and crawled under the gurney. Crowley's feet stopped before her face.

"Hello," he said.

He knows I'm here. He's going to kill me. What do I do?

"Veni huc," he said.

Latin. He wants me to come to him.

"Veni huc," he repeated.

No way, Mister Man. You come and get me. I'll kick your ass! She waited. Crowley's feet stepped away. *Maybe he's not talking to me.* Eliza looked around, desperate. She quietly crawled to a nearby workbench, expecting Crowley to spot her at any moment, and then ducked behind it. Crowley said nothing. *What's he doing?* She peeked around the bench and saw him turn a crackly page from a large book atop a medical cart.

My book!

Crowley studied it for a moment, then picked up a vial containing red liquid. He poured the concoction into the dead man's mouth, laid his hand on the man's chest, and mumbled something Eliza couldn't hear.

The dead man blinked.

Chapter Twelve

Jaime was cold. Not being-in-the-desert-at-night kind of cold. No. You could fix that cold with a jacket. Jaime couldn't fix this cold with anything because it wasn't anything. It was nothing. And, *nothing* was fucking cold.

Ven aqui.

Jaime's Spanish wasn't so good, but he'd heard that before. His grandfather used to say it when he wanted Jaime to watch television with him. Jaime would climb into the old man's Bar-calounger, and the two of them would watch some old movie or golf. His grandfather had never played a game of golf in his life, but he loved to watch other guys hit tiny balls into holes. Jaime thought it was super boring, but he liked sitting there, playing with his grandfather's gold ring that he'd gotten in some war somewhere. The old man would point to it and say, "Todos aman la vida. Pero el hombre valiente aprecia más el honor." Jaime didn't know all the words, but he knew that his grandfather was telling him to be an honorable man.

Jaime wished he'd listened to his grandfather instead of gang-banging and getting shot by some creepy guy in a black suit.

Ven aqui.

Jaime knew that voice. And he didn't like it.

Ven aqui.

Then there was a light. It was kind of weak and smoky at first, but then it got clearer until Jaime could see a face.

Badass Undertaker Dude.

Jaime yelled, "Who the fuck *are* you?" Only he didn't really yell because he couldn't talk. He couldn't even move his mouth. In fact, he couldn't move anything. All he could do was stare like a big pendejo at the dude who'd shot his stepfather in the face.

"Ven aqui," the dude said again. Only he wasn't actually saying these words in Spanish. He was saying *veni huc*. Dude didn't talk Spanish so good.

Jaime's stomach started to hurt.

"It's all right," the dude said. "You're safe here."

Jaime strained as hard as he could, and he managed to pry his lips apart.

Badass Undertaker Dude's eyes got all wide. "Yes?"

"Tums," Jaime said. At least that's what he wanted to say. What he really said was, "Aaaaargh."

"That's good," the dude said like Jaime had done something really smart.

Then the pain in his stomach got real bad like something was kicking and biting in there. The pain squeezed up from deep in his belly and into his throat, until he felt two little hands grab his tongue, and then this little dude crawled out of his mouth and hopped onto his chest. The guy was all slimy 'cause he'd been in his stomach, and he was super ugly. He had this big fat nose, and big ears, and no hair, and a really big wrinkly cock. He looked like a little old cholo, the kind that sat on his porch all day drinking whiskey out of a paper bag. Jaime should have freaked out 'cause little cholos don't usually come out of a guy's mouth, but he didn't, 'cause for the first time in forever, his stomach didn't hurt anymore.

The little cholo screamed. Then Jaime heard another scream. It was a woman. Jaime, Badass Undertaker Dude, and Little Cholo all looked across the room, and there was this girl poking her head up from behind a table. She had curly hair and big blue eyes, and she looked real worried, like she really cared...

Sandy, Jaime said to himself, and he knew everything was going to be all right.

Chapter Thirteen

Eliza screamed.

A repulsive little creature had crawled out of a corpse's mouth, and he was looking at her, so was Crowley and the corpse, who couldn't have been a corpse because dead people don't stare at you. Eliza's eyes went straight to the little guy's huge penis which swung back and forth as he balanced himself on the corpse's stomach. She pried her eyes off the terrible genitalia and looked at the thing's face. It had bugged out, gunmetal eyes, a large nose, fat cheeks, and no hair. It smiled at Eliza, and then it leapt onto the medical cart and grabbed her father's book.

Eliza forgot her fear and yelled, "No!" She rushed forward, but the creature darted under the gurney with her book.

"That's mine!"

"How did you get in here?" shouted Crowley.

The little man scrambled up a shelf, threw Eliza's book through a window, and dove out after it.

"My book!"

Crowley dismissed her with a snort and ran to a shelf full of jars.

"You've got to get it back!"

"What do you think I'm doing, woman?" Crowley exclaimed as he pulled a handful of wriggling earthworms out of a jar.

"That thing came out of his mouth!" Eliza shouted, pointing at the corpse. The corpse smiled.

Eliza screamed.

Crowley stuffed the worms into a paper bag. Then he pulled down a bottle full of seeds and poured them into a second bag. "Get out!" he commanded.

"My book!"

"Curses!" Crowley spat as he crammed the paper bags into his valise and ran out through a door Eliza had not seen.

"Curses?" Eliza repeated to herself, astonished that she could still feel charmed in the midst of all this madness.

"Wait!" she shouted and ran after him.

Night had fallen, leaving the warehouse district even more bleak than it had been during the day. Eliza caught up to Crowley as he marched down the sidewalk tracking tiny fluorescent-green footprints with a black light.

"What was that thing? Why did it take my book?"

"A homunculus, and I don't know," Crowley replied, never slowing his stride.

"Homunculus? They're not real. Are they? Oh, my God, they are! It was so gross. I thought you made a homunculus by putrefying semen in a horse's bladder."

"Sometimes they come out of a dead gang member's mouth."

"I didn't know that."

"Neither did I."

"You didn't make him on purpose?"

"No."

"That guy looked dead, and then he smiled, so he couldn't have been dead, right?"

"Go away."

"No! You stole my book. I stayed outside of your office for two days, and I finally had to break in. Not *break* in. I got the key. Don't ask me how. It was Ethan. But then there was this earthquake, and I fell through the wall and there were stairs and rats and the subway—"

Crowley spun on her. "You saw the subway? What else did you see?"

"Keep on Truckin'," she recalled with a disgusted shiver.

Crowley turned away and mumbled to himself as he continued his trek. "This could be no accident, but why her? What purpose could this puerile girl serve?"

"Hey," she objected.

"She must have some connection to the experiment... the book." He whirled back on her again. "Where did you get the book?"

"It's been in my family for generations. I told you—"

"Who *are* you?"

"Eliza Horowitz. Your student."

"Horowitz?"

"It belonged to my great-great-grandfather, Yosef—"

"Rabbi Yosef Horowitz?" Crowley whispered. He stuck his black light in her face and studied her eyes, mouth, nose, and ears. He gasped and stepped back. "Why didn't you tell me?"

"Because you never talk to me."

"Who is your father?"

"Jerry Horowitz. He's one of the most successful filmmakers of all time. Have you seen *The Lifeless Dead?*"

"That's redundant."

"It only grossed two-point-five *billion*—"

"And your grandfather made movies, too?"

"My great-grandfather. Jack Larson. He changed his name, you know, antisemitism and all. My father changed it back to Horowitz after it was okay to be Jewish. Jack Larson was huge—he practically created Hollywood. He died in the great Tinseltown Tragedy. I'm babbling, aren't I? Do you like silent films?"

Crowley glared at her with ferocious, unblinking eyes, then twirled around and bounded off.

I guess not.

Eliza scrambled to keep up with him. He led her past graffiti-covered walls, homeless men glowering from beneath mountains of soiled rags, and Spoor Gastric Bistro Pub. Eliza slowed to gaze at the hip thirty-year-olds drinking and laughing inside. She thought of Ryan. If only she could have liked Ryan, she wouldn't be following this crazy professor to find a stolen book and a tiny monster with an oversized penis.

At least you're not bored.

Eliza picked up her pace. She feared that running would make her look childish, so she walked as quickly as she could, which made her feel like an old woman power walking in a television commercial for some drug while an announcer read a long list of lethal side-effects.

"You look stupid," someone snorted. Eliza spun around. She saw no one.

"Who's there?" she yelled. No one replied. She must have imagined the voice. *Keep it together!* she commanded herself and ran after Crowley.

"Do you have to walk so fast?" she complained. He didn't answer or slow down. Eliza pressed on. "Who's the big guy with the tattoos? He looked dead. Then that thing came out of him. How did it get in there? And why would—?"

Crowley stopped abruptly and held a finger to his mouth. "Shh." He looked around, listening. Eliza did, too.

"I don't hear anything," she whispered.

"I know. It's pleasant, isn't it?" he said and resumed walking. Eliza followed with a frown.

The small green footsteps led them across train tracks and down a long, concrete incline to the enormous gutter whimsically named the Los Angeles River. Crowley stopped at the water's edge and turned back to Eliza. Distant streetlights cast dark shadows across his face, giving him the appearance of a malevolent wraith. Eliza scanned her surroundings. She was in a scary place with a scary, albeit extremely handsome, man.

Crowley stepped toward her. Eliza quickly raised her phone and *flash*! Crowley reared back. Eliza tapped her phone with blinding speed. "Sorry. I just thought I'd take some pictures in case I write a paper about this."

Crowley's face turned murderous.

"Or not," Eliza corrected herself. "I will never, ever write anything about this. Ever." Then she added, "Unless you want to write it together?"

"You sent someone my picture in case I try to kill you," he stated dryly.

"Maybe."

"That was the first intelligent thing you've done so far."

Crowley grabbed the two paper bags he had stuck in his valise and carefully poured some seeds and earthworms on the concrete beside the water. "Homunculi like wet places," Crowley declared.

"Like horse bladders full of semen?"

"Yes. And worms and persimmon seeds." Crowley backed Eliza away from the river and sat in the shadow of a bridge pilon.

"That subway. How did it—"

"Silence," he whispered. Eliza sat down beside him and remained quiet.

They waited, watching the water, saying nothing, until finally Crowley said, "They built the subway during construction of the UCLA campus. The line originally went from downtown to Venice Beach, which was quite the resort back in the 1920s, but an earthquake destroyed part of the tunnel, and they abandoned the project. Fortunately, the line between UCLA and downtown remains serviceable."

"But why—" Eliza started.

"Shh," Crowley commanded and pointed to something slithering through the river. Eliza watched, repulsed yet spellbound, as a small silhouette rose from the water and crawled across the concrete channel like a deformed spider. A car horn honked in the distance, and the creature froze. It cocked its head, sniffed the air, and crept forward slowly until, in a flash, it scooped up a handful of worms and crammed them into its mouth.

No one's going to believe this, Eliza realized, so she snatched her phone and *flash*! The creature leapt back into the water. Crowley jumped to his feet. "Revenito. Praecipio vobis!" he yelled, and slowly, the homunculus limped back out of the river.

"He obeyed you?"

"I fed him," Crowley replied. "Venit!"

The homunculus hesitated, trying to resist Crowley's command, but some overpowering impulse compelled him forward.

"Ubi est liber?" asked Crowley.

"Where's my book?" demanded Eliza.

"What do you think I asked him?"

"Quod liber?" the homunculus asked in a raspy little voice.

"Give it back!" Eliza yelled impatiently.

"He obeys only me."

"Because you fed him?"

"Of course. What do they teach in school these days?" Crowley turned to the homunculus. "Producat illum ad me."

The homunculus pouted. "Olim ego interficiemus te," he grumbled and stomped toward the bridge like an angry schoolboy. He scampered up a pilon and disappeared beneath the girders. Eliza and Crowley waited in silence for a long moment before something fell from the bridge. Time slowed for Eliza as she watched the book topple through the air, it's copper binding flashing green and red, until it splashed into the river. Eliza didn't hesitate. She jumped into what she assumed to be a shallow wash, but—due to an unusually long rainy season—turned out to be a rushing torrent that knocked her onto her face and sent her careening down the narrow channel. Fortunately, she had fallen onto the book, which she held onto tightly as she zoomed down the river, sometimes touching bottom, sometimes not until she crashed into the fender of a car.

Thank God for litter. Eliza tossed the book out of the water and crawled out after it. She scooped it up and ran her hand over the cover. It seemed intact. Cautiously, she opened it and found the tightly packed pages remarkably dry.

"Thank God," she sighed.

Her relief did not last long. A vague discomfort rose in her belly. She wondered if she had eaten something that disagreed with her. Then she remembered that she hadn't eaten all day. *I must be hungry*, she thought. She tried to ignore her mounting agitation, but it only grew stronger. *I'm not hungry*, she realized. *I'm afraid.* She looked around for the professor. She couldn't find him. Dread boiled inside her. Reproaches ricocheted through her mind. *I'm alone, I'm helpless, I'm worthless. Why didn't I bring a sweater? It's at the dry cleaners. It's been there for months. How long do they keep things—?*

She smelled it before she saw it. A putrid stench, like fruit rotting in a dumpster, rose from the river, coalescing into an opaque haze which blotted out the stars and the city. Eliza could feel the apparition's malevolence as it engulfed her. It hated her so purely, so self-righteously, that Eliza felt as if she had somehow brought the scorn upon herself. She tried to break free, but the miasma held her tightly. It yanked her arms back and plunged a filthy tentacle into her stomach. Eliza gasped as the cloud scavenged through her and latched onto something terrible deep inside her. It squeezed, and Eliza screamed in pain. Then it pulled, and out through her navel came a formless black malignancy. Eliza could feel its power, its outrage, and its savagery. She knew this creature. It had lived inside her all her life—suppressed, disparaged, and denied. The cloud had released Eliza's anger, and she reveled in its emancipation.

As darkness crept in from the corners of her eyes, she heard muffled staccato laughter, and an abrasive voice cut through her brain.

"You look stupid."

Chapter Fourteen

Eliza sits in a meadow atop a hill, overlooking the sea. Yellow dandelions sparkle in the windswept grass. The sun feels close and inviting. The little girl sits before her picking wildflowers. She offers one to Eliza. Eliza hesitates. She loves this little girl, and she loves this place. She always has. It's beautiful. Too beautiful. She doesn't know what to do with all this loveliness. She wants to grab it and claim it somehow, but she can't. It eludes her. It gnaws at her and taunts her. Her chest constricts. Her heart hurts. She yanks up tufts of grass and screams in frustration. She wants something so badly, but she doesn't know what. Her desire consumes her like fire. The mountain shakes. The ground cracks open, flames shoot up from the fissure, and Eliza falls.

Eliza sits with her English teacher on the beach at night, gazing into the bonfire. She had spent her entire senior year plotting to win Richard's love, and she had made no secret about it. She enlisted the aid of schoolmates and dismissed reprimands from teachers and staff. Nothing deterred her, not even Richard himself, who never expressed the slightest interest in her. Now her dream had come true. She had imagined the ecstasy she would feel once she could release all her pent-up desire and love Richard freely, but as they sit together on the beach, she doesn't feel ecstatic. She feels no wondrous gratification, only a vague sense of comfort and boredom.

Other couples sleep around the fire. Suzy, her high school friend, lies with Mr. Burger, their obese elderly biology teacher. *Yuck*, thinks Eliza. Two guys from the swim team snuggle inside a sleeping bag. *That's sweet*. Her mother lies with a sixteen-year-old boy, which doesn't surprise Eliza. What surprises her is that she sleeps with her eyes open. She looks more closely at the other couples. Suzy lies with her eyes open, too. Beside her, Mr. Burger, who now looks like Henry Kissinger, has flies crawling over his eyeballs. A bolt of terror shoots through Eliza.

"They're all dead," she gasps.

Eliza and David Tennant run through a pine forest to get help.

"Lift your knees when you run in the dark," David Tennant instructs her in his delightful Scottish lilt.

They find an escalator. Eliza runs up the metal steps. David Tennant remains stationary while he ascends. "You're defeating the purpose of electric stairs," he shouts.

"You're my favorite Doctor Who," she yells back but keeps running until she reaches the large Tudor-style house. She hears laughter and 1920s jazz with a scratchy voice singing about his sweet baby girl. Warm light sparkles through the window. Eliza steps closer. She pictures a large Christmas tree festooned with colored lights and a fire crackling in the hearth while beautiful people in tuxedoes and ballgowns chat gayly. She places her hand on the glass, looks inside, and the room turns black and silent.

Fear shoots up her spine.

She turns to David Tennant. Only he's not David Tennant or Richard. He never was. She sees his real face for the first time as he towers over her—a featureless black shadow with flaming red eyes, and long, curved horns like a bull.

Not again.

Chapter Fifteen

Eliza awoke with a gasp. She stared up at white nothingness, her heart pounding, her chest heaving. She closed her eyes. The bull glared at her. She snapped her eyes open. The beast waited for her in the darkness. She focused on the white blur above until it crystalized into a ceiling. She lifted her head and saw a pack of white-eyed ghouls chasing a young woman. She sighed with relief. She was in her room.

"You're drooling," said a deep male voice.

Eliza jumped. Oliver Crowley sat beside her bed, glaring down at her with his stony green eyes. Eliza scrambled away from him. *Oh, my God. He's in my room, he's in my room. How did he get here? What happened last night?* She looked down. She still had her clothes on, which reassured her but... *I must look awful.* She wiped her face, smearing mascara onto her hand. She pulled hair over her eyes and leapt out of bed.

"I have to... Be right back."

Eliza ran into the bathroom and choked back a scream when she saw her smudged racoon eyes in the mirror. She quickly washed her face, applied a touch of fresh mascara, gargled, thrashed her hair into submission, peed, unbuttoned another button on her shirt, and casually strolled back into the bedroom to find Crowley standing, valise in hand.

"You changed your tie," she observed with all the nonchalance she could muster.

"It's ten o'clock in the morning, Miss Horowitz. Let's go. We have no time to lose."

"Go where? Why?"

"We need to discuss last night's events in a more hygienic environment."

Eliza glanced at the clothes and candy wrappers strewn about her room. "Last night? What do you mean?" The stink of the strange cloud filled her nostrils. She gagged. The floor swayed beneath her feet as memories of the previous evening surged through her—the book, the smiling corpse, the tiny man, the big penis, the blackness coming from her navel. *Was it all a dream?* Eliza stumbled onto the bed, coughing and choking. She lowered her head between her knees, willing herself not to vomit. "What... happened?" she gasped. "Did I pass out? How did I get home? Where were you? Where's my book?"

"You were attacked by a demon. Yes. We brought you. I was there. The demon took it," replied Crowley.

Eliza blinked, trying to match his answers to her questions. "Wait. *What* happened?"

"A demon attacked you and took the book."

"A what?"

Crowley would not repeat himself.

"I remember a disgusting, stinky cloud coming at me, and then it felt like it went inside me, and it laughed and..."

"And it took the book."

"You're saying the cloud was a demon?"

"Yes."

"I thought demons had horns and hairy goat legs."

"They take many forms."

"You've seen demons before?"

"Not in the greater downtown area."

"Where then?"

"Hell."

"Hell? Like in *hell* hell with the devil and the pitchforks and the fire?"

"Sometimes."

"What happened to me? What did you see?"

"A putrid cloud popped into existence, called you stupid, then disappeared with the book and left you unconscious."

"It called me stupid!" she remembered. "That was mean. So, demons are mean, right?"

"Yes."

"Why didn't you wake me up? Or take me to the emergency room?"

"Modern medicine cannot treat psychic violations of this kind. Only rest can give your mind time to heal itself. Did you have terrible nightmares?"

"Yes," Eliza whimpered, recalling every detail of her dream.

"Good. Now, to retrieve the book—"

"Is there a song from the 1920s that says something 'sweet baby girl'?"

"Is there one that doesn't?"

"Never mind."

"Demons rarely infect the physical plane, Miss Horowitz, which raises two questions: First, how did it manage to manifest itself in this world? Second, why? A Half-Made has no use for the teachings of Thoth."

"Half-Made?"

Crowley exhaled, exasperated. "Demons often refer to themselves as The Half-Made. They claim to be God's abandoned children from an earlier creation. I don't know if that's true. Demons are tremendous liars, and God will rarely answer a direct question, either because He communicates through allegory or He doesn't exist."

"You've spoken to demons?"

"So have you, Miss Horowitz. Demons visit us all. They lurk in the shadows of our subconscious, sowing fear, guilt, and anger."

"Why?"

"Why are mountains high and valleys low?"

"Colliding tectonic plates."

"It was a rhetorical question, Miss Horowitz. I don't know why demons do what they do, but they do indeed do what they do."

"Excuse me?"

"You heard me."

"And who is Todd?"

"*Thoth*," corrected Crowley. "You have no idea what that book is, do you?"

"It's an illuminated manuscript from the middle ages."

"But you do not understand its contents. Your father never had it translated?"

"Why would he have to translate it? It's in English."

Crowley rolled his eyes. "That book, young lady, was written in ancient Chaldean, which proves its authenticity."

"I've been looking at that book my whole life. It's in English."

Crowley shook his head and extracted a binder from his valise. He flipped through a few pages then held it open for Eliza.

"I copied this from your book. Read it."

At first glance, Eliza saw a mishmash of triangular markings on notebook paper, but when she focused on the shapes, they coalesced into words, not English words exactly, but words that she could read.

"'Channel the spirit chard with a tincture of—'" she began.

Crowley snatched the notebook away, his eyes wide with astonishment. He showed her another page.

"'Where sulfur springs from mercury, and again mercury from sulfur—'"

"Dear God, woman! You can read it!"

"Can't you?"

"This is cuneiform. The oldest writing system on earth. I can only glean its meaning after hours of painstaking, often imprecise translation. The book has made itself known to you."

"I don't think so. I have no idea what a 'spirit chard' is."

"I do. Come. We must find this demon."

"What? No. Stop! This is crazy. There's no such thing as demons. None of this is real. You must have drugged me last night or hypnotized me or something."

"Why would I do that?"

"To get my book."

"Why would I be here if I already had your book?"

"I don't know, because you're insane and you want to murder me or maybe... seduce me?" she asked with a hopeful twinge in her voice.

He did not dignify her accusations with a response. He merely pointed to her nightstand. "Look in that thing."

My phone? Why—? Then she remembered. She snatched it off the nightstand, searched her photos, and groaned when she saw the wet, red-eyed homunculus with worms wriggling out of its mouth.

It really happened.

"Do you want to recover your book, Miss Horowitz?"

Eliza nodded numbly.

"Then accompany me to my office," he said and marched out of her bedroom.

"But..." Eliza mumbled to herself. "Your office is so ugly."

◈ ◈

When Eliza joined Crowley, she could hardly recognize her own living room. Beer bottles, half-eaten pizza slices, empty tortilla chip bags and condom wrappers, salsa jars, marijuana bowls, broken glass, an empty bottle of hot sauce, and puddles of vomit covered the tables, counters, and floor. A pair of men's underwear rotated slowly on the ceiling fan.

"What happened?" Eliza asked incredulously.

"When we brought you home last night, *that* one was throwing a party," Crowley replied, pointing to a dark-haired young woman asleep on the couch, hugging a bottle of vodka like a teddy bear.

"Tammy had a party?" The idea would not fit into Eliza's brain. Tammy had never had more than one or two nerdy friends over at a time. They never drank or smoked, and they certainly didn't have sex. "She must have been attacked, or drugged," Eliza exclaimed.

"She seemed quite lucid when she asked me to 'drop the bitch'—meaning you—and join the festivities."

"*Tammy* said that?"

"I checked on her periodically throughout the evening. She enjoyed herself thoroughly."

Eliza shook her roommate by the shoulder. "Tammy?" The girl coughed and nuzzled her vodka. "She's going to feel awful when she—wait a minute. She said 'drop the bitch'? Did you carry me to bed?" she asked with an eager smile.

"I said *we* brought you here."

"Who's we?"

"My associates—or rather, helpers—servants—*slaves* is an ugly word—*thralls*. Let's go with thralls. Come," Crowley commanded and started for the door.

"Wait!" Eliza called out. "Why do you want my father's book so much?"

"We don't have time for this. We must go. Now."

Eliza brushed crumbled corn chips off a chair and sat down. She raised her nose to flaunt her haughty indifference, picked up a dry slice of pizza and opened her mouth.

"Are you mad, woman?" Crowley exclaimed. "Heaven knows where that's been."

She chomped down on the pizza. "In my mouth," she burbled as she chewed.

Crowley pulled a gold pocket watch from his vest pocket and clicked it open. Eliza looked away. She didn't want him to charm her with his antiquarian ways. Crowley took a deep breath and raced through his explanation.

"The Jews were kicked out of France in 1394. They had to sell their possessions, so a rabbi sold a wealthy woman named Perenelle Flamel an old book with an inlaid copper binding—"

"My book."

"Don't interrupt. But, yes okay, obviously, your book. It turned out to be the teachings of Ambrelin, the ancient Egyptian mage, written in ancient Chaldean, which revealed the secret of the elixir of life. Although the book made her husband, Nicolas, quite famous, Perenelle was the true alchemist, one of the greatest of all time. She lived for more than two hundred years until Cardinal Richelieu stole the book. Richelieu wanted to make gold, but the book refused to work for him, and Richelieu rotted away covered in foul-smelling sores. Possibly the plague. Who can say? It's not important! The book disappeared for centuries until a scholar discovered it in the basement of an old synagogue... in Minsk."

"My great-great-grandfather?"

"Rabbi Isaac Horowitz."

"He was an alchemist?"

"Yes."

"Are *you* an alchemist?"

"Let's make a rule. If you can answer your own question, don't ask it."

"So, yes?"

"This book speaks to you, Miss Horowitz. It offers you access to the teachings of Thoth, the god of knowledge, the great mediator between life and death. Do you appreciate the magnitude of this? I have studied the alchemical arts for decades, and I have yet to encounter anyone with such a vital connection to the ancients."

"The ancients?"

"The age-old sages that guide us to alternate planes of consciousness. For some reason, you have a special link to these subconscious worlds. You can read the book. You may not comprehend its meaning, but I do. Together, we can decipher the gift of Thoth and complete the Magnum Opus."

"What's that?"

"The Great Work. The elixir. We can conquer death, Miss Horowitz."

"Call me Eliza. Why?"

"Why what?"

"Why do you want to conquer death?" she asked.

Eliza saw a depth of feeling in Crowley's eyes that she had not seen before. Then, like a tropical storm, it passed, and his face hardened.

"To live forever, of course," he remarked with a casual shrug.

"If I don't return that book, my father will never speak to me again."

"And that's a bad thing?"

"A *very* bad thing!"

"Fine. First, we get the book. Then we work out the details of our new relationship."

"Relationship?"

"Yes, Miss Horowitz. From this moment forward, you and I are a team. Together we will conquer the mysteries of the universe." Crowley held open the front door. Eliza stood and walked outside in a daze.

Relationship.

꩜ ꩜

Eliza and Crowley found Ethan sitting in the stairwell, fiddling with his phone. He leapt to his feet when he saw Eliza and his history professor walking toward him.

"Ethan," Eliza growled. "I told you not to pester me like this."

"I got the picture you sent," Ethan stammered, his eyes darting nervously between Eliza and Crowley.

"I'm fine. Go away," she snorted and stomped past him down the stairs. Crowley raised a disapproving eyebrow at Ethan and followed her.

Ethan shook off his initial shock and scrambled after them. "I need the key back," he explained.

"Not now," she yelled.

"I promised my mom I'd—"

Eliza spun around and pointed to a stair. "Sit!" Ethan plopped down obediently. "Stay," she commanded.

"But—"

"Stay!"

Ethan pursed his lips and said no more. Eliza whirled around and marched off. Crowley caught up to her. "You can be rather rude," he remarked with a hint of admiration in his voice.

"You have no idea," she replied curtly.

Crowley and Eliza marched up Bruin Walk through flocks of joyless students slogging to and from class. The campus seemed bleak, almost colorless. Eliza noted that someone had defaced the SAVE THE GLACIERS sign by crossing out the word "save" and writing in "fuck," which wasn't odd in and of itself—students committed vandalism from time to time—but she found it strange that the same activists stood by, apparently not concerned that someone had dramatically undermined their mission statement. While Eliza pondered this oddity, she almost bumped into a young couple walking hand-in-hand, crying—not whimpering or sniffling—these two students sobbed as shamelessly as Italian mothers in an old gangster movie. Eliza looked around to see if anyone else found their behavior odd. No one even glanced their way. Eliza quickened her pace to catch up to Crowley who, as usual, strode ahead, making it clear that, despite sharing a destination, they did not share the journey. As she reached him, she spotted the normally cheery gardener chopping violently at some elusive creature in the bushes.

"Things are weird," she said to Crowley. Several rats trotted across their path. "Ew!" Eliza cried and backed away. Other students stepped over the rodents without the slightest concern. "That is not normal!" she declared.

"I am a poor judge of normal, Miss Horowitz," Crowley replied calmly. A dissonant chord echoed through the quad. Crowley looked off and frowned. "Now *that* is unusual."

Eliza followed his gaze to a group of students listening to a jazz combo on the lawn. "Why? A lot of people like modern jazz."

"No. They don't," Crowley stated emphatically. "But I'm not referring to the terrible music."

"Then what?" asked Eliza. She saw nothing but a group of college kids and a seven-foot-tall, winged monstrosity snapping its fingers to—*Oh, my God!* Eliza clutched Crowley's arm. The creature stood on two legs, despite having the body of a lion, the head of a leopard, and the wings of an eagle. Its grotesque mouth hung open revealing rows of sharp teeth and a long black tongue that sloshed brown spittle onto the crowd. No one seemed to mind.

"What is that?" whispered Eliza.

"I believe that is Sytry, a great prince of hell. He claims to command sixty infernal legions, but demons love to exaggerate."

"You know that thing?"

"By reputation."

Eliza scanned the students placidly bobbing their heads to the music. "Nobody seems to care. Can't they see it?"

"People tend to overlook metaphysical abnormalities."

Eliza raised her phone to take a picture, but the demon spun around and hissed, its malevolent yellow eyes glowering at Eliza. Crowley lowered her hand slowly. "Nothing to see here," he announced to the world. "Just young people pretending to like jazz."

The creature smiled, and in a low scratchy voice, it declared, "He comes."

Crowley yanked her away. "Don't look back," he whispered.

"*Who* comes?" she asked.

"Probably another musician, maybe even…" Crowley shuddered. "A flautist."

"Why could we see it but nobody else did?"

"I don't know."

"Why is everything so weird today?"

"What part of 'I don't know' do you not understand?" he barked testily and turned into Kerckhoff Coffee house. Eliza paused, noting that Crowley's irritable demeanor had grown slightly more irritable, something she had not thought possible.

                        ☙ ❧

Crowley emerged several minutes later with two tiny espressos. He took a delicate sip from one cup and handed the other to Eliza. She downed it in one gulp.

"Can I have a double mocha frappuccino?" she asked.

"We are not animals," he scoffed and bounded up a staircase.

Eliza looked at her peers inside the coffee house, slurping down sugary iced concoctions from immense plastic cups and waving their arms wildly to mask the banality of their conversations. She decided that Crowley was right. *They are animals.* Satisfied with her sage superiority, she scurried after Crowley like a puppy dog.

She found the top floor dark except for one flickering fluorescent light off to her right. "Professor?" She heard footsteps and scurried toward them. She rounded a corner and crashed into the big dead guy from Crowley's lab. "Holy shit!" she cried, stumbling backward. The big guy remained still as a statue. He was shirtless, but at least he wore pants. *Thank God.* Eliza did not want to see any penises right now—except maybe one.

Crowley had called the brute a gang member. Now she understood why. He had tattoos all over his grey-brown skin—eagles, snakes, skulls, gothic letters, and a big scorpion on his face. The ink seemed to twitch and writhe under the strobing fluorescent light, which shadowed his eyes and accentuated a small crusty hole in the middle of his forehead.

"Miss Horowitz?" Crowley called from down the hall.

"Help," she called out as calmly as she could.

Crowley appeared behind the behemoth. "Movere deflectatis," he commanded, and the big guy backed up against a wall.

"What's wrong with him?" Eliza asked as she inched around the brute.

"He has a hole in his head."

"Is he dangerous?"

"No. Yes. Maybe. I don't know. The dead can behave irrationally."

The huge dead man opened his mouth, "San... dee," he croaked.

Crowley's eyes widened with surprise. "Incredible," he whispered.

"Why?" Eliza asked.

"Corpses do not normally speak."

"They don't walk either."

"Horsefeathers," he scoffed.

"What?"

Crowley stepped up to the tattooed man. "What is your name?"

The corpse stared at Eliza and said nothing. "Could have been a neurological reflex," Crowley murmured to himself. "Still a leap forward, old man."

"Sandy!" the big man cried and stomped toward Eliza. She gaped and backed up.

"Prohibere!" Crowley barked, and the corpse froze. The homunculus appeared on the tattooed guy's shoulder, sucked down an earthworm like spaghetti, and smiled maliciously at Eliza. Eliza gasped again. "Manere," Crowley commanded his thralls. "Quiet," he commanded Eliza and stomped over to a door marked DANGER HIGH RADIATION—AUTHORIZED PERSONNEL ONLY. Crowley took another tiny sip of his coffee, swung the door open, and motioned for Eliza to enter. She hesitated.

"Miss Horowitz, if this room truly contained toxic levels of radiation, a simple wooden door would not contain it."

"Is that true?"

"Yes. Probably—I don't know. Go inside."

Eliza stepped into a spare, elegantly appointed room, with lacquered blond wood-paneled walls, inlaid with intricate geometric designs that shimmered in dappled sunlight shining through a tall plate glass window. A richly varnished, round-cornered desk sat atop a rust-and-gold-colored rug. The space would have looked cutting-edge in 1930.

Crowley pointed to a black leather club chair. "Sit."

"Where are we?" she asked.

"My office."

Eliza sank into the chair with a sensuous sigh of relief. She inhaled deeply, relishing the subtle scent of leather and... cologne, perhaps? She couldn't tell. It didn't matter. The room was tasteful and manly and perfect. She watched Crowley hook his thumb into a vest pocket, take another sip of his seemingly endless coffee, and begin to pace the room.

"Demons are manifestations of our fears," he said. "Just as angels can be expressions of hope, lions of strength, birds of—"

"This is your *real* office," she purred.

"What? Yes. Of course. Pay attention. Everything is a manifestation of our psyche. Whether in the material or spiritual planes of reality, everything we see, hear, think, and feel is filtered through our minds. The universe is, in effect, our *collective* mind, and our mind *is* the universe. Do you understand?"

She had been watching his eyes sparkle green and gold in the morning light and missed most of what he had said.

"No."

Crowley frowned. "We do not exist here," he said, slapping the table. "We exist here." He tapped his temple.

Eliza touched her heart. "What about here?"

"Focus, Miss Horowitz."

"Call me Eliza. Yes. I'm sorry." She cleared her throat and forced herself to look serious. "So, are these weird things we're seeing real?"

"Yes."

She wanted to ask where he slept, but instead asked, "So, why have I never seen this stuff before?"

"Possibly Baader-Meinhof. It's a syndrome. You learn something new, and then you see it everywhere."

Eliza thought about this for a second, then shook her head. "That might be true for matcha tea and labradoodles, but everyone can see those things. Nobody sees demons, or they'd be all over the news."

"Have you watched the news lately?"

"Touché."

"Demons feed off negative feelings," he continued. "Perhaps this demon took your book to make you angry and afraid. It may have established a psychic connection with you. It could be feeding off you right now."

"Ew," Eliza scowled, sickened by the thought of that terrible stench rummaging through her mind. "But why me?"

"Perhaps your connection to the book has made you a more desirable victim," he mused as he sat on the corner of his desk and took another sip of coffee. *He's making that thing last forever.* He ran the tip of his tongue over his mouth to savor the taste, and Eliza's pelvis tingled. She watched his lips as he spoke and imagined how soft and warm they would feel against hers. It wasn't until he said, "...opened the gates of hell and destroyed the fabric of the universe" that she realized she should probably pay closer attention.

"What?"

"I'm just saying that it's probably not a coincidence," he concluded with a fatalistic shrug.

"What's not?"

He sighed with annoyance and explained, "That you stole the book, and I used it to retrieve a man from hell, and demons invaded the world. Most likely, these events are connected. Don't you think?"

Eliza blinked trying to process this information. "Wait, wait, wait. You brought that big guy back from *hell*?"

"I thought that was obvious."

"Hell? With the pitchforks and stuff?"

"You seem obsessed with pitchforks. There are far worse things in hell than farming implements, Miss Horowitz."

"How'd you do it?"

"Alchemy. Have you been paying *any* attention? I don't have time to teach you the Magnum Opus right now."

"So, there's really like a *gate* to hell?"

"Gate, door, portal—they're all metaphors for an anomaly in the structure of space and time where the metaphysical and physical bleed into one another. Think of it more as a tear or a *wound*."

"Can we fix it?"

"Typically, these injuries heal themselves. This one seems somewhat more... substantial," Crowley mused with a twinkle in his eyes.

"Can we stop this?" Eliza persisted.

Crowley studied her as if calculating his next move. "We must confront this demon and retrieve the book."

Eliza felt unwell. She wished she had gotten her mocha frappuccino.

"The only way to combat a demon," continued Crowley, "is to free yourself from emotion, good and bad. First, we must locate it. Demons dwell in the dream world. They adapt their appearance to fit our personal narratives—things we fear, shame we suppress. This demon has invaded your physical reality as well as your psychological one. You may have already seen it in another guise. It might be someone you fear or hate, someone who causes you distress."

"You mean, someone I know could really be a demon?"

"Possibly, but regardless of its corporeality, the demon primarily dwells in your mind, and that is where we shall find it. I must guide you through a meditation."

"Now?"

"Close your eyes and listen to your breath," Crowley said in a soothing voice.

"Maybe you should hold my hand," Eliza suggested.

"No. Just breathe... in and out... calmly, steadily. That's it. We will explore your memory by recalling sensory details—sights, sounds, smells, touch. Don't speak. Just note your thoughts and feelings without judgment. Now, let your breath in and out slowly. Good. First, picture a warm, comforting light in your heart."

Eliza envisioned someone placing a warm hand over her heart. It was a man's hand. It was Crowley's hand. Her heart beat faster. His hand was strong, insistent. Slowly, he moved it over her—

"Focus, Miss Horowitz," Crowley commanded.

"Huh? Okay."

"Now. Imagine that my voice is that warm light. My voice will calm you and protect you as we venture into darker realms."

A chill ran up Eliza's spine. She concentrated on his voice.

"Let's go back to the river," Crowley said.

Eliza inhaled sharply. She didn't want to go back there. She didn't want to think about that terrible cloud. She didn't want to smell it and hear it laugh. She wanted to run away, but then her father's face flashed into her mind. He looked worried and trusting. He always saw the best in her. He overlooked her childish failings and treated her like a rational adult. In his eyes, she was the person she wanted to be. Now, she pictured his eyes turn cold when he realized that she did not deserve his trust. She never had.

"See the city lights reflected on the river," Crowley continued softly. "Hear the water rushing down the channel. Feel the concrete under your feet. Can you see the bridge?"

She could.

"Look up into the shadows beneath the roadway. Watch the book fall into the river. Feel the cold water when you jump in. Feel the current as it sweeps you along. Feel the chill when you finally crawl out."

Eliza breathed more rapidly.

"Now, see the cloud."

Fear coursed up her spine. She pictured the putrid haze. She felt its hatred as it entered her and found the darkness within her. Eliza's cheeks flushed. Her hands tingled. Her jaw tightened. Her breath came in short puffs like a steam engine gaining speed. That cloud, that *thing*, had violated her. It had toyed with her. It mocked her. She felt the black fury growing inside her. She hated that demon. She hated it more than she had hated anything in her life, and she had hated many things, but she had always tried to hide her feelings. She had to behave like a rational adult so that her mother wouldn't lose her temper or cry or, worse yet, ignore her. She had swallowed her anger when her father sent Margarita to pick her up at the airport because he had to work. Work? The man made movies about glib superheroes who fought computer-generated monsters in computer-generated cities. She had kept quiet when her mother announced that they were moving *again* and introduced Eliza to another new boyfriend she had to pretend to like, then miss once he'd left. Eliza had suppressed so much rage over the years that if a thin layer of her skin was peeled away, only a viscous mass of pure anger would remain. Eliza yearned to set it free. She wanted to scream and break things and slash her way through crowds with a butcher knife.

A voice cut through her fantasy. "Miss Horowitz?"

Eliza inhaled sharply.

"Observe, Miss Horowitz. Do not judge, just witness. What do you hear?"

It said I looked stupid. And it laughed with this nasally, snorting...

"What do you smell?"

The stench of rotten fruit, cherry and...

Eliza's eyes sprang open. *Banana!*

"The demon is my motherfucking stepmother!" she cried.

"No, Miss Horowitz. Calm down," Crowley cautioned. "We have only begun to—"

Eliza didn't let him finish. She ran off to kill Aurora.

Chapter Sixteen

Where's the party, party, party? Gotta party right here. Where's the party, party, party? Gotta party right here. Wham bam, boogie, gonna wham bam boogie. Wham bam boogie, gonna wham bam boogie right here.

Shit.

Jaime couldn't get that song out of his head. They'd play it all the time at barbecues. Jaime loved those summer nights in the hood. All his homeys dancin' and drinkin' with the local ladies. Even Angel had fun. He'd be telling those bad jokes of his. "What did Batman say to Robin before he got in the car? Get in the car!" Angel would laugh 'til beer shot out his nose. Good times.

Jaime wondered if Sandy would like to go to a barbecue. He'd make sure his homeboys didn't get out of line with her. Hell, maybe she'd even like Angel's jokes. Some people did. Like Rita. She'd laugh and laugh. 'Course she was always pretty high. Rita also liked Jaime's scorpion tattoo that went up his neck and curled around the side of his face. When he first got it, Rita wouldn't stop kissing and licking on it. Made Angel real jealous. That was cool. He wondered what Sandy thought of his tattoos. She never said nothing, so she couldn't have totally hated them. Hell, she probably had tattoos, too, only classy ones that you couldn't see unless you were her boyfriend.

Jaime really wanted to see Sandy's tattoos. Where's the party, party, party? Gotta party right here.

He should say something to Sandy. She was on the other side of the door with Badass Undertaker Dude. He better not try to kiss her, or Jaime'd rip his face off. He planned to throw Badass Undertaker Dude out a window later, but right now he was too tired. He was so fucking tired, he couldn't even move. He just stood there. He should probably eat something, but he wasn't hungry, which was weird 'cause Jaime was always hungry.

He thought about that chicken he'd make at the barbecues. He got the recipe from his grandmother—tomato sauce, brown sugar, lots of chili powder. No one touched the grill but Jaime. He was the master chef. The ladies thought it was cute that a big guy like him liked to cook. Truth was, he just liked to eat, and nobody cooked as good as him. Gail was always hanging onto him while he was flipping chicken, rubbing his ass, and grabbin' his pecs. That girl had so many piercings, she would jingle-jangle when they were in bed together.

Wham bam boogie, gonna wham bam boogie—

Sandy burst out the door and ran down the stairs. She looked really pissed off. Did Badass Undertaker Dude tell her about Gail? He should follow her and apologize.

"Follow her!" Badass Undertaker Dude yelled.

It was the first smart thing that pendejo said. Jaime ran after Sandy. Well, he didn't really run. He just sort of clomped down the stairs as fast as he could. Badass Undertaker Dude and Little Cholo were faster, and they ran way ahead of him.

By the time Jaime got outside, Sandy was way down the hill with Badass Undertaker Dude running after her, yelling and shit. He hoped she got away, but he figured he should follow them just to make sure she was okay.

It seemed to take forever for him to plow through all the pendejos with their backpacks and get into the parking lot. He didn't see nobody, so he went upstairs and found Sandy in a big SUV. She looked super cool in that big pinche tank. Badass

Undertaker Dude was holding the door open, shouting something at her—Jaime couldn't tell what, but she was honking her horn and yelling, too. Everyone was talking so strange, like they were all at the bottom of a swimming pool, except when Badass Undertaker Dude talked straight at him. Jaime could hear him loud and clear.

"Stand in front of the car," he told Jaime.

Fuck you, thought Jaime. *I go wherever the fuck I want.* It just so happened that, at that particular moment, Jaime wanted to go to the front of the car. So, he did.

Badass Undertaker Dude got in the passenger seat, and Little Cholo hopped in back. They were saying stuff, but Sandy wasn't paying no attention. She revved up the SUV, leaned her head out the window and yelled something at Jaime. She looked real angry. Jaime wished he hadn't fucked Gail so many times and told everybody about it.

Then Sandy ran him over.

Jaime always thought it would hurt to have a suburban utility vehicle on top of him, but he hardly felt it. His body kept the front wheels from touching the ground, so no matter how much Sandy stepped on the gas, the wheels just spun in the air.

Then there was all this smoke, and the engine died, and he heard Badass Undertaker Dude say, "Come out from under the car." *Don't have to ask me twice, pendejo.* Jaime pushed the car off himself like it was made of cardboard. *All those years of pumping iron really paid off.*

Little Cholo opened the back door for him, and he got in. The interior was all clean and shit, but was kind of small. His knees were all scrunched up against the front seat where Badass Undertaker Dude was talking at Sandy. Sandy's eyes were big and red like some shit was about to go down, and then, sure enough, she stepped on the gas, and they were zooming down the ramp and out of the parking lot.

Sandy was a great driver. She was weavin' and bobbin' through traffic like they were on a Six Flags rollercoaster.

Wham bam boogie, gonna wham bam boogie right here.

Shit.

Chapter Seventeen

I knew she was evil. Oh, Daddy. I'm so sorry. I should have said something.

"Miss Horowitz," Crowley said from the passenger seat as she sped through campus.

"Call me Eliza," she commanded through gritted teeth.

Crowley kept his tone calm and steady. "Please, slow down."

She slammed on the brakes to avoid hitting a student, sending the homunculus crashing against the windshield.

"Occidere eam," he squeaked as he slid down onto the dashboard.

"Nondum," replied Crowley.

Eliza hit the gas and raced on. "Aurora is the demon. She smells the same, she laughs the same, she's the only one who could possibly know about the book, and I hate her fucking guts!"

"If and when we find the demon," Crowley pressed, "you cannot defeat it with anger."

"Then I'll use a baseball bat."

"Calm down."

"No!"

She ran through the red light at Sunset and Belagio and sped up the hill into Bel Air.

"Miss Horowitz," Crowley continued. "If you want to rid yourself of this demon, you must follow my instructions to the letter. Are you listening to me?"

"Yes."

"First, you must understand that we all exist on multiple planes of consciousness simultaneously. Altering the physical world alters the spiritual one and vice versa. So, when dealing with beings that dwell primarily in psychic worlds, we must first access our own…"

Eliza stopped listening. She would kill first; understand later. Aurora must have put some kind of spell on her father. Why else would he marry such a dolt? Sure, she was crazy beautiful, but her father was a major film producer. He knew plenty of beautiful women. He didn't have to marry one that said things like, "When I have a daughter, I hope it's a girl," and "Jew noses are cute."

Not that her own mother had been much of a catch. Her parents never got along. Katherine Flanagan, who described herself as "Jerry's shiksa trophy wife," was a difficult woman. She grew up in a small, Nebraska town that bored the hell out of her, so she dedicated her life to the pursuit of everything. The woman could not sit still. If she wasn't planning her next vacation, renovation, or holiday party, she was taking yoga, pottery, Italian, winemaking, beekeeping, salsa dancing, or creative writing classes. She claimed to love Eliza, but Eliza always felt that the only person Katherine loved was Katherine. Eliza blamed herself for subjecting her father to her mother for so long. If it wasn't for Eliza, they would have divorced much sooner.

After he left Eliza's mother, her father went through a slew of girlfriends—some smart, some stupid, all beautiful—but they didn't concern Eliza, because her father kept them away during her yearly visits, and more importantly, he didn't marry any of them.

Eliza thought back to the day she first met Aurora. Eliza had been living in L.A. by then, so she no longer had the intense yearly visits with her father. Now that she could see him all the time, she hardly saw him at all. Last year on her birthday, her father texted to ask if they could meet at the restaurant. No problem. She was almost nineteen, and apparently, this was how adults met for dinner.

She had arrived at The Ivy first and waited for her father at the table with her chin held high and her hands folded neatly on her lap. She discreetly tugged at her white gloves, which she had outgrown years ago, but The Ivy birthday ritual required gloves, and she hadn't wanted to buy new ones to wear only once a year.

She didn't recognize her father when he first entered the restaurant. The sight of a balding middle-aged man with a bushy beard in a floppy T-shirt with a big marijuana leaf on it just wouldn't register in Eliza's mind. Especially when the balding man stood next to the most beautiful woman Eliza had ever seen in her life. She had wavy blond hair flowing over sculptured bare shoulders, a short red dress that complemented her flawless figure, and high heels that made her tower over the dopey schlub beside her. But what caught Eliza's attention most were the woman's electric-blue eyes that scanned the crowded restaurant like a hawk searching for its prey. Eliza had flinched when they fixed on her.

Restaurant patrons gaped as her father led this creature to her table.

"Happy birthday, Pumpkin," he said.

Pumpkin? thought Eliza. He had never called her that before.

"This is Aurora," he blurted, giggling like a schoolboy.

"Happy birthday, Eliza!" Aurora cried far too loudly before kissing Eliza on the cheek—not a peck, but a hot, squishy kiss that made Eliza shudder.

Her father pulled a chair out for Aurora then turned to a waiter. "Another chair, please."

Those were the last words her father had said that evening. Aurora talked through dinner, barely pausing to take a breath. Eliza retained no memory of what she said, but the rolling whine of her voice and nasal chortling left Eliza nauseated for a week. By the end of the night, Eliza had learned three things. First of all, Aurora was stupid. Second, Aurora had some sort of strange hold over her father. Third, Eliza would never wear those stupid white gloves again.

But even this insult Eliza could forgive. People did stupid things, especially fifty-year-old men. But why did he have to *marry* her? Her father wasn't *that* stupid. It made no sense.

Until now.

"All right, let us review the plan," she heard Crowley say. "What is our first step?"

"Grab a butcher knife," Eliza snapped.

"What?"

By that point, they had reached her father's house. Eliza leapt out of the car and marched inside with Crowley, the corpse and the homunculus scrambling after them.

"Where are you, you soul-sucking succubus?" she yelled as she stomped through the living room, knocking sprite figurines off shelves. Crowley grabbed her by the arm and spun her around.

"Miss Horowitz—"

"Eliza!" she shouted.

"You are not behaving rationally."

"I don't care!"

"This anger you feel is not normal."

"I feel what I feel."

"Think. Have you ever felt this level of rage toward your stepmother before?"

"I've always hated her stupid guts."

"But to this degree? This rift with the netherworld—"

"Hell."

"Yes. Hell. These creatures we see are merely the tip of the iceberg. Worse demons lie within us. They yearn to break free and wreak havoc. But no matter how terrible these devils seem; they are merely feelings. Do not let them rule you, or you will be lost."

Eliza knew Crowley was right. Her anger was surreal. She knew that the light of reason would relieve her fury the way morning dispels a nightmare, but she didn't care.

"I feel what I feel!" she bellowed.

"Feelings are no more important than a spleen or an elbow. Do not put them on a pedestal and let them delude you into—"

Crowley stiffened. Something behind Eliza had captured his attention. Eliza spun around to see a framed poster for a film titled *The Son of Man* starring Charles Delamour. The advertisement featured Jesus on the cross gazing beneficently up to heaven while Mary Magdalene kneeled at his feet with her tunic draped suggestively off one shoulder. Crowley's eyes glistened. He cleared his throat but said nothing.

"That was my great-grandfather's last movie. Actually, he never made it."

Crowley nodded slowly, staring at the artwork with an anguished look on his face. Snorting laughter wafted from the back of the house.

"It's her," growled Eliza. She dismissed Crowley's odd behavior and followed the laughter to the swimming pool. She imagined holding Aurora's head underwater while she struggled, convulsed, and finally succumbed. Or maybe Eliza would just beat her face over and over until her eyes rolled back in her head, and then she'd beat her some more.

Eliza found Aurora gracefully gliding through the water while a new shirtless pool boy gazed at her adoringly. "You... " Eliza shouted, searching for the right words to express her outrage. The English language failed her, so she resorted to French. "J'accuse!"

The pool boy snapped out of his reverie and grabbed his shirt off a lounge chair. "No," Aurora commanded. The pool boy stopped, shirt in hand. "Eliza," she crooned as she glided to the stairs and emerged from the pool like Venus rising from the sea.

Eliza faltered. The woman was magnificent. Water trickled down her perfect body as she sashayed up to Eliza and graced her with a radiant smile. Eliza had to fight a powerful urge to bow her head in submission. Who was she to live in the same world as this stunning creature? Aurora was a goddess. Eliza was nothing but a curly-haired little troll who should crawl into a dark hole and die.

Crowley stepped up with the homunculus and the corpse. Aurora raised an eyebrow and ogled him lasciviously from head to foot. "Pleasure to see you again, O-li-ver," she whispered in a husky voice.

Crowley narrowed his eyes. "Have we met?"

Aurora stepped closer to him. "Oh, yes. We're old friends."

"You've changed your appearance?"

Aurora ran a finger down Crowley's chest. "Do you approve?"

Crowley's ears turned red. He furrowed his brow, confused and a bit flustered.

Eliza bared her teeth. She didn't care how incredible Aurora looked; she couldn't have Eliza's future lover.

"Give back Daddy's book, you demon," Eliza demanded.

Aurora gasped with exaggerated concern. "Did you lose one of your father's books?"

"You took it from me, with your stupid laugh and stinky breath."

"Your father doesn't seem to mind my... scent," Aurora purred and glanced at the pool boy. "What about you, Juan?"

"Robert," stammered the pool boy. "You smell great. Well, I should go and—"

"Stay," Aurora growled sweetly.

The pool boy looked frightened, but he stayed.

"You are a demon from hell!" Eliza yelled and turned to Crowley. "Right?"

To her horror, Crowley appeared lost in Aurora's eyes. "Hey!" Eliza shouted.

"Huh? What?"

Eliza screamed and rushed at her stepmother, but the woman stepped out of the way gracefully, and Eliza flew into the pool with a mighty splash.

"You're so funny," snorted Aurora.

Eliza did not emerge from the pool as elegantly as Aurora had. "Shut up!" she sputtered, cold and wet.

"Is this what you want?" Aurora asked, and suddenly she was holding the book. Eliza lunged for it, but she slipped on the wet cement and fell on her butt. Aurora doubled over with laughter. Eliza leapt to her feet and fell again.

"Stop. I can't breathe," Aurora snorted.

Crowley snapped back to his senses. "Madam, please return the book. It will not work for you."

"It's working great so far," Aurora blurted between guffaws.

"Please, give it to me," Crowley requested evenly.

"Sure," replied Aurora, holding out the book, but when Crowley reached for it, the book exploded in flames.

"Curses," barked Crowley.

"You!" Eliza shouted at the tattooed corpse. "Kill her!"

The corpse did not move.

"He obeys only me, Miss Horowitz."

"So tell him!"

"Occidere." He shrugged.

The corpse lurched toward Aurora, but she batted him aside with a casual swipe of her arm. The big man tottered into the pool and floated face down like a dead body, which he was.

With a puff of smoke, Aurora turned into a mammoth beast with a baboon face and blood-red lipstick slopped over grotesque swollen lips encasing a mouth full of jagged teeth. Her blond frizzled hair smoldered with flames that shot out of her ears. Two wrinkled breasts sagged over a bloated belly, which partially obscured the slimy black serpents wriggling in and out of her distended vagina. Only her electric-blue eyes and sickly stench revealed that this monstrosity was Aurora. Eliza grabbed Crowley's arm.

"She changed so fast," she gasped. "I thought she would have morphed slowly or something."

"Only in modern movies," Crowley explained. "The old films had it right. It's just a puff of smoke and—"

Aurora screeched. Robert, the pool boy, screamed as the demon wrapped one of her massive hands around his feet and lifted him into the air. Eliza watched in horror as Aurora stuffed Robert into her mouth headfirst. Blood gushed down her chin as she consumed the poor young man in seconds. She licked the blood off her lips with her thick, craggy tongue and smiled at Eliza. "You're fat," she quipped.

"Run," Crowley commanded.

Eliza, Crowley, and the homunculus raced into the house toward the front door, but an army of sprite figurines blocked their escape. Their friendly smiles contorted into vicious snarls, baring surprisingly large teeth. With a cacophony of "Ho, hos!" the tiny fiends attacked.

"Fucking dwarves!" Eliza screamed as she and Crowley kicked and stomped the little monsters and retreated into the kitchen. The homunculus did not fare as well. "Et tu Crowley!" he cried as the ravenous sprites dragged him away.

Crowley and Eliza found Margarita sitting at the kitchen counter, guzzling whiskey.

"Margarita! Run!" Eliza shouted.

Margarita pouted glumly. "He sacrificado mi vida por ese hombre," she slurred.

"Señora," Crowley demanded. "Donde estan los cuchillos?"

"Pero me trata como si no fuera nada!" she moaned.

Aurora's demon head crashed through the kitchen window and sneered at Eliza. "You really should wax that mustache, sweetie."

"I don't have a mustache!"

Crowley dragged Eliza out a side door. They circled around the outside of the house, but before they reached Eliza's car, Aurora dropped from the sky and flattened the SUV. She hopped down from the wreckage and glared at Eliza with contempt. "You're ugly," she sneered.

"Look who's talking! You're hideous!" Eliza screamed back.

"Quiet!" commanded Crowley.

"I thought you were supposed to face your demons, and then they go away or something."

"Nonsense. Always run away from demons. Especially when you don't have a gun. Apologize. Quickly."

"No!" Eliza cried, mad with fury.

Aurora took a big, clomping step toward her. "You think you're so special," she snarled. "Daddy's little darling."

"I'm no one's darling," Eliza shot back.

The massive creature bared her teeth, allowing globs of bloody saliva to dribble from her bulbous lips. "So untouchable."

"Say something nice about her hair," Crowley whispered.

"Her hair is terrible!" Eliza shouted.

Crowley shook his head in frustration, then pulled a silver crucifix from his pocket and thrust it in the demon's face. With barely a glance, Aurora backhanded him, sending him tumbling down the driveway.

"That never works," Crowley grumbled from the ground. When he got to his feet, Aurora struck him again. Crowley's eyes rolled back, and he dropped like a sack of rocks into a flowerbed. He did not rise again.

Aurora crouched down on her hairy haunches, and with a mighty grunt, she excreted slimy black snakes from her nether regions. The serpents slithered frantically beneath Aurora before crawling toward Eliza.

Terror overwhelmed Eliza's rage, and she ran. She raced around the side of the house, past the pool, and up the hill toward the faux Grecian temple. Just before she reached the rotunda, something grabbed her ankle and sent her sprawling face first onto the grass. She spun back and saw a black serpent coiling up her calf. She shook her leg, but the creature held on tightly. Another snake ensnared her wrist. Eliza flailed violently as more snakes encircled her arms and legs, spreading her limbs apart and pinning her to the ground. A pale-yellow serpent, larger than the rest, slipped around her neck and squeezed. Eliza could not scream or speak. She could barely breathe.

A shadow fell over her as Aurora glared down at her. "I've waited so long," she snarled. "But why put off for tomorrow what you can eat today?" She opened her hideous mouth.

This is really going to hurt, Eliza thought. A part of her wanted to surrender. The quicker it happened, the less she would suffer. Like most teenagers, Eliza had envisioned her death many times, usually at the hands of Nazis or vampires or a combination thereof, and in every scenario, she fought back. "They may kill me," she had always told herself, "but I'm taking one of them with me."

As the demon's jaws drew closer, Eliza tightened her muscles and arched her back, expanding her chest and shoulders. The serpents squeezed harder. Eliza gritted her teeth and pressed back. Her muscles swelled. Her body expanded. Just as Aurora's cavernous mouth enveloped her head, Eliza released her muscles, and, like a kid who jumps off a seesaw and sends their playmate crashing to the ground, her sudden retreat took the serpents by surprise. They slackened their grip, giving Eliza the opportunity to draw a breath and say something. She planned to curse Aurora, to shout her defiance and berate the hellish creature so that it would remember Eliza as the human she could not cow. The demon might kill her body, but never her spirit. Eliza sucked in air. The snakes recovered quickly and crushed her chest, and as the breath shot from her lungs, she only had enough wind for one word. In that fraction of a second, every expletive that she had ever heard flashed through her mind, but much to her surprise, no curse came from her, no shout of defiance, no proclamation of rage, only a soft, plaintive whisper.

"Daddy."

Then the world disappeared.

Chapter Eighteen

Jaime floated face down in the pool thinking about *The Little Rascals*. They were these super-old movies he'd watch with his grandfather where kids ran around calling each other "numbskull" and "palooka" and being cute in a weird black-and-white sort of way. One scene really stuck in Jaime's mind: The Little Rascals were swimming in a pond out in the woods somewhere, and this fat kid got on the diving board, but he was afraid to jump in the water, so all the other kids started yelling, "Jump, Fatty, jump!" So, Fatty looked right into the camera, straight at Jaime, and he sang the song "Asleep in the Deep" in this low, deep, grownup voice.

Fucking thing gave Jaime nightmares. Most of that old shit his grandfather watched scared Jaime because he knew that everybody in those movies was dead now. It was like watching ghosts that didn't know they were ghosts. It was spooky and sad.

Jaime kept on floating.

Many brave hearts are asleep in the deep, so beware...

Chapter Nineteen

Crowley opened his eyes to clouds of purple and white. *Petunias.* He spit dirt out of his mouth and rolled onto his back. He was lying in a bed of flowers, but he could not recall the location of the flowerbed or how he got there. Fortunately, Crowley had awoken in many unusual places over the years, and he had developed an effective procedure for dealing with such annoyances. First, do not panic. Second, he inspected his body for injuries and discovered a contusion on his cranium. That explained his insentience. He must have fallen or, more likely, someone had struck him. *But who?* Moving on, he focused on his breath to calm his mind and allow his jumbled thoughts to coalesce into a comprehensible memory.

The girl!

Crowley leapt to his feet, but a surge of nausea sent him toppling back to the ground. He spotted the demon in the distance, atop a hill beside a gaudy Grecian rotunda, menacing a prone figure covered in a writhing mass of serpents. *The girl.* He cursed himself for not bringing his Smith and Wesson.

As he sprinted toward them, he saw a small, bearded man running across the yard toward the demon. He could not see the man's face clearly, but his awkward gait revealed his age—early fifties—as well as his lack of athletic training. Crowley hoped the man had a gun or a club. Otherwise the monster would devour him. Crowley wondered at the man's courage. Who would rush headlong to his death to save this girl?

Her father.

Crowley stopped. Before he could shout out a warning, the father burst through the demon as if it did not exist. The monster and the snakes disappeared in a cloud of black smoke.

The father took no notice. *Had he seen the beast?* He lifted the girl and hugged her tightly. She wrapped her arms around his neck and buried her face in his shoulder. Crowley watched the tender scene in silence.

Then he vomited.

When he looked up again, he saw the father carrying the girl into the house. Sweat poured down Crowley's face. His head throbbed. The world listed like a ship floundering in a storm. Crowley had to grab hold of a tree to keep from falling. He took several raspy breaths to steady himself before he stumbled back to the patio. He fished the corpse out of the water with a pool skimmer, and then bumbled into the house, where he revived the homunculus, who lay bruised and bloody amidst an army of lifeless sprite figurines. Then, he led them away.

҈ ҉

Crowley left the corpse and the homunculus in a corner of his lab and lumbered to his desk.

You should not have left the girl, meyn zun, Crowley thought in an Eastern European accent.

"I know," Crowley grumbled to himself.

You should have explained zis to her father.

"She'll be fine."

You need her now, more zan ever.

"Tomorrow, old man. Tomorrow!" he shouted to himself as he picked up the porcelain doll and carried it to his meditation chapel. He pulled back the rug to reveal a trap door. He heaved it open and descended down a flight of rickety wooden stairs into darkness. Feeling along a roughhewn wall, he found a switch, and a soft light sprang on, illuminating a small chamber belonging to an older structure than the one above. It was empty except for a metal sarcophagus with a glass lid and one chair. Crowley stepped up to the casket and looked down at a perfectly preserved six-year-old girl who was wearing a frilly dress from the early twentieth century.

Crowley set the doll on the glass where the girl could see it, were she to open her eyes. He sat down and gazed at the child. It took a long time for his heartbeat to slow and his breath to steady, but gradually he regained his composure. He lowered his head onto the coffin, closed his eyes, and Oliver Crowley slept.

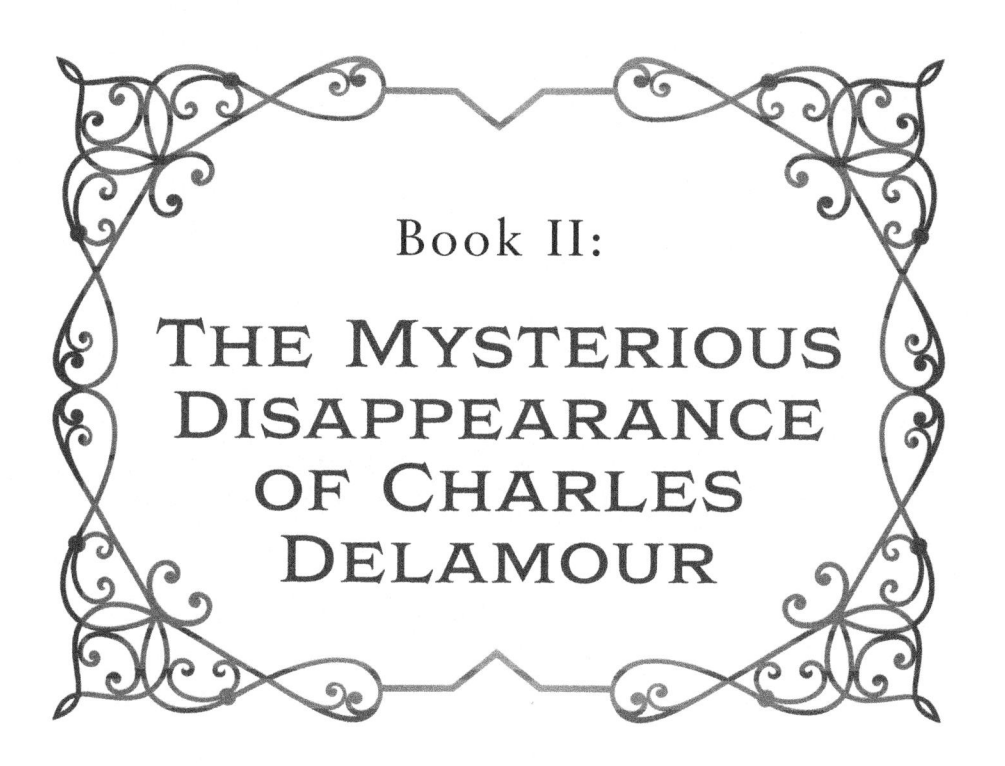

Book II:
The Mysterious Disappearance of Charles Delamour

Chapter Twenty

Five miles south of San Lazaro, Diego Cienfuegos had his farm, a few meager acres carved into the cliffs above the roaring California surf. Sea winds had beaten all color from his small wooden house and barn until they appeared as grey as the rocks to which they clung. Two horses, a shaggy cow, four pigs, and a dozen skinny chickens wandered the property.

Diego's son, Aurelio, sat atop a rose-grey mare on the road above the farm. Aurelio had recently turned eighteen, but his mop of black hair, downy face, and bright green eyes made him look much younger.

Aurelio shifted his weight in the saddle as the mare grazed on the yellow yarrow that lined the dirt road. The sun had almost crested the mountain to his left. It would get hot soon.

"Boy!" Diego yelled from the farm below.

Diego had asked Aurelio to saddle the horse so he could ride into town for salt and tobacco. "The tide has gone down," Diego had told his son. "While I am in San Lazaro, get to the rocks. There will be abalone to be found." But instead of bringing the horse to his father as instructed, Aurelio had taken it up the hill. Today was Friday, and every Friday morning, Dolores Belmonte traveled the old road that wound its way along the coastal mountains to visit the shops of Monterey.

"Aurelio!" cried his father. The boy feigned deafness and kept his eyes on the road. *Where is she?*

Finally, he heard the creak of wheels, and around the bend came a horse and buggy. Aurelio spurred the mare forward with an air of cavalier indifference. As he drew closer to the carriage, he saw her. She wore a blue and white striped blouse, a dark-grey skirt, and a large black hat with a bird on it. *A bird? No, wait.* It was a bow. *Thank God,* thought Aurelio. He did not want to have to inform Dolores that a bird had perched on her head.

Beside Dolores sat her chaperone, Mina Sanchez. Mina was a small dark woman with sharp Indian cheek bones, a hooked nose, and fierce black eyes that locked onto Aurelio the moment the carriage rounded the curve. Aurelio avoided Mina's glare and nodded to the buggy driver. The old man looked at him so sourly that Aurelio charitably conjectured that he must have urgent need of a latrine. Aurelio finally turned his attention to Dolores. He could not see her face beneath the generous hat, so he focused on her hand as it flicked open a purple laced fan and languidly waved it beneath her chin. She was near. His jaw trembled. *Behave normally. You happen to be riding down this road like any person who might happen to ride down any road.* When he reached the buggy, Aurelio tipped his hat to Dolores. She offered no response.

Aurelio and the carriage passed one another. He spun around, and as he watched her go, he evaluated this week's encounter. *She waved her fan. Was she signaling me? Inviting me?*

"Aurelio!" yelled his father. *Damn, that man has a thunderous voice.*

        ❧ ☙

"You demean yourself with that one," his father chided Aurelio as he climbed off the mare. "The Belmontes have no honor. Her father is naught but a shameless gambler."

"He is a financier," Aurelio explained, not for the first time. "He worships gold. He married his first daughter to a wealthy Americano, and I assure you, he will do the same with this one."

"Dolores is a free woman. She can decide her own fate."

Diego shook his head. "You cannot win a lady's heart by pestering her like a mosquito, my boy. 'Love is invisible, and comes in and goes out as he likes, without anyone calling him to account for what he does.'"

Diego loved to quote *Don Quixote*. It was the old man's bible, but Aurelio had read the novel as well, so he shot back, "'He who is down one day can be up the next...'"

Father and son finished the quote in unison, "'Unless he wants to stay in bed.'"

Diego chuckled. "Get the abalone. I shall make a stew tonight."

Aurelio watched his father cautiously guide his horse up to the road. *You have grown old.* Once, his father had seemed like a giant. He would gallop up and down mountains like a knight of old. His word was law, not just for Aurelio, his only child, but for the neighbors as well. Diego was renowned throughout the bay of San Lazaro for his honesty and fairness. He taught Aurelio to value honor over life itself. "You come from nobility," he'd said. "The Cienfuegos once ranched thousands of acres granted to us by the king of Spain. We were wealthy and respected until the Americanos drove us onto this precipice. We may no longer have riches, but we still have our self-respect."

Do we? A teacher once read Aurelio a speech from the American president, Theodore Roosevelt, declaring that, "All great races are fighting races." He feared that the old man had lost his fighting spirit. Aurelio needed to prove that the Cienfuegos were still great. Soon, he would join the Army and go fight the Kaiser. Aurelio did not know why America had entered the war in Europe, nor did he care. The conflict offered him an opportunity to prove his manhood and avenge his family's shame.

But first he would win Dolores' heart.

Aurelio's father regarded his love for Dolores as a childish infatuation. He was mistaken. Aurelio loved Dolores Belmonte more deeply than ever he had loved anything in his life.

It had begun long ago when Aurelio fell asleep during Sunday Mass, a pardonable sin for an eight-year-old boy. Normally, his father would have nudged him awake, but on this day, he received a sharp rap on the head. He awoke with a start and turned to his father who, Aurelio was surprised to note, had fallen asleep himself. He looked down the aisle and saw that the Belmonte family had just walked past him on their way to their pew. The Belmontes had accumulated such wealth that the church not only reserved the front pew for them, but it also allowed them to arrive at whatever hour they chose, thereby sparing them the tedium of the lengthy Introductory Rites. Father, mother, two sons, and one daughter filed silently into their seats, but the youngest daughter, dressed in a lacy pink dress, glanced back at him and smiled before she sat. Aurelio had seen Dolores before and thought nothing of it. She was a child. But, when she locked eyes with him that morning and gave him a gloriously mischievous smile, something inside Aurelio snapped. His chest ached and his stomach turned. For the rest of the week, Aurelio pondered his response until he reached the conclusion that, somehow, he had fallen in love with Dolores Belmonte.

Aurelio and Dolores exchanged clandestine smiles for several more Sundays until that fateful day when she fought by his side on the ramparts of Constantinople.

Diego had raised Aurelio on tales of heroic knights, dragons, and damsels in distress. When Aurelio played war with friends, he persuaded them to elevate their games beyond customary cowboy and Indian scuffles and reenact the adventures of legendary heroes such as Lancelot du Lac, Amadis the Gaul, and Sir Galahad the Pure. Craggy Huguenot Hill—named after a French Protestant who leapt from the rock after learning that his wife had left him for an Italian Catholic—served as their castle, which they defended with their lives until one of their parents called them to dinner.

One summer day, Dolores and two of her friends strolled up the hill to watch the boys reenact the fall of Constantinople. Inspired by their female audience, the boys fought particularly well that day. True to the historic event, the boys who played the evil Turks gradually overwhelmed the brave Greek defenders until only Aurelio, who portrayed the last Byzantine Emperor, remained alive. The Turks surrounded the doomed sovereign. Soon, his life would end and with it, the last remnant of the once-glorious Roman empire.

Then a miracle happened. Dolores raced up the hill, grabbed a stick from a dead defender and stood alongside Aurelio. "We shall never surrender, you Indian savages!" she yelled. Aurelio did not have time to correct her historical faux pas because their attackers let out an Indian war cry and surged up the hill. Aurelio and Dolores fought bravely, but they soon fell to the ground, side by side, mortally wounded. Dolores took Aurelio's hand, and gazing into his eyes, she groaned, "You have made me proud today, brave sir." She leaned in to kiss him, but before their lips met, she grunted and died.

As the victorious Turk/Indians cheered, Aurelio gazed at Dolores. His heart overflowed with such deliciously tragic ardor that he knew then and there he would love Dolores Belmonte for the rest of his life.

They had barely spoken since that heroic battle eight years ago. Dolores attended the Catholic academy, while Aurelio went to public school when he went to school at all. Occasionally, they saw each other at church gatherings, but rarely could he circumvent her family and friends to speak with her. Dolores remained visible but out of reach, which only increased his desire for her.

Finally, his chance to win Dolores had come. Next Saturday, San Lazaro would celebrate the Mexican victory at the Battle of Puebla with fireworks, music, and dance. The entire town would attend the fiesta. Of course, other men would compete for Dolores' attention, but Aurelio had two reasons to believe that he would triumph. First of all, many eligible men had already gone off to war; and secondly, Aurelio would employ witchcraft.

❧ ☙

Aurelio stared at the human skull glaring at him from behind the flowers and candles on the makeshift altar. Above the skull, a black mirror reflected the herbs and smoked meat that dangled from the rafters. The chamber reeked of burnt logs and sage.

"Who is that?" Aurelio asked, pointing to the skull.

"That is Raymond," replied the old Indian witch as she flipped her long white braid behind her back and began lighting candles. "He is not for sale."

"All right."

"I mean, he is not cheap."

"I do not want Raymond."

"You could call him whatever you like. Juan, Bob."

"No, thank you."

"Fine. Sit." She pointed a gnarled finger at a rickety chair and Aurelio sat.

"So," she began. "You are in love."

"How do you know?"

"Everyone knows. You have been following that Belmonte girl around for years. They make jokes."

"What kinds of jokes?"

"It does not matter. I know what you desire."

The old woman shuffled over to her shelves and fished through jars full of powders and animal parts until she found a small ceramic vial.

"Have her drink this. It will dim her wits. Then you can do with her what you will."

"I do not wish to violate her," Aurelio exclaimed, horrified.

"Truly? That is a first. 'Aurelio met his soulmate. Dolores did not.'"

"What?"

"That is one of the jokes people say. You see, it implies that you love her but she does not—"

"I understand," he interrupted curtly.

"I thought it was funny." She shrugged and then gingerly lowered herself into a chair and stared into Aurelio's eyes. Aurelio accepted her challenge and glared back. The woman's murky eyes discomfited him, so he fixed his attention on the fine lines fracturing her face. The woman had wrinkles within wrinkles, within wrinkles, within...

"You desire a *true* love potion," she whispered.

"Yes."

"They are expensive."

"I have ten dollars."

"Ten? I was going to give it to you for five. I will throw in Raymond."

※ ※

Emperor Maximilian the First burned at the stake. The flames from his tremendous papier-mâché head spewed sparks that swirled high above the plaza where women danced a zarzuela. Aurelio felt sorry for the Emperor. Granted, the French had imposed him on Mexico when they invaded seventy years ago, but he had tried to be a good king. He did not deserve to get shot like a common criminal. Most people at the festival knew nothing about Maximilian. They assumed that the fifth of May commemorated Mexican Independence. They did not know that the holiday actually celebrated a victory against the French; nor did they care. They simply wished to drink and dance. Aurelio did not care much either. He merely happened to have read about the battle in a book.

Aurelio read many books. His father had kindled Aurelio's love for a good story through his tales of knightly adventures, but the necessities of farm work had forced Aurelio to leave school after only six years. Fortunately, Aurelio's last teacher, Mrs. Frank, presented him a passport to all the wonders of the world: a library card. Since that day, Aurelio had ridden into San Lazaro every month to borrow books. By now, he had read the library's meager collection of adventure novels and histories several times over.

Aurelio owned but one book of his own, an illustrated copy of *Die Marchen der Bruders Grimm*. It had belonged to his mother, who emigrated to California as a child from Bavaria. Aurelio had no memory of his mother. She died when he was two years of age, and he had but one faded photograph by which to remember her. Aurelio would stare at her picture for hours, trying to understand the person behind the big round eyes that her father told him were bright blue. He thought she was the most beautiful woman in the world, an opinion shared by his neighbors. But Aurelio's father disparaged the picture. "The woman in that photograph is not your mother. She is too formal and serious. Ilsa smiled. She jested and laughed. She loved everyone. But, most of all, she loved you."

Aurelio had often wished that she had lived long enough to teach him German so that he could read her book. It took him years to learn that *Die Marchen der Bruders Grimm* translated to *The Fairy Tales of the Brothers Grimm*, and many more years before the book ceased to terrify him. His father had told him that his mother fled Germany to find a better life in America. After seeing the illustrations in her book, Aurelio could understand why. The engravings depicted a sinister world of dark forests where girls married frogs, witches ate children, and repulsive dwarves danced around bonfires and stole babies. Aurelio could not decipher the manuscript, but the pictures made it abundantly clear that Germany was a dreadful place, especially for children.

Aurelio no longer feared the book the way he did when he was younger. In fact, he regarded it as his most prized possession. But still, he would not look at the macabre images before going to bed.

Aurelio arrived at the fiesta wearing his best shirt and his father's red silk vest with a gold watch chain looped between the pockets. Diego had sold his gold pocket watch years ago to pay the taxes on their rock-strewn farm, but he had kept the chain. Aurelio gravitated toward the most crowded part of the plaza where women danced in swirling multicolored skirts and men drank. *Dolores will be at the center of the party*, he reasoned. He marched into the throng, and there he found her, flanked by her mother; two older brothers; and Mina, the chaperone. Dolores wore a bright red skirt with a white peasant blouse pulled down to expose her shoulders. Aurelio had not had a close look at her for months. Her youthful face had tightened, accentuating her cheekbones and her large brown eyes. She looked taller, leaner, and, if possible, even more beautiful. Aurelio fingered the love potion in his pocket. *Today she will be mine.* The Indian witch had told him to pour the mixture into a sweet drink to mask the taste and, most importantly, to stand before her when she drank, because the potion would engender irresistible ardor for the first soul she laid eyes upon. The witch had further cautioned Aurelio to keep Dolores away from rodents and cockroaches. "Those relationships always end in tragedy."

Aurelio purchased a cup of hot chocolate, poured his elixir into the beverage, and strutted toward Dolores, but Mina thrust herself forward and blocked his path. "Go away, Aurelio!" she enjoined.

"I thought Dolores might like some chocolate."

"She has had chocolate. And churros, and pilonsillo. Do you imagine that you are the first boy to molest her?"

"I do not molest her. I am her friend."

"She does not want your friendship."

"And why not?"

"Is that for me?" Aurelio and Mina turned to see Dolores strolling up to them.

Aurelio faltered. "Yes," he blurted too loudly and handed her the drink.

Dolores eyed him languidly from head to foot with amused approval. "I like your waistcoat," she purred and consumed the chocolate in one long, luxurious swallow. Aurelio thrust himself before her and held his breath, waiting for her eyes to meet his. But, as she lowered the cup from her lips, four other men swarmed in between her and Aurelio.

"Dolores! Care to dance? Nice dress. Remember me? Would you like to see a moving picture?"

Her eyes darted from man to man.

"Dolores!" Aurelio barked, compelling her to look at him.

"Yes?" she asked innocently.

He locked eyes with her. "Did you like the chocolate?"

"Yes. Could you bring me another?"

"Sure. How do you feel? Look me in the eye so I can..." Too late. Her suitors swept her off into a horde of drunken revelers. Aurelio's own witchcraft had foiled him, thus teaching him a profound truth that he would cling to for the rest of his days: Get better witchcraft.

Fireworks exploded over the plaza as Aurelio refilled his mug from a beer barrel. He had drained his third cup when Mina stomped up and reluctantly presented him a slip of paper.

"My young mistress commanded me to deliver this." When he took the note, Mina grabbed his wrist. "Do not read it."

Aurelio wrenched his arm free and read it anyway. "Midnight. The church. Bring tequila." Dolores had drawn a large heart around the word *tequila*.

A firework exploded in the night sky.

"Don't go," said Mina.

Aurelio was far too intoxicated with beer and love to hear the woman, so she slapped him.

"Ow!"

"Dolores is engaged to Bud McGregor."

"What? No."

"Yes."

"But Bud is so stupid."

"The McGregors are rich and powerful."

"She does not love him!" he shouted, flourishing the note. "She loves me. And I adore her. I am a good man, Mina. I do not deserve your scorn."

"It is *you* that concerns me, Aurelio," she explained.

Aurelio furrowed his brow to appear interested in what the woman had to say.

"I knew your mother."

Aurelio relaxed his face. The subject of his mother genuinely interested him.

"When my son got the typhoid, my mistress would not give me leave to care for him, so your mother sat by his side while I worked. She had work of her own to do. You had yet to be born, but she had many responsibilities on your farm. Still, she came to my house every day for two weeks. I am certain that my boy survived because of your mother's kindness. So, Aurelio, you can trust me when I tell you that Dolores Belmonte will only bring you sorrow. She is a child of her class—pretty, charming, yes, but also vain and willful. She *will* marry McGregor. He comes from a powerful family, and if you covet their property, they will harm you."

Aurelio said, "Thank you. I will consider your words carefully," but he thought, *Where can I buy tequila?*

֎ ֍

Aurelio sat on the church steps, beneath the full moon, rehearsing for his impending assignation. "Greetings, Miss Belmonte." *Too formal.* "Hey, doll face." *Absolutely not.* "Hello, Dolores." That sounded terrible as well. He decided to leave his dialogue to chance and react spontaneously. *I must practice behaving spontaneously.*

He pulled the small bottle of tequila out of his pocket. Mr. Chang, the grocer, had assured him that it was the finest brand available. Aurelio had noted that it was the *only* brand available in his store, but of all the markets in San Lazaro, only Mr. Chang had the entrepreneurial foresight to remain open on fiesta night, so Aurelio had little grounds for complaint. He contemplated imbibing a smidgen to calm his nerves but decided that he should present the bottle to Dolores unopened. He did not want her to imagine that he abused spirits, so he returned the bottle to his pocket. *What time is it?* Aurelio reached for the pocket watch he knew was not there, then balled his hand into a fist. *Calm down, man.*

The sound of a bolt scraping against metal drove Aurelio to his feet. The church doors behind him began to open. Aurelio bolted off the steps and ran ten yards before he heard, "Where are you going?"

He turned back to see Dolores standing in the church doorway. He glanced around nervously. Had anyone else witnessed his cowardly flight? Seeing no one, he cautiously returned to the church.

"How did you get inside?" he whispered.

"The back door," she replied, too loudly to calm Aurelio's nerves. "Did you bring it?"

"What? Oh, yes." He pulled the bottle out of his pocket. She snatched it away and marched into the church. He glanced around once more before following her inside and closing the large doors.

Moonlight from a circular window above the altar cast a silver halo upon the statue of the crucified Christ as Dolores twisted the cork off the bottle and took a large gulp of tequila. "Oh, Lord! That is terrible!" she coughed.

Aurelio flinched, hoping that her exclamation had not offended Jesus. He bent a knee and crossed himself before scurrying up to her. "Mr. Chang said it was good."

"Chang is a liar." She grimaced. She took another swig and concluded, "That is the worst tequila I have ever tasted." She handed him the bottle. He swallowed a mouthful and gagged. "That *is* terrible."

She took back the tequila and peered at him. "How old are you?"

"Eighteen."

"You look younger."

"You know how old I am. You have known me for years."

"I remember playing cowboys and Indians with you."

He considered correcting her, but instead he said, "You were the only girl to ever play with us."

She slipped into a pew, drank some more, and offered him the bottle. He shook his head and sat beside her.

"I like it here at night. It's quiet," she sighed.

"Yes," he replied, avoiding eye contact with Jesus.

"Are you scared?"

"No," he lied. He took the bottle from her and forced himself to swallow more. He shivered.

"You will be handsome someday." She smiled.

"I am not handsome now?"

"You are a child."

"No, I am not."

She brushed her hand over his vest. "Is it silk?"

"I don't know. It belongs to my father."

Moonlight sparkled in her eyes. "I might let you kiss me."

"Let me know when you make up your mind" was what he wished he had said. What he actually said was, "Uh…" She interrupted his dull-witted riposte by lying back onto the pew and pulling him on top of her. His face was now inches from hers. He could feel her heart beating. Her breath smelled of alcohol and chocolate. He drew closer to the warmth of her lips until, for the first time in his life, Aurelio Cienfuegos kissed a girl, and not just any girl. He kissed the *only* girl. It was a soft, gentle, wonderful kiss. It was better than he had imagined it, and he had imagined it many times.

"I think it worked," she whispered after they broke the kiss.

Aurelio panicked. Did she know about the potion? "What? What worked?"

"The tequila," she replied.

"Yes. Bad booze good." Aurelio found that lying atop the woman of his dreams hampered his power of speech. "Good," he added for emphasis.

She reached between them and began to unbutton his vest. He felt an overwhelming urge to express his feelings. "Dolores, I have always—"

She quieted him with another kiss.

☙ ❧

Aurelio lazily pumped water into a bucket as he gazed down at the brilliant blue Pacific Ocean. Ordinarily, fog dulled the California coast on spring mornings, but not today. Today, the euphoria radiating from Aurelio's heart had beguiled the sun to burn away the clouds and warm the entire world.

We shall live in San Francisco, mused Aurelio. He had never been to San Francisco, but he had seen stereoscopic photographs of the wondrous edifices that, from the ashes of a terrible earthquake, now bejeweled the impossibly steep hills of that golden-gated city. After he returned from the war, he would enroll in the University of California and become an engineer or an archeologist. Of course, he might not return. His intoxicating optimism did not delude him into imagining himself immortal, but the prospect of dying no longer frightened Aurelio. He had won the greatest treasure life had to offer. He could die in peace if God so willed it. But he needed to formally propose to Dolores before he enlisted. He had imagined the joyous moment many times. He would take her to Huguenot Hill and present her with the ring that his father had bestowed upon his mother when—

The roar of a motor roused Aurelio from his daydream. An automobile wound its way down the cattle trail toward the farm. Aurelio had seen cars in San Lazaro, but he had never ridden in one, and he certainly could not distinguish a Ford from a Chevrolet. The automobile that currently approached him carried four men, Americanos all. It came to a halt several yards from Aurelio, and the men jumped out. As they marched toward him, Aurelio recognized the leader. It was Bud McGregor. *Here we go,* thought Aurelio.

Aurelio's father had ridden off that morning to sell eggs to Mr. Chang, so he had to face the Americanos alone. He assumed the most powerful stance he could muster. Like most Americanos, these young men were disturbingly tall, none more so than Bud McGregor. "Good morning, Bud," Aurelio smiled warmly. He recognized one of the Americanos that accompanied Bud. "Hello, Teddy."

"Hey, Aurelio," Teddy replied with an apologetic smile.

Bud gave Teddy a shove. "What the devil are you doing?"

"We were in Mrs. Frank's class," Teddy explained innocently.

Bud dismissed Teddy with a snort, then strode up to Aurelio, his red freckled face inflamed into a feral snarl. "I saw you and Dolores come out of the church last night. What were you doing in there?"

Aurelio met Bud's rabid glare with equanimity. "I am sorry, Bud. I regret not having spoken to you man to man before last night. Trust me, I never intended to shame you or your family, but events took on an inexorable life of their own and like unwary bathers on a storm-battered shore—"

"What the fuck are you talking about?" demanded Bud.

"Bud," Aurelio sighed sympathetically. "Dolores and I are now one."

"What?"

"I think he means he fucked her," one of his companions ventured.

"Did you fuck her?"

Aurelio raised his chin with righteous indignation. "I must ask you not to use such vulgar language in reference to my intended."

"Your what?" bellowed Bud.

"He fucked her," concluded his Americano compatriot.

Bud punched Aurelio on the side of his head. Another Americano smashed the other side of his head, and someone else struck him in the jaw. Aurelio's legs folded, and he crumpled to the ground.

"You dirty wop," Bud screamed and kicked him in the stomach.

Wop? Aurelio considered explaining that he was, in fact, a spic, but he doubted that the distinction mattered much to Bud at this point, and, in any case, he needed to concentrate on protecting his face and neck from the Americanos' boots.

When the thrashing finally ceased, Aurelio's head throbbed like a drum. The steady pounding grew stronger and louder until Aurelio realized that the pulsations came not from his head, but from the earth. They were the hooves of a galloping horse. Aurelio lifted his battered face and saw his father charging down the mountain on the rose-grey mare.

"Aw, nuts," exclaimed one of the Americanos.

Diego Cienfuegos sprinted his horse past the hen house and snatched up a wooden rake. He tucked it under the crook of his arm and advanced on the Americanos like Don Quixote tilting at windmills. The boys scattered. Diego gracefully swung the rake like a polo mallet and knocked an Americano off his feet. He spun his horse around and whacked a second one in the stomach, sending him to the dirt with a mighty "Ooof!"

Diego pivoted to face Bud, who stood, frozen with terror. Diego gave him a courtly nod, spurred his mare, and charged. Bud staggered backward. He reached behind his shirt, pulled out a revolver and shot Diego in the chest.

Diego flew backward off the horse. "NO!" Aurelio wailed. He struggled to his feet and hobbled to his father, who lay on the ground with a look of astonishment on his face. "Papá? Papá!"

"You shot Mr. Cienfuegos," exclaimed Teddy.

"He was going to kill me," Bud pleaded. His compatriots had no desire to argue the point and ran off in all directions.

Aurelio took a handkerchief out of his father's pocket and pressed it onto the blood bubbling from his chest.

"Papá!"

"It was self-defense!" Bud screamed as he ran away.

Diego's eyes fluttered. "Aurelio."

"Yes, Papá?"

"Aurelio," his father croaked. "It... It hurts."

And Diego Cienfuegos died.

Aurelio had seen death many times. He had chopped the heads off chickens. He had helped his father nurse their old gelding, Bucephalus, as it passed away; and last winter, he had slaughtered his first hog, which proved a challenging ordeal. He had cared for Bobo since birth. He'd pleaded with his father to spare him, but his father had simply replied, "Do you want to eat?" Diego scooped up some mud with his forefinger and rubbed a spot onto Bobo's forehead. He handed Aurelio the mallet and said, "Strike hard and fast, so the animal will not suffer." Aurelio obeyed, and Bobo dropped like a sack of dirt. The feel of the hammer cracking the animal's skull haunted Aurelio for many days to come, but what disturbed him most was the brusqueness of it all. One moment, Bobo was a living creature with desires and fears, and the next he was pile of meat. One second Bobo was; the next, he was not.

Now, his father was not.

Aurelio wept as he tightened the harness on the mare. The old man had grown so frail that Aurelio had no trouble lifting him onto the cart. He threw the spade down beside him and pulled himself onto the wagon seat, and then started up the hill to his mother's grave. The knowledge that his father would soon reunite with his mother only slightly mitigated the anguish he felt. The law would offer him no justice. The McGregors were the wealthiest family on the bay. Bud's uncle was the chief of police; his grandfather was judge. They would rule his father's death an accident, or more likely, they would accuse Aurelio of the crime, a charge which he had little desire to defend since his own actions had, in fact, led to the old man's demise. But Aurelio had not pulled the trigger. Bud McGregor had done that, and Aurelio had no intention of paying for the Americano's crime.

Aurelio had but one option.

※ ※

It was late by the time he arrived at Dolores' house. He peered at the sprawling two-story home from behind an old walnut tree. The Belmontes lived in the hills above San Lazaro where the rich Americanos built their mansions. Light shone through the parlor window, but Dolores' bedroom was dark.

The sound of tinkling metal seized his attention. Two great mastiffs emerged from behind the house and charged toward him. Aurelio ducked behind the tree. The clanging grew louder. Aurelio braced himself as the beasts rounded the tree and barked wildly at him, before they pounced and lathered his face with their wet tongues.

Aurelio had often chastised himself for spending long hours crouched behind the walnut tree, surveilling Dolores' home. It made him feel like a pitiable wretch, and he had no doubt that Dolores would find his prying reprehensible. Fortunately, her hounds did not. Aurelio had made friends with Gonzalo and Sam long ago, and despite his forlorn state of mind, he had not neglected to bring them each a leathery wedge of salted pork to quiet them while he made his way toward his beloved's window.

Aurelio procured a stepstool from the back porch and used it to climb onto her balcony. He found her window open and commenced to enter the dark room, but he stopped and gingerly touched his face. The Americano's beating had swollen his eye and lip. *Perhaps, I will frighten her.*

Whereupon, from inside the room, he heard, "Come in."

His heart bounded with delight. He cheerfully vaulted through the window and unwittingly knocked an unseen glass item onto the floor with a cacophonous crash.

"Dolores?" boomed a male voice from somewhere inside the house.

Dolores struck a match to an oil lamp and gasped at the sight of Aurelio. "What are you doing here?"

Aurelio stopped breathing. "You invited me," he squeaked.

"You can't be here," she whispered.

"Dolores!" echoed the male voice.

"I'm asleep!" she yelled, then turned back to Aurelio. "What happened to your face?"

"Bud," he replied simply.

"Bud hit you?"

"And he killed my father."

"What?"

"He saw us leave the church last night."

Dolores took a moment to absorb the import of Aurelio's words before whispering, "What did he say?"

"That he saw us leaving—"

"What did *you* say?"

"The truth."

"What?" she hissed.

"He had a right to know."

"Know what?"

"That we made love."

"You told him *that*?"

"Of course."

"What have you done?"

"I don't understand."

"Get out of here!"

"But Bud knows. We can go together."

"I am not going anywhere."

"But you love me."

"I love Bud."

"But we..."

"We did nothing."

The floor tilted beneath Aurelio. He stumbled against a dresser and tried to focus his mind. "But last night..."

"Nothing happened. Bud will believe me. We have had disagreements before. He has a passionate temper. He imagines transgressions. He rants and he thunders, but by and by, he listens to reason and begs my forgiveness."

"*Imagines* transgressions? Our transgression was real."

"No. It was not. You invented it to make yourself look like a big man. It was a joke. Do you understand?"

"No."

"Understand this: You must go, *now*. I am sorry about your father, Aurelio. Truly, I am. But the law will never punish Bud for his death. They will punish you."

"But you kissed me."

"Be quiet. Go and do not return."

Aurelio recoiled at the incontestable coldness in her eyes. He heard a car outside.

"That is Bud. Get out of here!"

Aurelio's vision blurred and narrowed. He tottered to the window like an insentient corpse doomed to wander the earth long after its heart had stopped. He tumbled over the balcony and lay on the ground beside the house in a cataleptic stupor until the dogs trotted over and licked him back to his senses.

Aurelio Cienfuegos forced himself to stand and, placing one foot in front of the other, he slowly walked away from San Lazaro, from his father's farm, and from the love of his life.

Chapter Twenty-One

Aurelio did not join the Army. His father's death had dispelled all thoughts of martial glory. He didn't want to see anyone else die, much less kill them, so he headed south, hitchhiking when he could, walking when he had to.

Aurelio had pictured Southern California as a paradise of sunshine and palm trees, but alas, he soon learned that heaven cannot exist without hell. In this wonderland, hell came in the guise of petroleum drilling. Vast forests of bleak oil derricks blemished the hills, valleys, and beaches of Santa Barbara, Ventura, and Los Angeles. Winding his way through skeletal towers that belched flame and smoke, he felt like he had descended into the inferno his priest had warned him about. Then Aurelio Cienfuegos had a dreadful epiphany: *I belong in hell.* He had caused his father's death. He deserved to suffer.

Aurelio found work as a roustabout on the rigs along Venice Beach. For ten hours a day, he hauled pipes, dug ditches, and repaired wells. When the work grew frustrating, he would recall his father telling him to "Use your head, not your hands." When his co-workers slacked off, his father's voice reminded him to "Do twice the work and never complain." And, when someone picked a fight, he knew to "Throw the first punch. At least you'll get one in." This backbreaking purgatory did not assuage his guilt as he had hoped it would, but it did strengthen his muscles and put money in his pocket. Two years of hard labor turned the slim boy from San Lazaro into a robust man.

One hot August afternoon in 1920, Aurelio ripped the tongs off a drill pipe, took off his hardhat, and looked forward to the beer he would soon have at Menotti's speakeasy. Aurelio never joined his workmates on their nightly revelries. Although his fellow roustabouts appreciated Aurelio's work ethic, they did not want to socialize with him. Dolores Belmonte's prediction had come true. Aurelio had turned into a handsome man, far too good-looking for his not-so-good-looking workmates to introduce to their not-so-trustworthy girlfriends, which was fine with Aurelio. He preferred solitude and a good book to idle banter, except on Saturdays. On Saturday night, after a week of hard labor, Aurelio enjoyed one mug of cold beer before heading down to the Abbot Kinney Pier for a hot dog and some saltwater taffy. On Sunday, he would lie in bed all day and read. Aurelio lived for Sundays when he could forget his past, his future, and most importantly, his present, and lose himself in someone else's wondrous adventures.

Aurelio entered Menotti's Grocery Store one Saturday night around eight o'clock. He wore his only suit, a white shirt, and, of course, a vest. He walked past a matronly woman squeezing oranges and a teenage boy buying peanuts. He nodded to Cesar Menotti, the grocer, and entered a back room where he found a narrow black door with a button beside it. He pressed the button and, after a short pause, a bell rang. Aurelio opened the door and squeezed into a coffin-like elevator, which descended slowly until it hit the ground with a jarring thud. Aurelio stepped out of the box into an ornate, smoke-filled saloon full of spruced up workingmen and perfumed ladies. He squeezed his way to the bar and nodded to the bartender, who quickly slid a frothing mug of beer into his hands. Aurelio lifted the brew to his lips, took one luxurious sip, and sighed.

"Aurelio!" shouted a man.

Aurelio lowered the mug and saw a young Americano pushing

his way toward him. When the man removed his hat, Aurelio knew his name.

"Teddy?" Aurelio blurted.

"Hey," Teddy replied sadly. "How ya doin'?"

Aurelio felt like punching him in the face; not for his involvement in his father's death—Aurelio did not blame Teddy for that—but rather for the contrite expression on his face.

So, he did.

Aurelio's right cross knocked Teddy backward into a stocky woman, spilling her beer onto a barrel-chested fellow with a walrus mustache, who gasped with horror at the stain on his shirt before punching Teddy in the stomach, sending him stumbling into another guy, who hit him in the temple.

By the sixth or seventh punch, Aurelio decided that Teddy had had enough and pulled him free of his attackers only to get clobbered over the head with a beer bottle. Aurelio punched his assailant, and the entire bar exploded into a befuddling free-for-all of blows and kicks and shouts. Something hard struck Aurelio in the back of the head. It took him a moment to realize that it was the floor. He was on the ground, getting trampled by the brawlers above. Someone grabbed him by the collar and dragged him across the room. When he had cleared the melee, he looked up and saw Teddy's battered face.

"You okay, Aurelio?" he garbled through his bloody mouth. Aurelio sat up and smiled at Teddy.

"You look awful."

"Feel pretty bad, too," Teddy added, returning Aurelio's smile.

*   *

"You were smart to get out of town," Teddy said as he passed the flask of gin.

The alcohol stung Aurelio's cut lip, but it felt warm going down his throat. He handed back the flask, dug his bare feet into the cool sand and gazed at the moon perched over the ocean.

Teddy continued, "Bud told everybody that you killed your daddy because he was always drunk and you hated him. He tried to get me to go along with his story, but I wouldn't do it. Your daddy weren't no drunk. He was a nice man. He used to give me rides on that pony of yours when we was little, remember? I weren't gonna sully his memory, and Bud didn't have to make up no story. You was already gone. He got Dolores all to himself—they got married and had a kid—I told him he should just leave you alone, but he wouldn't do it. He was real angry at you. At me, too, 'cause I wouldn't lie for him. His stinkin' uncle threw me in jail; said they was gonna tell everybody that *I* killed your daddy! But, then one night, right before they was going to take me to court, they left my cell door open, so I went home. Mama said I should run away like you did. She knew this fella that had a lumber yard in San Gabriel, so I worked for him for a bit. Then I came to L.A., and now I got me this keen job at Matador Studios, haulin' lumber and building sets and things. I bet I could get you a job there, too, if you want. I'm just glad you ain't dead. They sent guys after you. Did you change your name? You should. You look different. How ya doin'?"

Aurelio took a moment to sort through all the information Teddy had thrown at him then asked…

"What's a set?"

Chapter Twenty-Two

Matador Studios was located in the lovely Los Angeles district of Edendale. The one-hundred-acre lot bordered Griffith Park, Silver Lake Reservoir, and the Los Angeles River, giving it access to a variety of natural landscapes with plenty of space to build lavish sets for Westerns and biblical epics—the two staples of the booming film industry.

One Friday afternoon, six months after Aurelio had run into Teddy, famed director William Desmond Taylor was trying to finish the final sequence of *The White Horseman*, starring Art Acord. Aurelio and Teddy had just installed the saloon window, which was made of sugar glass so the actors could crash through it without getting hurt. Aurelio and Teddy put down their hammers to watch Art Acord ride through town on his white Palomino. Aurelio loved watching the actors perform their amazing stunts, which never looked as thrilling on screen as they did in real life. These performers were fearless, especially the cowboys. It helped that most of them had been real cowboys before they went into show business.

Teddy had told him that in the early days of the nickelodeons, the studios had shot Westerns in New York City. When they came to California, they found that the wild west was gone, but the cowboys were still there. They needed jobs, and Hollywood needed cowboys. It was a match made in heaven.

Aurelio loved watching the former cowhands flaunt their horsemanship for the cameras. Their skill in the saddle was surpassed only by their lust for alcohol and fighting. Staged fights often led to real ones, which delayed shooting and inflated budgets.

Nobody loved to fight more than Art Acord, who, at this very moment, raced his horse through the make-believe town, blasting away with his six-shooters.

"You missed your mark! Get off the bloody horse!" yelled William Desmond Taylor in his effete British accent.

Art didn't think much of directors. He referred to them as "highfalutin bootlickers" when he felt charitable. "Assholes" when he did not.

"Did you say sumpin', asshole?" Art yelled as he spun his horse around and galloped back down the street, vaulting from one side of the animal to another before bouncing up into a headstand. Then he rolled backward off the saddle and somehow landed on his feet. Aurelio and the entire film crew applauded. Art belched drunkenly and staggered up to angelic little Mary Miles Minter, the heroine of the movie, who puckered her lips to welcome her cowboy hero.

Art shoved her to the ground.

"Motherfucker!" screamed Mary.

"Cut!" yelled William Desmond Taylor, but the cameraman kept on cranking. Art's antics were too delicious not to record.

Art burped some more and lurched over to Aurelio and Teddy, who watched the fun from behind a light stand. Aurelio had seen Art work long enough to know what was coming; and so did Teddy, because he ran away. *Good thinking*, thought Aurelio. But, before he could follow his friend, Art grabbed him by his collar. Aurelio had hoped that a job in the entertainment industry would involve less fist fighting than working on oil rigs, but he was mistaken.

Art spun Aurelio around, but Aurelio was ready and smashed his fist into the movie star's jaw. Art flew backward onto the dirt, and there he remained, snoring peacefully. Aurelio inspected his hand, surprised by his own strength. Everyone gaped at him in silence. Then Mary Miles Minter rose to her feet and clapped. William Desmond Taylor joined in, and soon the entire crew applauded Aurelio.

William Desmond Taylor marched up to him. "Well, done, young man. You're fired." Then he whirled on the crew. "I need a volunteer to kiss Mary!" A slew of dirty cowboys rushed forward, but Mary Miles Minter shoved them back and stomped up to Taylor.

"I'm not letting any of these drunk sons of bitches near me!" screamed the young lady.

"Mary, darling," pleaded the director. "We can't end this fucking movie without a fucking kiss. We'll put one of these monkeys in Art's costume. With the hat, nobody will know the difference."

"Then you better get another girl, because the next cocksucking cowboy who lays a hand on me will be picking his bloody balls up off the street."

"Darling, you have to kiss *somebody*."

Without hesitation, Mary Miles Minter pointed at Aurelio. "Him."

◈ ◈

The boots were too big. Aurelio almost fell when the assistant director rushed him onto the set and left him alone on the dusty street while the crew set up the last shot of the day. Perspiration trickled down his armpits, soaking Art Acord's red-sequined shirt, which already reeked of sweat and whiskey. A wardrobe assistant plopped a hat onto Aurelio's head, stuffed two six-shooters into his belt, and scampered off.

"Pull the hat down over your face," barked Taylor.

Aurelio complied. Now he could see nothing.

"You're going to walk up to Mary and give her a kiss. Think you can handle that, young man?"

Aurelio peeked out from under the big hat at Mary Miles Minter, who stood a few feet away, swarmed by beauticians powdering her face and picking at her curls.

"Mary?" Taylor asked.

Her entourage skittered away, revealing the beatific vision of virginal loveliness that was Mary Miles Minter. She smiled coyly at Aurelio and nodded.

"Okay!" shouted the Director. "Camera? Ready and..."

Aurelio stomped up and gave Mary an awkward kiss.

"Wait until I say action!"

Aurelio backed away from Mary, tripped over his spurs and fell on his behind.

"Eager boy," Mary tittered, and the crew burst out laughing.

Aurelio flushed. He rose to his feet and glared at all the red, blotchy Americano faces contorted with laughter. He thought of Bud McGregor. *You dirty wop*, and Dolores, *Are you an idiot?* He faced Mary Miles Minter, the instigator of his latest abuse, and all the rage and humiliation that he had stifled for so long exploded through his chest and propelled him toward Mary like a missile. She froze when she saw the fire in Aurelio's green eyes. He grabbed her by the waist, and, before she could scream, Aurelio pressed his lips against hers and let all his pent-up anger surge into the young woman through the most passionate kiss the eighteen-year-old starlet had ever known.

It was not a short kiss. Aurelio had kept his inner beast caged far too long, and it was hungry. Initially, he felt her flinch when he pressed himself against her, but gradually, she yielded with a soft moan. Aurelio would later learn that the starlet had spent her short but illustrious career living off cottage cheese, lettuce, and foul-breathed cowboys who kissed like they hog-tied calves—hard and fast. Mary Miles Minter was hungry, too. The make-believe kiss turned into something primal. The crew stopped laughing.

The wild-west set grew quiet but for Mary's muffled sighs. When Aurelio finally released her, he and Mary glared at each other like predators inflamed by their first taste of blood.

William Desmond Taylor whispered to the cameraman. "Tell me you got that." The cameraman gave him a thumbs-up.

Without taking her eyes off of Aurelio, Mary declared, "I need another take."

Chapter Twenty-Three

Charles Delamour stood on his balcony, sipping soda water and gazing down at the tide of gaudy color and hilarity and strangely shorn hair undulating beneath the colored lights of his spacious garden. Paul Whiteman & His Orchestra played *Nothing Could be Sweeter*, while old men pushed young women in graceless circles on the canvas dance floor, and single girls danced alone. Rounds of cocktails floated through the swelling chatter and the sporadic shrieks of instantly forgotten introductions.

Delamour looked away from his garden to the lights of Hollywood glimmering in the valley below. The speed with which the small town had grown in the last five years astonished him. *Astonished? No. Annoyed.* He was glad to live outside Tinsel Town in Beachwood Canyon. He would have preferred a smaller house, but the "Thief of Hearts" needed a proper palace to entertain his illustrious lovers. At least that was what the studio had said in *Photoplay Magazine* after his hit movie, *The Thief of Hearts* and its equally successful sequel, *The Son of The Thief of Hearts*. The house was a faux Tudor mansion with high-beamed ceilings, plate glass windows, and eighteen stone fireplaces. Studio designers had covered the walls with gloomy portraits of British aristocrats and display cases full of medieval weaponry. Although Delamour enjoyed swinging the occasional battle-ax, he liked only two things about his home—its secluded locale and its library.

The band began playing *Love Me*, which meant that it was midnight, time for Delamour to make an appearance at his party. Of all the roles Charles Delamour played, he found jovial host the most tiresome. But whether portraying a pirate, a knight, a flying ace, or a devil-may-care playboy, Delamour committed fully to every role. Pretending came easily to him. Before becoming an actor, he had dreamt of being one of the heroes from the books he'd read. Now, he could pretend to be all of them. Best of all, he no longer had to play the only character he despised—the naïve, foolish, Aurelio Cienfuegos.

"May I, sir?"

Delamour turned to see his butler, a tall, regal black man in tails, holding a sport coat and gesturing to the water glass in Delamour's hand.

"Sure thing, sport," replied Delamour as he handed over the glass. He knew that the butler didn't appreciate being called sport, but Delamour didn't appreciate having a servant, so he figured that made them even. The studio had forced him to take on a large serving staff in order to promote his well-heeled bachelor mystique, and, Delamour suspected, to keep an eye on him. They shadowed him day and night, except on Sundays when he had the house all to himself. Delamour lived for Sundays. The butler, whose real name Delamour refused to learn, set the water glass down on a small table and helped Delamour slide a blue blazer over his white flannels. While most of his male guests wore tuxedos, the Matador Studios Publicity Department had suggested that less formal attire would enhance Delamour's reputation as a lady's man who slipped on clothes as casually as he slipped them off. Delamour gratefully followed their advice. He hated monkey suits.

The moment he stepped out into his garden, two young women in twin yellow dresses fluttered up to him.

"Hello!" they cried together. "Why did they have to hang you?"

They were referring to his latest film.

"I *was* a thief, after all," joked Delamour.

"But you were so handsome!" said one of the girls. "You don't remember us, do you? We were here last week. You said we looked like twins."

"Of course I remember," Delamour replied with a warm smile. "You're Honey Pie, and you're Sweetheart."

"No," said the other girl. "I'm Honey Pie, and *she's* Sweetheart."

"Of course."

The girls laughed, and Delamour moved on.

He squeezed past Art Acord, who had his arm around stunt man Yakima Canutt. "No fighting tonight, Art," Delamour teased.

"Too late." Acord laughed, turning his head to reveal a badly swollen eye.

Yakima Canutt smiled, displaying a missing tooth. Delamour shook his head in mock disapproval and walked on.

He soon found himself wedged between an inebriated man with large owl-eyed spectacles and a rowdy little girl who gave way, upon the slightest provocation, to uncontrollable laughter.

"You look familiar," observed the drunk man. The girl laughed. "Do you come to these soirees often?" he asked.

"I do," Delamour replied sincerely.

The girl shrieked with mirth.

"The host is some big-shot movie star," confided the drunk man. "And boy, oh boy, is he rich. You see his library?"

"It's nice?"

"It's huge! It belongs in a castle somewhere. It's got carved wood shelves two stories high, just loaded with books. And the amazing thing is..." He leaned in close to Delamour and whispered, "They're real. They got pages and everything. I thought they'd be cardboard, you know, just for show. No-siree-Bob! This guy's got class."

The girl pointed at Delamour and choked with laughter.

"More champagne?" Delamour offered graciously.

"Don't mind if I dippy-do!"

Delamour snapped his fingers, and a server handed the drunk man a fresh glass of champagne.

"Chuck!" a woman called.

Only one person called Delamour "Chuck." He turned with a smile. "Marquise."

"Shut up and dance with me."

Gloria Swanson had just returned from making a movie in France, where she married the Marquis de la Falaise, a proud French nobleman who had fallen on hard times. The marriage made Swanson a Marquise and gave the Marquis some badly needed cash. The press celebrated their fairytale romance despite rumors that she had already begun an affair with Joe Kennedy. Gloria Swanson was a superb actress, who enjoyed life thoroughly. In fact, she had enjoyed life with Charles Delamour on more than one occasion.

Delamour motioned to Paul Whiteman, and the band seamlessly switched their selection to a tango. Swanson raised an approving eyebrow as Delamour swept her into his arms and glided her across the dance floor.

"And the Marquis?" he asked looking around.

"Fixing a castle somewhere. Rudy brought me." She tilted her head to Rudolf Valentino who chatted at the bar with several delicately handsome young men.

"And Rudy's wife?"

Swanson craned her head to scan the crowd, grimaced and pointed. Delamour spotted Rudolph Valentino's wife, Natacha Rambova, standing alone beneath a Chinese lantern. People streamed past her like water around a rock. She wore an ornate oriental gown topped by a tightly wound black turban, pinned with a jewel-encrusted brooch. She exuded the dark, angst-ridden mystique of a Russian artiste, even though she came from Utah. Her real name was Winifred Shaughnessy. Fortunately, nobody cared about the truth in Hollywood. Only image mattered. Delamour felt sorry for Natacha. Rudy did not make a good husband.

"They both brought you?"

"Yes, but I doubt they'll be taking me home," she crooned with a mischievous smile.

Delamour pulled her closer, and for a split second, he left his body and looked down upon himself with amazement. How had a poor farm boy with a sixth-grade education found himself fielding propositions from the biggest female movie star in the world while dancing the tango in his own Hollywood mansion? How? Easily.

The public knew that Hollywood peddled fantasy, but they didn't understand the depth of the film industry's deception. Magazines like *Photo Play*, *Screenland*, *Motion Picture*, *Silver Screen*, and *Screen Romances* transformed movie stars into modern-day Olympian gods who floated from party to party and marriage to marriage, free from the petty morality of the common man. The public worshipped them, but only from afar. Mortals did not mingle with gods.

What the public did not know, or want to know, was that actors, directors, and producers were really just carneys. Most of them came from vaudeville, music halls, circuses, and bordellos. They were lowlifes who no decent family would have invited to dinner, much less allowed their daughters to pine for. Charles Delamour had little trouble fitting in. If anything, a lifetime of reading had almost rendered him too cultured for the raunchy lifestyle of the rich and infamous.

When they released *The White Horseman*, starring Art Acord, the press raved about the grand kiss at the end of the film. Studio president, Jack Larson, knew a profitable product when he saw one and hastily announced that Matador Studios had found a new star, the suave and utterly irresistible, Charles Delamour. After six months of acting, dancing, and fencing lessons, as well as meticulous instructions on how to comport himself in public, Charles

Delamour was ready for his first starring role as swashbuckler Don Rodrigo of Seville, who used his superior swordsmanship and disarming smile to defeat the evil black Moors—played by white actors in blackface—and rescue the princess, played by the lovely Mary Miles Minter. *Silver Screen* magazine called his performance a "tour de force," adding that "the romance between Miss Minter and Mr. Delamour was electric." *Motion Picture Magazine* called it a "tour de force," and *Screenland* enthusiastically proclaimed, "It was a tour de force!" Matador Studios had so many reviews to write for their own films that they could only supply one article for all the magazines to share.

Most importantly, the movie was a hit at the box office, and Charles Delamour rocketed to stardom. Alas, Mary Miles Minter did not fare so well. Police found her monogrammed underwear in the bungalow where William Desmond Taylor lay dead with a bullet in his back. The murder of the famed director became the greatest unsolved mystery of its day. Lurid tales of drug-fueled orgies, pederasty, blackmail, and racketeering filled newspapers and magazines throughout the world. The press implicated half of Hollywood, but no one drew more salacious attention than Mary Miles Minter. Although the police officially exculpated her, leaving lacy undergarments in a dead man's apartment devastated the actress's virginal mystique. After the arrest of Fatty Arbuckle for rape and murder four years earlier, the Studio would not tolerate another scandal. They terminated Mary's contract. Mary went on to gain an inordinate amount of weight and sue her manager-mother for stealing all her money.

Fortunately, Mary's downfall had no effect on Charles Delamour's career—the Studio had plenty of other beautiful ladies to pair him with, on and off the screen—nor did it disturb him personally. Very little did anymore. Over the last five years, Delamour had found the key to inner peace: *Don't give a damn about anyone.* Dolores Belmonte had taught him that love was a farce, and the film industry showed him that people were chumps, so he learned to imitate love rather than feel it. He simulated heartache and rapture, grief and ardor, without having to suffer them. He felt liberated. Detachment brought him serenity, wisdom, and power, which he used to satisfy his urges, and Delamour had many urges.

"Küchle," Delamour said as he dipped Gloria Swanson.

"Excuse me?" she asked when he raised her up again.

"It's a Bavarian pastry. My mother's recipe. They're delicious with coffee in the morning."

"Oh," Gloria replied with a gleam in her eyes. "I think Rudy lost one of his ladies tonight."

Delamour glanced over at Rudolf Valentino, who was whispering into the ear of a very dapper young man.

"He'll be heartbroken," Delamour quipped.

Gloria Swanson smiled and pressed herself against him. She glanced over his shoulder and lifted one of her remarkably expressive eyebrows.

"Look busy. Here comes the boss."

"I'm working as hard as I can," he replied, never taking his eyes off her.

"Charles," exclaimed a male voice.

Delamour released Gloria Swanson and turned around.

"Jack," he said with his trademark debonair smile.

Jack Larson was a spooky little man, hence his nickname, "Spooky." Larson spoke in a lethargic monotone, which, coupled with his Eastern European accent and placid grey eyes, gave him a bovine quality that unnerved both friend and foe alike. Beside him stood his latest discovery, a young starlet who towered over the balding studio head. "I will make her a goddess!" Larson had promised Delamour, but Delamour knew better. Larson made a new discovery every few months, and none of his beauties had yet to appear in a film, let alone attain godhood. But, Delamour couldn't fault Larson's taste. The woman was stunning.

"Lovely party, Charles," Larson droned.

"Thank you, Jack."

"Gloria, you look glorious as always."

"Thank you, Jack."

"You have all met before, no?" Larson asked, gesturing to his companion.

"Of course," Delamour replied. The starlet held out a limp hand. Her electric-blue eyes sparkled mischievously as Delamour bent to kiss it.

"No. I haven't had the pleasure," Gloria interjected.

Delamour raised an eyebrow. He had seen Gloria greet the starlet on several occasions. The young woman's lip curled with annoyance. Delamour stifled his amusement. *Round one, Gloria Swanson.*

Larson took Gloria's hand. "Sweetheart, could you do me a grand favor and ask Rudy to dance with you? Too much time with the young men is not so good."

"Of course, Jack," Gloria smiled warmly and headed off to ruin Rudolf Valentino's evening.

Larson snapped his fingers and two enormous bodyguards lumbered up. Larson referred to the hulks as "the boys," but everyone else called them Tweedle Dee and Tweedle Dum. The brutes wore black suits and round dark glasses which made them look like murderous accountants. They never spoke or smiled. Delamour didn't know why Jack needed such menacing protection, but Jack Larson was a secretive man. Delamour knew little about him beyond what he read in press releases. Larson had emigrated from Russia thirty years ago with no money, but plenty of grit and brains, and he built the largest fur business in Buffalo, New York. When a client took him to an amusement park that featured one of Thomas Edison's new marvels—moving pictures—he left the fur business, and with astonishing speed, he built a small empire of highly profitable motion picture theaters. Not satisfied with playing other people's films, he began to make his own, thereby controlling both production and distribution of his product.

Larson knew what audiences wanted. They wanted *more*—more adventure, more glamour, more romance, more sex, but most of all, more cowboys. He decided that filming Westerns in front of painted backdrops in New York City imposed too many limitations, so he took his cameras to Southern California where he found all the open space, sunshine, and cowboys he could ever want.

"Charles, may I speak with you privately?"

"Of course."

"Sweetheart, let the boys accompany you to the punchbowl."

Tweedle Dee and Tweedle Dum stepped up alongside the starlet as if they intended to arrest her. She glanced at them with mild amusement then turned to Jack. "Don't leave me alone too long," she purred. "There's no telling what kind of trouble I might get into."

Delamour and Larson watched her strut away. They said nothing. There was no need.

Delamour escorted Jack to a secluded table and had a waiter bring coffee, which the studio head consumed day and night.

"You are Jesus Christ," Larson proclaimed.

"Excuse me?"

"This Christmas, MGM will release *Ben-Hur*. It will do well," Jack admitted with a dismissive wave of his hand. "So, next Christmas, *we* will release *The Son of Man* and destroy MGM, metaphorically speaking, of course."

"You want me to play Jesus?"

"I want you to *be* Jesus. While you portray the savior of mankind in the greatest epic ever made, you, Charles Delamour, the great sinner, will be reborn. You will find God and change your evil ways. *Ben-Hur* will be just another movie. *The Son of Man* will be the real thing."

"I have to go to church?"

"For a few months."

"Will people buy it?"

"Yes. Because you will fall in love. A nice Christian girl will win your heart and teach you how to be good. It will be a love story for the ages. It will inspire audiences around the world to find the goodness in themselves, so like the real Jesus Christ, you, Charles Delamour, will save mankind and make a lot of money."

"Which girl?"

"I make a list. You choose. After the movie is big hit, you keep her, you give her away, you decide."

Larson lowered his chin and glared at Delamour like a bull about to charge. "Will you do this, Charles? For me?"

"Sure, Jack," Delamour replied with a casual shrug. Larson patted his hand.

"You are a good boy. We will have a big party right here, like it is ancient Rome with the soldiers and the slave girls. We have the press and the cameras, and we will make big announcement about the new movie, and we say goodbye to all this fun, at least for a little while. Yes?"

A chauffeur in a robin's-egg blue uniform stepped up.

"Mr. Delamour, there's somebody who wants to see you—"

"I'm speaking with Mr. Larson," Delamour snapped.

"It's real important, Mr. Delamour."

"Not now."

"It's all right, my boy." Jack stood. "Enjoy your party. We shall begin our new project in a few weeks."

"Thank you, Jack." They shook hands and Jack Larson stomped off into the party. When he was out of sight, Delamour whirled on his chauffeur.

"Goddammit, Teddy. You know not to interrupt me when I'm with Spooky."

"This is real important, Aurelio—"

"Don't call me that! I'm not telling you again."

"Okay, okay. Look, you got a bigger problem than what I call you."

Teddy pointed to a pair of portly men, smoking cigars.

"Who are those guys?"

"No. Behind them to the right."

Delamour saw a woman standing beneath a porchlight, her face obscured by cigar smoke. When the smoke lifted, he noted that she wore a long overcoat and a big hat with a bird on it. Or was it a bow?

Dolores.

Chapter Twenty-Four

Dolores looked small and fragile in her ridiculous hat from another era and her long grey coat, which she clutched tightly as if to protect herself from the whirlwind of gaiety raging around her. She looked at Delamour with large, determined eyes.

Delamour's heart stopped, and for a sliver of a second, he became an eighteen-year-old boy gaping at the object of his desire, overwhelmed by conflicting thoughts and feelings that coalesced into one overriding emotion: fear. His heart shot back to life with a tremendous thump. He took a slow, deliberate breath, clenched his fists to keep his hands from trembling, and walked to her.

"You filled out," she said to him with a tentative smile.

He studied her. She had the same radiant eyes that he remembered, but her face had grown thinner, harder, her lips more pinched. Delamour turned to Teddy, who could only offer an apologetic shrug.

"You have a beautiful home, Mr. Delamour," she said.

"What are you doing here?" he asked as evenly as he could.

"There's someone I'd like you to meet," she purred as she looked down.

The surprise of seeing Dolores again had so befuddled Delamour that he had failed to notice the little girl standing beside her.

"This is Bonnie. Your daughter."

"Holy cow," murmured Teddy.

"Bonnie?" Dolores said in a sweetly authoritarian lilt. "Say hello to your father."

The child peeked up at him. She had long brown hair, olive skin, and clear blue, frightened eyes. She did not speak.

"Bonnie," Dolores repeated. "What do we say?"

The child buried her face in her mother's skirt. Dolores clenched her jaw.

"She's tired."

"Chuck!"

Gloria Swanson waved at him from the dance floor. Jack Larson stood beside her; his eyes fixed on Dolores.

"Take her to the library," Delamour ordered Teddy.

Delamour watched them go, and then marched off to offer his excuses to the biggest movie star in the world and her boss.

℘

Delamour refilled Dolores' glass with champagne.

"Bud was terrible," she said.

Delamour looked at the little girl lying on the couch. Could she hear them? He had brought them upstairs to his library because it was private, and he felt safer ensconced within his fortress of books.

"He was all right at first, before Bonnie was born, but when she came out with dark hair and not even one freckle, he knew she was yours."

She paused to allow Delamour to respond. He didn't. His training as an actor had taught him to search for truth in a person's eyes, not in their words. He studied Dolores closely.

"Bud got so jealous," she continued. "It got so I couldn't go to the bathroom without him accusing me of going there to meet some man. He got violent. *You* know how violent he gets. He called me horrible names, and... he hit me. Many times."

Delamour offered no response.

"And poor Bonnie, he won't even look at her. It broke my heart to see that girl pining after a father who never gave her the time of day. He hates you most of all, Aurelio."

"Charles."

"I'm sorry. Charles. He never stops talking about you. Says he wants to kill you. He doesn't know that you're a big star yet. He doesn't go to movies, not romantic ones at least, but it's just a matter of time. I'm so afraid for you."

She covered her mouth and whimpered, but Delamour noted that her eyes remained dry.

She's lying.

"He's mean and stupid. The man's never read a book in his life. Not like you," she exclaimed, waving her arm at the towering bookshelves. "Did you read all these?"

"No."

"It's so good to see you," she said and laid her hand atop his.

Delamour finally understood why he had been afraid of seeing Dolores again. He wasn't scared that she could disclose his true identity or ask him for money. No. He was afraid that he might still be in love with her. Wanting her had destroyed him once. It could do so again. Fortunately, time and her mediocre performance dispelled his apprehension. He realized, with a sigh of relief, that he no longer loved Dolores Belmonte.

"How much money do you want?"

Dolores recoiled as if he had slapped her. Her eyes widened with rage, which she quelled with a deep breath. "You're still angry at me. I don't blame you. I wasn't very nice."

"I'm not mad. I'm just cutting to the chase. Bud kicked you out—"

"I *left*," she declared holding up her chin.

"And you saw me in a movie."

"*Hearts of Passion*. You were very handsome."

"So, you come here and tell me this girl is my daughter."

"She is."

"Dolores, I'm not the same idiot I was seven years ago. I'm not the first guy you took to that church. That could be anybody's kid."

Dolores dropped all pretense. Her eyes turned as cold as they had been the night she kicked him out of her room. "She could only be yours or Bud's, and she's not Bud's. They got this new blood test. If you want, we could—"

"It doesn't matter. How much do you want?"

Dolores flashed him a brilliant smile.

"Maybe I just want my little girl to have a daddy."

"She has a daddy," he stated flatly.

"Maybe I want to meet Rudolf Valentino and Douglas Fairbanks and John Gilbert—mostly Rudolf Valentino." She downed the champagne in one gulp. "We've been traveling all day. Is there a room in this fucking palace where your family can get some sleep?"

Delamour studied her. He had to proceed cautiously. He thought of poor Fatty Arbuckle. Even back in San Lazaro, Delamour knew about the comic movie star. Although he had never seen one of his films—or any film, for that matter—he had seen Arbuckle's pictures in magazines. His father would point to them and laugh. "He is so big, but his clothes are so little." Aurelio had liked how happy Fatty Arbuckle looked.

Delamour hadn't seen a happy picture of Fatty Arbuckle in a long time. Four years earlier, the comedian had taken a break from his busy filming schedule and gone to San Francisco with two buddies. They checked into the St. Francis Hotel and invited some female friends to their suite. During their carousing, actress and model Virginia Rapp fell ill. Arbuckle called the hotel doctor, who concluded that she was only drunk, but Rapp's condition grew worse, and four days later, she died. Her friend, Bambina Maude Belmont, told a doctor that Fatty Arbuckle had raped Miss Rapp and crushed her to death with his massive weight.

Doctors never found any evidence of rape. Virginia Rapp had suffered from protracted bladder infections due to several botched abortions, which, along with her chronic alcoholism, most likely killed her. But, Bambina Maude Belmont, against whom California police had filed at least fifty counts of extortion, bigamy, fraud, and racketeering charges, stuck to her story, adding that Arbuckle had violated Miss Rapp with an icicle. The press embellished her tale by turning the ice into a champagne bottle and then, most famously, a bottle of Coca Cola.

After three trials, the courts finally exonerated Fatty Arbuckle, but the damage was done. Theaters banned his films, and he never worked again. Jack Larson once told Delamour that "Fatty ruined his career because he called the doctor before he called me. I would have made his problem go away. Instead, I had to make Fatty go away."

Charles Delamour would not make the same mistake. He would call Jack tomorrow. He would make his problem and her daughter go away.

Chapter Twenty-Five

He's on the farm. The morning sun glimmers over the craggy mountains as he tosses a saddle onto the grey mare. The horse snorts and bobs her head. He strokes her neck gently before he bends down to cinch the saddle.

"How do I look?"

He rises to see his father smiling cheerfully. The old man has his grey hair parted down the middle, and he wears his red silk vest.

"Fine. What's the occasion?"

His father's smile widens. "I'm bringing her home."

"Who?"

"Your mother."

Aurelio's throat tightens. "But she's dead."

"She has been waiting for us all this time."

"Did you talk to her?"

"Yes. She wants to see you."

"But," he stammers, tears welling in his eyes. "She won't recognize me."

His father gives him a kindly pat on the cheek and says, "She will know you." Then he vaults onto the horse and proclaims, "One man scorned and covered with scars still strove with his last ounce of courage to reach the unreachable stars; and the world will be better for this." He spins his horse around and gallops up the mountain.

He rides like a young man again. As if he was still alive.

◦◦ ◦◦

Delamour awoke with a gasp. He stared at the ceiling, relieved and heartbroken that it had only been a dream. He looked at his clock: 8:30 a.m. He hadn't slept much. He rubbed his dry, swollen eyes and picked up the telephone beside his bed and dialed. It was early Sunday morning, but he knew that Jack Larson's secretary would be at her desk. The woman never stopped working.

"Jack Larson's office."

"Margaret. I need to see Jack. Today."

He could smell the coffee as he walked downstairs. *Curses. She's already up.* The studio had trained Delamour to say "curses" instead of using real curse words. He had learned his lesson so well that he could no longer swear properly, even in his thoughts. But this morning, he had misdirected his sanitized profanity, because when he entered the kitchen, he found only the little girl sitting at the table, sipping coffee and whispering to her porcelain doll. She wore a yellow summer dress with mismatched striped socks and worn boots. She had her hair pulled back into a lopsided ponytail.

"You're awake," he grumbled.

She glanced at him and replied, "You're wearing blue pajamas."

"You made coffee."

"You have black hair." She turned to her doll, "This is a silly game, isn't it, Ilsa?"

Delamour stopped. Ilsa was his mother's name.

"You named your doll Ilsa?"

"It was Mina's idea."

Delamour pictured the dark Indian woman who had warned him about Dolores.

"How is Mina?" he asked.

"She's in heaven."

"I'm sorry."

"She's happy. She lives in a nice house with lots of flowers, and her friends visit her."

"In heaven?"

The girl nodded. Delamour did not want to debate the afterlife with a six-year-old, so he kept quiet and poured himself some coffee. The brew was far too strong, but he drank it anyway.

"You're not my father," the girl remarked.

"I know."

"My father's home. He's going to take me to the World's Fair."

"That's nice."

"There was a World's Fair in San Francisco. It had a tower made of jewels and a rollercoaster and a painting of a woman that really breathed. Only I couldn't see it."

"Why not?"

"Because she didn't have any clothes on, and the World's Fair went away."

"Then how can your father take you?"

"There's going to be another World's Fair."

"Oh." He grimaced as he swallowed more bitter coffee.

"In Barcelona. That's in Spain."

"Bud's going to take you to Spain?"

"Yep. He promised," she asserted. Then she scowled at her doll. "That's mean, Ilsa."

"What?" Delamour asked wearily.

"Ilsa said that Daddy's not going to take me to the fair anymore because Mommy made him angry. But it wasn't *my* fault. I didn't yell at him and break things and take his money. It's not fair, Ilsa."

The girl listened to the doll for a moment then sighed, "I know."

"What?"

"She said life is not fair."

"Smart doll."

"Ilsa's the smartest doll in the world," she said as she glumly stared at her empty cup.

"More coffee?" he asked.

She nodded then added, "Can *you* make it? I make bad coffee."

He dumped the old coffee grounds into the trash and refilled the pot. After starting the percolator, he leaned back against the counter and studied the girl. She sat at the table with her back straight and her chin held high like a fine equestrian, like his father. *Curses,* he thought. She licked her lips and exhaled slowly, struggling to maintain her composure. Delamour wondered what she wanted. He took a wild guess.

"Hungry?"

"Ice cream!" she exploded. "You have some in that giant icebox that doesn't have any ice. How can you have an ice box without ice?"

"That's a new *electric* icebox. It's called a refrigerator."

The girl's jaw dropped. "An *electric* icebox?" She glanced at Ilsa. "You're right." She turned to Delamour. "Ilsa says you should take your electric icebox to The World's Fair. She thinks everyone would love to see it."

"I'll think about it."

Delamour took a carton of chocolate ice cream out of the refrigerator and a spoon from a drawer.

"Ilsa likes ice cream, too."

He grunted and grabbed a second spoon.

"Is Rin Tin Tin real?" the girl asked after she'd stuffed a mound of ice cream into her mouth.

"What do you mean?"

"Mama says he's fake. She says they use a bunch of dogs to do different parts of the movies, and there isn't really a dog called Rin Tin Tin."

"She's wrong. There's a Rin Tin Tin. I've met him. He's a beautiful dog. His owner rescued him—"

"From the war when he was a puppy." She beamed. "And then he became a big movie star. Did you see the one where he jumped in the frozen river, and he rescued that girl, and then he kept her warm until she woke up, and he let her hug him? He's the smartest, bravest dog in the world." She pursed her lips and looked at Delamour with big, worried eyes. "Do you think…?" She stammered. "Do you think… he'd like me?"

Delamour felt a pang in his heart, and it angered him. He didn't want to feel any pangs or pity or even civility. He wanted to hate this kid. He needed to say something cruel to drive her away.

But he couldn't.

"Sure."

The girl's face broke into the most gloriously unguarded smile that Charles Delamour had ever seen in his life. *Pang!* went his heart.

Curses!

Delamour left candy for the kid and a note for Dolores saying that he had business to tend to. He snuck out the back door and headed through his garden toward the garage.

"Could you hand me a towel?"

He turned to see Dolores languidly wading in his swimming pool. She pointed to a towel lying on a lounge chair. He did not move. Dolores sighed and rose from the pool. She wore a skimpy modern swimsuit and a rubber bathing cap. Her face may have grown harder, but she still had a striking figure. She tore off the cap and shook loose her long brown hair. He watched her slowly rub the towel over her bare arms and legs. He certainly did not love her. He didn't even like her. And yet…

"I borrowed a bathing suit," she said. "You have a lot of women's clothes in that room. For anyone in particular?"

"I have friends."

"I'll bet." She smiled. "Where are you going?"

"Business."

"Don't let me stop you."

He turned to go.

"Have you seen your daughter?"

He stopped, but he didn't take the bait.

"The child is in the kitchen."

"Your daughter's sweet, isn't she?"

"Stop that," he snapped.

"You don't have to be so angry."

"What do you want, Dolores?"

"We're old friends. We have a lot of catching up to do."

"No, we don't."

"We're family, Aurelio."

"Don't call me that," he snarled.

"You take your roles seriously, don't you? Fine. *Charles Delamour*. It's a bit theatrical, but I suppose it worked. You're a big star."

"What's your plan? Just tell me, please."

"Your daughter and I need a home."

"I'm not her father."

"We'll let a doctor decide."

"Even if I'm *physically* her father. I'm not legally. My name's not on her birth certificate. I'm not the man who raised her."

"Bud hardly raised her."

"To her, he's her father. She wants to go home."

"We can't."

"You chose Bud, Dolores. You kicked me out. I came here with nothing, and I made something of myself. And now, you see me in a movie, and you figure I'll make a better sugar daddy than Bud, so you come here to feed off me like a succubus."

"Who?" she asked, clenching her fists.

"A demon who sucks the life out of her victims."

Dolores' face contorted with rage, making her look like the very demon Delamour had described.

"You think I like doing this?" she hissed. "Do you think I like dragging my child down here to beg?"

"Then go home."

"I have no home! There's no going back. It's over. Look, I loved Bud. I really did. What happened with you and me was just a fling. I had too much to drink, and you were so needy, and it just happened, but I tried to be a good wife to Bud. I was nice to him and his stupid mother and father—who was always pawing at me, by the way. Then Bonnie came, and Bud got mean. He'd stay away for weeks doing God-knows-what, but my kid needed a home, so I put up with him for six years. What choice did I have? I'm a woman. I have to depend on a man to survive. So here I am, asking another man for help."

"Why didn't you go to your parents?"

"They knew Bonnie wasn't Bud's. They didn't want us. But, even if they had, I'd have still come here. The kid needs her father."

"And I'm a movie star."

"That's right. I got to do what's best for Bonnie."

"Bonnie wants to be with Bud."

"She's a child. She doesn't know what she wants."

"What will it take for you to go away?"

She frowned for a beat then snapped into a coquettish smile that terrified Delamour.

"This bathing suit," she decided, sliding her hands down her hips. "And a dress like the one Gloria Swanson was wearing last night and some nice shoes. Lots of nice shoes, and I want to cut my hair short like Louise Brooks, and to smoke through one those long cigarette holders. I want to go parties and drink champagne and sleep with Rudolf Valentino."

"Good luck with that."

"I want Bonnie to go to a fancy private school and marry a rich man. And…" She fixed Delamour with a fierce glare.

"I want to never, *ever* have to ask another man for anything for the rest of my life."

"Asking? Is that what you call this?"

"I've done my research, Aurelio."

"I told you not to call me—"

"Aurelio Cienfuegos!" she screamed. "That's who you are, and I'll tell the world. I'll tell everyone how you abandoned your daughter and *murdered* your father."

His face hardened into a lifeless mask.

"The law is after you, Aurelio. You're still a wanted man."

"I never murdered anyone," he whispered.

"Neither did Fatty Arbuckle, and look what happened to him. A story doesn't have to be true. It just has to be good. Newspapers love this stuff, don't they? I know about the morality clauses you people have to sign and the new censorship rules. One big scandal and poof! There goes your career."

"Why would you want to ruin my career?"

"I don't. I want you to be the biggest, *richest* movie star in the world," she declared with a malevolent smile. "For the sake of your family."

Chapter Twenty-Six

Delamour sat in Jack Larson's luxurious office, sipping coffee. The room looked like an old Victorian study with heavy velvet curtains and overstuffed leather chairs. Grand pastoral landscapes hung on the walls, illuminated by the soft, warm glow of Tiffany lamps. If not for the huge stuffed bull's head hanging above the fireplace—Matador Studio's recently deceased mascot—the room would have felt quite welcoming. Delamour figured that Jack displayed the fearsome creature to intimidate his minions. It didn't bother Delamour. He had a monster of his own waiting at home. Beneath the bull sat an empty, old wooden chair.

Jack Larson's chair.

The bald little man with the funny accent had amused Delamour when they first met, but Delamour had been an ignorant youth from San Lazaro back then. He knew better now. Jack Larson wielded enormous power in Hollywood and beyond. Because of the film industry's importance to the American economy, Larson controlled key sectors of both local and state government. Today, Delamour felt intimidated, not by the theatricality of the bull, but by the austerity of the chair. Only a man who eschewed comfort to pursue his goals with remorseless resolve would choose such a grim chair. Or, a man with a bad back. Either way, Larson was a spooky guy.

Tweedle Dee and Tweedle Dum lumbered into the room and flanked the doorway like stone towers. After an uncomfortably long pause, Jack Larson marched in. Delamour stood as the studio head lowered himself onto his dour throne.

"What may I do for you, Charles?" Larson asked, motioning for Delamour to sit.

"You said if I had a problem, I should come to you first."

"Absolutely," he replied, raising an eyebrow.

"There's a woman..."

"Ah," Larson sighed knowingly.

"This was seven years ago, before I began to work for you. I was only with this woman once."

"You have an illegitimate child."

"She says I do. I don't know. I mean, there *is* a resemblance, but this woman didn't want me. She married someone else. I didn't even know she'd gotten pregnant. Her husband raised the child, but now she's left him and come here."

"Does the child bear your name?"

"No."

"Then you have no legal obligation to this woman. How much does she want?"

"She says she wants to live with me."

"Impossible."

"That's what I told her. But..." Delamour took a deep breath. "There's more. Before I left San Lazaro, that's where I'm from, her fiancé attacked me, and in the fight, he shot my father. Killed him. His family controls the whole town, and they accused me of the murder. I ran away and came here. Now she's threatening to tell the police that I'm a wanted man. I'm innocent, Jack. I have witnesses, but it could be an awful scandal."

To Delamour's surprise, Jack Larson laughed. He had never seen the little man express such sincere delight.

"The perfidy of human beings never fails to amuse," he said, wiping a joyful tear from his eye.

Composing himself, Larson continued, "Charles, when I took you under my wing, what did I asked of you, the most important thing?"

"That I become a new man."

"A new man," Larson repeated. "And to do that, you promised to leave your old life behind."

"I did, but it's hard to hide when your face is on every movie screen in the world."

"I do not want you to hide, Charles. I want you to become a new man."

"I have a new name, a new—"

"You do not understand."

Larson studied Delamour for a moment.

"When I look in your eyes, Charles, I see that you are not entirely here. You watch the world from a distance. You do not lose yourself in the petty concerns of mortals. Few people achieve this detachment, but it is the essence of greatness. Do you understand?"

"I think so," Delamour lied.

Larson took a deep breath and continued, "I have done great things, Charles. I crawled out from the bowels of an immigrant ship and fought my way to the top of the mountain, here, in the richest country in the world. Many people tried to stop me, throw me back into the sea. Where are they now? Zukor, Goldwin, Laemmle? They are insects for me to step on when I please, and they are the lucky ones. They are still here. The others? Gone, and who will remember?"

Larson leaned closer to Delamour.

"Do you want to know my secret, Charles?"

"Yes," Delamour said, although he didn't.

"Sacrifice," Larson whispered.

Delamour nodded as if Larson had uttered great words of wisdom rather than a tired cliché.

"Life…" Larson continued. Delamour moaned silently. "…is chaos. It is a storm of desires and regret, fear, guilt, and then more guilt. It is a bad melodrama, starring a terrible actor who learns no lesson before he dies. All this noise is good for only one thing, to distract us so we shouldn't notice that life has no meaning."

Larson paused to gage Delamour's reaction to his words of wisdom. Delamour wished he hadn't come. He avoided Larson's glare and focused on the stuffed bull's head. He recalled how the studio mascot had been killed by a trolley on Cahuenga after a publicity shoot.

"Poor Minos," Larson sighed, reading Delamour's thoughts. "A beautiful beast."

Delamour nodded.

"Do you know why I named this company Matador Studios?"

"You like bullfights?"

"I do, but that was not the reason. When I was a boy..."

Delamour took a deep breath and braced himself for a long story.

"In the shtetl, there was a bull. He was the center of our village, the patron saint, like you Christians say. They kept him in a big field with plenty of grass to eat and cows to inseminate. He ruled his world like a god. I would watch him for hours, behind a fence, of course. He scared me, but I admired his strength and his noble spirit. One day he got sick with the foam on his mouth, and he was jumping up and down, charging everything and everyone—crazy, you know? He had to be put down, but the villagers were frightened little men. One of them had an old musket in his cellar. Very illegal in The Pale. Goyim would have strung him up if they knew. The man took the gun, and from behind the fence, he shot the bull, but the man was a poor shot. The bull did not die. He just got angry, and he charged into the fence, almost broke it. The man shot him again, but still the bull did not die. The man shot again and again. The memory of that mighty beast pecked at by those pathetic little men. It sickens me to this day. Finally, the poor animal was wobbling around. One more shot would kill him. I was crying, tears running down my face. It was a terrible sight. The beast saw me, and he walked up to me, to the fence, and he looked at me with those big black eyes that bulls have, you know? Cold eyes that show no emotion, but I could feel the pain inside of him. He looked at me, deep into my soul, and he saw me, the real me, the part I share with no one, and in that moment, his spirit passed into me. I felt his strength, his pride, his anger. They became my own. Boom went the gun, and the beast dropped, never to rise again, but that bull, he is inside me still."

Larson paused. Delamour had found the story irrelevant and disturbing, but it made him feel some compassion for the little man.

"Why do I tell this story, Charles?"

"Um..."

"The beast died and gave me his strength. Only through his sacrifice, could I benefit. Do you see that?"

"Yes."

"Sacrifice is the key. Sacrifice here," he said pointing to his head. "And, most of all, here." He tapped his chest. "Are you willing to sacrifice, Charles?"

Delamour pretended that he needed a moment to ponder a profound decision.

"Yes," he said decisively.

"*Are* you?" Larson demanded with a cold, hard glare.

Delamour flinched. He braced himself and, facing Larson's eyes with a steely glare of his own, he replied, "I am."

Larson leaned back, mollified.

"We shall take care of your problem. You will be Jesus Christ."

"Thank you, Jack," Delamour exhaled with relief.

"Go home. Treat this woman well. Give her money, clothing, jewelry, whatever she wants. Give her no reason to go to the police. I shall be out of town for a while, but I will have a chat with this creature before our big party to launch the movie. On your way out, tell Margaret everything about her, the child, the husband. The more we know, the quicker we can resolve this. Yes?"

"Yes. Thank you, Jack."

Larson smiled beneficently. "No need to thank me. I am not doing this for you. I am doing it for Jesus."

※ ※

Delamour saluted to the studio guard as he eased his roadster out the gates and almost hit an old derelict who had stepped in front of his car. Delamour slammed on his brakes. The old drunk stood his ground, glaring at Delamour. Delamour placed his hand on the car horn, but something about the old man arrested him. He wore a black overcoat and a wide-brimmed black hat. Two large grey eyes glared from behind his tangled white hair and beard. The old man opened his mouth to speak when the studio guard yelled, "Beat it, rummy!"

The old man ducked his head and shuffled away, never taking his eyes off Delamour.

I should have given the old coot a dime, Delamour thought as he turned onto Franklin Avenue.

※ ※

Delamour entered his house that afternoon, carrying a large bouquet of roses. His butler took the flowers and slipped off his sport coat.

"Welcome home, sir. I took the liberty of rescheduling your *Vanity Fair* interview."

"That was this morning?"

"I set it for Thursday. I left the details on your desk along with your phone messages and mail. Should I put these in water?"

Delamour noticed small muddy handprints on the butler's white vest.

"What happened to you?"

"The child, sir. She requested my help with mud pies."

"Where's the mother?"

"She had the chauffeur take her shopping."

"Teddy took her shopping?"

"Yes, sir. The child is in the garden."

"Thanks, sport."

The butler nodded with a slight scowl and marched away. Delamour headed to the back door but stopped when he spotted muddy footprints in the kitchen. He followed the mud up the stairs and down the hallway. They led into his bedroom.

Curses.

He burst into his room and found his carpet covered with muddy tracks.

"Hey!" he yelled angrily.

He heard banging inside his closet.

"Come out," he commanded.

The rustling and shuffling continued, but the noisy intruder did not emerge. He flung open the closet door and spotted little feet protruding from behind his sport coats. He pushed the clothes aside, and there stood the girl in a muddy smock, with her hands behind her back and a terrified look on her face.

"What are you doing in here?" he demanded.

Her lower lip trembled with fear.

"Come out," he said softening his tone. "I'm not going to hurt you."

"Promise?" she squeaked.

"Yes."

She cautiously sidled out of the closet, facing Delamour and, keeping her hands behind her back, sidestepped toward the door.

"Stop."

She screamed, startling Delamour.

"Don't do that," he commanded. "What's behind your back?"

"Nothing."

"Show me your hands."

She held out one hand, and a large book dropped to the floor behind her. Delamour quickly snatched it up. It was his mother's book.

"Did you get this dirty?" he asked, anxiously.

"No. I washed my hands," she claimed and pointed behind him.

He turned and saw footprints heading into his bathroom. He inspected the book and found no stains.

"Okay," he exhaled, relieved. "This book is very important to me. You must never touch it again. Do you understand?"

She nodded vigorously.

"And you are never ever to enter this room. Do you hear me?"

She nodded. Tears welled up in her eyes.

"All right. Go."

She didn't move. She opened her trembling mouth to speak, but words didn't come.

"What is it?"

"I... uh..."

"What?" he demanded with more force.

Tears rolled down her cheeks. "Are you...?" she stammered. "Are you going to tell my mother?"

"I should."

The girl began to cry.

"Why don't you want me to tell your mother?"

"She'll pinch me."

"Pinch you?"

The girl raised the hem of her smock, revealing hideous purple and yellow bruises all over her thigh.

Delamour gaped with disgust. "Your mother did that?"

She nodded, and through whimpered spasms, she explained, "When I didn't... call you... daddy."

Delamour felt nauseous. "I won't tell your mother. I promise."

Relief released the child's emotional floodgates, and she began to bawl. Delamour quickly shut the door.

"Stop that. Here."

He handed her his handkerchief. She rubbed it against her face smearing it with tears, mucus and mud. She tried to hand it back to him.

"Keep it."

She had to take several wheezy breaths to compose herself, at which point, she straightened her back and said, "Thank you."

"You're welcome."

"You have a nice room," she added, in a brave attempt to sound mature.

"Thank you."

"And I like your book. It's very funny."

"Funny?"

"Yes. I can't read it. I mean, I can read other books, but I can't read this one."

"It's in German."

"I see," she mused in as sophisticated a tone as a six-year-old girl can muster.

"What was funny about it?" he asked.

"The pictures."

"Really? Which ones?"

"Well." She thought. "The girl dancing with the wolf on page thirty-two."

Delamour furrowed his brow and turned to page thirty-two where he found a picture of the wolf trying to devour Little Red Riding Hood.

"You remembered the page number."

"You have green eyes," she said, then added, "Am I playing this game right?"

Delamour snorted and studied the engraving of a beast attacking a little girl. The picture had disturbed him greatly as a child.

"Why do you find this funny?"

"Because the wolf is dressed like an old lady, and he has glasses on, and his eyes are crossed."

Delamour looked more closely and, indeed, the wolf's eyes looked crossed. He had never noticed that before.

"And the little man on page seventy-seven. He's goofy and his nose is really big."

Delamour turned to the page and saw a demonic dwarf dancing around a fire. He knew that the dwarf in this story planned to steal a baby if their mother couldn't guess his name, but this girl saw something entirely different.

"Who do you think this is?" he asked.

"Bob."

"Bob?"

"I don't know for sure, because it's in German, but he looks like a Bob."

"Why?"

"Bob's a funny name."

"Why is he dancing?"

"He's happy because it's springtime. See the flowers? And he's having a cookout in the woods. I camped with my grandfather once. We made popcorn. I like the forest. Don't you?"

No, he didn't. Forests scared him. But he liked her story better than the real one.

"And dwarves are always happy because people think they're cute and give them pennies and candied apples. At least, I would if I ever saw a dwarf. Have you ever seen a dwarf?"

He had once worked with a dwarf actor, Stewart... something-or-other, on the film *Circus Magic*, and Stewart was indeed a good chap.

Delamour flipped through the book to another picture, a beautiful, dark-haired queen.

"What about this one?" he asked.

The girl's face dropped.

"I don't like it. It's scary."

Upon closer inspection, Delamour understood her reaction. The queen looked like Dolores.

"Have you eaten?" he asked the child.

"I had some candy."

"I mean real food."

She looked up and thought about it. Delamour reasoned that if a girl who could effortlessly recall page numbers in a book couldn't remember her last meal, it was time to eat.

"How about a hamburger?"

Her eyes lit up.

Chapter Twenty-Seven

Delamour needed time to regroup before he could face Dolores, so he took the child to the studio commissary. He felt safe on the lot. There he was a prince among princes, revered yet familiar.

And they made a damn fine hamburger.

The girl had already finished her burger, two bags of french fries, a soda, and she was halfway through dessert before she looked up at Delamour.

"Arbaba," she said through a mouthful of cherry pie.

"It's good?" he asked.

The girl nodded and swallowed. She exhaled dramatically and sat back to peruse the cowboys, princesses, Roman soldiers, and clowns eating lunch all around them.

She screamed as several half-naked, hairy men walked by.

"They're making *The Lost World*. It's about cave men and dinosaurs."

Her eyes darted around the room.

"The dinosaurs aren't here. In fact, they're really just puppets."

"Cavemen fight puppets?" she asked incredulously.

"They look real on film."

"But they're not?"

"Nope. Movies are all make believe."

Gloria Swanson stepped up wearing a stunning gold-sequined evening gown.

"Charles," she exclaimed with one of her million-dollar smiles. "You abandon me at the party, and now I find you with another woman."

Delamour stood and kissed the movie star's cheek.

"Gloria, this is... uh..."

"Bonnie," the girl blurted, gaping at the movie star.

"She's the daughter of an old friend."

"And *he* has you babysitting?"

"It's a she. But we're just... friends."

Gloria gave him a skeptical grunt and turned to the girl.

"Bonnie. It's a pleasure to meet you."

The awestruck child whispered, "You are so beautiful."

Gloria Swanson heard this compliment a dozen times a day, but it never failed to delight her.

"Why, thank you, Bonnie. So are you."

The girl gasped with joy.

"Please tell your mother's friend here," she said, motioning toward Delamour, "to give me a call sometime."

"Call her," Bonnie sternly commanded Delamour.

"I will," he chuckled.

"I like this girl," Gloria Swanson announced before strutting away.

"Are you going to marry her?" Bonnie asked when she had gone.

"No," he replied with mock sadness.

"But she's so pretty."

"She already has a—"

"The bum!" Bonnie screamed and pointed.

Charlie Chaplin had just entered the commissary in full costume, chatting with a studio executive.

"The *Tramp*. Not the bum," whispered Delamour.

"I saw him in a movie," she yelled. Chaplin looked over at her. She waved, and much to Delamour's relief, Chaplin instantly assumed character and waved back with an impish grin.

"Ha!" Bonnie cried with delight. "He's so funny. Did you see the one where he kept falling down?"

"Probably."

"Mina used to take me to the movies before she went to heaven. Then Pablo did. That's her son. He's very nice, but he was really sad when Mina left. I was sad, too, until I saw her new house. Mina said I can visit her anytime I want. So, I do."

"In your dreams?"

"Yes. Mina says we can visit anyone who dies—Mina died."

"You said."

"You can visit them anytime in your dreams. And after I die, I can live with her if I want. But…" she added with an exaggerated scoff, "that won't be for a *long* time—popcorn!" Bonnie pointed to a man carrying a bag of popcorn.

"You want some?" asked Delamour.

Bonnie composed herself and lifted her chin with modest elegance. "If it's no trouble," said she.

Pang!

Curses.

☙ ❧

Delamour took the girl to watch Buster Keaton film his new movie. She gaped at the comic as he performed one incredible prat fall after another. She screamed every time Keaton hit the ground and laughed every time he got back up.

Delamour had always dismissed movie fans as fools. They were so easily conned and so willingly fleeced. Delamour knew how the Hollywood sausage was made, and he disdained those who gobbled it up, but the genuine delight he saw in Bonnie's eyes reminded him of his own reaction to *Treasure Island* and *King Solomon's Mines*. Those books had brought magic into his mundane childhood. Perhaps movies could do that, too. Maybe, just maybe, he wasn't as big a charlatan as he thought.

Of course, Bonnie charmed the cast and crew. The cameraman let her turn the crank, and Buster Keaton let her wear his little flat hat. After another meal, topped off with chocolate cake and a carriage ride through the backlot, Bonnie was blissfully exhausted.

The child had fallen fast asleep by the time they returned to the house. Delamour carried her inside, skirting the living room where he heard music playing, and up the stairs. The butler appeared and offered to take her from him.

"No thanks, sport. I got her. Put the foldaway bed in the library. I think she'll like waking up in there."

☙ ❧

Delamour kept Larson's instructions in mind as he stepped into the living room and found Dolores dancing with Teddy, jazz music blaring from his phonograph. Delamour noted how intimately his old friends capered across the carpet. When Teddy saw him, he backed away from Dolores. She turned to Delamour and smiled languidly.

"Hello," she purred. Teddy leaned against a chair to steady himself. They had been drinking. Delamour walked over to the phonograph and lifted the needle.

"Have fun today?" he asked.

"Loads," proclaimed Dolores. "Do you like my new dress? I charged it to you. Hope you don't mind."

She wore a glittering ball gown. Teddy looked away in shame.

"It's very nice," Delamour replied graciously. "I hope you haven't been worried about Bonnie—"

"She was with you. Your colored man told me."

"Yes," Delamour sighed. "I put her to sleep in the library."

"You're such a good father," she teased.

He bit his tongue and smiled.

"Well, goodnight."

"Wait!" she commanded. "I want to wear this dress in public. With you."

"Of course," he replied with his trademark movie-star smile. "I'm working this week but—"

"You're making a movie?"

"We're preparing to, yes."

"What's it about?"

"Jesus Christ."

"And you're playing Jesus?"

"Yes."

Dolores squealed with laughter. Teddy laughed, too, although he probably had no idea why.

"You? The son of God!" she guffawed.

Delamour kept the smile fixed on his face and offered her an apologetic shrug.

"This, I gotta see," she declared. "I want to watch you make this movie."

"We don't start filming for a while."

"I want to see the movie studio. I want to meet your friends and tell them about us. I want to wear my beautiful dress!"

Delamour decided to change tactics. He contorted his face with terror, just like he had when he faced the Army of the Dead in *The Black Tomb*.

"Please, don't say anything, Dolores," he pleaded believably—he was a movie star after all. "Not yet. I'm going to have a party, like the one I had on the day you arrived. I'll introduce you to everyone then. I promise."

"Will Rudolf Valentino be there?"

"Of course. All the big stars will be there."

She scowled at him, then relaxed into a smile.

"Okie-dokie," she slurred.

She placed her hands on his chest and leaned in closely.

"I wish you still liked me, Aurelio. We could have so much fun."

He pushed her away gently.

"We will."

"I should go," Teddy said.

"No!" Delamour commanded. "Stay. Enjoy yourselves. I'll see you both in the morning."

"Aw, hooey," pleaded Dolores. "You got so many swell records. Let's dance."

Dolores began rifling through his recordings.

"Nothing happened between us," Teddy whispered to Delamour dramatically. "I swear to God almighty."

"Make love to her all you want. In fact…"

Delamour pulled out his wallet and handed Teddy a wad of cash.

"Paint the town red."

"You're a good egg, buddy-boy," Teddy said, putting his arm around Delamour. "I'm sorry your daddy got shot."

"Me, too. Have fun."

He shoved Teddy toward Dolores and darted upstairs.

Chapter Twenty-Eight

He walks along the verdant mountains that tower above the Pacific Ocean. He had hated this place once. The cliffs had felt like prison walls keeping him from the wondrous adventures that awaited beyond. But he has to admit that it's beautiful. Sunlight passing through the billowing ocean mist splinters into evanescent rainbows. The scent of sage and lilac and caramel fills the air. *Caramel?* It reminds him of saltwater taffy and Sundays. He searches for the source of the enticing aroma and there, perched high upon a steep precipice, he sees a small cottage with smoke rising from its chimney.

It has whitewashed adobe walls with a red-tiled roof. Flowering vines border the windows and door, all of which are open. A small dark woman steps out. He cannot see her face clearly from where he stands, but somehow, he knows that she is smiling. She waves to him. He waves back.

The woman turns to the mountains beyond, and her visage changes. She raises a hand to her face and points. He turns and sees black smoke rising from a distant valley.

"She needs you," rasps the bearded old derelict he had seen outside the studio, who he realizes has been with him all along.

He does not have to ask the old man who needs him. He knows.

"Mama!" he yells.

꧁ ꧂

He awoke with a gasp. He sat up in his bed and turned on the light. *Curse these dreams!* Then, from somewhere inside the house, he heard, "Mama!"

Delamour found the child wandering through the dark hallway, clutching her doll. She screamed when she saw him.

"It's okay, it's just me. Charles."

She hugged his leg.

"It's okay. You want your mother?"

She whimpered and nodded. The butler appeared.

"Is everything all right?" he asked.

"Just a bad dream," Delamour assured him.

"Hi, Oliver," Bonnie whispered.

"Hello, Bonnie," replied the butler with a kind smile. "Would you like a glass of milk?"

She shook her head.

"It's okay. I got this."

The butler nodded and retreated down the stairs.

"What did you call him?" Delamour asked the girl.

"Oliver. That's his name. He knows a lot of songs, and he's good at patty cake."

"The butler sings?"

"What's a butler?"

"It doesn't matter. Come on, I'll take you to your mother."

She didn't release her grip.

"I'm going to need that leg to walk," he joked.

She reluctantly released him. He took her hand and walked her down the hall.

"I'm sorry. I thought you'd like it in the library."

"It was dark."

"I should have kept a light on."

"There was a monster."

"Really? What kind of monster?"

"She was wearing a red robe and she was pretty, but then her face disappeared, and she laughed, and I woke up, and I was all alone."

"It was just a dream. Here's your mother's room."

As Bonnie reached for the doorknob, a dreadful thought struck Delamour.

"Let me look inside first. Just to make sure it's the right room."

He cracked the door open and saw Teddy grunting atop Dolores on the bed. He quickly shut the door.

"She's not here," he whispered and dragged Bonnie away.

"But I heard something."

"That was the... gardener. He likes to garden at night." The stupidity of his lie made him wince.

"Where is she?" Bonnie asked getting scared again.

"She went out to... buy you some toys."

"At night?"

"Yes. In Hollywood, the best stores are open all night. She wanted to surprise you."

She doesn't believe me. It doesn't matter. Just get her back to sleep. He couldn't take her to his own room. That would look bad.

"I'm going to take you back to the library."

"No!"

"I'm coming with you. Don't worry."

"But the monster."

"That was just a dream. We're going to turn on all the lights, and we're going to find a nice book, and we're going read as long as we want."

"And you won't leave?"

"I won't leave. I promise."

He pulled up a comfortable chair beside Bonnie's bed and, sheltered behind towers of books, he read to her from *The Wonderful Wizard of Oz*. The girl fell asleep within minutes, but he continued reading until he had finished half the story. Dorothy's worries helped him forget his own, and he slept soundly in the chair until late morning when he felt something kick him in the shin. He opened his eyes and saw Bonnie standing before him holding two steaming mugs.

"I made us coffee," she said, smiling.

He looked into her large blue eyes and finally accepted the truth that he had tried so hard to deny. The girl had his mother's eyes. He smiled back. He knew that this would be the best terrible cup of coffee he would ever have.

And, it was.

After he had cooked up some eggs and made a pot of better coffee, he asked the girl if she would like to take a walk in the woods.

"Are there dwarves?" she asked excitedly.

"No, but there are squirrels and rabbits."

"I want to see the rabbits!"

She pulled him by the hand toward the front door, but he stopped her.

"I have a better idea," he said with a conspiratorial grin.

He led her back into the library, to a lone shelf beneath the staircase that led to the second tier of books.

"Watch this," he said.

Delamour pushed the shelf aside and uncovered a small door.

"Jeepers creepers," Bonnie exclaimed with wide-eyed wonder.

He opened the door to reveal a flight of stairs descending into darkness.

"Jeepers creepers," she repeated, far too amazed to think up a new exclamatory phrase.

"This is my secret escape tunnel. Nobody knows about it but me and now, you. It goes out into the woods."

"To the rabbits?"

"That's right."

He switched on a light to reveal that the stairs led to a door one flight down.

"Hold on to the handrail," he said, and off they went.

Chapter Twenty-Nine

Delamour spent the next two weeks with Bonnie. He left her with the butler when he had business to tend to—Bonnie and Oliver had become good pals. Apparently, the elderly domestic had a way with children. He maintained his aloof deportment while sharing a cup of imaginary tea with Bonnie or teaching her how to fashion pies from mud, but always with a twinkle in his eyes that belied his fondness for the child. For the first time since the studio forced a household staff upon him, Delamour felt grateful for his butler's presence. He tried to leave Bonnie with her mother, but Dolores did not want the child spoiling her fun. As far as Delamour knew, Bonnie did not see her mother once during those weeks, which was fine with him. He enjoyed taking care of her.

Not that it was easy. The child demanded constant attention. She didn't need his help with the basics—food, clothing, hygiene. Lack of attention had made Bonnie self-sufficient, but it had left her craving human contact. The kid needed to talk, and she had an opinion about everything.

"Chocolate's the best ice cream unless you're having chocolate cake. Then you have *got* to have vanilla. Santa Claus knows magic, but he's not a god like Jesus. He can just fly and give kids toys really, really fast. It's okay to kill a cockroach but not a mouse."

She concocted elaborate stories about talking animals and dancing dwarves and funny tramps with little mustaches and beautiful women in gold-sequined gowns. Every tale featured a girl who defeated a big, bald monster or an evil witch with the help of friendly animals and a good huntsman, who, with each passing day, looked more like Charles Delamour. And the girl had an unquenchable curiosity.

"Who's that guy on the corner? Why did God make mosquitos? Do birds sleep? Why don't you button the bottom button of your vest? What is your favorite animal? Do dogs go to heaven?"

The girl climbed trees, fences, and hills fearlessly. She scrambled up anything that could be scrambled up, and some things that could not. Delamour couldn't decide whether to applaud her courage or scold her foolishness, so he did both.

But the girl also knew fear. She was afraid of bad dreams and monkeys and loud noises. Most of all, she was afraid of her mother. Delamour noted how Bonnie flinched every time Dolores changed moods, which she did often and without warning. Yet, she never complained. When something frightened her, she would not scream or cry. Instead, she would grab Delamour's hand and squeeze tightly, as if she could force the fright away.

The child utterly exhausted Delamour, and he grew to love her more than he had loved anyone in his life. He had not known that such profound love existed. Had his mother and father loved *him* this much? Even as he asked the question, he knew that they must have, and it filled him with wonder. He felt as if God had shared a great secret known to everyone in the world except him.

But he knew it now, and it changed him. He would not let her go.

☙ ❧

One typical, sunny Los Angeles afternoon, Delamour drove Bonnie up Beachwood Canyon toward his house. Bonnie leaned her head out the passenger window looking for rabbits. She had yet to see one, but hope sprang eternal.

Delamour welcomed the silence to review his plan. It had been two weeks since he spoke to Jack Larson about Dolores, and he no longer wanted Dolores and Bonnie to go away, at least not Bonnie. He had formulated a plan whereby both he and Dolores could get what they wanted without involving Jack Larson. Delamour would offer to support Dolores and Bonnie if Dolores promised to stay close. Delamour wanted to help raise Bonnie, possibly adopt her. Of course, Dolores would have to refrain from destroying his career, but he doubted that she would kill the goose as long as it kept laying golden eggs.

He needed Dolores to agree to his plan before the party tomorrow. He wanted to reassure Jack that he had handled the situation and *The Son of Man* could proceed as planned.

When they entered the house, they found an open steamer trunk full of glittery dresses and lingerie blocking the reception hall. Teddy gamboled down the stairs with more dresses.

"Hey, stranger," Teddy exclaimed.

Dolores trotted down behind Teddy. "Did you bring down my hat boxes—? Oh, Hi, Aurel—Charles. Sorry about the mess."

"This is all yours?" Delamour asked.

"I have good news and bad news. The bad news is, yes, you bought all this for me. The good news is, you won't have to spend another penny on me ever again. Bonnie and I are going to Paris!"

Bonnie squeezed Delamour's hand tightly.

"What?"

"I got a part in a movie with *John Gilbert!*" she exclaimed with a big smile. "It shoots in Paris. We're leaving right after the party tomorrow."

"A movie?"

"Jack told me what you said."

"Jack Larson?"

"I know you only did it to get us out of your hair, but it worked. Jack called me into his office yesterday. I got to admit, I was pretty nervous, what with all the fancy furniture and that awful bull's head. But then he had this director, 'King' something-or-other, make a short movie with me—a screen test, they called it. Jack wants me to play the lead role in his new movie. It's about the war and France and stuff. He's sending tickets for a train to New York tomorrow night, then an ocean liner to Paris, first class cabin. I'm going to buy you so many dresses, Bonnie, you won't look like a bum anymore."

"You mean tramp," Bonnie murmured. "Are we going away?"

"To the most beautiful city in the world."

"For how long?"

"Forever, hopefully."

"Forever?" The girl gasped and pressed herself against Delamour.

"Bonnie, go upstairs," Delamour commanded gently.

"But..."

"You, too, Teddy."

Teddy glanced at Dolores suspiciously before turning away.

"Leave my dresses!" Dolores barked.

Teddy laid the gowns on the trunk. Delamour waited until he and Bonnie had gone before he turned to Dolores.

"Dolores, you're not going to be in a movie."

"The hell I'm not."

"I never said nice things about you to Jack. I asked him to get rid of you."

"And he found the perfect way, didn't he?"

"Movies cost a lot of money. He's not going to gamble on some unknown."

"He said I was so beautiful—"

"There are thousands of beautiful women in this town with far more experience."

"He gave me a check for a *thousand* dollars."

"Getting you out of his hair might be worth a few thousand dollars and a boat ticket, but he's not going to keep you up in Paris or make you a star. Once you land in France or wherever that ship takes you, you're going to be on your own."

A look of disgusted comprehension came over her face. "You're jealous. You can't stand that I might have something of my own, something you can't control."

"It's Bonnie," he said. "She really is my child."

"Oh, my God."

"I want to help you."

"You want to take her away from me."

"No. I just want to be there for her. I could give you enough money to live comfortably for the rest of your life if you just stay close."

"You think I want a sugar daddy?"

"I wouldn't be—"

"You think I want to depend on you? So you can order me around?"

"Dolores, I love Bonnie, and she likes me, too, and—"

"Bonnie likes anything in pants. The poor girl's starving for a father."

"I want to be that father."

"You missed your chance, buddy. Bonnie and I are going to Paris, and I'm going to be famous and rich, and I'm never going to see your sad, stupid face ever again. Teddy!"

Teddy ran in.

"Take this trunk up to my room. We'll finish packing there."

And, with one last murderous look to Delamour, Dolores stomped up the stairs.

Delamour stood, dumbfounded, as Teddy closed the chest and tried to drag the behemoth upstairs.

"Can you give me a hand?" he asked Delamour with an ingenuous smile.

Delamour spun on his heels and left the house.

Delamour drove up to Matador Studios to find the gate closed and the guard booth empty. *Where the hell is everybody?* He was about to honk his horn when the old derelict that accosted him before—the one who had wormed his way into his dream—grabbed his car door. "Meyn zun," pleaded the old man with large, crazed eyes that reminded Delamour of an engraving from his father's copy of *Don Quixote.*

"What?" asked Delamour, but before the old man could respond, a studio guard grabbed ahold of him from behind.

"Sorry, Mister Delamour. Gate's open. I'll take care of this bum."

"Thanks, Hank," Delamour replied, avoiding the old man's piteous glare.

As he eased his roadster onto the lot, he glanced into his side mirror and saw the guard shoving the old man onto the ground. Delamour almost turned his car around to help the old coot, but he didn't. The derelict rattled him. *Why?*

Two policemen guarded the entrance to Larson's office building. *Something's wrong.* The cops eyed Delamour suspiciously when he pulled to the door, but their faces lit up when they recognized him.

Larson's office felt smaller and tawdrier than before. The ornate furniture that had once awed Delamour now looked like cheap hand-me-downs, the bull like tacky décor from a Mexican restaurant. Jack Larson ruled Hollywood from this room. It represented the pinnacle of every actor's, writer's, producer's, director's, crewmember's, and messenger boy's ambition. *How sad.*

Larson stood looking out his window. He wore no jacket over his shirt and vest. Sweat beaded on his bald head, and most uncharacteristically of all, he had knotted his necktie crookedly. The studio head exhaled with annoyance at the sight of Delamour.

"Charles. I was not expecting you."

"What's with the cops?" asked Delamour.

"Ever the same. You climb to the top; people want to drag you down."

"Has someone threatened you?'

"Feh," Larson spat with a dismissive wave. "How can I help you, Charles?"

"Are you really going to put Dolores in a movie?" Delamour asked cautiously.

"Who?"

Delamour took a deep breath to steady himself.

"Jack... Her little girl. She *is* my child."

Larson narrowed his eyes but said nothing.

"I know it sounds crazy. It surprised me, too. I never wanted kids. I liked being the happy-go-lucky lady's man, but then I got to know Bonnie, and—you don't have kids, do you? It's hard to explain but... She needs me, and I need her."

Jack remained still as stone.

"Give her mother some bit parts in town. I'll pay for it out of my salary. Just keep her here, at least until after the Jesus film. Please, Jack. I love the kid."

Larson continued to glare into Delamour's eyes and then, seemingly, into his very soul, which Delamour knew, would prove a fruitless search. If he had a soul, it harbored no secrets. Not anymore. Larson turned to the window, closed his eyes, and let the sunshine warm his face.

"Do you know the story of Jesus Christ?" he asked.

"Sure."

"God loved mankind so much that He sacrificed his only begotten son so those who believed in him might live forever."

"Yeah."

"What is the moral of that story?"

"God loves us?"

"Then why did he not simply grant us immortality without killing his son?"

"Because of Adam and Eve and original sin?"

"God was owed a sacrifice. Because all gods since creation have required sacrifice. Gods grants nothing without one. The greater the loss, the greater the gift. It is the law of the universe, the prima materia, the essence of all existence."

Larson turned to Delamour with voracious eyes.

"The gods have given you fame and fortune, Charles. They offer you immortality. But they demand payment. I told you that you must sacrifice the life you live today and become like Jesus. Did you think I spoke in metaphors? No! Jesus Christ did not have bastard children. You must choose between Jesus and this girl. *This* is your sacrifice, Charles."

The sunlight gleaming off Larson's bald head cast shadows over his eyes, making him look like a vengeful goblin.

"I can't do it, Jack. I'm sorry."

"Sorry? You give me an apology? Like I have asked for a favor? I do not ask. I tell. You belong to me, Charles Delamour. I invented you. You do not exist without me." Larson faced the window and held his arms out to embrace the studio he had created. "You are nothing without this. This is—"

Jack Larson stopped mid-sentence and pressed his forehead against the glass. His eyes widened with terror. He clutched his chest and staggered backward onto the floor.

"Jack!" Delamour rushed to his side. Larson gurgled and gasped for air. Delamour grabbed the telephone and dialed zero. "Get a doctor to Jack Larson's office. Hurry!"

He hung up on the startled operator and glanced out the window. Someone sat in his car. *The derelict. How did he get on the lot?* The old man locked eyes with Delamour for a split second before policemen dragged him away.

"You!" shouted Larson.

Delamour turned back to find Larson pointing at him. "Ingrate! Traitor! I made you! How could you? You're done. I will destroy you. Get out!"

"Jack—?"

"OUT!"

Larson's two bulky bodyguards burst into the room; their expressions masked by their little dark glasses. Delamour gave Larson one last confused look and stumbled out of the office.

※ ※

Delamour got in his car and stepped on the gas. He didn't know where he was going, and he didn't care. *What have I done? My career's over. I'm ruined.* Maybe Jack really had a heart attack. Maybe he's dead— *No, too much to hope for. It's Charles Delamour that's dead. I killed him. But, if he's gone, who am I? Nobody, I'm nobody at all. So, what? What's so great about being somebody? The money. Okay, sure, the money's good, but it's all a sham. Great actor, ha! I'm a trained monkey. Stand over here, walk over there, smile, cry, pretend like you care about something. All I want is a good book and for everyone to LEAVE ME ALONE... except Bonnie. I care about Bonnie. She's real. She needs me. I can't let her down. So, I won't be a movie star? She won't care. Dolores will. I just ruined her career. Sure, it was fake, but she doesn't know that. She thinks she's going to do a movie with John Gilbert. When she finds out she's not going to Paris, and it was all my fault, and I'm not even a movie star anymore, she's going to...*

Take Bonnie away.

Delamour slammed on his brakes. Behind him, tires screeched as a car swerved to avoid smashing into him. The driver yelled obscenities that Delamour ignored. *I have to get to Dolores before she talks to Jack. Where the hell am I? Mulholland Highway? How long have I been driving?*

Delamour spun his roadster around and raced down the mountain, zooming past cars and stop signs, skidding around sharp curves and dim-witted pedestrians until he reached level ground and screeched to a halt. Traffic. This was Los Angeles. There was always traffic.

"Go, go, go!" he screamed, banging on the steering wheel. When cars ahead of him failed to obey, he drove into oncoming traffic, on sidewalks and, at one point, across the lawn of a neighbor's Spanish Colonial mansion, taking out a mailbox and a couple of iron jockeys. Finally, he skidded into his driveway, roared up to the house, and screeched to a bone-jarring stop behind a black Rolls-Royce. It was Jack Larson's car.

He was too late.

Chapter Thirty

Delamour ran into the house and crashed into Tweedle Dee and Tweedle Dum, who blocked the entrance hall like a couple of moronic monoliths.

"Move it, lug heads!" he yelled.

He tried to shove them out of the way but only succeeded in pushing himself backward. Then, from the living room, Delamour heard something entirely unexpected, laughter.

He squeezed between the two bodyguards and entered the room to find Jack Larson and Dolores chatting gayly.

"Hello, Charles," Jack said with a friendly smile.

"There you are!" Dolores guffawed. "Jack was just telling me how stupid you looked in Art Acord's cowboy hat."

"It was a tad large," Jack explained with an apologetic shrug.

"Uh..." Delamour responded stupidly. In the corner of the room, he spotted Bonnie with her face buried in a book and her lower lip curled into an angry pout. She did not look at him.

"This is a surprise," Delamour ventured.

"Yes, I imagine it is," Jack replied. Turning to Dolores, he explained, "Charles and I had a bit of an altercation. I came to apologize. If you will excuse us?"

Jack rose to his feet.

"No, *we'll* go. I've still got a lot of packing to do. Come on, Bonnie. Let's let the men talk. It was wonderful to see you again, Jack."

She held out her hand, and Larson kissed it. She giggled and sashayed out of the room. Bonnie followed her, glumly ignoring Delamour.

"I am sorry, Charles. My behavior today was inexcusable," Larson said once they were alone.

"I thought you had a heart attack."

"No, no. Nothing like that. I received bad news today, about my father..." Larson paused to stare deeply into Delamour's eyes.

"Is he ill?" Delamour asked.

Larson grunted and continued his explanation. "No. He is missing. He lives in Russia. He has never left home before, and back there, it is dangerous to leave one's village. I fear the worst."

"I'm sorry."

"Thank you, but it is I who must apologize. I have treated you badly. It was very wrong of me. Of course, you can do the movie about the Jesus and also be a father to this little girl. She is very pretty. We can make it part of your rehabilitation. You should both be happy, but also, we must keep the mother happy, so she should not make the scandal, yes? I have a plan. Tomorrow night, at our big party, we announce the movie, but we must let the mother think that she will still go to Paris with John Gilbert, at least until *after* the party. The next day, I will tell her that I am so sorry, but the movie has problems, and so I will give her a nice job here in Los Angeles. She will stay. She will make money. She will be happy. You will be happy, yes?"

Delamour sighed with relief. "Yes. Thank you, Jack. I am so sorry about your father."

"I am sorry, too."

Larson patted Delamour on the cheek and left the house with Tweedle Dee and Tweedle Dum clomping behind.

༄ ༅

Delamour found Bonnie in the library, curled up in a big stuffed chair with a book in her lap.

"What are you reading?" he asked.

She did not answer.

"You're upset. Is it about going to Paris?"

She turned away dramatically and covered her face with the book.

"I'll take that as a yes."

Delamour ached to tell her that she would not have to go, but he couldn't trust the child with such an important secret. Bonnie loved to talk. One careless word and Dolores would learn the truth and ruin everything.

"They say Paris is beautiful," he said.

She dropped the book and looked at him with appalled disbelief.

"They chop off everybody's head!" she exclaimed.

He looked at her book.

"The French Revolution?" he asked, impressed and amused. "That's a grownup book."

"I know." She raised the book and read, "'The streets ran red with blood as the goo-eye-low-tine worked day and night.' Do you know what a goo-eye-low-tine does?"

"Guillotine," Delamour corrected.

"It chops off people's heads!"

"The French Revolution was a long time ago, sweetheart. They don't do that anymore."

"How do you know? Have you ever been there?"

"No."

"Are you going with us now?"

"No."

"Because you're afraid. I hope when they chop off *my* head, they send it to you so you can see my head all the time, and then you'll be so sad because my head will be chopped off and it'll be your fault."

She leapt onto her fold-out bed and buried her face in a pillow. Delamour stifled a smile and sat beside her.

"I will never let anyone chop your head off or any other part of you. I will keep you safe, no matter what. I promise you."

She lowered the pillow. "You can't promise because you won't be there," she declared then shoved the pillow back onto her face.

"I can promise, and I do."

"You're leaving me alone," she muttered from beneath the pillow.

"You'll be with you mother."

The moment he said it, he realized that he'd made a mistake. Bonnie began to cry. He reached out and gently stroked her hair.

"I am not leaving you. I will never leave you. I can't explain it right now, but I will soon, and you're going to be happy. I promise. Do you want me to read you a bedtime story?"

"I'm going to see Mina," she whimpered.

"Mina?"

"In heaven."

Oh, jeez.

"Stop it. You're not going to see Mina for a long, long time. Everything's going to be okay, Bonnie. I'll see you in the morning."

Chapter Thirty-One

Delamour did not see her in the morning. He slept badly, and by the time he got out of bed, Dolores had taken Bonnie out to buy her new clothes for the party. Delamour took a long walk along the Silver Lake Reservoir while work crews transformed his fake Tudor home into a fake Roman villa, complete with columns, statues, and fountains that spewed wine from the orifices of grotesque mythological creatures. He gave them permission to do whatever they wanted with the house as long as they didn't touch his library. Normally, these parties bored Delamour, but this one made him nervous. He had a lot riding on it. The sooner it was over, the sooner he could get on with his new life.

He saw Bonnie only briefly after she returned from the stores. He tried to cheer her up.

"They'll have music at the party and ice cream and real live peacocks!" he exclaimed with desperate enthusiasm.

"I don't like peacocks," she replied brusquely.

"Why not? They're beautiful—"

"I'm not going," she snapped.

"You'll change your mind," he said with a pathetic smile.

She didn't. The girl had a will of iron.

That evening he squeezed into a tuxedo and waited in his bedroom for the publicity people to summon him to the bacchanalia.

He tried to distract himself by skimming through his favorite passages from *Don Quixote*. Perusing the book made Delamour appreciate how much he had changed over the years. Once he had admired Don Quixote the idealist, but now he felt closer to slow-witted Sancho Panza. Sancho harbored no foolish dreams of glory. He just wanted a good meal and a warm place to sleep, but still, he did his duty. He stuck by Don Quixote and kept him safe. *Sancho was the real hero,* thought Delamour.

Outside, Paul Whiteman & His Orchestra played "Yes Sir, That's My Baby" over the growl of the well-oiled crowd.

He heard a knock on his bedroom door.

"Come in."

Oliver entered.

"Bonnie's gone to bed."

"Did she eat anything?"

"I left a glass of milk for her in the library. She's very sad, sir. She would appreciate a visit from you."

"First thing in the morning, I'll— No, wait." He couldn't let Bonnie suffer all night. He had to tell her the truth and trust that she could keep a secret. "Tell her I'll be right there, sport. I mean... Oliver."

"Yes, sir."

Oliver nodded politely and marched out the door as Jack Larson burst in with a tall, beautiful redhead.

"The hour is nigh!" Larson exclaimed.

"No, it's almost midnight," squealed the redhead in a nasally New York accent.

"What I meant, sweetheart, was that—"

"Oh, my God!" shrieked the woman. "You're Charles Delamour!"

"I'm afraid so," Delamour replied kindly.

"Oh, my God! You're even more handsome in color."

"That's very kind of you."

Larson stepped between Delamour and the young woman.

"Charles, meet Betty, my new discovery. Soon, she will be a big star."

Betty snorted gayly. "He says that, but I think he's just trying to get into my bloomers."

Larson laughed too loudly. "Sweetheart, do me a grand favor and get me a drink."

"Can I have one, too, poopsie?" she cooed.

"You can have two."

Betty winked at Delamour and sashayed away.

"Nice girl," Delamour offered after she had gone.

"Not really. May I?" he asked, pointing to the balcony.

"Of course," replied Delamour.

Larson strode outside. Delamour followed.

"I have seen you up here, looking down at your guests like a Roman Emperor. It is good here."

Delamour nodded politely. Below him, publicity people anxiously cleared the dance floor to make room for this evening's main event—him. He felt like a Christian about to be thrown to the lions.

Larson gazed beyond the party to the distant lights of Hollywood. "When first I came to this place, it was nothing but farms and orange trees and sheep. Hollywood Boulevard was a dirt road. The night was black. But then I said, let there be light. And look now!"

"It's quite an accomplishment," Delamour agreed.

"Yes," Larson growled. "But, like everything, it will not last."

Larson gazed upon his creation wistfully as if it would soon vanish before his eyes, as if all human efforts led to naught but death, rendering them futile and meaningless. Delamour knew this feeling well.

"You're worried about your father."

"Yes," Larson smiled ruefully. "Very much."

Below them, the band began to play "Love Me."

"That is your signal," said Jack. "Go to the party."

"I just need to make one little stop before—"

"No time. Go now! I will make my announcement from up here like I am the Caesar."

Flashbulbs exploded in Delamour's face as he entered the garden. Reporters peppered him with questions. "What's the new movie?" "Another Bible pic?" "When ya gonna settle down, Charles?"

Delamour responded by flashing them his trademark smile and keeping his mouth shut. An eager publicity flunky ushered him past the press and deposited him on the empty dance floor, leaving Delamour encircled by the hungry spectators like a gladiator awaiting battle. He prepared himself by casually pulling a cigarette from a silver case and popping it into his mouth. He sauntered over to the crowd, and a dozen lighters fired up. Choosing the closest one, he lit the cigarette, and with a grateful wink, he strolled back to the center of the arena.

While he puffed on his cigarette, willing himself not to cough since he only carried cigarettes to offer female admirers, he surveyed the crowd. Serving girls in nymph tunics dispensed cocktails while Roman soldiers stood guard wearing armor and short skirts meant to titillate more than intimidate. He saw Gloria Swanson sitting at a table with her Marquis husband and the lovely actress, Maude Fealy. Could Maude be the woman Jack intended him to marry? She had quit movies and returned to the stage, yet there she was. *Not a bad choice,* thought Delamour objectively, but there were many other young starlets at the party that could play the role. *No point guessing.*

He spotted Rudolph Valentino whispering to a debonair young man. At the opposite side of the garden stood his wife, Natacha. The once stately woman looked frail in her geometrically patterned shroud and headdress, which had been all the rage after the discovery of King Tut's tomb several years earlier but now seemed kitschy. A wave of pity washed over Delamour, not just for Natacha, but for everyone at the party, for all of Hollywood, for a world full of people trying to hide their desperation behind glittery disguises. Delamour pulled at his tight collar, stomped out his cigarette and made his way to Natacha.

"I like your brooch," he said, referring to the pin that held her turban in place. Natacha flinched, startled to be addressed directly.

"Oh? Yes, thank you. It's a scarab. From Egypt. It represents Atun, the first man on earth. Scarabs roll big balls of dung into holes where they lay their eggs. The babies eat the dung and come out of the hole fully grown, like a man rising out of the earth. So, according to the Egyptians, men came from a pile of shit."

Delamour decided that he liked this woman.

"Would you care to dance?"

Again, she flinched with surprise.

"No," she replied curtly but added more softly, "Thank you."

As Delamour inched his way back through the crowd, he saw Dolores tittering at a man whose face Delamour could not see. Whoever he was, Delamour felt sorry for him, having to endure one of Dolores' puerile diatribes. Then the man turned around, and Delamour's heart stopped.

It was John Gilbert, one of the biggest stars in Hollywood, and the man who would star with Dolores in her upcoming film, if such a film existed, which it did not. What the hell was Gilbert doing here? How could Larson have allowed him to come tonight of all nights? Delamour saw John Gilbert shake his head and shrug. Dolores' bright expression darkened into confusion, disbelief, and finally, rage.

The music stopped abruptly, and Jack Larson appeared on the balcony. He raised his arms commandingly, and the throng quieted to a murmur.

"Welcome, my friends, to this joyous celebration," he proclaimed. "Tonight, I want to announce our new extravaganza. A movie like no other. It will have the biggest cast, the grandest settings, the most beautiful girls dressed in the most beautiful clothing, the most exciting action, and, most of all, it will have the greatest love story ever told. The love between God and mankind. A love that can never die."

Delamour stopped listening. He watched Dolores turn her back on John Gilbert and glare up at the studio mogul who had lied to her, her lips moving in a murderous monologue that, thankfully, he could not hear. She marched toward the house. Delamour considered trying to stop her, but what could he do? Only Jack Larson could fix this problem.

People turned to Delamour and clapped, so he returned his attention to Larson's speech.

"Some of you might ask, 'The Thief of Hearts playing our Lord and Savior? Have you gone mad, Jack?' Perhaps, but let me remind you that Jesus Christ was not just God. He was also a man. And, Charles Delamour is a man, too, is he not?"

The audience applauded.

"But more importantly, Christ said, 'I came not to call the righteous but the sinners.' We do not make this film for those who are already saved. No! This epic will be a beacon of hope and redemption for sinners and reprobates, you know, people like us."

The crowd laughed.

"Prepare the way. He comes! My good friend, Charles Delamour, the Son of Man!"

Fireworks shot into the sky, and the crowd erupted with applause. Rockets rose into the night one after the other, bursting into multicolored flowers of light. Jack Larson lifted his arms, embracing the fiery heavens like an ancient god.

Until the house exploded. A huge ball of fire burst through the roof. Spectators screamed as flames curled high into the night sky, and burning debris rained down upon them.

Delamour looked to Jack Larson on the balcony. The movie tycoon glanced at the burning roof, and then ran into the bedroom only to be driven back by a cloud of black smoke. Flames shot up from the floor below him. Larson had no escape. He gripped the rail and glared out at the city lights with a stoic smile as fire engulfed the balcony.

The mob swept Delamour away from the house in a chaotic tangle of elbows, screams, and curses. One thought cut through his jumbled mind.

Bonnie!

Delamour charged into the tide of fleeing revelers, shoving, punching, kicking, getting pushed back, almost knocked to the ground, redoubling his efforts, barely moving like in a nightmare, until finally, he broke free of the crowd and raced toward his front door where he found Betty, Larson's latest starlet, watching the flames with a childlike fascination. Delamour had no time for her foolishness. He reached his front door and pulled the handle.

It was locked.

What the hell?! He looked around frantically, found a potted plant, and threw it through a window. Kicking away stray shards of glass, he climbed into his house. A blast of hot air sucked the breath from his lungs. Covering his mouth, he ran toward the stairs only to collide with Tweedle Dee or Tweedle Dum—it didn't matter which.

"Help me," Delamour commanded. But, when he tried to lead the bodyguard upstairs, the brute shoved him back.

"There's a child up there!" shouted Delamour.

The bodyguard remained still as stone. Delamour lowered his head and tried to charge past him, but the brute batted him away like a fly, sending him tumbling onto the living room floor. When he raised his head, he found himself staring into a pair of lifeless brown eyes.

They belonged to Dolores. She lay on the rug beside him, twisted and broken.

Before his mind could fully register the gruesome sight, someone grabbed him by his hair and lifted him to his feet. Delamour twisted around in time to see Tweedle Dee or Dum rear back his fist. Fortunately, Delamour had not risen empty handed. He held a fireplace poker. Using his fencing training, he lunged, ducking the bodyguard's punch, and plunged the poker into his belly.

The brute didn't even wince.

"What are you?" yelled Delamour.

The bodyguard shot his other fist at Delamour's face. Delamour managed to dodge this blow, too, and the brute's hand punched through the wall behind him. Delamour tried to yank the poker from his belly, but the Tweedle backhanded him into a coffee table.

The brute yanked his hand from the wall and stomped toward him. Delamour frantically searched for a way to get past him. *The chandelier*. He jumped atop the table and leapt onto the iron chandelier, just like he had done in *The Son of the Thief of Hearts*. He hoped that his momentum would swing him over the bodyguard, but unlike movie chandeliers, real ones cannot hold the weight of a fully-grown man. Delamour and the heavy lighting fixture crashed down onto the bodyguard. Delamour sprang over the prone brute and ran up the stairs without looking back. As he reached the second floor, another explosion shook the house. Flames shot up from below, setting the staircase behind him on fire. He rushed down the hallway, but before he reached the library, something smashed him against the wall.

It was Tweedle Dum or Tweedle Dee—again, who cared? This one had lost his dark glasses, and he glared at Delamour through milky dead eyes. Gashes across his arms and chest revealed that Delamour had not been his first adversary that evening. The inhuman brute grabbed Delamour by the neck and walked him backward toward the burning staircase. Delamour kicked and punched and tried to pry the creature's fingers from his throat, all to no avail. Stars exploded before his eyes as the world grew dark. He was losing consciousness. He felt the heat of the flames rising from below.

Then Tweedle's head exploded, spraying Delamour with fetid brain matter. The beast loosened his grip, giving Delamour a chance to scramble onto the landing. Gasping for air, he saw Oliver standing behind the beast, holding a bloody medieval battle-ax. The creature stumbled forward, somewhat disoriented by the loss of his cranium, and toppled down the burning stairs.

The butler, coatless, his shirt torn and bloody, let the ax fall from his hand and limped to Delamour. "Bonnie!" he yelled.

Delamour dashed down the hall, through the acrid stench of burning carpet, past portraits of faux ancestors blistering in the heat, with Oliver close behind. Smoke stung his eyes and burned his throat as he dove for the library door.

Then the ceiling fell. Burning rafters crashed behind him in an explosion of heat and flame. Spinning around, he saw Oliver trapped beneath a mountain of fiery debris. Delamour reached for him, but the butler shook his head.

"Tell my son..." He gasped. "Daniel... Union Georgia... Please, tell him I'm... sorry."

In the fraction of a second that it took for the butler's words to coalesce into comprehension, memories of the man lying before him flashed through Delamour's mind. He had treated Oliver badly. He had demeaned the man to make himself feel superior. Oliver had endured Delamour's pettiness with poise and integrity. He was, by any measure, a far better man than Charles Delamour. And, he had a son. Delamour reached through the burning debris and grabbed the man's hand in a futile attempt to pull him free.

"Go," protested Oliver.

"You saved my life," Delamour wheezed.

"Now, save the girl."

"I don't even know your last name."

"Crowley."

Then the floor gave way, and Oliver Crowley fell into the burning cauldron below. Delamour stifled a scream and staggered away from the pit.

He ran into the library. The bookshelves had ignited into flaming towers, filling the room with black smoke. "Bonnie!" he cried. He could see nothing, so he took a deep breath and ran into the room blindly. He knocked into her bed before he saw it. Bending down, he found the girl.

"Bonnie!" She lay limp in his arms as he picked her up. He saw her porcelain doll lying on the floor. He left it and carried Bonnie to the back of the library. Flames had not yet reached the bookshelf beneath the spiral staircase. Gasping with relief, he shoved it aside with his leg and ran down the secret passageway out of the house. The foliage outside had caught fire. Delamour had to wind his way down the hillside to the creek bed that bordered his house before he cleared the conflagration. He set the child down on a patch of dry grass.

"Bonnie? Bonnie!"

The girl did not move. He felt for her breath, her heartbeat, a pulse, but her cold skin and half-opened, unfocused eyes told him what he had known all along.

Bonnie was dead.

Delamour let out a primal wail that echoed through the rocky canyon. He howled and howled until he had purged every last vestige of humanity from his heart, and then he yelled some more. Gradually, his screams weakened and sputtered out. He placed Bonnie's head on his lap, and he sat in a silent stupor, gazing at nothing.

Delamour didn't turn to look when he heard footsteps crackling through the dry weeds. He felt no surprise when the old derelict with the white beard crouched down, touched the child's forehead, and then looked at him.

"Come with me."

Book III:

Perchance to Dream

Chapter Thirty-Two

Eliza sits at the prow of the boat. She shields her eyes from the sunlight sparkling off the ocean swells and gazes up at the foam-washed cliffs, crowned with yellow and purple wildflowers.

I should come here more often.

"It's really cool, Sandy," grunts a husky male voice.

Eliza turns to see the tattooed corpse sitting at the back of the boat. The creature's great bulk weighs down the stern, stabilizing the vessel. Eliza notes that the dead man doesn't seem all that dead, and, more importantly, that she's not afraid.

"My name is Eliza."

The corpse furrows his brows and blinks.

"Okay," he mumbles then points. "My friend lives there."

Eliza looks up and sees a small white house perched atop a bluff. It's too far to see clearly, but somehow, she knows that it's surrounded by flowers. She and the corpse stare at it in silence for a moment before Eliza says, "Something bad is going to happen, isn't it?"

"It usually does." Jaime shrugs.

His name is Jaime.

"You should probably wake up," he adds.

"No." Eliza sighs. "Let's stay here a little longer."

And they do.

❦ ❧

When Eliza saw Willy Wonka, she screamed. She had woken up in her old bed at her father's house, wearing a pair of his flannel pajamas. She examined the poster of Willy Wonka glaring down at her from the ceiling with his crazed blue eyes. *No wonder I was such a nervous kid.* She took a deep breath and tried to fall back asleep. She wanted to keep dreaming. The dream had made her happy, but the harder she tried to recapture it, the more it slipped away until she had forgotten it altogether.

Eliza started to get out of bed, but she remembered Aurora's grotesque face and dove back under the covers. *What happened? Why am I still alive?*

She heard the bedroom door open, and a female voice crooned, "Little Lamb?" Eliza peeked out from beneath the comforter and found Margarita standing by the bed. "Thank the gods. We were very concerned," she whined and began typing into her old flip-up phone.

"It didn't get you?" Eliza asked.

"It probably did. Everything does sooner or later," Margarita sighed, slipping her phone into her jacket pocket.

"I mean the demon."

"Demon?" asked her father as he burst into the room.

"Daddy?" she cried and sat up.

"Relax," he commanded with a concerned frown. "You got quite a bump on your head. We thought we might lose you."

"Bump?" Eliza felt the back of her head and winced. She did not remember getting hit. She heard a knock, and the pool boy poked his head into the room.

"I just dropped by because I heard the little lady had quite a fall and—" He smiled when he saw Eliza. "Well! She seems all right now."

"Juan! You're alive!"

"Robert. Yeah, I think so," he joked, running his hands over his buff torso.

Eliza grabbed her father's hand. "Aurora. She's a—"

Aurora stepped into the room.

Eliza leapt to her feet. "Call 911!"

Aurora stepped back, startled. Dressed in a T-shirt and jeans with no makeup, she looked more like a scared young woman than a demonic vixen.

"Bubelah! What's wrong?" asked her father.

"She's a demon! She tried to kill me!"

"Now, now, Eliza," her father chided gently.

"It's true! She's a monster with big teeth and fire shooting out her ears and terrible, terrible hair, and the snakes, and they grabbed me and— Tell him!" Eliza screamed at her stepmother. "Tell him the truth, demon. I command you!"

Aurora's eyes filled with tears.

Eliza growled, "Don't you even— She's a liar! Daddy, listen. I borrowed your book, the illuminated manuscript—I know, I'm not supposed to know about it, but I do. I'm sorry. Then this gross little man, a homunculus—they're supposed to come from horse's bladders, but this one came out of a dead gang member's mouth— he stole the book. I got it back, but then this cloud took it, and it smelled really bad just like Aurora because it *was* Aurora and poof! She became a huge demon, and she was so ugly, which is ironic because she called *me* fat. You have a vagina full of snakes! That's a whole lot worse!"

"I don't understand. I'm sorry," Aurora whimpered and started to leave.

"Wait," Jerry commanded. Aurora backed into a corner but remained in the room.

Her father exchanged a sympathetic look with Margarita. "That sounds like quite a dream, Bubelah," he said gently.

"No, this was real! And you were there," she said, pointing to Margarita. "And you were there." She pointed to the pool boy. "And Oliver was there."

"Oliver?"

"My history professor."

"Was that the man who came with you?"

"Did you see him?" Eliza asked.

"No. He left before I got home, but Aurora did. Sweetheart, would you please tell Eliza what happened?"

"I'm making her upset. I should go," Aurora whined.

"Please."

Aurora sniffled and swallowed. "I was in the pool," she said meekly. "And Eliza, ran up with this guy in a suit, and Eliza started yelling at me about some book. She said I stole it. I don't even read books. Why would I steal one? I was trying to calm her down, but her friend, this man, he pushed her at me."

"That's a lie!" yelled Eliza.

Aurora gasped. Jerry held up his hand to calm everyone, then turned to Aurora. "Please continue, my love."

Aurora took a deep breath. "Eliza ran at me, like she wanted to kill me or something, and she slipped, and she hit her head on the side of the pool and fell into the water. Robert and I jumped in and got her out." Aurora turned to Eliza and sobbed. "You were unconscious, and then your father came home, and we took you to the doctor. I thought you were dead or something."

"I never went to the doctor."

"I took you to the emergency room myself, Bubelah."

"I don't remember," Eliza said, starting to doubt herself.

"The doctor examined you. You answered her questions."

Eliza furrowed her brow. "I did?"

"She said you might have some memory loss. You told her you smoked marijuana. She said some people have psychotic reactions—"

"I wasn't high. She was a demon!"

Her father gazed at her with tender concern.

He doesn't believe me. Why should he? I need proof—the homunculus. "Where's my phone?"

"It went into the pool. I'll get you a new one."

Damn. "I need to use your computer."

"Why? Who do you want to contact? This professor?"

"No." *I don't know how.*

"What's your relationship to this man? Are you... more than friends?"

"We're not *even* friends."

"Why was he here?"

"To help me in case Aurora was the demon."

"So, he put these crazy ideas into your head."

"No. I mean. Sort of." Eliza sat down on the bed and rubbed her temples. "I'm confused."

"You're all right. That's all that matters," Jerry said, stroking her hair.

"No. It really happened, Daddy. She burned your book."

"You mean *this* book?" Her father stepped over to the dresser, picked up the illuminated manuscript and handed it to Eliza. She ran her fingers over the copper binding before cracking it open to find the hand-painted king and queen.

"How..." she asked, dumbfounded.

"You brought it with you, Bubelah."

"No, I didn't. Did I?"

"You didn't have to steal it. You could have just asked me."

"But you hid it from me. It was your secret. I thought you'd be mad."

"Mad? I'm proud of you. I knew you snuck into my library. I've always known. I even knew you'd found the manuscript. All the trouble you went through just to read books? I loved it."

"You did?" she asked weakly.

"Absolutely," he replied with a warm smile. Then his face darkened. "But I'm worried about this teacher of yours. Why did he involve himself in your life?"

"He was interested in the book."

"Why?"

Eliza hesitated. She couldn't tell him that Oliver Crowley used the book to raise the dead. That sounded crazy. *Because it was crazy.* A warm wave of relief washed over Eliza as she realized that none of the horrors that she remembered could have happened. *It's impossible.* She must have dreamt it all, or she had brain damage. She touched the bump on the back of her head. The pain soothed her. *Thank God,* she thought. *It's just a little brain damage.* She sank back into the bed with a serene smile.

"His name is Oliver Crowley," she explained calmly. "He teaches one course a year at UCLA. This year it was Cultural and Intellectual History of the Fourteenth Century—you know black death, alchemy, terrible music."

Jerry and Margarita exchanged a knowing look.

"Which explains the demons, right? I don't know how to contact him. He lives downtown somewhere, by the river, but I don't remember where exactly."

Jerry's eyes flared. "You went to his house?" he rasped.

"It's more of a lab. Who lives in a lab? I must have dreamt that, too."

"I'd better have a talk with this man."

"Okay. If he's real," she sighed, settling back onto the bed.

"Get some sleep."

"I have school—"

"Not today. We'll see how you feel tomorrow."

Eliza recognized the futility of arguing with him. "Okay."

"Are you hungry?"

"Yeah."

"Good. I ordered us some pizza."

"Canadian bacon and tomato?"

"Of course."

Eliza smiled and closed her eyes. *There's no place like home.* She breathed deeply and listened to everyone whisper as they shuffled out of the room. She rolled onto her side, cracked her eyelids open, and caught Aurora's reflection in the dresser mirror as she glared at Eliza with hungry eyes and blew her a malicious kiss before walking out.

Eliza bolted upright. It wasn't a dream. It had all happened just like she remembered. The monster was real, and it was waiting for her behind that door.

Chapter Thirty-Three

Crowley marched across campus. The previous day's extraordinary events filled him with dread and hope. The day of reckoning was at hand. Everything depended on the girl. He had to find her.

Surely, ze child is mit her father, Crowley thought in an Eastern European accent.

"She has to return to school. I am her only hope."

If she still lives.

"Her father saved her," Crowley muttered somberly.

You should talk to him. Explain everything.

"And tell him what, old man? That his daughter and I released an army of demons into the world, including his own wife?"

Ze wife was here before you used ze book, no?

Crowley stopped. In all the chaos, he hadn't considered this. If he didn't conjure the father's demonic wife, who did? Crowley banished the concern. "The demons are here. The portal is wide open. That's all that matters."

The child is in danger.

"Quiet!"

Crowley spent years trying to get the old man's voice out of his head, but over time, he grew to accept it. The banter kept him sharp, and it brought the old rabbi back to life, at least in his mind.

You have lost ze book.

"I took copious notes. The girl can decipher them. That will suffice. It has to. We're close, old man. Finally, after all these years, we're so close."

You should tell Eliza ze truth.

"No."

Crowley stopped at the corner of Gayle and Strathmore beside a herd of students who talked too loudly, laughed too much, and looked impossibly young. While he waited for the light to change, a Mercedes Benz pulled up alongside him with a large, winged weasel perched atop it. The students paid it no mind. *They still can't see.* As the car passed, the creature vomited a stream of gold coins onto the street. Crowley's eyes burned with eager determination.

"The hour is nigh."

                          ❧ ☙

The scraggly haired Asian girl opened the apartment door and looked up at Crowley with bloodshot eyes. "What do you want?"

"I'd like to speak to Miss Horowitz, please."

The girl rubbed her eyes and took another look at Crowley. Apparently, she liked what she saw this time because she grinned and opened the door wide. "Come in. Sorry about the mess."

Crowley stepped over beer bottles and pizza boxes and studied the young woman. She wore an oversized T-shirt featuring a flaming skull beneath the words, "Pig Slayer," and underpants (he hoped). "Is Miss Horowitz here?"

The girl scowled and shouted, "Eliza!" She waited a few seconds then shrugged. "Nope."

Crowley pulled a pen and notepad from his coat pocket, scribbled something, and handed it to the girl. "Can I trust you give this to her?"

The girl read the note, then smiled at him with ferocious eyes. "*I'll* come to your office if she won't," she purred.

"So, the answer is no," Crowley stated. "Good day, Miss."

Crowley stepped toward the door, but the girl blocked his way. "You could wait for her here," she suggested with affected innocence.

"Tammy!" boomed a male voice. Crowley turned to see a naked young man emerge from the hallway. The nude youth stopped when he saw Crowley and ducked behind a corner. "Sorry! Tammy, have you seen my clothes?"

"Who are you? Go away!" the girl shouted.

"Connor, and I can't 'cause I'm naked."

The girl rolled her eyes. "Boys."

"Please give Miss Horowitz my note. I need to see her urgently." Crowley pushed his way past the girl and out the door.

"Hey!" she shouted indignantly. "Don't you shove *me*, Mister Man. I'll report you to—"

Crowley shut the door behind him, pulled a jackknife from his pocket, and deftly scratched the words, "My office. C," onto the apartment door.

Chapter Thirty-Four

Aurora was going to kill her, and her father didn't believe it. Why should he? No one could see demons except Eliza and Crowley. *Crowley.* This was all his fault, raising people from the dead like some modern-day, super-handsome Doctor Frankenstein. She had to make him close the portal to hell before Aurora murdered her and her father and God knows who else? Maybe the whole world. She had to find Crowley.

What if he's dead?

Icy terror shot through her. The last thing Crowley said was "run" before Aurora struck him. Had Eliza lost him? Before they'd even *kissed?*

Eliza had to get out of her father's house without anyone seeing her. Unfortunately, the bedroom door opened onto a landing that overlooked the living room. Anyone sitting down there would see her the second she stepped out. She scurried into the bathroom and tried to escape into the adjoining room, but the door would not budge. *They locked me in! Don't panic!* She glanced at the bathroom window. *Too narrow.* She tiptoed back into her room and pressed her hands against the large bedroom window. She knew that it didn't open. *Fucking modern homes.*

Eliza tried the bedroom door. The knob turned. They hadn't locked it. She put her ear to the door. She heard nothing. Okay,

okay. Open it slowly. If someone sees you, just ask for some water. Nothing weird about that. Everyone drinks water, right? Okay, okay... Carefully, she turned the doorknob as far as it would go. Then, ever so slowly, she pulled the door. It creaked. She stopped and waited. She heard no footsteps. No one called to her. She resumed pulling. The door creaked again, and again she stopped. The more slowly she opened it the more noise it made. She needed to fling the door open quickly and confront whatever awaited her on the other side. Eliza took a deep breath and yanked the door open with one mighty pull.

Aurora stood in the doorway.

Eliza yelped and stumbled backward. Aurora smiled mischievously. She wore a black jumpsuit and high-heeled boots, making her look like an assassin from a James Bond movie. "Where you going?" she asked coyly and entered the room.

Eliza searched for a weapon. She snatched up a table lamp, but she couldn't get the cord unplugged from behind the dresser, so she grabbed a stapler and held it out like a sword. "Help! Daddy! Help!"

Aurora laughed and stepped closer. "He's gone." She pouted. "You know your father. Work, work, work."

Eliza lunged at her with the stapler but struck only smoke. She whirled around and found Aurora standing behind her.

"You're fun," she cooed as she knocked the stapler out of Eliza's hand and backed her up against the wall.

"Help! Someone help me!"

Long black claws sprouted from Aurora's fingertips. She reached out and stroked Eliza's hair.

"It would look better cropped short and black."

"I know," whimpered Eliza. "Why are you doing this to me?"

Aurora's face turned to stone. Her eyes vanished, leaving only two gaping black holes. A terrible screeching voice tore through Eliza's brain.

"You have stolen what is mine. Feel my pain!" shrieked Aurora. Eliza felt the irresistible pull of the fiend's empty eyes, wrenching her into a bottomless pit of agony, born of a need too profound to resist or satisfy and fueled by rage so absolute that it could obliterate entire worlds, let alone a scared nineteen-year-old girl with a bad haircut. Eliza felt herself falling into the black vacuum, powerless and alone.

"Pizza," announced a woman's voice.

Eliza snapped back to reality. She turned to see Margarita standing in the doorway with a pizza box. Eliza looked at Aurora. All her demonic features had vanished.

"Pizza!" Aurora exclaimed, eagerly clapping her hands.

"Miss Aurora, you should not be here," Margarita droned in her perpetually disillusioned tone.

"I just wanted to see if Eliza was okay," Aurora explained innocently.

"Mister Jerry said that you upset her, and you should go away."

"Aw." Aurora pouted and turned to Eliza. "See ya soon," she chirped and sashayed out of the room.

Margarita called after her. "He say you should leave the house!" Margarita waited until she heard Aurora's footsteps recede in the distance before turning to Eliza. "I am sorry, Little Lamb. I will see that she does not bother you anymore."

"We've got to get out of here, Margarita. She tried to kill me. She's evil."

"She is evil, but she would not kill you. That would make your father very angry."

"She's a demon, Margarita, a *real* demon! Please, you have to believe me!"

Margarita sighed compassionately. "Little Lamb, you have hurt your head, and you see things that do not exist."

"No—"

"Shh! I will stay with you, and she will not come back. Okay? And we will eat the pizza." Margarita opened the box, filling the room with the succulent scent of garlic and bacon. Eliza hadn't eaten for a long time, so she grabbed a slice and furiously tried to formulate an escape plan.

"Rarabrabory?" she asked through a mouthful of pizza.

"Yes, Canadian bacon is very good," Margarita mused. "Which surprises me because Canada is a terrible, terrible place. Isabela wants to go there, probably to steal more children, because in Canada they do not love their children like we do here."

Eliza swallowed. "Tell me a story."

"What?"

"Like when I was little."

Margarita's eyes welled with tears. "Of course, my Little Lamb."

Eliza sat on the bed, leaned back against the headboard, and patted the mattress beside her. Margarita joined her and sighed contentedly. "Did I ever tell you the story about Tom the Troll?"

"Tell me again."

"Once upon a time there was a troll. His name was Tom. Tom lived in the forest. He spent his days picking wildflowers and eating berries and nuts and virgins. He was very happy."

No wonder I was such a weird kid.

"One day, Tom saw a pretty maid. She had plump, rosy cheeks and big blue eyes. Tom thought, 'Whoopie! Lunch!'"

Eliza closed her eyes as Margarita's disturbing story droned on, slowed, and eventually petered out. Eliza waited until she heard soft, regular breathing. She opened her eyes and saw that indeed, like always, Margarita's story had failed to put Eliza to sleep but had knocked Margarita out cold.

Eliza eased out of bed and rummaged through her drawers for clothes and weapons. She found a pair of cut-offs and a T-shirt that still fit her but nothing with which to battle a shapeshifting demon. *If only I had my phone… Margarita!* Ever so gently, Eliza reached into the sleeping woman's jacket pocket and took hold of her phone.

Margarita lurched. "Enki, Enki, Enki…" she murmured. Eliza froze until the woman settled down and eased the phone out of her pocket, flipped open the old thing and dialed, 9-1— She stopped. *What good would the police do?* They couldn't stop Aurora. *Crowley.* He was her only hope.

Eliza snuck into the bathroom, locked the door behind her, and looked around. Eliza didn't know if she could fit through the narrow, horizontal window, but she had to try. *Fucking modern houses.* Shoving Margarita's phone into her pocket, Eliza climbed onto the sink, opened the window, and squeezed her head through it. She saw no one outside, so she forced her shoulders into the slender opening and shimmied out until her upper body hung from the window. *Now what?* She was more than two floors above the ground. If she fell, she would land headfirst into the bushes. She had to come out feet first. She tried to wriggle back through the window, but she had no purchase. The more she squirmed, the more she slipped down. She decided to squeeze one leg outside and try to use it to leverage her body around, but she only succeeded in dropping even further. Now she held herself up by only one leg. She couldn't hold on much longer. She scanned the bushes below. They did not look inviting. She determined which one seemed the leafiest and angled herself over it. She hyperventilated to rev herself up for the fall. *One... two...*

Aurora emerged from the house and stopped right below her.

Eliza gasped and pawed at the wall, trying to push herself back into the bathroom, but her hands slid uselessly on the cement. She expected Aurora to look up at any moment and see her, but the demon stood still as a statue. Eliza's leg throbbed as she strained to keep herself up. *Don't fall, don't fall, don't fall.* She didn't fall.

But, Margarita's phone did.

It slid out of her pocket and landed beside Aurora with a loud plop. Eliza clenched her entire body, awaiting Aurora's assault. It never came. The demon just glared off into the distance as if she were in a trance. *What's she looking at?* Eliza twisted her head around and saw bubbles burbling in the pool. A black sphere began to rise from the water. Eliza didn't have the time to find out what it was. She was about to drop. She looked around desperately and spotted a drainpipe two or three feet away—maybe five. Eliza was terrible at estimating distances, especially when she was hovering upside down above a sadistic fiend. She stretched but couldn't reach it. Her leg faltered, and she dropped another inch. Twisting her hips, she swung her body away from the drainpipe to build momentum and lunged for it. She got a hold of it, but only for a split second, and she swung back again.

Her escape plan was not going well.

Eliza looked down at Aurora. The creature had not moved. Eliza glanced at the pool. A face emerged from the water. The pool boy. Eliza ignored her predicament for a brief moment to watch Juan, or Robert, or whatever the hell his name was, rise slowly from the water. Sunlight sparkled off his wet, muscular torso. Eliza wondered if he was naked. When she saw his penis, she fell.

Eliza landed in the bushes in a painful tangle of limbs and branches. Pops and swirls danced before her eyes. She had to clear her mind before Aurora pounced on her, but Aurora did not pounce. *Why?* Eliza stifled a moan as she peered through the leaves. Her stepmother and the pool boy now stood several yards away. Both of them were naked. The two magnificent specimens of humanity, almost too perfect to be sexy—*almost*—stared at each other in silence, oblivious to her presence. This was her chance. She snatched up Margarita's phone and pushed herself backward through the bushes. Every inch of her body ached, but her limbs responded, and she continued to crawl. She began to think that she might get away when she heard a terrible wail, so anguished and childlike that it tore through Eliza's chest, filling her with the same desperation she had felt when she called out to her father in her nightmares.

The shriek had come from the pool boy. Eliza lifted her head over the foliage to see the strapping young man wilt into a pale, emaciated child. The pathetic waif gazed up at Aurora with bulging, plaintive eyes and crushed himself against her naked belly.

Eliza had no time to ponder the creepiness of *that*. She continued to back away carefully, wincing at every crunch and crackle she made along the way.

Then something leapt onto her back. Eliza stiffened. She had no idea what it was. It was heavier than an insect, but lighter than a dog. She tried to shake it off without making too much noise, but the thing held on tightly. Eliza took a deep breath and spun onto her back. She saw nothing. Whatever it was, it had gone. Eliza exhaled with relief.

Then the largest rat she had ever seen in her life leapt onto her chest. Eliza reared back. The rat glared at her with mad, pink eyes. It bared its teeth, screeched, and lunged at her face, biting off a chunk of her cheek before she could whack it away. Eliza spun onto her belly and began to scramble madly through the bushes. Another rat appeared before her. It leapt at her face. Eliza backhanded it away, but it was not alone. Rats began burrowing out of the ground all around her until she could see nothing but writhing fur and leathery tails. Eliza buried her face in the dirt as the horrible creatures ran through her hair and over her back. Soon, hundreds then thousands of rats covered her body. Eliza braced her hands on the ground to raise herself, but the army of rodents held her down. Eliza screamed helplessly into the dirt. She tried to suck in air, but there was none. She couldn't breathe. Her body spasmed as she suffocated, waiting for the rats to devour her bit by bit. A wave of nausea washed over her as she began to lose consciousness. Just before the world turned black, a vague thought forced itself into her muddled mind.

They're not biting me.

Rats ran over her body, but they did not attack her as the first rat had done. Eliza willed herself to remain awake as the terrible horde trampled over her, then eventually, moved on.

Eliza raised her face from the ground and sucked in air. She rolled onto her back, wheezing and spitting dirt. She would almost welcome Aurora's deadly attack after that ordeal. She raised herself to a crouched position and looked behind her. The rats surrounded Aurora, chirping on their hind legs in a grotesque spectacle of obeisance. A murder of crows circled over her head, joined by bizarre, winged creatures with furry limbs and ancient, craggy human faces. Eliza dared not move or make a sound.

Then Margarita's phone rang.

Eliza ripped the battery out of the antiquated device and ran.

Chapter Thirty-Five

Jaime watched the naked little cholo chase a cockroach around a table in Badass Undertaker Dude's laboratory, and he thought, *Órale, Jaime, you really are in hell.*

He remembered Angel's head exploding and Badass Undertaker Dude's gun. *He must have shot me, too.* But why was Jaime in hell? He hadn't hurt nobody. Sure, he'd put Chango in the trunk, but it was Angel that shot him. Jaime didn't want to kill him. He didn't hate Chango, even if he was a Filero 13. They'd all been on the same soccer team back in eighth grade. Chango had even kicked the winning goal at the CIF Championship. When Jaime had asked Angel why he picked Chango to kill, Angel had said, "What the fuck does it matter?" Jaime didn't say anything at the time, but later he figured it probably mattered to Chango and his homeys, and his mom.

But I didn't do nothing. Why should I be here?

Jaime thought about all the bad things he'd done in his life. He'd shot *at* a few people, but he never hit them. And, yeah, he beat up a lot of dudes, but they were big, and they wanted to fight. His grandfather taught him never to hit anyone little, or a girl, 'cause it made you look like a coward, even when they had it coming, like the time Gail broke his nose with a coffee pot; he didn't hit her.

Angel hit girls all the time. He treated Rita real bad. Jaime hated seeing them fight. Like that last party when Angel beat the shit out of her. It made Jaime sick, but what could he do? You don't get between a brother and his ruca, and Rita knew that. She had her tats. When she begged Jaime for help that night, she knew he couldn't do nothing. It wasn't his business. If she couldn't keep peace with her man, what was Jaime supposed to do about it?

And sure, Jaime felt shitty when they found Rita's body in that dumpster. He wished it hadn't happened, but he didn't do it.

So, why am I in hell? I didn't do nothing. I didn't...
Oh.

Chapter Thirty-Six

Eliza burst into Crowley's office, filthy, bloody, and torn, and found him sitting at his desk sipping an espresso. His eyes glistened with what Eliza took for relief until he exclaimed, "If you're done wasting time, we have a great deal of work to do."

A sob of joy rose in her throat. *Thank God he's alive,* she thought, but she said, "I'm going to get the plague!"

"Excuse me?"

"A rat bit me in the face! Now I'm going to get boils and puss and vomit blood, and it's all your fault!"

"Stop!" commanded Crowley. "First of all, I'm glad you paid attention in class. Secondly, you cannot get the plague from a rat bite."

"You can't?" she asked, still dazed from her ordeal.

"No. Rabies perhaps—"

Eliza screamed.

"Quiet," Crowley commanded, less unkindly than before. He stepped up, grasped her chin and turned her head to examine the wound. Eliza calmed slightly, placated by the scent of his cologne and the touch of his hand. "It's nothing. A little iodine and you'll be fine."

Eliza pulled back, angered by his dismissal. "It's not nothing! It's a lot of things! Rats and spiders and rats and—Aurora's going to kill me! And no one believes me—" A terrible thought crossed Eliza's mind. "You believe me, right? You saw the demon, too, didn't you?"

"Of course, Miss Horowitz," Crowley sighed irritably. "Stop being so dramatic. Let's go."

"I'm not going anywhere until you send Aurora back to hell."

"Do you think I can simply snap my fingers, and poof she's gone?"

"Yes!"

"We can only stop these demons by mending the tear in the universe that allows them into this world. The wound does not exist in this office or anywhere else in the physical world. It lies here." He tapped his temple. "And, since you created this breach, you must close it."

"Me?"

"If you hadn't given me the book—"

"If you hadn't stolen it!"

"Let's not quibble about who destroyed the universe first. You can read the book. I understand it. It will solve our problems."

"But my father, I left him with Aurora. She's got rats and crows and giant spiders. She's going to kill him."

"If she hasn't killed him by now, she must need him alive, most likely to feed off his lifeforce in order to maintain her corporeal existence."

"Like a vampire?"

"Oh, no," Crowley assured her with a wave of his hand. "Much worse."

Eliza moaned.

"Miss Horowitz!" Crowley barked. "We can only save your father by closing the breach, and we must do it together. Do you understand?"

"Yes," she grumbled.

"Then come with me."

"To your lab?" Eliza asked, wiping muddy tears from her face.

"Yes."

"How long will it take?"

"Days. Weeks. I don't know," Crowley marched out of the room.

Jumbled images flashed through Eliza's brain—Aurora's vacant eyes, the waif, snakes and rats, the pool boy's penis, pizza—but one thought burst through the rest and sparkled before her mind's eye.

He wants me to spend the night.

Chapter Thirty-Seven

Ethan waited outside Eliza's apartment for two hours, but she never came out. He was about to terminate his morning surveillance shift when he heard someone coming up the stairs. He ducked around a corner and saw Professor Crowley march up to Eliza's apartment and knock on the door. Her stupid roommate let him inside. *I knew it!* Ethan thought, stomping furiously up and down the hallway. *Crowley! He's probably forcing her to have sex with him for a good grade. Teachers do that all the time in graphic novels and pornography. When he comes out, I'm going to break his face! I'm going to—* Crowley walked out and Ethan ran back around the corner. He heard scratching sounds before Crowley's footsteps receded down the stairs. He poked his head out and saw that Crowley had written something on the door.

"My office, C," he read aloud. *I have you now!* Ethan ran down the stairs and followed Crowley, across Strathmore Drive and onto campus. He shadowed the professor, adroitly ducking behind trees or casually looking away when he thought Crowley might turn around. He never did, but Ethan kept up his stealthy routine because it made him feel super cool.

Crowley surprised Ethan by going to Kerckhoff Hall rather than his basement office in Boelter. Ethan watched him race up a flight of stairs and disappear into a room marked DANGER

RADIOACTIVE MATERIAL. *I knew he was evil!* Crowley probably had Eliza imprisoned in that room right now, tied to a chair, or a bed, naked, so he could do terrible things to her. The idea filled Ethan with righteous rage, and it gave him an erection. He pondered ducking into a bathroom to relieve his tension when he heard someone coming up the stairs. He dashed behind the corner and spied Eliza marching into Crowley's office and slamming the door behind her.

Eliza's appearance unnerved Ethan. She had on torn, dirty clothes, and her face was bloodstained. Crowley had obviously assaulted her, and she had come to confront him. *She's so brave.* He thought of calling the police, but first he needed proof of Crowley's perfidy. He tiptoed down the hall and put his ear against the door. He heard muted voices, a scream, silence, more muffled talk, and then the door flew open. Ethan almost fell into the room, but in what he would later recall as a brilliantly executed sequence of parkour acrobatics—which was in fact a clumsy stumble onto his rump, followed by a frantic crawl around a corner—Ethan managed to avoid detection. Whatever satisfaction he could have taken from his stealthy escape evaporated when he saw Eliza meekly follow Crowley down the stairs. *What kind of insidious hold does he have on her?*

He followed both of them southward through campus. Eliza stopped abruptly. Ethan dashed behind a vending machine and saw her waving her arms at Crowley. He opened the binoculars app on his phone and zeroed in on her. She was really angry. He zoomed in on her mouth. Ethan couldn't read lips, but it seemed to him that she was saying, "I love Ethan. I love Ethan." Of course he couldn't be certain, but he would stick with that theory for now.

A young woman stepped up to Ethan. "Prepare the way. He comes!" she chirped blissfully.

"Go away," Ethan hissed.

Eliza and Crowley marched off, and Ethan scurried after them. As they neared Boelter Hall, a crowd of students in red beanies charged into Ethan, shouting, "Burn! Burn! Burn!" waving signs that read, "Down with the System," "Our Day Has Come," and other nonsense. By the time Ethan had untangled himself from the melee, he had lost sight of Eliza. No matter. He knew where Crowley would take her to have more sex.

Ethan sprinted through the back entrance of Boelter Hall just before Eliza and Crowley walked in the front. He ducked into the men's room and peeked out the door to watch them walk by. Only they didn't. *Where'd they go?* Professor Crowley answered his question by bursting into the bathroom.

"She's out there," he remarked casually as he headed to a urinal.

Ethan failed to come up with a witty response, so he locked himself in a toilet stall and waited for Crowley to finish his business before he ventured outside. He raced down the stairs in time to see Crowley's office door slowly closing. He slid headfirst at the door, smashing his head against the wall and jamming his hand into the doorway. Ethan stifled a howl of pain when the door crushed his fingers. He listened for sounds coming from the room. He heard only ringing in his ears from the blow to his head.

Ethan considered sneaking away before they found him lying on his belly, holding the door ajar with an aching hand, but the image of Eliza so beat up and upset steeled his nerves. *So what if they find me?* he reasoned. He took Crowley's class, too. He had a right to speak to his professor. He just had to come up with a credible excuse, a question, something casual yet pertinent.

How much will the midterm count toward our final grade? *Brilliant.*

Ethan stuck his other hand into the doorjamb and pushed it open. He saw no one, so he stood and boldly walked inside. The room was empty except for an old desk, a chair, and a poster of an ugly cartoon man. *Where'd they go?* He looked for an exit but saw none. *There has to be another way out of here.* Fortunately, Ethan had a way to find out. He pulled a thermal imaging camera attachment from his backpack, clicked it onto his phone, and spotted the heat imprint that his hand had left on the office door. Scanning the rest of the room, he found weaker heat signatures on the opposite wall, which must have been made by Eliza and Crowley. He pushed on their thermal handprints and a door popped open. He peeked inside. It was pitch black.

He heard a scream. *Eliza*. Ethan gasped with fierce determination. *Now I can save her!*

"Eliza!" he shouted. He ran into the dark room, and the floor disappeared.

Time slowed as Ethan fell into a black abyss, giving him an opportunity to appreciate the marvels of gravity. One second he was charging forward like a conquering hero, and the next he was tumbling down a flight of metal stairs like a useless sack of meat. He hit bottom with a bone-jarring thud. Fortunately, the backpack secured to his back—with two straps, despite Eliza's admonitions—helped cushion his fall.

He remained still for a long time before he summoned the courage to stand. His knees and elbows ached, but he hadn't broken any bones. He couldn't see Eliza, or anything for that matter. The place was pitch black. He switched on his phone's flashlight. Everything looked foggy and out of focus.

My glasses!

He got down onto his hands and knees, which hurt so badly that he had to lie flat on his belly. Using his hips and shoulders, he slithered across the ground, desperately searching for his glasses.

He heard footsteps.

He switched off his phone light. *Clump, scrape, clump, scrape.* Someone was coming. *Clump, scrape, clump, scrape.* Someone with a bad leg. He saw no other light. How could they see in this darkness? *Clump, scrape.* They were getting closer. Ethan considered calling out but concluded that he really didn't want to meet anyone who limped through dark basements.

Clump, scrape, clump, scrape. Ethan could hear the person gasping for air. No, wait. That was him. He tried to quiet his breathing, but it was too late. He felt a foot strike his thigh. Ethan clawed at the ground to drag himself away. His hand landed on something small and plastic. His glasses. He put them on and turned on his light.

Above him, stood a hollow-eyed corpse with leathery skin and a lip-less mouth that hung open in a silent wail of agony. With a loud creak of cartilage and bone, it tilted its head toward Ethan and smiled.

Ethan screamed.

Chapter Thirty-Eight

Crowley opened the elevator door, and Eliza burst out. "I'm never going down there again!"

"Your screaming did make the ride rather unpleasant," Crowley remarked as he marched toward his laboratory.

"What *were* those things?" she demanded.

"Things?" asked Crowley.

"In the tunnel. Something was moving around."

"You mean maintenance?"

"People work down there?"

"Subways do not run themselves, Miss Horowitz. They require constant attention, electrical systems, water pumps—"

"Why don't you just get a car?"

"We traveled from Westwood to downtown in fifteen minutes. Try that on the ten at rush hour. Plus, a direct line to the University allows me to transport materials for my work."

"You take things from school?"

"It's a public university, and I am a member of the public. More importantly, we need the equipment."

"We?"

"We are partners now, Miss Horowitz, an inseparable team dedicated to unlocking the mysteries of the universe."

Eliza softened. "Partners?"

"More like master and servant, but inseparable nonetheless, until we finish our work."

They entered the lab and found the tattooed corpse standing motionless in a corner.

"Hi, Jaime," Eliza said.

The corpse turned to face her.

"What did you do?" Crowley asked incredulously.

"I said, hi," Eliza replied.

"How do you know his name?"

"Didn't you tell me?"

"No."

Eliza furrowed her brows. "I think I dreamt it."

Crowley glared at her fiercely. "Sometimes you surprise me, Miss Horowitz."

"I'm also a great kisser."

"Sometimes you don't."

Crowley marched to his desk and began rifling through stacks of papers. Eliza glanced around impatiently. The lab had changed since last she saw it. *What's different?* She noticed the light streaming in through the windows. *It's daytime.* The sun spoiled the lab's medieval mystique and made it look more like a prefab warehouse in some industrial park. *Except for the old furnace*, she thought. *And the walking corpse and...* "Oh, God!" She grabbed Crowley's arm.

"Stop that," he remarked without looking at her.

"It's eating a rat!" Eliza cried and pointed.

Crowley looked. The homunculus sat on a stool sucking the blood from a rat's decapitated torso.

"We have to stock up on blood," mused Crowley.

Eliza grimaced and turned to Jaime. "What about him? What does he eat? Please don't say brains."

"The dead do not convert organic matter into energy. They function outside the life cycle."

"But you brought him back from hell, right? He moves around, he does what you tell him. He's alive."

Crowley continued organizing his notes while he explained, "I have reanimated his body but not his essence. How did I do it, you ask?"

"I didn't ask."

"Reviving the dead involves three stages: First, one administers the elixir of life to a properly preserved corpse. This restores basic bodily functions but not cognitive abilities, leaving the subject much like a brain-dead patient on life support. Second, another human being ingests the elixir while maintaining physical contact with the corpse. This gives the living person access to the dead person's soul, for want of a better word, in the afterlife—hell, in my experience. If the dead person's soul can see the living person in hell, and often they cannot, the living person can return the soul to its body fully restored, at least in theory."

Eliza frowned at Jaime.

"I have yet to succeed completely. All the dead I have rescued from hell return damaged. They can move about and obey—not just in Latin, in any language—but little else. Jessie is the best I've done so far."

"Jaime."

"He has attempted crude vocalizations, and he responds to you, Miss Horowitz, which suggests some crude cognition. I credit this progress to your book, which I fear, I translated poorly. We will do better next time."

"Next time? You're going to bring more dead people back to life?" she asked incredulously.

"We both are."

"Are you crazy? That's what caused all this trouble in the first place."

"Miss Horowitz, I have rescued many people from the clutches of hell, and it has never unleashed a horde of demons on Los Angeles. The only difference this time is you. You came into my life and changed everything."

Eliza blinked. "It sounds kind of romantic when you put it like that."

"It's not. It's frightening, yet full of possibilities."

"Still sounds romantic."

"If you want me to close the gates, I must go to hell, and I can only go there through the psyche of a deceased person. I know of no other way."

Eliza backed away. "You have another dead body?"

"Of course."

Eliza glanced around nervously. "Where?"

"In the freezer, along with other perishables, including a year's supply of frozen dinners. I hope you like Salisbury steak."

Eliza grimaced. "That's so gross."

"It is not so bad. It includes a delicious apple cobbler, although the portion is rather small."

"I mean the body."

Crowley's eyes crinkled, betraying a hint of amusement. "I know. Do not worry, Miss Horowitz, I have stored the cadaver well away from the food."

"Who is it? Is it a man or a woman? How'd they die? Where'd you get it? Is there more than one body?"

"I don't know. A man. Gunshot wound. I have sources—hospitals, morgues, funeral homes. Sometimes I employ brokers, although they can prove unreliable, and no."

Eliza took a moment to connect Crowley's answers to her questions then asked, "Is this legal?"

"No."

Eliza took another moment to ponder the implications. Although she fancied herself a rebel among the student hoi polloi, she had never broken a law that could land her in jail. "So..." she continued carefully. "You're going to revive this dead guy and use him to go to hell where you'll find this opening and close it?"

"Yes."

"How do you know you can find it?"

"It takes no great skill to find an opening to hell. We all have wounds that connect us to our personal demons. The alchemist learns to exploit the wounds of the deceased to journey to different planes of consciousness. These wounds tend to be small. They very rarely grow large enough for beings from one dimension to bleed into another. This breach must be severe, therefore easily detected. I hope."

"And how will you close it?"

"I don't know."

"It all sounds kind of vague."

"Do you have a better idea?"

Eliza fell silent for a moment then asked, "What's it like? Hell?"

Crowley stopped sorting notes, picked up a drawing pad, and showed Eliza a pencil sketch of a kindly old woman sitting beside a small Christmas tree decorated with candy canes.

"Hell is a sweet little old lady?"

"It is if you're Kevin Ritter. Every Christmas, Kevin's mother would ask him to put up a candy cane tree, and every Christmas, Kevin failed. The tree was always too big or too small. It had too many candy canes, or too few, and always, it was crooked. Why couldn't Kevin put up the candy cane tree properly? Because, as his mother constantly reminded him, Kevin was stupid, lazy, and fat. She lamented not having aborted him during pregnancy or smothering him soon thereafter. Kevin disliked his mother a great deal, but he feared her even more. He did not, however, fear prostitutes, so he killed twenty-three of them and decorated his own Christmas tree with their bones. Kevin now spends his afterlife putting up candy cane trees for his eternally dissatisfied mother."

"How do you know all this?"

"Because I was there."

"In hell?"

"In Kevin's hell."

"There's more than one hell?"

"We all exist on many planes of reality simultaneously. We create these worlds ourselves. We fashion them from our hopes and fears, from the stories we tell ourselves and the dreams we dream. When our lives end in this reality, our dreams continue in others."

He showed Eliza another picture. She recoiled with disgust.

"What are those things all over her?"

"Cockroaches. Sarah Beckman was deathly afraid of cockroaches, so…"

"You saw this, too?"

"I drew all these pictures from memory."

"They're so detailed. How do you remember it so well?"

"Because they're now my hell, too. These realms do not exist independently from us. In these worlds, if a tree falls in a forest and no one is there to hear it, it does *not* make a sound. When I journey into someone else's dreams, it becomes my dream, too, subject to my own hopes and fears, to my perception of reality. I must remain vigilant lest I lose myself in these dreams. I remember the details because, for better or worse, I helped create them."

"How do you know what's real?"

"Everything is real."

"Did you try to get this woman out of there?"

"She could not see me. Most people resign themselves to what they know rather than look for alternatives, even when it involves cockroaches."

"That's horrible."

"We all have our crosses to bear, Miss Horowitz."

Crowley turned to another drawing.

"Is that Jesus Christ?"

"No, that's Ramon Gonzales. Some people's crosses are more literal than others."

"Why do the Roman soldiers wear wristwatches?"

"I don't know."

"What does 'Adaru fourteen' mean?"

"Where do you see that?"

"All over the Roman shields, and on the wall behind the candy cane tree, and the red cockroaches spell it out, see?"

"No, I don't. There is no red, Miss Horowitz. I drew these pictures entirely in black pencil."

"I see lots of red and some green."

"What else do you see?"

"Adaru fourteen, fourteen Adaru, Adaru..."

"On all the drawings?"

"Yeah."

Crowley strode over to a workbench and began rifling through a large book until he found an engraving of an old circular calendar. "Adaru is the final month of the Babylonian calendar. Each month begins with a new moon. This year, the fourteenth day of Adaru marks the end of a twenty-year cycle. These transitions between cycles were sacred days for the ancients. Sit-at-home, do-nothing days. Very volatile. On the Gregorian calendar, Adaru fourteen falls on the twenty-fourth of June, seven days from today. These dreams are telling us, or rather, telling *you* that something will happen on Adaru fourteen, or has happened on Adaru fourteen, or it's utterly meaningless."

"That's my birthday."

"You were born on Adaru fourteen?"

"June twenty-fourth."

Crowley glared at her with fiery eyes. "The plot thickens."

"What does it mean?"

"Only one way to find out."

"How?"

"Go to hell."

Chapter Thirty-Nine

Ethan ran into a wall. He staggered backward but managed to stay on his feet. It was utterly black. He dared not turn on his phone and draw attention to himself, so he listened for footsteps. He heard nothing. He kept one hand on the wall and, taking a deep breath, he began to inch forward. He heard three loud booms. He froze. *What is that?* Again. The booms echoed through his chest. *It's your own heart, idiot. Okay. Okay, okay. Just keep moving. One step at a time.* He followed the wall around a corner. His sneakers splashed into water. He stepped away and bumped into another wall. He was in a tunnel.

Calm down. It wasn't a zombie. It was just a homeless guy, a dirty, deformed homeless guy limping in the dark, smiling at young men.

Now Ethan wished it *had* been a zombie. Zombies he understood. They just clomped around eating human flesh until you shot them in the head or set them on fire.

He kept splashing through the water as quietly as he could until he could no longer feel the walls. *I'm out of the tunnel.* He waved his arms around gingerly and took another step forward. He stopped to listen. Still no sound. Whoever he had seen had not followed him. He pulled out his phone and clicked on its flashlight.

He was surrounded by zombies.

Ethan switched off his phone. *Those are definitely not homeless people.* He held his breath and waited for the living dead to tear into him. They didn't. *Why don't they eat me? Who cares? Do something!* He considered charging through them like a football player, but Ethan had only played football once in his life when his father had forced him to join a game in the park. He'd left after one play with a bloody nose and a humiliated father.

Think, dude! Do you have a gun? No. Do you have fire? No—wait a second... Ethan switched on his phone's cigarette lighter app and held up the small digital flame.

The zombies screeched and lunged at the phone. Ethan flung it away and ran. He didn't get far. He crashed into a column, stumbled back, and hit another one. He bounced from column to column like a pinball until he bashed into a counter of some kind. He rolled over it and crouched down. *Do... not... make a sound.*

The booms again. *Fucking heart!*

Chapter Forty

Crowley carefully pulled the white-hot matter out of the furnace with iron tongs.

Ze Dry Way is dangerous. It works mit ze raging fires of our lower nature. It can drive you mad.

"I'm not a novice, old man," grumbled Crowley.

The object hissed and crackled when he set it down on a metal tray. A red crust formed on its surface as it cooled. Crowley scraped the coating into a stone mortar and chanted the sacred words of Hermes Trismegistus—Thrice Great Hermes. "That which is above is as that which is below. The sun is its father, the moon its mother, the wind hath carried it in its belly, the earth is its nurse."

"What's next?" he asked the girl, who sat on a stool furiously transcribing his notes.

She flipped through a stack of papers. "Mix in two debens and three kites of pul-vis solaris."

"Two debens? Impossible." Crowley stomped over to check the notes. "That symbol means *two*?"

"I just see a two."

Crowley grunted. He combined a small amount of black powder into his red mixture and poured it all into a glass of water.

Ze girl is not ready.

"Nobody is ever ready," Crowley blurted.

"What?" asked Eliza.

"Nothing."

She is cold.

Crowley glanced at the girl, hunched over a table, her brows knit, writing and mumbling.

"She's fine."

She has my eyes.

Crowley pictured the old man's smile, and he felt a sting in his heart, which he quickly shook off. No time for emotions. He had to prepare this girl. She had no idea of the danger, which was just as well. When it came to the horrors of hell, ignorance was bliss.

Unless it kills her.

The elixir would allow them to enter a subject's postmortem dream together. That was the easy part. The hard part was staying together once there. If the girl got caught up in the drama, and dreams always involved drama, it could lead her down an infinite maze of thoughts, and she would be lost forever. It happened to the famed alchemist Nicolai Lorga, who followed his subject into her darkest sexual fantasies and spent the rest of his days in a padded cell singing "If Mama was Married" from the Broadway musical *Gypsy*.

Crowley held the glass of red water up to the light. He detected a faint orange glow that pulsed like a heartbeat then settled into a deep purple. "A good start," he mused.

You should tell her ze truth.

Crowley grumbled, picked up an old sweater from the back of a chair and wrapped it around the girl's shoulders.

"Thank you," she said with a smile which Crowley did not return.

Ze poor darling is scared.

"Quiet!"

"Sorry," blurted Eliza.

"Not you. What's next?"

Chapter Forty-One

Ethan spent three days hiding behind the counter in the dark. Actually, it was only about an hour, but it felt like three days, so Ethan went with that.

The zombies had not attacked. *Why?* He saw their gruesome faces emerging from the blackness all around him. He even saw them when he shut his eyes, which meant he only imagined them, but it didn't matter. Every breath he took felt like his last. He almost wished they would hurry up and eat him and end the torturous anticipation.

On the fifth day (thirty minutes later), Ethan recalled that the hero of every horror movie he'd seen always reached a point where he or she, *or they*, stopped running and fought back. They had to risk their lives to survive. Ethan inhaled deeply and exhaled slowly. He rose to his feet and winced in pain. His leg had fallen asleep. Ethan ignored the excruciating pinpricks and took a fighting stance like Goku did when he battled Frieza Number Four in *Dragon Ball Z*. If he had to die, he would die like a man.

"Bring it on!" he yelled.

The zombies responded with a screech that nearly burst Ethan's eardrums. He leapt back against a wall, which gave way, and he fell through a door into another chamber. He jumped to his feet, and in complete darkness, he tried to shut the door behind him, but the zombies jammed their way in. He pushed on the door with all his might while bony zombie hands reached through the opening and pawed at his arms and face. There were too many of them. He couldn't hold them back. Bit by bit, they pushed the door open.

"Help me!" Ethan screamed. The skeletons screamed back at him and pushed even harder. "Leave me alone!" he whined, and with one final gargantuan effort, Ethan somehow found the strength to shove the zombies back and close the door.

Frantically, he fumbled around until he felt a bolt. He had to hit it several times with his palm before the metal moved, and he locked the door. He staggered back and looked around. He saw nothing but blackness. "Help!"

The zombies lunged themselves against the door. Ethan ran, hit a wall, and the world disappeared.

༄ ༅

Fireworks exploded before Ethan's eyes. *So pretty.* Gradually, the bursts of color waned into irritating flashes of pain.

My head.

Ethan found himself still in utter darkness. He listened for the zombies. They had stopped banging on the door. He started crawling quietly, but his knees still hurt from his fall, so he got to his feet. He reached out his hand, praying that it didn't touch a zombie face, and limped forward. He felt something soft and flinched. He stood trembling for a long time before he mustered the courage to extend his hand once again. It touched something smooth and flat. A wall covered with velvet. Wallpaper. He ran his hand along the wall, past a framed picture, until he found a button, two buttons, one directly above the other. He pressed the lower button. Nothing happened. He pressed the higher one.

The room exploded in light.

Ethan flinched. Blinking through the brilliance, he saw that the light came from a crystal chandelier reflecting off a huge mirror.

Stools, glasses, and empty bottles of liquor littered the dusty floor. Ethan spotted his own footprints coming from the door he had bolted shut. It had a sliding peephole. He stepped up, pulled it open, and found himself staring into a pair of milky-white zombie eyes. He slammed it shut and backed into the center of the room.

Ethan shook his head. *Get your wits about you, man!* The fifth doctor in *Doctor Who* used that expression all the time, and Ethan thought it was cool.

Where am I? Spider webs covered a set of beer taps on a long counter. *A bar.* Yellowed ads for soda, cigarettes, and Model T cars lined the walls. *A really old bar with a peephole in the door. What's it doing way down here?* Ethan looked around. He found a small bathroom with a crazy-old toilet and sink. They both worked. Behind the bar, he discovered a cardboard box containing two dozen candy bars, a jar of olives, five tins of sardines, a stack of *Los Angeles Evening Herald* newspapers from 1925, and two unopened bottles of gin; but he found no way out other than the way he had come in. He needed a plan. He pulled his tablet out of his backpack and fired it up. He had no phone or internet service, but he did have several seasons of *Doctor Who* and *The Simpsons*. If there was a working outlet, he would have something to pass the time until he came up with a plan.

He tore open a candy bar, which was rock hard but tasty, turned on season three of *The Simpsons*, and settled down to think.

Chapter Forty-Two

"First Matter, the essential element of all time and space, exists in a state of perpetual chaos and potential," Crowley said as he poured red liquid into a kettle full of putrid brown goop he called rebis, producing a vapor cloud that reeked of vinegar and rotten eggs.

Eliza covered her nose.

"To form the material universe," Crowley continued, gently stirring the fetid filth with a copper spoon, "first, matter organized itself into four elements—earth, water, air, and fire—which represented the different humors of the spiritual and physical world. By manipulating these four elements, the alchemist can create a fifth element—"

"A quintessence," Eliza interjected impatiently, "which you use to make the elixir. Got it." Eliza had labored with Crowley for two days, and as far as she could tell, they hadn't made any progress. She had translated reams of notes and listened to him drone on for hours about white, black, and red phases; phoenix birds; and transmutations. Despite learning a great deal about alchemy, a subject she absorbed with preternatural ease, she felt no closer to saving her father than she did when she'd first arrived.

"Bring out the dead guy. Let's do this thing," she urged.

Crowley ignored her and kept stirring. "The gods gave humanity the elixir twelve thousand years ago during Zep Tepi—The First Time…"

Eliza groaned.

"...when a group of gods brought their advanced technology to earth. Unfortunately—"

"Isn't there only one God?" she asked, annoyed at having to sit through the story again.

"No."

"What about *God* God from the Bible?"

"He controls everything. Or, he gives us free will to do as we please. Or, he doesn't exist. I don't know. Now, when the other gods arrived, they became overwhelmed with lust for human women and bred a race of giants who terrorized mankind for thousands of years. One of these supernatural visitors—"

"What happened to the giants?"

"Humans exterminated them."

"What about the gods?"

"They're still here."

"Where?"

"Everywhere. The gods flitter from universe to universe doing what gods do. Politics, mostly. They plot against each other, make alliances, fight wars, that sort of thing. They rarely concern themselves with human beings, which is a good thing. They can be quite dangerous and rude."

"Have you ever seen one?"

"Yes."

"What was it like?"

Crowley frowned for a moment then snapped, "Do you want to save your father?"

"Yeah."

"Then stop interrupting." Crowley took a deep breath and continued stirring his concoction. "One of these gods, Thoth, later called Hermes by the Greeks, Mercury by the Romans, took pity on humans and gave them the secret of immortality. He preserved his writings inside two massive pillars just before the Great Flood, but only the Emerald Tablet survived. It began with the enigmatic phrase—"

"That which is above is as that which is below," Eliza complained. "I know this already."

"You know nothing," Crowley retorted. "The elixir of life is not some banal recipe. It is a mystery to contemplate over and over again. I have just introduced mercury, the White Queen, to sulfur, The Red King."

Crowley placed the kettle atop the furnace. "Now we must invite them to mate."

"Mate?"

"Yes. Through meditation, we will visualize their loving union."

Eliza smiled. Maybe this wouldn't be so bad after all.

Eliza sat cross-legged in the oratorium, Crowley's name for the curtained-off vestibule where she once found him staring into a black mirror beside a creepy doll. The room had scared her back then, but now she found the candlelight and incense comforting. Best of all, the dark mirror blurred the blemishes on her face.

"Focus on your breath," Crowley instructed evenly. He sat beside her, still wearing a vest and tie, except... His tie was red before. Now it's blue. When did he change it? Where did he change it? Where does he sleep? Does he sleep? Does he wear pajamas?

"Eyes closed," he continued. "Concentrate on the air passing through your nostrils, in and out, in... and out."

Eliza inhaled. "It stinks in here," she grumbled as she exhaled. "Which is probably a good thing 'cause then I can't smell myself. I haven't showered in days. How old are you?"

"Breathe in... breathe out."

Eliza took another breath. "You look forty, forty-five at the most, but you take that elixir a lot, right? 'Cause you're always bringing people back from hell, so you could be like a hundred or a thousand. Did you live in the middle ages and that's how you know so much about it?"

"Do you want to save your father?"

"Okay, okay." Eliza breathed in and out a few times. "Have you married a lot of women? Sorry. It's just, I can't stop thinking."

"Stop talking."

"'Do you not know I am a woman? When I think, I must speak.' That's Shakespeare."

"You don't have to stop thinking," he said. "Just stop letting your thoughts distract you. Concentrate on your breath."

"Got it." Eliza continued breathing in silence for a few moments. Then... "Have you—? No, wait. Sorry. Got distracted. Back to my breath." She inhaled and exhaled several more times. "The problem is my thoughts are much more interesting than my breathing. I mean, air goes in, air goes out. Boring."

"That's the point," Crowley responded patiently. "A repetitive action improves your ability to concentrate. Trust me."

"Okay." She breathed in and out, in and out, in and— "It must be sad if you're immortal and your wife grows old and dies but you don't. Or your *husband*. Do you have a husband? Because that would really ease the tension between us, which, you got to admit is pretty intense."

Crowley clapped his hands loudly. "Miss Horowitz!"

"Sorry. I've only slept a couple hours in three days."

"We must remain focused while we're in hell, or we will not find our way back."

"Why do I have to go? I know I can see things you can't, like Adaru fourteen and stuff, but I don't know what it means."

"I do."

"Then *you* go."

"Your presence greatly enhances my chances of success. Focus, Miss Horowitz. These dream worlds communicate through symbols and metaphors. You must clear your mind to see them, and you must keep your wits about you at all times, especially when talking to demons."

Eliza flinched. "There's demons?"

"We *are* going to hell, Miss Horowitz. That's where they live, but beware. They do not receive many mortal visitors, and they can get rather chatty. Be attentive and polite, but do not trust them or have sexual intercourse with them. And most importantly, do not eat their food."

"Will it damn me forever?"

"No, but it's awful."

Eliza began to hyperventilate.

"Calm down."

"How? I'm supposed to talk to demons and not have sex with them, which implies they're going to want to have sex with me, and why wouldn't they? Everyone does, except you—"

"Breathe, Miss Horowitz."

Eliza exhaled slowly.

"That's it. Now breathe in."

Eliza inhaled.

"That's all you have to do. Breathe in and breathe out."

Eliza complied. After a few minutes, her breath steadied.

"We have placed the sulfur and mercury compound on the fire," he said in a steady voice. "We must help the White Queen and Red King join in the sacred marriage. Envision the Queen. She wears a white flowing gown. Her crown gleams with pure white light. She carries a white flower. Can you picture that?"

"Yes," replied Eliza.

"Good. Now, the King approaches. His red cape hangs over his silver breastplate, leather tunic, and greaves. He carries a spear. They see each other. The heat of the furnace melts their fear and distrust. It burns away their resolve to remain apart. They draw closer to one another."

Eliza's breath quickened.

"The King reaches out his hand. Slowly, ever so slowly, the Queen slides her hand into his."

Eliza's face flushed.

"The heat rises. The King and Queen step closer together. Closer and closer and…"

Eliza grabbed Crowley's hand and an explosion shook the lab.

"Curses!" cried Crowley. Eliza followed him out of the oratorium into a cloud of black smoke. Crowley ripped off his vest and threw it to her. "Cover your nose and mouth," he shouted as he disappeared into the black cloud. In a few seconds, Eliza heard the roar of a motor, and a powerful vent sucked the smoke into the rafters and out of the lab. Crowley doused the burning remnants with a fire extinguisher, leaving the lab covered with white foam and charred gunk.

"Is this a good thing?" Eliza asked meekly.

Crowley responded by thrusting a broom into her hands.

⁂

Two days later, Eliza consulted Crowley's notes while he worked on a new batch of elixir. He had passed the torturously difficult black phase of *nigredo* where he reduced the prescribed elements to their bare essences, and through *albedo*, the white phase, where he cleansed the remaining matter to a new level of purity, and he had now embarked on the final step, the red or *rubedo* phase, where he attempted to merge the purified matter into one quintessential element packed with enough energy to restore life.

Crowley chanted quietly while he worked, occasionally stopping to ask Eliza for a translation, but mostly lost in his alchemical reverie. Eliza hadn't changed clothes or showered in five days. She had only slept a few hours a night curled up in uncomfortable chairs, and she had eaten only microwaved Salisbury steak, which did not taste as bad as she had feared. Crowley allowed her no comforts, and she had asked for none. She had not spoken to her father since she fled his house, and every hour that passed increased her anxiety. Aurora could kill him at any time. Maybe, she already had. Eliza yearned to put the battery back into Margarita's phone and call him, but if her father used the phone to track her, he would send police and prevent them from completing their mission. To ease her mind, Eliza talked incessantly. She told Crowley everything about herself, and he never judged or criticized, primarily because he never listened.

"I have intimacy issues. I won't deny it. Dating a single guy my age makes me nauseous, not just because they're boring and childish, but because they like me *so* much. Why? I do nothing to deserve it. They're like dogs, not cute dogs, but needy, yappy dogs. The idea of getting stuck in a relationship with one of them feels like someone's putting a pillow over my face. Frankly, I'd prefer the pillow. It's quicker—"

"Twelve grains pulvis solaris and then…?" asked Crowley.

"Liquor hepatis, one half shekel," she replied without having to consult her notes.

"Hepatis? At this stage? Impossible," he barked.

"Don't believe me then." Eliza shrugged.

Crowley grunted and did as she instructed. Eliza continued, "My mother wanted me to see her therapist when I told her I was still a virgin. Like I need some stranger to tell me that I have daddy issues and I don't trust men. So what? Feelings are feelings. I can't just wish them away. I have to accept them and move on—I wonder if that applies to demons and jazz?

"But maybe I don't *want* to move on. Maybe I want to live my own life, not someone else's. It's not like I don't know that all my problems come from my mother. It was just the two of us most of my life, and she was not the most stable person in the world. She'd be sweet one second and blow up the next. I didn't know what would set her off. I never felt safe as a kid unless I was alone. Fortunately, I was alone a lot.

"I always thought my mother drove my father away with all her craziness, which she probably did, but he can be a handful, too. He's always busy, and he can be distant and unavailable. So yeah, I'm attracted to smart, mature, independent men. Why isn't *every* woman? I mean, I'd take King Arthur over Lancelot any day.

Maybe I'd have an *affair* with Lancelot, but Arthur has depth and soul. Even when his wife's cheating on him, he chooses the greater good over his male ego. *That's* who you fall in love with, not some boring French knight, and let's be clear, I'm talking classic King Arthur. Give me *Camelot* and *The Once and Future King*, not all this new crap where Arthur is some stupid *Roman* fighting barbarians. I want shining armor and jousting and damsels, not a bunch of raggedy druids wallowing in mud. I should have been born a long time ago. I don't understand people today. I don't understand *anything* really, except this weird ancient writing, which says it all, doesn't it? The only thing I can relate to is some dead language. That's probably why—Ew!"

Eliza covered her nose as a stinky cloud rose from Crowley's concoction.

"It's ready," Crowley announced and placed the kettle on the furnace. Eliza backed away, wary that it might explode again.

"Time to meditate."

"Curses," groaned Eliza.

☙ ❧

Eliza and Crowley sat in the oratorium.

"This time we will concentrate on the *metaphysical* implications of the union between mercury and sulfur, and *please* keep your hands to yourself."

"Whatever," Eliza grumbled.

"Look at your reflection in the mirror. Relax your vision and breathe, in and out, in... and out."

Eliza obeyed.

"Now picture the Red King. The King represents the masculine spirit—the sun, energy, aggression, intellect. See the White Queen. We associate her with matter, passivity, contraction, and emotions."

"So the man is intellect and the woman is passivity?"

"Yes."

"Alchemy's pretty sexist, isn't it?"

"Yes. He craves action and adventure. He seeks objective truth. She values memories and reflection. She prefers storytelling over theorizing. Her language is art and music. These opposing character traits exist in all of us, men and women. We must accept both sides of ourselves before we can help the King and Queen consummate their marriage."

Eliza yawned. The dark room and deep breathing had quieted her anxiety and allowed her exhaustion to catch up to her. She felt an overwhelming urge to curl up into a ball and sleep.

"Focus!" snapped Crowley.

Eliza jolted awake. "I got it, I got it. We have to accept the masculine and feminine inside us."

"Correct."

"Doesn't that take years of therapy?"

"No. Do it now."

Eliza shrugged. "Okay." She closed her eyes and thought, *Male, female, both cool* and *Boom!* A blinding white light flashed, and the earth shook.

"Oh, no," moaned Eliza.

Crowley leapt out of the oratorium. Eliza followed cautiously, but instead of black smoke, she found a dazzling golden light radiating from atop the furnace. An uncharacteristically buoyant look ignited Crowley's face. He donned a pair of dark goggles and cautiously approached the kettle. Even with his protective glasses, he had to look away to drop a heavy lid onto the pot and lift it off the fire.

"Zounds!" he exclaimed.

"Is *zounds* good?" Eliza asked as she lumbered up, shielding her eyes.

"It is the spark of life, Miss Horowitz. My master and I nurtured many incarnations of the elixir. All of them tapped the source of creation to some degree, but never so profoundly as this!"

"You had a master?"

"Of course, just as he had a master before him, and you have one now."

"Who's my master?"

"I am."

The word *master* offended her, and it turned her on.

"Do you know what this means, Miss Horowitz?" Crowley asked eagerly.

"Um..." she replied, rubbing her tired eyes. "We're ready to enter hell and close the gates and stuff?"

"Yes!"

"Great."

"You don't sound very excited."

"I'm exhausted, Oliver, I mean, Mr. Crowley, or master, or whatever it is you want me to call you."

"Professor is fine."

"Professor. I've hardly slept for days. I feel achy and gross. I need to rest, just a little, just... rest."

"We have almost achieved our mission, Miss Horowitz. How can you stop now?"

Eliza propped herself against a table and closed her eyes. "I don't know. I just... just..." She almost slid onto the floor. Crowley helped her to a stool and studied her in silence.

"We're *all* tired, old man," he whispered.

"You're talking to yourself again," she sighed as she laid her head on the table and fell asleep.

Chapter Forty-Three

Ethan was going to die. He had run out of candy bars days ago. He'd even eaten the sardines and olives, which he hated. Worst of all, he had no more *Simpsons* or *Doctor Who* to watch. The end was near.

Over the last week (real time, not Ethan time), he had concocted many escape plans. He thought of using a barstool to fight his way out; or disguising himself as a zombie to slip away unnoticed; he considered making a cannon like Captain Kirk did when he battled the Gorn—all he needed was sulfur, charcoal, and saltpeter, none of which he had. He could have made a torch if he had matches, or a Viking sword if he found a deposit of iron ore and a furnace hot enough to remove impurities.

Ethan was losing his mind.

Every time he slid open the peephole, zombie eyes glared back at him. Ethan was a coward, and he knew it. He would die alone in that basement, and that would make his mother very sad. She could be annoying at times, but he didn't want to upset her. He needed to find the courage to fight his way out of there. Then he realized that he'd had it all along. It was waiting for him on the bar.

Ethan had only had one sip of alcohol in his entire life. His mother had let him taste the red wine she drank every night. He hated it and never touched the stuff again. But today, as he scrolled through the movies that he wished he could download, he came across *The Evil Dead*, a horror comedy where zombies tore off the main character's arm, so he jammed a shotgun into the stump and began blowing them away. Ethan fantasized about having an arm-stump shotgun. Then he thought about amputations and how much they must have hurt before anesthetics. He figured that people back then must have gotten drunk to dull the pain. Then he remembered that he had alcohol. *Maybe booze will make my death less painful.* He stepped over to the bar, twisted the cork off a bottle of gin and took a sniff.

It smelled like poison.

"It's a good day to die," he declared and took a big swig.

Ethan doubled over, gagging and spitting. His chest and throat burned. His stomach heaved, but somehow, the gin stayed down. Ethan sat behind the bar and tried to catch his breath.

How can anyone drink this crap? What is wrong with people? Are they insane? I'd rather be torn apart by zombies. No, you wouldn't. Yes, I would. No, you wouldn't. Yes, I would! Oh, yeah? Prove it, coward!

"I will!" Ethan shouted. He stood up and stumbled against the bar. "Just watch me. I'm gonna get eaten so bad!" He snatched up the gin and took another swallow. "So terrible!" he growled. "Where's my backpack? There you are!"

Ethan stuffed his belongings into his pack and strapped it on.

"Two straps. In your face, Eliza!"

He marched to the door, slid open the peephole, and gasped, like he always did, at the sight of the milky-white cadaver eyes. Only this time, he didn't shut the slot.

"What are you looking at?" he scoffed. "You looking at me? Huh? You looking at me? Feeling lucky, punk? When I want your opinion, I'll beat it out of you. I'm your worst nightmare. Yippee-ki-yay, motherfucker!"

The zombie did not seem impressed by Ethan's repertoire of film quotes.

"Okay. Here we go." Ethan reached for the bolt then stopped. "Wait, wait, wait." He ran back to the bar and took two more gulps of gin. "Man, that's good." He stomped back to the door and pointed at the zombie.

"Back away, punk!"

The zombie retreated into darkness.

Bile and fear surged up Ethan's throat. *It's a trap. It wants me to come out so it can eat me.* The combination of terror and tainted booze made the world spin. Ethan collapsed onto the door. Darkness closed in from the edge of his vision. *This is it. Now or never!* He shook his head, and with a mighty yell, he unbolted the door, yanked it open, and staggered backward.

Light from the speakeasy illuminated an army of semi-decayed human beings. Some of them still had remnants of dried skin and muscle. Others were no more than walking skeletons. All of them stood motionless, glaring at Ethan.

White-hot electric fear shot up his spine and exploded in his brain, blasting him backward, down a long, dark psychic tunnel until the outside world looked distant and trivial. Ethan hiccupped, hooked his thumbs through the straps of his backpack, and said, "Step aside."

The zombies parted like the Red Sea.

Ethan belched. "Thank you. Now, could you direct me to an exit?"

The floor rumbled in response. A spotlight pierced the darkness. The roar grew louder, and the light grew brighter until a subway train screeched to a halt before him. "Thank you," said Ethan.

Then he barfed.

Chapter Forty-Four

Eliza's eyes wafted open slowly. She allowed them to remain unfocused so she could linger in the delicious limbo between sleep and wake. Eventually, her vision sharpened, and she found herself looking at a ceiling decorated with ornate metal tiles. She had no idea where she was, and she didn't care. She loved those old tin ceilings. She yawned and stretched languidly. She was in a warm bed with soft cotton sheets and plush down pillows. She was fully dressed, which meant that nothing too embarrassing happened the previous night.

She sat up, rubbed the sleep from her eyes, and took in the spacious room. It had decorative Persian rugs atop a hardwood floor and a large plate glass window looking out over the Los Angeles Warehouse District. Ashes in a fireplace on the opposite wall left traces of pine and charcoal in the air. But what impressed Eliza most were the floor-to-ceiling shelves full of books.

This had to be Oliver Crowley's bedroom. *He must have put me to bed while I was asleep.* Although she knew that Jaime had probably lugged her there, the thought of Crowley carrying her to his bed like Clark Gable in *Gone with the Wind* made her happy, so she stuck with that explanation.

She strolled to the books and ran her fingers along the bindings. She expected to find antiquarian volumes in Latin and Greek.

Instead, she saw *Mysterious Island*, *The Adventures of Tom Sawyer*, *The Call of the Wild*, *The Return of Sherlock Holmes*. They were the books of a boy. Eliza had never imagined Crowley as a child. The notion filled her with wonder and affection.

She noticed an open door and stepped into a spotlessly clean bathroom with black-and-white hexagonal floor tiles and marble countertops. A stack of fresh towels rested by the sink. She turned on the shower, and steam filled the room. She shed her grungy clothes and stepped into the hot spray. She sighed as the knots in her neck and back loosened, releasing days of pent-up apprehension. A new feeling crept into her heart, something she had not felt for a long time.

Hope.

Eliza descended a dark flight of stairs to find Crowley meditating in the oratorium. He had hidden the entrance to his bedroom behind a curtain in his meditation chapel. *Sneaky*.

"Good morning," she sighed languidly.

Crowley inhaled deeply and exhaled slowly. "It's afternoon."

"Thank you for letting me sleep in your room."

"Don't get used to it." He opened his eyes. "I didn't give you permission to wear one of my shirts."

"May I wear one of your shirts?"

He huffed and stood. "Come. We haven't a minute to lose," he declared as he strode into the laboratory. Eliza followed.

"I love your books. Have you had them since you were a boy?"

"No."

"Do you speak German?"

Crowley picked up a small glass vial full of red powder. "Why?"

"Your copy of *Grimm's Fairy Tales*, it's in German."

"Did you look through my drawers, too?"

"Yes. I was hoping to find something incriminating."

"I have no secrets that will fit into a drawer," he quipped as he pulled the cork from the vial and poured some powder into a drinking glass.

"Do you speak German?" she asked again.

"Not if I can help it. My mother gave me that book when I was a child. I lost it, so I purchased another copy."

"Was your mother German?"

Crowley ignored the question. He poured water into the glass and stirred it with a copper rod.

"I *love* the pictures. In the book. They're funny."

Crowley froze.

"Those old engravings are so full of life. I love the dancing dwarf and the forest and the rabbits. I love rabbits."

Crowley tossed the stirring rod into the sink sharply and stomped away.

"Something wrong?" she asked.

Eliza found him standing before a gurney. The soothing effects of a good night's sleep and a shower melted away the moment she saw the cadaver beneath a white sheet. "Our guide to hell?" she asked, straining to sound casual.

Crowley pulled the sheet off the body, revealing a dead young man. He had a shaved head, several teardrops tattooed on his cheek, and a black hole in the center of his forehead.

Crowley and Eliza heard a gurgled scream behind them. They turned around to see Jaime backing away.

"What's wrong with him?" Eliza asked.

"He may recognize the deceased. If so, it could mean that a part of Harry's mind survives. This bodes well for our mission, Miss Horowitz."

"*Jaime*. They knew each other?"

"Yes," Crowley replied as he secured the body with leather straps and attached sensors to its chest and wrist. "His name was Angel Matamoros."

"How do you know?"

"I checked his wallet."

"Did you kill him?"

"In self-defense. Murder would corrupt the alchemical process."

"They attacked you?"

Crowley did not respond to obvious questions.

"Does anyone else know what happened to them?"

"No. We are perfectly safe."

"I mean their friends and family. Do their mothers know they're dead?"

"They chose lives of crime, Miss Horowitz. I am under no obligation to redress their sins. If this ruffian helps us achieve our goal, then we shall grant his worthless life a shred of value."

Jaime complained with a muffled cry.

Crowley lifted the glass. The red powder had dissolved, leaving a clear liquid that pulsated with bright golden light. "Ready?" Crowley asked gravely.

Eliza backed away. "Right now? Just like that? Shouldn't we pray or make a speech or something?"

"Today is the day, Miss Horowitz. Adaru fourteen. The stars have aligned, the elixir's power has reached its zenith. The portal is wide open. It's now or never."

"It's my birthday," Eliza squeaked.

"Happy birthday. Let's go to hell."

Chapter Forty-Five

Eliza backed away. She had worked feverishly with Crowley for the last week. She knew the theory behind the elixir. She understood the profundity of its mythos, in some ways, better than Crowley did. She had helped create it. "The sun is its father. The moon, its mother." *I am the moon. It will work*, she told herself. *It has to.* She would drink the elixir, but she had never spent a birthday away from her father. *He must be worried sick.* He had no idea where she was or what condition she was in. She could be dead for all he knew. He could be dead for all *she* knew. What if they failed? What if something went wrong and Eliza never returned from this bizarre astral trip, which could turn out to be nothing more than some deranged professor's delusion? What if Jaime wasn't really dead? He could just be some brain-damaged vegetable. Could it all be a lie? *No. The demons were real. Aurora was real.* She did not doubt that, but she could not know how Crowley's concoction full of poisonous chemicals like mercury and vitriol—whatever the hell that was—would affect her. She might drop dead or wind up like Jaime. But, what choice did she have? *Aurora is out there.* Eliza took a deep breath.

"I need coffee," she blurted and ran to the kitchen.

"Now?" complained Crowley.

"I just woke up!" she called back to him as she put a kettle on the stove, but she did not wait for the water to boil. Instead, she ducked down a short hallway that led to a large metal door. She had not left the laboratory for a week, and she had never used this exit. *Please open.* The door squeaked and scraped loudly.

"Miss Horowitz?" Crowley called out.

Eliza managed to yank the door wide enough to slip outside. She ran five blocks before she stuck the battery back into Margarita's phone and called her father. He answered immediately.

"Bubelah?"

"Yes, Daddy."

"Oh, my God. Where are you? Are you all right?"

"I'm fine, Daddy. I just wanted to see if you're okay."

"I'm *not* okay. I've been worried to death about you. I called the police, private investigators. You're on TV, the internet, newspapers. The whole country is looking for you."

"Curses."

"What?"

"Nothing. I'm okay, Daddy."

"He kidnapped you, didn't he? This professor. The FBI's looking for him."

"No one kidnapped me."

"He brainwashed you, filled you with crazy ideas, turned you against me—"

"No. I'm fine. Really. I'm sorry I'm going to miss our birthday dinner."

"No! You can't! Stay on the line. I'll be right there."

"Sorry, Daddy. I'll see you soon."

Eliza ended the call, took out the battery, and headed back toward the lab. She hadn't taken three steps before she heard a plaintive wail echo down the street. She looked around, and two questions crossed her mind simultaneously. *Who yelled?* And, *Where is everybody?* The universe answered her first question when a shadow passed over her. She looked up and saw an immense bird soaring above the city, only it wasn't a bird because birds didn't have arms and legs and snaky spiked tails.

The weird creature spiraled downward and hovered above the corner of Eighth and Santa Fe, beating its powerful feathered wings and glaring down at Eliza with bulbous, black, vacant eyes. It growled, threw back its squat canine head, and screamed like an adolescent girl.

Eliza ran.

A manhole cover blew open in front of her, and a three-foot-tall white-haired mammal of some kind, carrying a spear, a round shield, and wearing a helmet with two eye slits, leapt out of the sewer. Eliza stopped. The little beast raised its weapon, cried, "Meum nomen est Tom," and charged.

The creature scrambled toward her awkwardly, giving Eliza the opportunity to plan her defense. She would deflect the spear with her left arm then kick the little bastard in the face. She felt confident that her plan would work, but she never got a chance to test it because at the last moment, Jaime stepped in front of her. *Where the hell did he come from?* The creature punched his spear clear through Jaime's torso. The big man didn't flinch. The little monster tugged on his weapon, but he couldn't free it from Jaime's sizable belly. Jaime took hold of the shaft and slowly drew it out himself. Blood oozed from his belly onto the street, but Jaime didn't flinch.

He really is dead.

Jaime gripped the spear like a baseball bat and swatted the little beast clear across the street. "Uh," commented Jaime and stomped off, whacking more furry warriors all the way back to the laboratory.

☙ ❧

"The demons found me!" Eliza cried as she burst into the lab with Jaime on her heels.

"You could have ruined everything," Crowley barked, barely restraining his rage.

"This thing with wings and this mouse-type thing, it stabbed Jaime and—" She noted that the corpse's wound had stopped bleeding. "Aurora's going to come and kill us!"

"It would serve you right, but no. Demons cannot enter this lab. I have placed natron crystals and pulvis poultices—"

"Who cares? Let's go."

Crowley inhaled sharply and exhaled slowly. He picked up the elixir and stepped over to the corpse. "You are not prepared for this."

"Thanks for the pep talk."

"You have not mastered your thoughts, nor developed the proper focus to navigate through the hellish nightmare we will encounter. I shall have to guide you." Crowley took her hand. Eliza gasped. *He touched me.* She had fantasized about this moment for weeks. Now that it had come, it felt oddly mundane. "When your mind wanders," he continued, "when you feel scared and overwhelmed, and you will, squeeze my hand. It will remind you that I am with you. Always." Eliza nodded rapidly. "I also brought you a weapon."

Crowley handed her a plastic cocktail sword.

"What will this do?"

"You can transform this into a real sword, or a spear, or an orangutan, anything. This bobble will help remind you to use your will power. You have the ability to control your own destiny in these dream worlds. Very few people grasp that concept, let alone master it."

"Will I have pockets to keep this thing in, or will I be naked?"

"That's up to you."

"Will you be naked?"

"No."

Using an eyedropper, he squirted some elixir in the dead man's mouth. Nothing happened for several seconds, then Angel Matamoros' head flew back, and his back arched off the gurney. He spasmed, then collapsed. Bright red blood bubbled from the hole in his head and ran down the sides of his face. Crowley pressed a towel onto the wound and waited, periodically checking the injury. When he finally took the towel away, the blood had coagulated, sealing the wound.

"Wow," said Eliza.

Color returned to the dead man's face, and the heart sensor beeped, showing a regular heartbeat.

"He's alive," she gasped.

"The elixir has restored the body's basic motor functions. Now we go to hell and bring back the man."

"How do you know he's in hell?"

"I've done this before."

"Is anyone in heaven?"

"I hope so."

"You never go there?"

"I experiment on reprobates who have nothing to lose, but also… I have not found heaven. I want to believe that it exists, that some of us have good dreams after death, not just nightmares, but I have yet to see one."

"Why?"

"I don't know, Miss Horowitz. Perhaps it is because of my own failings. Perhaps, I cannot conceive of heaven, or I haven't looked hard enough."

"So, you've only brought back bad people?"

"*Bad* is a poor description. *Fearful* is closer to the mark. Fear justifies bad behavior. It puts self-preservation above all else, encouraging us to retreat into ourselves, trapping us in cycles of terror and anger, making our world smaller and smaller. Hell is a little place, Miss Horowitz. It is a land of isolated prisons, some no larger than a thought. I imagine heaven to be somewhat more… expansive."

Crowley brought the glass to his lips and took a sip. He inhaled sharply. "Zounds."

"Zounds? That's good, isn't it?" Eliza asked.

Crowley's eyes gleamed triumphantly. He handed her the glass. Eliza hesitated. "So, what exactly am I supposed to do in hell?"

"Look for signs, talk to demons."

"Should I ask them where the gate to hell is?"

"Sure. Drink."

"And they'll tell me?"

"Yes, no, maybe—just keep the demons occupied, and I'll take care of the rest. *Drink*."

Eliza eyed Crowley suspiciously. He seemed uncommonly agitated. Of course, under the circumstances, it would have been more uncommon to *not* be agitated. She shook off her apprehension, took a deep breath, and drank. The liquid exploded into a kaleidoscope of indescribable flavors when it touched her tongue. Eliza had never tasted anything so delicious. It was the nectar of the gods. It was life itself.

"Zounds," she whispered.

Gripping Eliza with one hand, Crowley reached out to Angel with his other.

"Hold on."

Chapter Forty-Six

Eliza runs. It's gaining on her. She dashes into the driveway of a beige stucco house with barred windows and doors. Dodging trashcans, clotheslines and skateboards, she sprints through the backyard and scrambles over a wall just as a giant stinger crashes into the cinderblocks behind her. She races toward the back porch. She hears its legs thumping across the lawn. She'll never outrun it. She flings open the screen door and rushes inside, past the dirty dishes in the sink, across the threadbare avocado carpet and up the stairs. The huge thing bangs and clatters after her.

She runs into a bedroom, shuts the door and locks it. She backs into the center of the room and looks around. The bed is unmade. Clothes litter the floor. Posters of psychedelic skulls, flaming guitars and bikini-clad women toting machine guns line the walls. She holds her breath and listens. She hears nothing. Then...

CRACK! A giant black scorpion smashes through the window. Eliza backs into a corner. The massive arachnid squirms into the room with startling speed. It shakes broken glass off its scaly back and faces her. Eliza grabs a soccer trophy off a dresser and throws it at the beast, but it clanks off its shell harmlessly. Then, Eliza remembers that she has a weapon. She reaches into her pocket and pulls out a cocktail sword. She wills the plastic utensil to transform into a real sword, and *Poof!* It turns into a cocktail umbrella.

"Goddammit!" she yells.

The scorpion arches its spiked tail and clacks its claws as it closes in on her.

"Stop," says a male voice.

Eliza feels a strong hand yank her away, and she finds herself facing Oliver Crowley.

"This is not your dream," he says.

Eliza turns around. Now, she's across the room watching the scorpion hover over a naked little man covered in tattoos. Angel Matamoros. The scorpion raises its orange-tipped tail.

"No, please!" screams Angel. "Help me, Rita! Please!"

A dark-skinned teenage girl appears beside the scorpion. She wears a frilly white dress that clashes with the scorpion tattoos covering her arms.

"Please, baby. Make it go away!" Angel begs the girl.

She smiles sweetly. "No way."

SNAP! The scorpion's tail plunges through Angel's stomach. His eyes gape in agony as the arachnid lifts him off the floor and swings him around, spraying the room with blood. Crowley pushes Eliza forward. "Say hello."

"What?"

Crowley rolls his eyes and calls out, "Excuse me!"

The scorpion and the girl turn to look at him. Angel is too preoccupied with the stinger in his gut to respond.

"Sorry to interrupt, but we were wondering if we might have a word with you?"

"I know you," the girl says to Crowley. "You've visited us before."

"Yes, but may I say, I have yet to encounter a more thrilling scenario than what you've created here. Congratulations."

"That's kind of you to say," says the girl. "Our leading man brought a wealth of material to work with."

Angel moans.

"But it takes a brilliant mind to craft that material into a dynamic storyline. Did you create it on your own?"

The girl glances down with a modest smile. "Yes."

The scorpion whips Angel around the room violently.

"Breaking through the window was her idea," the girl admits with a nod to the scorpion.

Angel shrieks as the scorpion wags its tail.

"Please join us," the girl says to Crowley.

"We don't want to be a bother."

The girl lowers her chin and glares at him with hungry eyes. "No bother at all." She motions to the scorpion. The creature flings Angel off his stinger, snaps its claws and heads for Crowley.

Crowley pulls out a revolver and shoots the scorpion in the face. The giant creature turns into a small mound of white blubber wearing a nun's veil.

"Ex nihilo nihil fit," grumbles the blubber and slithers out of the room.

"How come you get a gun and I only have a plastic toothpick?" Eliza whispers.

"Lack of imagination."

"Enough!" snaps the tattooed girl. The bedroom disappears, and Eliza finds herself in a murky haze with no walls, no top or bottom. Angel floats off aimlessly, curled in the fetal position, yet Eliza still feels ground beneath her feet. The tattooed girl has also vanished, replaced by a tall, emaciated creature with the head of a vulture, wings made of rippling hair, furry muscular legs, and a lion's tail.

"Ragmentor," Crowley exclaims with a deep bow. "You honor us with your presence." He squeezes Eliza's hand. She takes the hint and bows as well.

"Yes, I do," Ragmentor squawks. Crowley remains bent at the waist as the demon draws nearer. Eliza glances up to find herself at eye level with the creature's large, leaky phallus. *What is it with demons and disgusting groins?*

"You flout the laws of space and time to come here. Why?" asks Ragmentor in a shrill voice. Crowley straightens and starts to respond, but the demon cuts him off. "Don't answer. I know. You want to master the secret of life. You want to be the most powerful human of all. Am I right, Al-chem-ist? Of course, I am! And who is this girl?" Eliza rises. "Wait, don't tell me. I know." The demon turns its head to glare at her with one unblinking raptor eye. "You are his concubine, are you not?"

"Not exactly," Eliza says.

"You sexually debase yourself for this human, don't you?"

"Not at the present time."

"What is your name?"

"Eliza Horowitz."

Lightning crackles through the mist. Thunder booms. The demon shrieks and drops to its knees. "Forgiveness, Blessed One. Forgiveness."

Eliza glances at Crowley for an explanation. He cocks his head in confusion.

Angel screams.

And in a puff of smoke, Eliza stands in a pine forest at night, gazing into a bonfire. She reaches for Crowley, but she can't find his hand. Her heart begins thumping wildly.

He abandoned me!

No. He may have released her hand, but she can still feel his presence standing beside her. Her heart slows with relief. She looks at the couples sleeping around the fire, only they're not sleeping. They're dead. Eliza's looks up the hill and sees the large Tudor mansion with light shining through its windows.

Eliza and Crowley run through the forest. Black shapes watch them through the trees. The foliage grows thick and gnarled. Her feet sink into rotted vegetation. It takes all her strength to put one foot in front of the other.

Eliza climbs onto the front porch. Warm light sparkles through the windows, and she hears a familiar tune play on a phonograph, with the words "sweet baby girl." She pictures glamorous people in tuxedoes and ballgowns chatting and laughing. She longs to join them by the roaring fire and the Christmas tree, but she can't. She has tried many times, in many dreams, but the comfort of home always eludes her.

This is my hell.

Eliza pushes the door open. The house goes black and silent as it always has, but this time something has changed. *She* has. After studying with Oliver Crowley, Eliza understands what she could not before. She knows what this place really is.

This is the gate.

Normally, she would run away at this point in her dream. This time she does not. She has to walk through the door if she hopes to heal this cosmic wound.

She braces herself and steps inside only to find herself back on the front porch. Light and laughter radiate from the house. She opens the door again, and once again, the house goes black. She steps in, and she's back on the porch. She goes through the door over and over again, and always she finds herself on the porch.

"What's happening?" she asks Crowley. He doesn't respond. Fear clenches her chest. The man standing beside her isn't Crowley. Crowley abandoned her, left her here, in hell, alone with... She hears a deep, harsh laugh.

It towers over her, a featureless black shadow with flaming red eyes, and long, curved horns like a bull, and it whispers...

"Moloch comes."

Chapter Forty-Seven

Eliza awoke, standing beside Crowley while he examined Angel Matamoros' pupils.

"What happened?" she asked, bracing herself against the gurney.

"It worked. Mr. Matamoros? Can you hear me?"

"What worked? The gates of hell. I was there. I stepped through the rift."

Crowley shot her an anxious look. "You didn't close it, did you?"

"I didn't know how. I couldn't figure it out."

"Good," Crowley exclaimed with relief.

"Good?"

"We got our man, Miss Horowitz! Mr. Matamoros?"

Angel opened his eyes.

"It's okay," Crowley told the young man. "You're safe."

Angel blinked and opened his mouth.

"Where were you? Why did you leave me?" Eliza asked.

"Quiet," barked Crowley.

"Wa..." croaked Angel.

Crowley snapped his fingers at Eliza. "Water." She looked at him blankly. "Curses." He strode over to the watercooler, returned with a cup, and helped Angel drink. "What is your name?" Crowley asked him.

Angel stared back dumbly.

"Where were you born?"

He gave no reply.

"Do you remember anything? Anything at all?"

"You..." he rasped. "Owe me money."

Crowley smiled with such unbridled joy that Eliza no longer recognized him, but finally, she understood him.

"Yes. I do," Crowley replied to Angel. "I owe you more than you can possibly imagine."

"You never wanted to close the gates of hell," Eliza stated evenly. "It was all a lie."

"I want my fifty thousand dollars," Angel said, looking around. "Where am I?" He tried to rise but found his arms strapped to the gurney. "Get these things off me!"

"Of course!" Crowley unbuckled the restraints.

"You want the gates to stay open so you can bring more dead guys back to life," Eliza continued.

Angel slid off the gurney and crumbled to the floor. "Puta madre!"

"Your muscles are weak," Crowley said as he lifted him up. Angel brushed him off and fell again.

"Cabrón!"

"Huc veni," commanded Crowley. Jaime clomped over and yanked Angel to his feet.

"Dude!" Angel exclaimed, recognizing his friend. "What the fuck's going on? You don't look so good."

The homunculus popped out from behind the big corpse's shoulder and smiled.

"Omnes moriendum est," said the homunculus.

Angel screamed and toppled back onto the floor. Crowley motioned for Jaime to stand back.

"You have been through a traumatic experience, Mr. Matamoros. Can I get you anything?"

"Fifty thousand dollars, puto!" he growled as he grabbed a table and pulled himself to his feet, at which point, he noticed that he was wearing a hospital gown. "And my clothes! And my wallet, my phone, and my Glock!"

"He wants his gun!" Crowley chuckled. "Isn't that wonderful, Miss Horowitz? He wants his possessions as if nothing happened!"

Eliza glared back at him with disgust.

Angel looked to Jaime. "Homey! What the fuck is this?"

The big man stared blankly. Angel turned on Crowley. "What did you do to him?"

"I shot him in the head."

Angel snatched a pair of iron tongs off the table and lunged at Crowley. "Back off!"

"That's it!" cried Crowley. "Come closer. One step at a time. Excellent!"

Angel veered away from Crowley and hobbled off.

"Brilliant! Muscular atrophy healing rapidly, no sign of necrosis," Crowley commented as he followed him.

Angel reached a wall and spun around. "Let me out of here!"

"What is your date of birth?"

"What?"

"I need to test your mental acuity. When were you born?"

"You ain't testing nothing."

"Do you remember the scorpion?"

Angel's eyes widened with terror. "Rita," he whispered.

"He remembers! Oh, isn't this glorious! We brought a human being back to life, and he remembers hell! Miss Horowitz, I couldn't have done this without you. I am eternally grateful. Now, we must hurry. We have just enough elixir for the final phase, and it is a notoriously unstable substance. Mr. Matamoros, under normal circumstances, we would have spent a great deal of time getting to know each other, but alas, that cannot be. Remember this, you have the power to change, even in hell." He pointed to a door. "Please let yourself out. Goodbye."

"What about my shit? My clothes, my wallet? My money? That scorpion. What the fuck did you do to me?"

Crowley pulled a revolver out from behind his back and leveled it at Angel. "Goodbye, Mr. Matamoros," he growled with ice-cold malice.

Angel scurried out the door.

Crowley put down the gun and gave Eliza a big smile. "Shall we get to work, Miss Horowitz?"

"You left me in that horrible place all alone so you could play Frankenstein. You don't care about me, or my father, or anyone."

"We can deal with that later. We have work to do," Crowley yanked back the curtain to the oratorium, opened a wooden chest that lay hidden behind the altar, and pulled out the porcelain doll that Eliza had seen when she first found Crowley meditating before the dark mirror.

"The demon said that Moloch is coming," Eliza declared.

Crowley stopped and turned to her.

"I walked through the door again and again," she continued, "but every time, I ended up back where I started. Then the demon with the horns and the red eyes—the one that's been in my dreams since I was a little girl—he said Moloch was coming. He'd never said that before. What does it mean?"

Crowley glared at her for a moment before replying, "Nothing. Demons lie."

"You're the liar," she countered.

"We don't have time for this. Help me or go!"

Eliza looked into Crowley's bloodshot eyes and realized that she had fallen in love with the semblance of a man, a fantasy she had created to fill a hole in her heart. The real man stood before her now, exposed and fragile, and she did not know him. She only knew that this man, this stranger, had used her, then left her to die in hell. And worst of all, he had made a fool of her.

Eliza turned and walked away.

Chapter Forty-Eight

The gardener was crying. Tammy had no idea why. He certainly hadn't been crying when he crashed the party last night, drank two bottles of Pink Chablis, and sang Mexican songs at the top of his lungs. Tammy had slept with him because he seemed like a fun guy, and he had stayed awake longer than anyone else. She didn't remember the sex. That happened a lot lately. She'd be partying one minute and the next she'd wake up with some frat guy snoring in her bed. Tammy preferred forgetting. That way she could have all the fun and none of the regret.

She shoved the gardener. "Hey, Paco! Go home!"

"My name is George," he sniveled as he picked up his clothes from the floor and lumbered into the bathroom. Tammy noted that he had bite marks on his butt. *Cool.*

Tammy liked sex—the flesh, the grunting and sweating—but, more than anything, she loved the hunt that preceded it. She felt so powerful knowing that she could have any man she wanted. A little smile, a squeeze or two, and he was hers, at least for half an hour. Men were such sheep. She couldn't believe that she had once been afraid of them. That was her mother's fault. She had told Tammy that men were animals who only wanted to use women then toss them away. The most important thing a woman had was her dignity, she'd say. If she lost that, she had nothing. Then came the day that Tammy had her grand epiphany. *Was it just a week ago?* On that day, the truth hit her like a punch in the face. Dignity was nothing but a word old people used to keep young people from having the kind of fun they couldn't have anymore. That very night, Tammy had sex for the first time and decided that if she couldn't eat it, fuck it, or dance to it, she didn't want it.

She looked at her phone. *12:30?* She was late. "Julio! Get out of my bathroom!"

A few minutes later, Tammy had put on the black beanie she had knitted herself and headed to the march.

It was the third straight Day of Rage at UCLA, and this one promised to be the wildest one yet. Initially, Tammy joined the *I Am* movement to protest academic authoritarianism, but when the group allowed a faculty member to speak at their meeting, she joined the splinter group, *You're Not!* which vowed to never compromise with authority. Then, she joined the more radical, *You're Not, too!* which advocated violent resistance, before finally co-founding the even more radical *You're Not, too, too!* because they had cooler beanies.

Kids in multicolored hats crammed Wilson Plaza. As Tammy squeezed through the crowd, she heard, "We are people," countered by "No, you're not," "Jews will not replace us," "Muslims go home," and "Death to The Association of Free Lutheran Congregations!"

The press of bodies excited Tammy as she worked her way toward Janss Steps where a band blasted electric noise through mammoth amplifiers. Tammy began bobbing her head to the beat of the teeming mob. She looked for members of her group but didn't really care if she found them. There were plenty of hot bodies to keep her entertained. The band stopped and the crowd yelled. Tammy yelled, too, although she had no idea why.

Then, from the sea of hip protesters, emerged a young man in a blue button-down shirt, white pants, and topsiders. He had short blond hair, blue eyes, and a golden tan. With a supremely confident, casual air, he trotted up Janss Steps to the microphone and took in the crowd with a friendly smile. Students shouted and jeered. He seemed to enjoy it.

Tammy pushed her way through the throng to get a better look. She had seen him before, but she couldn't recall where, which disturbed her because he was super handsome.

Gradually, the heckling subsided.

"Hey, guys!" he announced with an easygoing smile.

Men jeered. Women hooted.

The young man laughed, delighted by the crowd's reaction.

"You guys," he continued with a clear voice that carried to every corner of the plaza, "are beautiful!"

People cheered and whistled.

"It's morning in America! You are the change we can believe in. We are stronger together, and as long as we keep hope alive, we will keep moving forward. Can we make America great again? Yes, we can! Why? Because we, the people, are in charge. We, the people, have the power. We, the people, can do anything!"

The crowd cheered. The young man waited with his hands folded before him until they quieted down. Then he leaned into the microphone and whispered.

"Except it's all bullshit."

The plaza went silent.

"We can't do anything. We have no power. We're just nano bytes in the System. The System tells us what to wear, what to eat, what to say, who to hate. It keeps us drugged with religion, and sex, and smartphones; and we think we're so smart with our tweets, and our marches, and pink hats, red caps, cat videos, and angry raps to make us feel cool, but we're not cool. We're stupid."

Angry shouts erupted from the audience.

"Me, too! Look how I'm dressed. I've been a good nano byte. I conformed when the System told me to be polite and get good grades, obey my parents, not talk with my mouth full, and smile—smile and the whole world smiles with you. I say please, and thank you, and shake hands, and brush my teeth, and get my vaccines. When the System says 'Jump,' I ask, 'How high?' I let it mold me into its idea of a good citizen, and in the process, it crushed any genuine emotion I ever had. I'm just a cog in the wheel... on the outside. But inside? Inside, I am so full of rage that if I let even a tiny bit of it out, it would burn down the whole world."

His audience let out a mighty roar of approval.

"Sounds like some of you might know what I'm talking about."

They roared and cheered more loudly.

"So, who made this System? Politicians? The rich? The Pope? Sure. They benefit from it. But here's the thing they don't want you to know: They created it, but they don't control it. The System has outgrown them. It's spread all over the world. It governs nations, economies, churches. It rules us because it's wormed its way into our minds. It's that voice in your head that says, 'Don't want too much. Don't aim too high. Don't say the wrong thing. Don't make trouble. Don't fight for what you know is right!'"

The students yelled angrily.

"We've lived with the System so long, we think these voices are normal, that they're just a natural part of the human psyche. Bullshit! Do you think our paleolithic ancestors worried about having a bad hair day? Or speaking out of turn? Or loving who they loved? Or defending themselves when someone attacked them? Do you think they thought they didn't deserve to get what they wanted? If they had thought that, humanity would have gone extinct a long time ago. No! Our ancestors were wild, and beautiful, and FREE!"

Students wailed like happy animals.

"Freedom! That's what the power-elite can't tolerate. They created the System to break our spirit, to keep us weak and afraid, dependent and docile. Why?"

He paused to build tension.

"Because they're afraid of us."

Students whooped and hollered.

"The wildfire still burns inside us. The System's almost put it out, but not quite. They know that if we give it just a little fuel, the fire's going to get bigger and hotter until it burns their System down, and we take back what's rightfully ours!"

The crowd howled. The young man dropped his head, exhausted by his exhortation and humbled by the audience's approval.

Tammy finally recognized him. He had come to her apartment with flowers for Eliza. The thought filled her with jealous fury. How could such a smart guy go out with that slouch? Tammy wanted to grab Eliza by her moppy hair and beat her face into a squishy mass of bloody meat. She searched the crowd but didn't see her. He must have dumped her. "Pathetic loser," snorted Tammy.

"I don't know about you," resumed the young man, "but I'm going to feed that fire."

The crowd hollered some more.

"And I bring good news. We are not alone. There's someone coming to help us, someone far greater than me, someone who will lead us out of this desert and back to the garden. Look in your hearts. You know that what I'm telling you is true."

Tammy did. She didn't know his name or his face, but she felt the flame of recognition just the same. He was coming. He would free them all.

"Prepare the way! He comes!" shouted the young man, and the crowd went crazy. Electric chords screeched through the quad and people danced. Tammy threw off her hood and writhed to a pounding rhythm that seemed to rise from the depths of the earth. She found herself pressed against a shirtless young man. She squirmed against his sweaty skin. She inhaled deeply and licked his neck. He tasted so good. She bit down hard.

Blood filled her mouth.

Chapter Forty-Nine

Angel marched toward the Sixth Street bridge, looking as badass as a guy in a hospital gown can. He held the back flap closed with one hand and gripped a knife he'd snatched from the crazy dude's lab in the other. He ignored the cars that slowed down to look at him. This was Filero 13 territory. If gangbangers spotted his tats, he was dead, and if he died again, he might end up back with that big fucking bug.

It was just a nightmare. There's no bug, there's no bug, there's no bug.

A car honked at him. He put his head down as it passed him by. He needed clothes. He spotted a thrift store across the street with shirts and pants hanging on the door. *Perfect.* He started to cross the road, but a fucking blue Prius almost ran him over.

"Motherfucker!" Angel screamed as the car sped away. He looked to his left. Coast was clear, so he stepped out in the street again, and the same pinche Prius clipped his hand coming the from the other direction, sending the knife clanking across the asphalt.

"What the fuck?" Angel grabbed his sore hand. The car was driving on the wrong side of the road. *Driver must be wasted.* Angel scurried into the street and picked up his blade in time to see the hybrid pull a 180 and come back at him.

"Shit!"

Angel got off the road. So did the car. It raced down the sidewalk, mowing down trashcans and shop displays to get to him.

Who is that? A gangbanger in a pinche Prius? He didn't have a lot of time to think about it. The hybrid was coming fast. Angel ran. He dodged a street sign, and the Prius crashed through it. It was right on top of him. *Do something!* He spun to his right, dodging the car like a bullfighter, and ran back the way he'd come. The car spun around and came at him again. Angel ducked into an alley, and the Prius zoomed by. Angel peeked out. The crazy car made a turn, and it was gone.

"Ho... ly... shit," Angel panted. Fuck the clothes. He was only a couple miles from home. He could make his way back on small streets. He jogged through the alley, but before he reached the end, the Prius zipped up and blocked his escape. *Goddammit!* Angel turned and ran, but pinche Priuses were made for pinche alleys, and it came at him full speed. Angel's legs started to give out. They were pretty shaky, what with having been dead and everything. His feet were getting torn up running on the craggy asphalt, and his chest hurt. He wasn't going to make it to the other end. He spotted a rusted metal dumpster. Giving it all he had, Angel sprinted to the big trash can and leapt inside just as the Prius crashed into it, rattling him against the trash bags and cardboard boxes inside.

The Prius didn't stop. Its tires burned rubber as it pushed the dumpster down the alley. Angel raised his head to get a look at the driver. Through the tinted windshield, he saw some old white dude with a shit-eating grin.

Who the fuck is that? Angel was about to yell something at him when they both shot out onto the street. Then this big fucking truck came out of nowhere and blew the Prius away and its crazy fucking driver, too.

Thank you, mister truck.

The dumpster spun around in circles and stopped in the middle of the road. Angel crawled out. He was banged up pretty bad. The scorpion flashed through his head. *The bug wants me back.* He tried to shake off the fear. *Get some cojones, dude! There's no giant bug. It was just some crazy dude in a hybrid. A dead crazy dude. The bug is not real.*

Angel stayed close to the dumpster, waiting for the traffic to clear long enough for him to get off the street. Up ahead, he saw the semi-truck screech to a stop. It shifted into reverse, trying to shake the Prius off his grill, but that mangled hunk of metal wasn't going nowhere. The truck driver must have seen Angel get out of the dumpster because he made a big-ass U-turn and started driving toward him. Angel didn't want to stick around to talk to no pinche truck driver about no accident, so he started to make his way to the sidewalk. The truck sped up. Sparks shot up from the mangled car's fender, scraping asphalt. Fucking thing looked like some mechanical fire-breathing dragon coming at him. It took Angel a second to realize that the truck driver didn't want to talk to him. He wanted to kill him.

The bug is real!

Angel ran. He heard explosions from the truck smashing into other cars as it got closer. Angel made it into a Salvadoran Market just as the truck crashed through the window, plowing into shelves, hurling produce everywhere.

Angel ran out the back, down small streets, and into a park where he curled up under some bushes and cried like a baby. Angel hadn't bawled like that since he was little and his mother would slap him and say, "Stop whining like a little bitch and kick some ass."

I can't, Mama. The bug's too big. I can't fight the bug. Why is this happening to me? Why, Mama? Why?

The dude in black, pendejo, answered the mother in his head. *He fucked you up.*

His mother was right. She was always right. That weird dude with his vest and his tie had shot him, stolen his money, messed up his homey, and locked him up with that scorpion and Rita— *fucking bitch.* Angel's fear turned to rage like fear usually does.

I'm gonna make that dude fix me. Then I'm going to get my money, and my clothes, my phone, and I'm gonna waste his ass.

❧ ☙

Angel stood by the door to the dude's place. It was locked. If only he still had that knife, or a screwdriver, or something. He looked around for an open window. Then he heard a woman's voice, and he crouched down. He spotted the white chick from the lab standing on the corner, talking on her phone. *Órale, Mama.* He hadn't noticed how hot she was. He didn't know how long he'd been out of it, but he was all woke up now. He wanted this chick bad, which was perfect, 'cause now they could have a little fun and then he'd force her to let him into the lab. Angel smiled, but then the pinche door flew open and whacked him in the face.

Jaime walked out from the building and headed toward the white chick. He walked slow like a zombie. *That dude really fucked you up, homey.* Angel grabbed the door before it closed. He watched Jaime try to catch the white chick, but she got in a cab and it drove away.

"Catch ya later, baby," Angel whispered. Then he slipped into the lab.

Chapter Fifty

Crowley gazed at Bonnie through the glass lid. She looked fresh and vibrant as if she could open her eyes at any moment and smile, but of course, she didn't. Not yet.

Sweat trickled down Crowley's brow. He had identified the symptoms of fear long ago—rapid heartbeat, shallow breathing, obsessive thought patterns, nausea. He had learned to observe them dispassionately and keep the emotion from clouding his judgment. He could not do that now. The magnitude of the moment breached his rational defenses. Crowley had spent most of his unnaturally long life working toward this day. From that first horrible night when the rabbi had rescued him—and throughout the years when they worked together and when Crowley had worked alone, perfecting the process and himself, shedding all earthly attachments—he had spent every waking moment searching for her. Today he would bring her back. Or not, and then his life would cease. He did not fear death. The justice of going to hell comforted him. The thought of partially succeeding and bringing back an abomination that he would have to destroy—*that* filled him with terror.

The time had come. It was now or never. He wiped his brow again and prepared to remove the glass lid.

She is in grave danger.

"I know what I'm doing, old man," Crowley said as he carefully unscrewed the clamps that kept the air-tight chamber sealed. "This elixir is pure."

You know who I am talking about, meyn zun.

"She'll be fine. She's smart."

Moloch comes.

"How many times have we heard that nonsense? The Half-Made lie. It's their modus operandi."

Moloch ze bull comes.

That stopped Crowley. He knew the legend, of course. The Old Testament warned the righteous about Moloch, the Canaanite god who sacrificed children. For many years, historians regarded the Bible's claim of human sacrifice as Hebrew propaganda against a rival god until they found the charred bones of children in the ruins of Carthage. Demons, satanists, and heavy metal bands with permed hair and impractically large penises embraced Moloch as their mascot, assuming that celebrating child murder made them edgy. Crowley thought it made them stupid. He had mocked many a demon when they mentioned the old god (mockery being one of the few pleasures Crowley allowed himself during his long, reclusive quest). Moloch was merely a legend, but...

He was the bull god.

Miss Horowitz' father and her great-grandfather, Jack Larson, had both surrounded themselves with bull paraphernalia—heads, horns, matadors. *A coincidence*, he told himself, and he resumed unfastening the coffin lid.

Why does Eliza's father possess ze Book of Thoth?

Crowley stopped again. "The girl said it came from you, old man."

The gentiles burned my library in ze pogrom. I had no ancient books. You know zat.

"Did you? Once?" Crowley asked. "Before the pogrom, did you own *The Book of Thoth*?"

The old rabbi did not answer because he was, after all, only a figment of Crowley's imagination. Crowley realized that he had never contemplated the book's origin. It could help him bring Bonnie back. Nothing else mattered to him. Perhaps it should have. Somehow, the girl's mediocre film producer father possessed the greatest tome of alchemical knowledge known to man, *and* he married a demon. Miss Horowitz' father could be an alchemist. Perhaps he planned to summon Moloch. It did not matter if Moloch really existed. It only mattered that someone *believed* that he did. Faith moved mountains. It built pyramids, cathedrals, and democracies. It also burned witches and gassed Jews. If Eliza's father believed in Moloch, if he summoned demons like his wife into this world to serve him, if he convinced others to believe...

"The elixir is ready *now*, old man!" protested Crowley. "It took almost a century for the universe to align itself so perfectly, to find the book and the girl, to open the gates. They won't stay open long. Even now, I can feel the elixir's power fading."

The demon will kill her.

"She's managed to survive this long."

She has found ze wound between worlds.

"Thankfully she could not mend it."

So, you will bring Bonnie back to life in zis world full of hellish fiends?

"I'll heal the wound later."

How will you do zis without Eliza?

"To hell with her!" Crowley cried. "I have sacrificed lifetimes to rescue my *only* child. You think I won't sacrifice some wanton teenager and her father and everybody in this cursed world? May they all rot in hell!"

Crowley laid his forehead on the glass and stared at Bonnie. After a long silence, the old man whispered.

Is one dead child not enough?

"Curses!" Crowley shouted and slammed his palm against the thick glass. With a defeated growl, he resealed the sarcophagus and walked up the stairs.

Chapter Fifty-One

Angel hid behind a bunch of dead lizards in glass jars, watching the dude messing with test tubes and shit. For the first time since he woke up, Angel was glad that he had no shoes on, 'cause now he could creep up behind the dude super quiet with the knife that he found in a sink. Angel had never stuck nobody. He had a Glock, two Berettas, a snub-nose .38, and an AR-15. He didn't need no pinche blade. But he didn't have his guns now, and that dude had the biggest fucking revolver he'd ever seen.

Then he got lucky. The dude took his gun out from behind his back and set it on a table. Angel moved quick. He snatched the gun, and when the dude turned around, he whacked him upside the head with it. The guy staggered back and got ready to come at Angel, but he stopped when he saw his own gun pointed at his chest. Angel could see him figuring out if he was close enough to grab it before he got shot. Angel cocked the gun, and the dude realized his chances weren't so good.

"What the fuck did you do to me?" Angel demanded.

"I brought you back to life," the dude said all calm, like this kind of shit happened all the time.

"After you killed me."

"You drew a gun on me."

"You didn't give me my money."

"You want the money?"

"You bet your ass I do. And I want you to make it go away."

"What?"

"The scorpion, cabrón."

"I can't do that."

"Why not?"

"Because it's *your* scorpion. You created it. Only you can kill it."

Angel tilted the gun to one side like you do when you're shooting a semi-automatic out a car window so the shells fly over the roof of the car. He wasn't in a car, and shells didn't fly out of revolvers, but it looked cool anyway. "Don't fuck with me, man. There weren't no giant bug 'til you shot me. You drugged me, didn't you? What you give me? This?" Angel picked up a bottle full of blue liquid and threw it against the wall, shattering it to pieces. "This?" he yelled, grabbing a tiny bottle with some red powder.

"Don't touch that!" yelled the dude.

"Whoa. Is this the good shit?" Angel raised the bottle as if he were about to smash it on the floor.

"Don't! I'll take away the scorpion. I'll fix everything!"

"Bullshit." Angel was about to throw the bottle when the dude rushed him. He grabbed the arm holding the bottle. He should have grabbed the arm with the gun, 'cause Angel used it to bash him in the head again. The dude went down hard.

"You're just a big pussy," Angel said and kicked the dude in the head, knocking him onto his back. He blinked up at Angel all goofy-like, blood oozing out his nose. Angel aimed the gun at his head. "Nobody fucks with me." He was about to blow the dude's face off when something bumped into him from behind. He whipped around. It was Jaime.

"Bro! Don't sneak up on me. I almost wasted you!"

Jaime didn't look like he knew what Angel was saying.

"Hey, dumbshit. You understand me?"

Jaime raised his arm in the air and said, "Ree-ta." Then he brought his fist down on Angel's head.

Angel's in his old room. The scorpion crashes through the window, shakes the glass off its back and closes in.
Not again.

Chapter Fifty-Two

Jaime may have hit Angel a little too hard. He didn't mean to break him. He just thought about Rita and how she was all black and blue and begging Jaime for help, and it pissed him off. But, like that cartoon moose used to say to the squirrel, "Guess I don't know my own strength." Jaime had always been strong, but going to hell had made him like Superman or something.

He watched Badass Undertaker Dude crawling on the floor and grabbing a little bottle out of Angel's dead hand. Then he tried to stand up, but he was real wobbly. Angel must have kicked him real good. He held out his hand to Jaime. "Help me."

He looked so pitiful with his nose all bloody that Jaime gave him a hand. The dude stumbled over to a table, poured the powder into a plastic baggie, and held it up to the light. Then he stood still for a long time like he was thinking, which he probably was. Jaime looked down at Angel. *Why do people look like babies when they're dead?* Sandy wouldn't like that Jaime had killed his best friend. Even if he didn't mean to do it, she still probably wouldn't want to go out with him. Then he remembered that he was dead and Sandy wasn't, so he couldn't go out with her anyway. That made Jaime sad.

The other girl, the one Jaime thought was Sandy until she told him she wasn't while they were on the boat, she seemed pretty cool for someone in hell. Maybe she'd go out with him. "Eee-lie-zaah," he said out loud.

Badass Undertaker Dude looked at him all surprised. "Very well," he said. Jaime had no idea why. He couldn't understand most of the stuff the dude did. "Take your friend to the freezer," he said.

Fuck you, thought Jaime, but then Badass Undertaker Dude said something he'd never said before.

"Please."

Okay then. They shouldn't leave Angel on the floor anyway. The girl who wasn't Sandy might see him and think that he killed Angel on purpose and not want to date him, or she might want to date him more, which would make her kind of crazy, so they couldn't hook up long term, unless the sex was really, really good; then, you know, whatever.

But before Jaime could pick Angel up, he heard this real loud scream. Badass Undertaker Dude looked behind Jaime and said, "Curses."

Jaime turned around and saw all these pinche skeletons, like from a haunted house or something, running at him. *This is more like it*, Jaime thought as the skeletons knocked him on his ass and started scratching and chewing on him.

Now this is hell.

Chapter Fifty-Three

"I am the lord of darkness come forth from the underworld to rule mankind!"

Ethan stood with his arms held high as his skeletal minions destroyed Oliver Crowley and his tattooed henchman.

Until Crowley shouted, "Sedeo!" And his whole zombie army sat down.

"What are you doing?" Ethan screamed at the zombies. "Get up!"

The zombies clattered back to their feet.

"Sedeo," said Crowley, and they sat down again.

"Up!" shouted Ethan.

"Sedeo," Crowley repeated with a bored sigh. "We can do this all day."

"But, they're *my* army. They obey *me*," whined Ethan.

"They obey everybody. They're mindless drones. Ideal maintenance workers."

"That's not fair."

"You look terrible, young man. Where have you been?"

"I spent forty days and forty nights in hell!"

"I saw you in the bathroom a week ago."

"It's a metaphor! I completed the hero's journey. I survived my ordeal in the underworld, and now I am back to kill my father and fulfill my destiny!"

"I am not—"

"It's a metaphor!"

"Calm down. You need food. Would you like some Salisbury steak?"

"Yes, I would!" he shouted angrily. He looked around. "Where's Eliza?"

"She's gone."

"Oh, man!" He stomped his feet like an angry toddler.

"She may be in grave danger. Exurgo!" The tattooed goon stood up. The zombies had taken a few bites out of him, but that didn't seem to bother him.

"Where are you going?" Ethan asked.

"Her father's house."

"I'll go with you."

"No, you won't. You will walk to that freezer and get a TV dinner. Do you know how to use a microwave oven?"

"I'm not an idiot."

"Yes, you are. You cannot win a lady's heart by pestering her like a mosquito, my boy. If we survive the next twenty-four hours, I will give you some valuable advice. Now, eat."

The zombie army began biting one another.

"Not you," Crowley barked.

"Eee-lie-zaa," moaned the tattooed guy.

"Yes. Sequi me," Crowley told the big guy. Then he turned to this monkey with a big dick, who was sitting on a shelf, and said, "Et vos," and they all walked away.

Ethan clenched his fists. "You may have won this round, Professor Crowley, but I will have you in the end!" He laughed like a diabolical madman until he realized that what he'd said wasn't all that funny.

He popped a frozen dinner into the microwave and calculated his next move.

Chapter Fifty-Four

Why can't I get through the door? Eliza had stood on that porch, with all the happy people inside the house, so many times, but she never managed to join them. She understood the metaphor, of course. Her mother had dragged her from house to house, stepfather to stepfather, making her long for the happy home she never had, but the doorway signified more than her troubled childhood. It was the key to this whole mess. *It's the gate to hell.* She needed to understand it. Why was everyone in her dream dead? Why did everything disappear the moment she opened the door? Eliza could feel the answer coming to her. She was right on the verge of seeing it when something hit the taxi from behind. Eliza turned and saw a gigantic rhinoceros-like skeleton with flames shooting from his nose and eyes. It hit them again, showering the taxi with sizzling sparks.

"Faster!" Eliza yelled at the driver. The old man behind the wheel smiled serenely and sped up, leaving the beast behind.

The driver's placid reaction unnerved Eliza. Did he see the demon? Was the driver a demon? Eliza took a deep breath. It didn't matter as long as she made it to her father's house. Her father wouldn't betray her like Oliver Crowley had. He would protect her.

If he can. "Please let him be all right," she murmured to herself. If anything happened to him, Eliza would blame herself. She had started this mess. She knew that the tear in the universe, the demons, Aurora, they all centered around her. She knew she could fix it somehow, but how? *Why can't I get into that house?*

Something landed on the roof of the cab. "Faster!" shouted Eliza. The obliging driver hit the gas, and something tumbled down the back of the car onto the street. Eliza didn't look back. Out of sight, out of mind.

I need the Book of Thoth. Thoth had to know about gates of hell. *He's a friggin' god, for God's sake.* If *he* couldn't help her, who could?

※ ※

A huge crowd of young people blocked the canyon road that led to her father's house. They carried signs that read Our Time, Burn Down the System, and The World Belongs to Us, while chanting, "Burn, burn, burn!" Eliza didn't know what they wanted to burn, nor did she care. She just wanted them gone.

The cab driver showed admirable tenacity by easing the car through the throng slowly. As they inched forward, Eliza saw a couple of students from the Literature Department and a girl from Honduras who had taken a Shakespeare class with her last quarter. She had hardly spoken English back then. Now, she was perched on a guy's shoulders yelling "Fuck" at the top of her lungs.

The American Dream.

Eliza didn't know what had made the students so angry until she saw several hairy giants marching with them. The ogres, or trolls—Eliza never understood the difference—stood more than twice the height of a human being. They had massive, sloped shoulders and muscular arms that they waved in the air, egging the crowd forward like a squad of Neanderthal cheerleaders. Students made way for the beasts, waving them on. *They see the demons. This can't be good.*

The driver stopped before the gates to her father's house, which was mobbed with students, and honked his horn, which sounded more like a roar. Students backed away from the cab. An ogre stomped up to Eliza's window and bent down to peer at her with squinty black eyes. Globs of saliva oozed onto its grizzled beard, and its breath fogged up the taxi window. It grinned.

Eliza backed away. "Do you see this?" Eliza asked the driver.

The driver didn't respond. He just kept looking straight ahead with the same friendly smile he had sported throughout the drive. A cloud of smoke engulfed Eliza. When it cleared, she found herself sitting atop a scaly, creature of some kind that reeked of sewage and tar. Even as Eliza screamed and scrambled off the reptilian monster, a part of her mind remained lucid enough to quip, *No tip for you.*

"You whore!"

Eliza spun away from the monster taxi and found a wild-eyed young woman with a mane of tangled black hair glaring at her.

"Tammy?"

"He's mine!" she screamed as she grabbed Eliza by the hair.

"Tammy! What are you doing?" Eliza cried.

Her roommate responded by trying to bite Eliza's face. Eliza twisted away from Tammy's teeth, but the crazed young woman kept hold of her hair. Eliza jammed her hand into Tammy's neck to hold her off. She watched in horror as her rabid roommate growled and snapped, her eyes flared with bloodlust—no, that wasn't the word... *pleasure*, that was it. This lunatic found Eliza's fear amusing.

But Eliza wasn't afraid. She was angry, and she was strong. She tightened her grip on Tammy's neck. The girl's eyes widened as Eliza squeezed. She released Eliza's hair and tried to pry her hands off her neck, but Eliza held on tightly. Tammy's mouth slackened. She gasped for air. Eliza pressed harder, drawing on a bottomless reservoir of rage born of all the times her mother had forced her to move to a new city, every school play and soccer game that her father had not attended, every frat guy who tried to get into her pants, every grown man who had rejected her, and every goddamn romantic comedy where the two stars ended up living happily ever after—as if the audience didn't know that they would from the start, as if anyone, anywhere had ever been or could ever be happy.

Eliza decided to kill Tammy.

"Stop!" yelled a megaphoned voice.

The crowd parted to make way for a good-looking young man carrying a bullhorn.

"Ryan?" Eliza asked incredulously, releasing Tammy, who staggered away sucking air into her lungs.

"Eliza, are you all right?" Ryan asked with genuine concern.

Eliza looked around. Students stood by, silently watching her. Beyond them, she could see the gate to her father's house.

"No," she admitted, trying not to cry. "My father lives here. I want to go inside."

"Of course," he reassured her gently. "Make way," he said without the aid of his bullhorn, and students cleared a path for her.

"What's going on, Ryan? Why's everyone so mad? Why are you at my dad's house?"

"No one's mad. This is a celebration!" he exclaimed while several students dragged Tammy away.

"Celebration of what?" she asked.

"You," he replied with a smile.

Eliza refrained from asking what the hell he meant. Ryan had probably fallen under a demonic spell like everyone else. She forced herself to smile and chirped, "Cool," before she ran to the front gate, punched in the code and entered her father's property.

☙ ❧

"Daddy!" Eliza yelled as she ran into the house.

Margarita appeared atop the stairs dressed in black with her hair tightly braided into a bun like Mrs. Danvers in Alfred Hitchcock's *Rebecca*.

"Margarita! Where's Daddy? Is he okay?"

Margarita clutched her hands over her chest and in a booming operatic voice, she began to sing the song from Eliza's dream. *"Sweet baby girl..."*

"What are you doing?"

"Wishing you a happy birthday," Margarita replied innocuously.

"Where's Daddy?"

"In the temple."

Eliza ran from the woman, who had obviously gone crazy just like everyone else.

"Little Lamb!" Margarita cried behind her. "Your dress!"

Eliza ignored her and rushed in the direction of the backyard, but she stopped short when she heard dramatic piano music coming from her father's screening room. She peeked inside and saw an old silent film playing on the screen with no one watching. The sight of a melodramatic actress gesticulating wildly would normally have made Eliza laugh. Today, it frightened her.

She sprinted into the garden and found her father, beneath the Grecian rotunda, watching the sun set behind the mountains.

"Daddy!" she shouted.

"Bubelah!" he cried and raced down to hug her.

"Are you all right?" Eliza asked holding him tightly.

"Me?" Jerry cried as he stepped back to examine her. "Are *you* all right? You have no idea what you put me through."

"I'm sorry, Daddy. I'm okay."

"Did that man hurt you or molest you?"

"He didn't touch me."

Jerry Horowitz let out a tremendous sigh of relief and threw his arms around her again.

"Where's Aurora?" she asked while he kissed her forehead.

"It doesn't matter."

"Yes, it does. I need the *Book of Thoth*."

"Bubelah, if anything had happened to you, my life would have been over."

"Where's the book?"

"The book doesn't matter anymore. Nothing does. Just you. Twenty years ago, on this night, you came into this world."

The crowd outside roared.

"Daddy! Listen to me. Horrible things are happening. I know you don't believe me, but there are demons out there and ogres—or trolls, I don't know which."

"Ogres," said her father.

Eliza froze. "What?"

"They're ogres. French. Generally larger than the Scandinavian trolls."

"You see the ogres?" she asked.

"Of course," he replied innocently.

"And the demons?"

He nodded.

"But you said you didn't. You didn't believe me about Aurora. Do you know about her?"

Jerry gazed at her with sad, loving eyes. "Eliza."

A bolt of dread shot up her spine. "Have you known all along?"

"My one and only. I love you more than I have ever loved anything in this terrible world. You cannot possibly know the joy you have brought me."

A long black blade appeared in Jerry's hand. "And the heartache."

Eliza stepped back. "What are you doing?"

His eyes filled with tears, and he stepped closer to Eliza.

"Daddy! Stop! Listen to me! The gates of hell are open. People are going insane. You don't know what you're doing!"

"Oh, but he does," purred a sultry voice.

Eliza spun around. Aurora stood before her wearing a black hooded cloak. The beautiful demon's jaw dropped open grotesquely and snakes spewed from her throat onto Eliza's face. She screamed and flailed, trying to disentangle herself from the slimy serpents, but more came, winding around her torso, arms, and legs, binding her to the columns of the rotunda.

Flames burst into the sky all around her. The mob cheered. Aurora laughed.

Chapter Fifty-Five

Jaime liked this car. It was a '64 or '65 Chevrolet Impala with a mint green interior and a V-8 that purred like a tiger. Jaime couldn't believe that Badass Undertaker Dude had let him drive it. *Angel must have kicked him in the head real good.* At first, Jaime thought he wouldn't be able to do it, what with him being dead and all, but it all came back to him like he'd been driving this car all his life.

"Faster," said Badass Undertaker Dude.

I can't go faster than the cars in front of me, Jaime replied in his head, but his mouth said, "Uh!"

Badass Undertaker Dude rubbed his temples. "Please do not shout."

Jaime sped up a little.

"Turn right here."

Puta madre, this guy's as big a pain in the ass as Angel.

Jaime turned onto a winding road with swanky mansions all around. He remembered this place from when Sandy—*Eliza*—drove them up here.

"Curses," Badass Undertaker Dude said, 'cause there were all these people blocking the road, dancing and yelling and shit.

Little Cholo jumped on Jaime's shoulder and whispered, "Kill them all."

"Uh," laughed Jaime.

Badass Undertaker Dude leaned over and hit the horn, which was a big mistake 'cause everyone went nuts and started banging on the car. Jaime kinda felt sorry for Badass Undertaker Dude 'cause they were gonna wreck his super-fine lowrider. If it had been his car, he'd have gone out there and kicked some ass, but it wasn't his car, 'cause even though it looked just like it, his car had the Virgin of Guadalupe and two plastic boobs hanging from the rearview mirror.

The mob started bouncing the car up and down real hard, and something rolled off the dashboard onto Jaime's lap.

A pair of plastic boobs.

"Kill them now," whispered Little Cholo.

Jaime jammed the car into neutral and revved up the engine. He was going to plow through those motherfuckers.

"No!" yelled Badass Undertaker Dude. "You'll kill somebody."

Little Cholo clapped his hands all happy and shit. "Kill, kill, kill!"

"Just back up slowly."

Jaime growled, but he did what the dude said. Then the car hit something hard. Jaime looked in the rearview mirror and saw two hairy trees. Then the trees moved 'cause they weren't trees. They were legs, and they belonged to this huge dude who stomped over to his side of the car, ripped off the door, and dragged Jaime out. Jaime was big, but he only came up to this dude's belly. The giant grabbed him around the neck with one big-ass hand and lifted him up in the air. He brought Jaime's face close to his and sniffed. Then he made this ugly face like Jaime smelled bad, so Jaime punched him in the eye. The giant roared and threw Jaime through a brick wall.

Good thing I'm dead or that woulda hurt.

Jaime was lying under a pile of bricks, and he thought, *This is nice.* Jaime would have stayed there forever if this voice in his head hadn't said, *Help!* It was Badass Undertaker Dude. The ugly giant was probably killing him. *I guess I should go watch.* Jaime knocked the bricks off himself and stomped back to the street. The giant had smashed up his beautiful car and left. He'd probably killed Badass Undertaker Dude and Little Cholo, too. Jaime wanted to cry.

He loved that car.

Chapter Fifty-Six

Crowley waded through the mass of crazed students with the homunculus perched on his shoulder.

"Omnes interficere," whispered the homunculus.

"Nondum," replied Crowley.

"Professor Crowley!" shrieked a protester.

Crowley ignored her. "Professor!" yelled another student, then another, and another. Students began crowding around him. They would have pilloried any other teacher who dared crash their rally, but Crowley's contempt for humanity validated their youthful cynicism, making him the only professor they trusted. They wrapped their arms around him, pumped their fists in the air, and chanted "Crowley! Crowley!" Soon, he had a private bodyguard propelling him through the crowd toward the Horowitz house.

The homunculus bared his teeth and snarled. The mob found him adorable. They laughed and cooed at him in baby talk.

"Volo enim vos omnes occidere," he whined.

"How could you possibly kill them all?" Crowley snorted.

The homunculus shrugged.

"Next time, plan ahead."

The homunculus lowered his head in shame.

When Crowley reached the front gate, a young woman threw her arms around his neck and kissed him. Crowley pushed her away.

"Professor!" cried Miss Horowitz' roommate. "I knew you'd come!"

"No, you didn't," Crowley replied matter-of-factly. "I need to see the owner of this house."

"He's not accepting visitors," said a young man who looked like he had just stepped off his father's yacht.

"It's quite important," Crowley assured him.

The hale young man smiled pompously. "This is a gathering for young people, Professor. I'm afraid that—" The young man stopped mid-sentence and cocked his head. A second later, Crowley heard an ear-piercing screech. He looked up and saw an enormous black beast—part dog, part vulture—gliding over the house. Crowley did not find the creature particularly remarkable. It looked like your run-of-the-mill demonic abomination. What disturbed Crowley was the young man's reaction. He saw the demon without looking.

The boundary between the material and the ethereal had blurred. Worlds were merging. Hell had come. Crowley gave the student his most withering glare. "Moloch awaits me. Do not disappoint him."

The young man drew back in fear. He nodded to a group of shirtless male students, and they opened the gates. Crowley brushed passed them and entered the property.

༄ ༅

The sight of Miss Horowitz strung up like a hog for slaughter amidst the flames and the shouts sent Crowley reeling back, one step, then two, then one hundred years to another fire at another mansion atop a hill.

Once again, he felt the heat of the explosion tearing through the roof of his movie-star home. He felt the crush of sequined gowns and tuxedos. He smelled the smoke. He looked into the milky dead eyes of the brute who clutched his throat. He saw Dolores, broken on the floor, books burning, and Oliver trapped beneath burning rafters, begging for him to find his son, which he never tried to do. He felt Bonnie's limp body in his arms as he carried her outside.

The old derelict had said something to him that night, but he hadn't heard it over the roaring fire. It didn't matter. When the old man strode off, Delamour had held Bonnie tightly and followed, putting one foot in front of the other, letting gravity drag him down the hill, away from the burning house, through a firelit maze of manzanita, sagebrush, and stone until they reached a shadowy figure smoking a cigarette beside a parked car. The glowing ember lit up his face.

Rudolf Valentino.

"We almost left you!" he scoffed at the derelict in his sing-song Italian accent. He stiffened when he saw that the old man was not alone. "Charles?"

Valentino knocked on the car window and signaled his wife, Natacha Rambova, who stepped out holding a handkerchief over her nose. She lowered it when she saw the girl.

"Oh, no." She reached out to touch Bonnie, but Delamour pulled her away. "It's okay, Charles," she said. "We'll take her to a doctor." She looked to the old man, who shook his head sadly.

"And your son?" she asked.

The old man wiped a tear from his grizzled cheek and, with a heavy Eastern European accent, declared, "We must go now. Very fast."

Natacha held open the car door. "Come, Charles. Maybe there's still something we can do."

While Rudolf Valentino drove them to his Beverly Hills estate, the old man explained that his name was Itzak Horowitz. He had recently come from Russia to find his son, Moshe, who had fled to America many years ago and changed his name to Jack Larson. The old man, whom Natacha referred to as Reb Horowitz, was an alchemist. So was Natacha. They belonged to a secret worldwide network dedicated to the mystic arts. When Reb Horowitz had come to Los Angeles, he stayed with his fellow mystic, Natacha, much to her movie-star husband's displeasure.

When they arrived at Valentino's estate, Natacha led Delamour and Reb Horowitz into her private laboratory behind the stables and laid Bonnie in a bathtub full of ice. The old man and Natacha cooked up some foul-smelling goo which they smeared onto Bonnie's forehead, chest, stomach, and feet. Reb Horowitz unwrapped a chunk of red stone from a silk cloth, chipped off a portion, ground it down in a mortar, and dissolved it in water. Using an eyedropper, he placed some of the liquid into Bonnie's mouth. Color returned to Bonnie's face, and a spark of life returned to Delamour as well. Reb Horowitz instructed him to take Bonnie out of the tub and lay her on a bed.

Horowitz drank some of the red liquid, sat beside Bonnie, and took her hand. The old man closed his eyes and sat perfectly still for a day and a half. Natacha told Delamour that he was searching for Bonnie in the other world. Delamour sat with them without eating or sleeping until Horowitz emerged from his spell and whispered, "Ze elixir is weak. She would not look at me. Someone she trusts must go to her. You, young man, you must find her." Delamour shook his head. He did not want to continue this charade. He would bury Bonnie properly and, if he had the courage, join her in death.

"I spoke to a woman in ze dream world who knows ze child," Horowitz continued. "A small dark woman. Mana or Mani..."

"Mina?" Delamour asked incredulously.

"Yes," replied Horowitz. "She says she looks for Bonnie, too. She had rabbits for her to play with, and she gave me zis." Horowitz pulled Bonnie's porcelain doll out from beneath his coat.

Over the years, Crowley would confirm the doll's ephemeral nature when it disappeared and reappeared randomly, usually at the most inopportune times.

When Bonnie's corpse had not decomposed in the slightest for three days, Delamour felt a shred of hope. With Natacha's help, they'd packed the girl in a passenger trunk and sailed through the Panama Canal to Europe. In Paris, Delamour discreetly transferred his savings to a Swiss bank. He purchased a new American Passport under the name Oliver Crowley, which he used to travel to Slomir, a sad little town in Belarus, where Crowley and the old man began years of labor that took them around the globe, eventually landing them back in Los Angeles, where their quest had begun. Over the years, Crowley had learned to control his emotions and detach from ordinary human concerns. Tonight, his training failed him.

He gasped for air as his thoughts flashed chaotically between past and present. It wasn't just the flames shooting up into the sky that took him back to that terrible night in 1925, or the screaming crowd around the property, or even the sight of another girl in peril. It was the man standing beside the girl, his face contorted in a demonic smile.

"Jack Larson."

Chapter Fifty-Seven

Crowley had only whispered the name, but somehow, over the rumbling flames and the young woman's screams, Jack Larson had heard him. Their eyes locked. Larson's face hardened.

"Charles," he growled.

"Professor!" cried the young woman. A snake coiled around her face. "Daddy—" she pleaded before the serpent covered her mouth.

"Shh, Bubelah. You'll hurt yourself."

Crowley strained to make sense of the scene before him. Jack Larson—a man he had watched die a hundred years ago—stood beside Miss Horowitz, and she called him Daddy. Judging by the snakes entwined around Miss Horowitz and the long knife in Larson's hand, she was in grave peril.

Moloch comes.

The realization of what Larson intended to do hit Crowley like a shot in the chest.

"Don't, Jack."

"Don't what?" Larson sneered.

"It won't work. This will not summon Moloch. There is no Moloch."

"There will be." Larson grinned.

"This demon," Crowley said, glancing at Larson's fiendish wife. "She's not your friend. She wants to destroy you."

"She's saved my life countless times."

Crowley thought back to the fire. "Jack, I saw you die."

"You saw what I wanted you to see."

Crowley stopped breathing. He pictured Larson atop the balcony, engulfed in flames. The man hadn't screamed or tried to escape. He looked resigned—no, *satisfied*.

"You... started the fire?" Crowley whispered.

"Of course. I needed to disappear. I left a burnt body with my identification. The world assumed Jack Larson had died, and I was free."

"You killed Bonnie."

"Who?"

Crowley pulled out his revolver and shot him.

The explosion echoed through the canyon. The girl screamed. Smoke filled the air. When it cleared, Larson's demonic partner stood before him. She opened her fist to reveal the bullet in her hand.

Crowley shot her in the face, and she turned into a lanky beauty with a Louise Brooks haircut. Crowley recognized her as one of Larson's girlfriends from long ago. He shot her again, and a stunning redhead appeared—another of Larson's silent era starlets. He shot her again and again, and each time she changed into different women from different eras—the 1930s, the '40s, '50s. He ran out of bullets, but she kept changing—the '60s, '70s, 2000s, until she resumed her most recent guise as Miss Horowitz' stepmother.

Aurora snatched the gun from Crowley and tossed it away. "You're fun," she purred. Her eyes vanished, leaving two empty black sockets. Her skin ignited with a sickly green light, and a thunderous voice tore through Crowley's head. It spoke in a language he had never heard and hoped never to hear again. It sounded like the wail of a fawn being torn apart by wolves. He could not make out the words, but he understood their meaning.

"Now and forever. I am."

Crowley stumbled backward. This creature was no ordinary demon, no Half-Made he could outwit and exploit. This was a primordial force, a cosmic archetype, unassailable and eternal.

A god.

Crowley forced himself to look away from her and focused on Larson. The little man had barely changed since he stood atop that burning balcony in 1925. He dressed differently, of course, and he had lost his Eastern European accent—*he's had time to practice*—but behind those seemingly placid eyes burned a fierce drive and something Crowley had not recognized before. *Fear.* This fearful little man thought he commanded the malevolent goddess at his side. The fool. She was obviously using him, but to what end?

"Jack. You started the fire to disappear. Why?"

"To get away from you, of course."

"Me?"

"And my father. He tracked me halfway around the world to get his precious book back, and you were helping him."

"What are you talking about?" Crowley asked, utterly confused.

"I saw him in your car, Charles. At the studio. The day you told me that you wanted to throw away your career to raise a bastard child. Did you really expect me to believe that? I knew you were up to something. Then I looked out my office window, and I saw my father in your car. That's when I knew I had to disappear."

"Your father was in my car?"

"Don't treat me like an idiot, Charles!"

"Yes. I remember now, but I promise you, Jack, I never spoke to your father until after the fire."

"So, you're not an alchemist? You're just an average one hundred thirty-year-old schmo who pals around with golems and homunculi? My father taught you the art, didn't he?"

"Yes," Crowley admitted. "Your father trained me, but only *after* Bonnie died. I swear to you."

Larson glowered. "Then you were a useful idiot."

"You were already an alchemist back then," Crowley realized. "Tweedle Dee and Tweedle Dum?"

"Golems, like the one you brought to my house."

Crowley glanced at the deity beside Larson. "Jack, has this creature duped you into trying to conjure Moloch?"

"I'm not going to conjure Moloch. I'm going to *become* Moloch."

She promised to make him a god. He'll rule the world, and she will rule him. "Jack, you're a fool."

Miss Horowitz struggled against her bonds. Crowley looked into her frightened eyes, peeking out from inside her serpent cocoon. Did she know what was happening? Could she sense the goddess's power? Crowley felt a pang of remorse. He had betrayed this young woman, so she ran to the only person in the world she thought she could trust. Crowley could have prevented this. He could have saved her.

"Inca priests sacrificed their children during famines," Larson explained. "Agamemnon sacrificed his daughter to save his fleet. Yahweh sacrificed his only son to save mankind. They loved their children so much that their terrible gift shook the world and laid heaven at their feet."

Larson caressed one of the snakes that confined his daughter. "The more painful the sacrifice," he continued forlornly, "the greater the reward. I conceived Eliza twenty years ago for this purpose, and when I offer her up to the gods, on the day she becomes a woman, still unsullied, as foretold in the epic of Gilgamesh and the sacred ziggurat of An, I shall restore the great pantheon my Hebrew ancestors destroyed. I shall rule over the true Olympus as Ba'al, Kronos, Moloch the bull. I shall restore order from chaos. Heaven and earth shall weep for me and worship me. I will be immortal."

Miss Horowitz moaned.

"I'm glad your father died before he saw this," Crowley spat.

"My father was pathetic."

"Your father was a great man. Honest and kind. He spoke of you often, all those years we worked together. He didn't come to California for the book. He came for you. To apologize."

"That's a lie."

"He loved you."

"He loved nothing! When the goyim came to my village, burning and killing, he hid in the temple. He let those monsters beat my mother to death while I watched. She begged me for help, but what could I do—a scrawny thirteen-year-old boy? My father could have stopped them. He had a golem. He could have killed them all, but no. He was afraid. That was when I learned the only truth in the universe—the strong live and the weak die. I vowed to be strong. I set fire to his house, burned all his books but one, his greatest treasure, the thing he spent his life studying while he ignored my mother and me. I took the book and came to America. I worked in sweatshops, while I learned the art, but I needed help. I needed a teacher. Then I found my angel."

The goddess gave him a loving smile.

She found him, more likely.

"With her help, I deciphered the book and so much more. She taught me secrets Thoth would not divulge."

"Thoth is a coward," Aurora snorted.

"She showed me the golden path," Larson pronounced as he raised the knife. Serpents slithered apart to expose Miss Horowitz' neck.

"No, Jack! There are other ways. I can help you. Together, we could create a new elixir—"

"Elixir? That sop prolongs life, but it won't make you immortal. Only blood can do that. I know. I have shed enough of it over the years, but none of it with the purity of my greatest love. My beautiful child."

"Daddy," Eliza pleaded in a strangled voice.

Larson's eyes welled with tears. The knife trembled in his hand. "There's no other way, my sweet baby girl."

"She's not a baby, Jack," Crowley interjected. "She's an intelligent young woman. She can read Chaldean; did you know that? She has a greater facility for archaic symbolism than anyone I've ever met, including your father. And, she's brave. She has gone to hell and faced demons that would have broken the strongest of men. She cares deeply and loves passionately, which takes more courage than anything. She can serve you much better alive than dead."

Tears poured down Larson's face. "No. Eliza's my little baby. I have to protect her from this terrible world. Better she leave it now before she learns that there are no angels or saviors, no Lancelots to sweep her away on a white horse."

"She prefers Arthur."

Eliza looked to Crowley. "You listened."

And her father cut her throat.

Chapter Fifty-Eight

First there was this big flash, and then there was this big earthquake, and this big ball of fire shot up in the air, and Jaime thought, *Whoa.* Then he thought...

Eliza.

All the pinche people cheered. One of the hairy giants bashed a hole in the wall, and everybody rushed through it. Jaime did, too. People were going around the sides of the house to get to where all the fire was, but Jaime smashed down the front door and went *through* the house. It was empty except for some loca in a black dress standing on the stairs singing opera or something. She was super creepy, which was cool, but Jaime didn't have time for crazy chicks right now.

Eliza.

Jaime smashed through a glass door and stomped into the backyard, around the pool that the babe threw him in, and up this hill where fire was shooting up into the sky like fireworks, and people were shouting. Jaime didn't know why until he saw the devil.

Finally!

The devil was sitting on this big old throne on top of this mountain of stone, and there were flames all around, but he wasn't burning up 'cause he was the devil. He was real big, and he was all swole up like he'd been liftin' heavy, and he was kind of brownish-red, and he had these big red eyes that looked like they were on fire, too, and he had horns, of course. Wouldn't be no devil if he didn't have horns. And he was shooting lightning bolts from his hands and crisscrossing them in the sky like spotlights at a movie premier, and he was yelling, "Freedom! Freedom!" And, the crowd was hollering, "Moloch! Moloch!" Jaime got all dizzy 'cause besides the big devil, there were thousands of tiny devils on everybody's cell phones, 'cause when the devil comes to town, you video that shit.

Jaime figured he better cheer, too, so the devil wouldn't get mad at him, but then he thought, *So what?* He was already in hell. What else could he do to him? Jaime had always done what people told him to. For once in his pinche life, he wasn't going to follow the crowd. He was going to do what *he* wanted to do.

Find Eliza.

Jaime shoved his way through all the people partying with giants and animals with heads that didn't match their bodies.

"The system is dead! Long live the first kingdom!" yelled the devil. The devil was loud.

Then Jaime heard this quiet voice in his head. *Help.* It was Badass Undertaker Dude. He wasn't dead. Jaime started looking for him. *Help.* People were really packed in tight around the devil, so Jaime had to bash some heads to get through. When he got close to the fire, which must have been super hot for dudes who weren't dead like him, he saw a gap in the crowd, like people didn't want to step on something nasty. Jaime shoved his way closer, and there was Badass Undertaker Dude, down on his knees, bowing to the devil. He must have gotten cut up or something, 'cause when he looked up at Jaime, his hands were all bloody.

"Help," he said.

Then Jaime saw that Badass Undertaker Dude wasn't cut, and he wasn't bowing. He'd been keeping people from stepping on someone.

"Ee-lie-zah," Jaime moaned.

Jaime had seen a lot of messed up things in his life. He'd seen guys crying like babies when they got shot. He saw Manny El Loco fall from the Fourth Street bridge and pop like a blood balloon on the street. He saw pictures of Rita when they pulled her out of the dumpster. But he'd never seen anything more messed up than this. Maybe it was because Eliza looked like Sandy, or because she'd been nice to him, or because she was real ballsy, but mostly it was the look on her face. She looked like one of those black velvet paintings of kids with really big eyes that they sold at the gas station on Whittier and Soto next to the fake Persian rugs. Jaime couldn't look at those things for too long 'cause they made him feel all achy and shit, like he should do something to help those kids, but they were just stupid paintings so he couldn't do nothing.

Jaime felt like that now.

"Blessed be the children of the new kingdom!" shouted the devil.

Badass Undertaker Dude picked up Eliza and held her head to his chest so it wouldn't flop around. "Please, help me get her inside."

Jaime charged back to the house with Badass Undertaker Dude right behind him. People cussed and yelled when he crashed into them, but they made good progress until he smacked into this big, hairy thing. Jaime looked up and saw that it was a giant's belly. The giant smiled down at him and asked in a weird squeaky voice, "Going somewhere, are we?" Jaime couldn't tell if it was a boy giant or girl giant, so he punched it in the groin. It squealed and fell down on his knees.

It was a boy.

"Hurry!" shouted Badass Undertaker Dude, and Jaime started going again, but then there was this loud siren. *5-0!* Jaime looked around for a police car. Fortunately, the noise was just coming from a monster that plopped down in front of them. This guy had bat wings and all these horns sticking out of his head and this really ugly, hairy face with big crazy eyes, and he was screaming like a fire engine or something. He had pretty big teeth, too.

"Run!" shouted Badass Undertaker Dude, so Jaime ran, but Badass Undertaker Dude didn't say which way to go, so Jaime ran straight into the monster and knocked him down. Then the monster bit Jaime's shoulder. It didn't hurt, but part of his shoulder was gone along with his tattoo of Jesus downing a Schlitz Malt Liquor tall, which Jaime loved 'cause Jesus may be God and all, but he's also a cool dude. Jaime got pissed. *Don't fuck with Jesus, monster man.* Jaime knew how to wrestle. He hugged monster man close so he couldn't bite him again, but then the monster whacked him in the head with his tail. Jaime hadn't seen no pinche tail. The monster kept whipping it around, whacking Jaime. Then he wrapped it around Jaime's neck and began to squeeze. *Good thing I don't breathe,* he thought, but then Jaime heard bones in his neck crack, and he realized that monster man wasn't trying to choke him out, he was trying to rip his head off. *This sucks.* Jaime didn't want to be no lame head rolling around the grass with no body.

Then Little Cholo came out of nowhere and climbed onto his shoulder. *Great,* thought Jaime. *He'll save me.* But, Little Cholo just started poking Jaime in the eyes and laughing. Normally, Jaime would have laughed, too, but at that particular moment it was pretty annoying. Jaime might be dead, but he still needed his eyes to see.

Then Little Cholo ran away, and the monster stopped yanking on his head. Jaime didn't know why until he saw all these skeletons climbing all over the monster, biting his head and arms and ass.

Hell sure is loco.

Monster Man started swinging his tail around trying to knock the skeletons off him, but those skeletons wouldn't let go. They grabbed his wings, and the monster went nuts. He tried to fly away, but the skeletons weighed him down, so the monster just took off running with skeletons hanging all over him.

Then the skinny punk from before walked up and yelled something Jaime couldn't understand, and all the skeletons came back and stood at attention like a super creepy army. Jaime thought that was cool until the punk pointed at him, and the skeletons jumped all over *him*, biting and shit. Then Badass Undertaker Dude yelled, "Stop!" and the skeletons stopped.

Jaime thought Badass Undertaker Dude had run off without him, but he was still there with Eliza, probably because there were tons of people between him and the house. The skinny punk stomped around, all angry and shit, until he saw Eliza. Then he got real quiet.

"Give Moloch thy seed and thou shalt be free!" yelled the devil. The punk noticed the devil for the first time, and he did like in the old cartoons where the coyote's mouth drops open and his eyes pop out of his head.

"Please, help me get her inside," asked Badass Undertaker Dude.

The skinny punk started freaking out pretty bad, but he did what Badass Undertaker Dude said. The skeletons pushed punks out of the way, and they all went into the house.

Chapter Fifty-Nine

Crowley carried Miss Horowitz past the maid, who stood atop the staircase singing a surprisingly adept rendition of "Someday My Prince Will Come," and into an empty room where a most unpleasant surprise awaited him:

Charles Delamour.

Crowley had entered Jack Larson's private screening room where *The Pirate King*, starring Charles Delamour, was playing. Crowley paused to watch Delamour stab one Moor after another—all played by white men in blackface—while diving over tables, swinging on chandeliers, and making suggestive faces at Mary Miles Minter.

Poor Mary. Crowley hadn't thought of her in years. She had needed a friend. Instead, she got a fatuous opportunist who discarded her the moment she no longer served his career.

Watching Delamour kill people, Crowley remembered that the fight sequence had taken two days to film because Delamour couldn't decide which colored scarf to wear around his head, as if color mattered in a black-and-white film, as if a movie star's problems mattered, as if *anything* mattered.

You killed another girl.

Crowley laid Miss Horowitz down in front of the screen. Blood gurgled from the cut in her throat. She was white and ice cold. "Bar the doors," he ordered the skeletons. "Bring water," he instructed the skinny young man.

"Water? We gotta call 911!" He reached into his pocket, then wailed, "My legions took my phone!"

"Breathe, young man," Crowley said evenly and pointed to a wet bar behind the seats. "Please, bring me a glass of water."

"Okay, okay, okay," the young man said, panting, and ran to the bar.

The homunculus squeezed past the skeletons dragging Crowley's revolver. "Ego sum iens ut interficias omnis ex vobis!" he cried as he tried to lift the gun, but it was too heavy for him. Crowley snatched it away.

"Gratias."

Crowley shoved the revolver into his belt and bent over the young woman. He should have helped her close the gates of hell. He should have protected her. Perhaps he could still save her, but he only had enough elixir for Bonnie, and its potency wouldn't last. He could already feel the powder cooling in his pocket.

For one hundred years, Crowley had labored obsessively, venturing to the darkest corners of the earth and the foulest depths of hell, only to revive one brain-dead abomination after another. Regular doses of the elixir had slowed his metabolic aging, but spiritually, he was an old man. Each failure eroded his resolve until he had lost all hope of saving Bonnie, but still he kept trying, day after day, year after year. His work became his penance. He could not stop until he died, and he could not die until he had paid for his crime.

The only thing that gave Crowley any pleasure was the class he taught each spring. Yes, he treated the students harshly, but secretly, he admired them. They sparkled with energy. They laughed too hard and worried too much. They devoured life as if it were a glorious feast prepared just for them. Crowley envied their passion, but he could not share it. He had lost his taste for life long ago.

Then this girl showed up. Because of her, he had brought a healthy human being back to life for the first time. Of course, he didn't know if he had succeeded completely. If the corpse hadn't killed him, Angel Matamoros might have dropped dead in a couple of days or grown two heads—something Crowley had seen before and did not care to see again—but it was without question the greatest accomplishment of his life. Crowley had to try to bring Bonnie back tonight. He would not get another chance.

The skinny young man brought him water. Crowley drank half of it. Confronting evil gods and studio executives had made him thirsty. *Time to go.* He had failed to save Miss Horowitz. He must not fail Bonnie.

You did this to her.

"No, old man. Jack Larson had planned to sacrifice the girl from the day she was born."

You stole the book.

"She gave it to me. She was an adult. She bears responsibility for her actions."

Of course, he could not have made the elixir without her help. If he brought Miss Horowitz back to life, they could make more elixir, couldn't they? Not likely. One did not *make* the elixir of life so much as beckon it. The elixir was a confluence of intention, chemistry, space-time, grace, and luck. It might take decades for the universe to align itself properly to call forth elixir as potent as the one he now held in his hand. Crowley had to awaken Bonnie tonight or never.

"Leave now! Go to Bonnie!" he shouted to himself.

Unfortunately, Crowley's body did not obey his command, and he was surprised to see that he had already dissolved the red powder into the glass of water and poured half of it into Miss Horowitz' mouth.

Curses.

Crowley took one last look at Charles Delamour on the screen, laughing atop a pile of dead Moors, and he drank the last of the elixir.

Chapter Sixty

Oliver Crowley climbs through knee-high oat grass, past golden poppies and purple shooting stars, toward a small white house perched high atop a cliff. A verdant river valley ringed by pine-crested mountains lies to the east. To the west, the golden sun turns the ocean purple and red. He takes a deep breath. The smell of sea and meadow make his chest ache for a past that he can barely remember let alone reclaim.

Is this Miss Horowitz' afterlife?

Crowley recognizes the house from his childhood, or was it a dream? It's an old adobe cottage, a type of structure that Crowley had only seen in ruins or replicated in concrete and plaster by the Americanos. Yet, this house looks new, with freshly whitewashed walls, bright blue shutters and a sturdy wooden porch. An old-fashioned swing hangs from a giant oak tree that casts dappled shadows over the front door. A lazy wisp of smoke rises from the chimney.

Crowley's chest tightens. His jaw quivers. He finds each step harder to take than the last. Demons lurk in that house that do not belong to Miss Horowitz. They are his. He shuts his eyes to clear his mind. When he opens them again, he's at the front door.

Crowley lurches back from the porch.

He has traveled through Europe, the Middle East and China. He has seen men blown apart by artillery and women shot by firing squads. He has barely escaped enslavement by Ruwalla tribesmen in Syria and execution by the Imperial Japanese Army in Shanghai. He has confronted demons both real and imagined, but he has never felt this kind of fear before. Crowley realizes that he has spent his entire life steeling his heart for this moment, and it hasn't been enough. This, he cannot face.

He hears something rustle. He peeks around the oak tree and finds a white rabbit poking its head out of the tall grass. The rabbit glares at him with fearless curiosity.

"That's Buster," says a girl.

Crowley spins around, and there, on the porch, stands Bonnie. Crowley's legs give way, and he falls back against the tree.

Bonnie wears the same mismatched outfit she picked out for herself all those years ago. Her wavy dark hair is pulled back into a ponytail except for an errant strand that dangles over one of her big blue eyes. She blows the hair out of her face and smiles. "Do you have a carrot?"

The lump in Crowley's throat prevents him from replying. He had followed Miss Horowitz to her afterlife but somehow found his own. After decades of sacrifice and failure, Bonnie stands before him, and he doesn't know what to do. He had once fantasized about raising Bonnie should she return. He had envisioned her room, the vacations, gifts, schools. He had rehearsed his apology for the past and his promises for the future. But that had been so long ago. Facing Bonnie now made all his plans seem infantile. Here stood a little girl who he had known for only a short time, a child who could not possibly understand a parent's heartache, nor should she. A wave of despair washes over Crowley. He had never been trying to save Bonnie. He had been trying to save himself. Maybe she's happy here. Maybe she doesn't want to see him. Maybe she doesn't even remember him.

He pats his pockets. "I'm afraid I... Oh, wait." He pulls a small carrot out of his pocket.

"Thanks," she exclaims and snatches the carrot. "Here, Buster!"

The rabbit bounces up, sniffs the carrot then shuffles away.

"I keep telling him that rabbits love carrots, but he doesn't believe me. Do you want to see my swing?"

"Uh... okay."

Bonnie plops down on the wooden seat. "I can go as high as the sky. Watch." She begins to undulate back and forth but goes nowhere. "Can you push me, please?"

Crowley steps up and places his hand on her upper back. He holds it there for a moment. She feels so real. Then he gives her a gentle push.

"Harder."

He obeys.

"Harder!"

He keeps pushing. She swings higher and higher. "I'm flying! Stop!"

He grabs the ropes and slows her down. She jumps off and gives an exaggerated sigh of relief. "That was scary! Let's do it again!"

Crowley gives her half a dozen more rides, each one ending with a panicked command to stop followed by an exhilarated laugh. When she gets off the swing for the last time, she takes Crowley by the hand, "Wanna see the World's Fair?"

Crowley nods, afraid to speak lest he ruin the moment. Bonnie leads him behind the house where the hillside slopes gently into a wooded valley. Far away, shrouded in a violet mist, Crowley sees the outline of a sparkling jeweled tower, rollercoasters and a Ferris wheel.

"I'm going to go there."

"When?"

Bonnie looks up at him with a furtive smile. "Soon. You want some coffee?"

"Sure."

"Don't move." Bonnie runs back toward the house, stops halfway and turns back. "Don't move."

"I won't!" he shouts back. He watches her disappeared into the house then turns back to gaze at the wondrous fair rippling in the distance.

"She wouldn't go without you."

Mina, Dolores' fiery chaperone, stands beside Crowley. Crowley studies the small woman's dark face. Her black eyes once filled him with dread. Now, he finds them profoundly comforting.

"She should have gone a long time ago," Mina continues.

"What do you mean?"

"Look around. It's a big world full of wonderful things. She needs to see it. She needs to grow up, but she's been waiting for you."

"For me to die?"

"No, you idiot. For you to live."

"Here!" Bonnie thrusts a mug of coffee into Crowley's belly. "Just like you like it."

He takes a sip. It's horrible. "Mm-m. Thank you."

"Okay, child. Don't stay out too long," Mina tells Bonnie before reaching up to pat Crowley's cheek. "It's good to see you, boy." With one parting smile, Mina ambles back to the house.

"You want to see my tree house?"

"Of course."

"Finish your coffee."

Crowley holds his breath and gulps down the nasty brew. Bonnie smiles and dashes off. Crowley follows her back to the oak tree where he finds a wooden ladder, which he had not seen before, or perhaps, it had not existed before. Bonnie scrambles up like a monkey.

"Careful," Crowley hears himself say.

"Come on," she shouts as she disappears into a yellow tree house with a green-gabled roof and a window box full of daisies.

Crowley starts to set his empty coffee cup on the ground but discovers that he no longer has it, so he climbs the ladder and joins Bonnie. He has to crouch inside the tiny house, which is lovely and somehow familiar. He scans the white curtains and the sky-blue ceiling painted with clouds and flying horses. This is the room he had planned to make for Bonnie when she returned. Has he imagined this into existence? Or, did Bonnie know?

Bonnie sets two teacups and saucers on a miniature table.

"Would you like one lump or two?"

"One, thank you," he replies as he contorts himself into a tiny chair.

Bonnie picks up a teapot and, to Crowley's relief, pours imaginary tea into their cups. She settles herself into a chair, straightens her back and, with her pinky extended, takes a sip of nonexistent tea.

"Is it too sweet?" she asks.

Crowley takes a pretend sip. "No. It's quite delicious."

Bonnie suppresses a giggle to maintain her aristocratic decorum. "So, how is your business?"

"My, uh…?"

Bonnie snaps her head to one side. "Ilsa," she chides.

Crowley turns to see the porcelain doll sitting at the table, its lifeless blue eyes staring at nothing.

"We are having a grownup conversation. This is no place for children." Bonnie pauses to listen to the doll. "I am, too. Now, please don't interrupt the grownups."

Bonnie turns back to Crowley. "She's glad that you like your tea. Well, *my* business is doing very well. We are doing important things, and we are making a lot of money, and we are going to buy a lot of farms and factories."

Crowley and Bonnie enjoy their teatime discussing important adult things, after which, Bonnie leads him out onto the fields where she impresses him with her cartwheels and her ability to leap over small rocks. She asks for candy, which, of course, he has, but he refuses to give her more than one piece because it might spoil her appetite. She pleads with him, but he stands firm, so she asks him to play tag, which he does. She stops to point out a rainbow and inform him that leprechauns hide their gold there. He explains that rainbows are caused by the diffraction of light through clouds, which makes her laugh because it sounds silly.

They run and laugh and play for hours, and the sun does not move in the sky.

Crowley asks Bonnie no questions. He fears that the slightest rational thought might wake him from this wonderful dream. When they grow tired, they lie on the grass quietly, letting the sun that does not set warm their faces. And, for the first time in many, many years, Oliver Crowley does the unimaginable: He allows himself to be happy.

"You want to see my friend?" Bonnie asks after a long rest.

"You bet," Crowley responds.

Bonnie jumps up, takes his hand and leads him toward the sea. When they crest the ridge of the hill, Bonnie points to a woman sitting on an outcrop of rock several yards away, gazing down at the ocean. Crowley inhales sharply.

"Miss Horowitz."

The young woman's face glows in the golden light of the afternoon sun. She looks profoundly content.

"You know her?" Crowley asks.

"Eliza's my friend."

"Since when?"

"Since always. Ilsa says you don't have friends. Why don't you have friends?"

"I've been busy. Trying to find you."

"Then why didn't you talk to me?"

"When?"

"When I came to see you."

"When did you come to see me?"

"All the time, but there was always fire. I tried to show you my house and tell you about Buster and the World's Fair, but you never heard me 'cause the fire was too loud. And, every time I saw you, it made you sad, so Mina said I should stop seeing you. But, I didn't want you to be sad all time, so I sent Ilsa to keep you company, but she says you're still sad. So, I visit Eliza and Jaime."

"Jaime?"

"Yeah, he's funny. He says things like 'Homey,' and 'Yo loco' and bad words Mina doesn't want me to say. I showed him my house, too."

"Are you talking about dreams? You came to me in my dreams?"

"I stopped because of the fire."

"You came to Miss Horowitz in her dreams?"

"She likes scary movies, but she's nice."

"How did you know about her?"

"The bad man who was going to send me to *Paris*—yuck—he was going to hurt Eliza, so I told her to see you so you could help her and then you'd have a friend, and you'd stop being sad. Mina said it wouldn't work. She's tired of staying here. But it *did* work, 'cause here you are, and there's Eliza, so now you can help her. You're going to, right?"

"How did you know that the bad thing was going to happen?"

"We're on a mountain, silly. You can see real far from here."

"You helped Eliza find me?"

"I told her to take your class 'cause you're funny, and then I invited her to come over. The old man with the beard said you'd come, too, and you did."

"The rabbi was here?"

"Lots of people come to visit. Mina's son, Diego, and Rin Tin Tin. He's so big! I was scared at first, but he was so nice. And, Oliver came. He said you were lost, but you're not lost, 'cause here you are."

"Where are they all now?"

"They went exploring. Mina's going to take me exploring, too, now that you're happy."

Crowley crouches down to face the girl. He feels that he understands everything, but he knows that the ephemeral logic of a dream rarely survives the harsh light of day. He should ask her many more questions, but he only has one.

"Bonnie, do you want to come back with me?"

The child's eyes widened with apprehension. "I want to go to The World's Fair. Mina's going to take me."

Crowley swallows hard and forces himself to smile. "I can't wait to hear all about it someday."

Bonnie glances around conspiratorially and whispers in Crowley's ear. "They have elephants."

She steps back and gives him a glorious smile. "Bye!"

He reaches out and hugs her tightly. The warmth of her small body loosens the last knot of remorse in his chest.

"I love you, Bonnie," he whispers.

"I love you, too, Daddy."

And for the first time since his father died, Aurelio Cienfuegos cries.

Chapter Sixty-One

Eliza watches a tight formation of pelicans glide over the translucent waves that sparkle white and gold in the afternoon sun. She can see hills beyond the sea, valleys, cities, people, past and present. She sees the panoply of random events and responses that have coalesced into a curious creature named Eliza. She laughs at her life's insignificance and weeps at its beauty. A warm serenity washes over her. She closes her eyes and lets the wind blow back her hair.

When she opens them again, the sea has darkened to steel grey. Colors fade as a fog bank rolls over the rocky shore and up the cliff. Eliza doesn't want to leave the mountain, but she must. She vows to cling to the elation of this moment, but she knows that she will not. Bliss does not linger long in the real world. Eliza throws back her head to welcome the cool mist that washes through her, melting the world to white.

                                                         ࡍ ࡏ

Faint shadows danced and swirled, growing darker and sharper until they crystalized into the black-and-white image of a man standing atop the mast of a ship, laughing. The man wore tights with a ridiculously large scarf tied around his head. Music swelled as he grabbed a rope and swung down to fight pirates who looked like they had smeared shoe polish on their faces.

Silent films are dumb.

"Miss Horowitz?"

Oliver Crowley's face blocked her view of the movie. "Miss Horowitz, can you hear me?"

Eliza sat up slowly. She was in her father's screening room.

"What do you remember?" he asked.

Everything. Eliza looked into Crowley's anxious eyes and felt a rush of sympathy. "She's wonderful."

Crowley blinked and cleared his throat. "Yes," he managed to say.

He helped her up. Eliza saw Jaime, and the homunculus, and an army of decomposing skeletons, which should have intrigued her, but didn't. Someone screamed. She turned and saw Ethan drop to the ground.

"He's happy to see you," Crowley explained.

Eliza nodded. *Poor Ethan.* She looked down at her blood-drenched clothing and ran her fingers over her neck.

"How do you feel?" Crowley asked, reaching his hand out to her, but stopping short of making contact.

"Okay," she replied. In fact, she felt wonderful. She had yet to lose the euphoria from her time on the mountain. She tried to define the feeling. If she could find the right word to describe her epiphany, she could hold onto it, or at least recall it from time to time. *Happiness?* No, too general. *Peace of mind?* Yes, but more than that. *Wisdom?* Again, too vague.

She heard screams and explosions outside. The room shook. Her ruminations would have to wait. She needed to go out there. She didn't bother to consider the danger. Everything that had happened—the book, the demons, the dream, the prolicide—they all revolved around her. Eliza had to confront her father and… She didn't know what she would do precisely, but as sure as the sun rose in the morning, she had to face him. She took a deep breath and stepped toward the door.

"Where are you going?" asked Crowley.

"To close the gates of hell." She stopped before the mob of skeletons who blocked the exit. "Excuse me," Eliza requested politely. The skeletons shuffled aside.

Crowley stopped her at the door. "You should not go out there."

Eliza studied Crowley's face. He looked calm, not in his typically cold, detached manner, but with a warmth that she had not seen before. He was being kind. Was that the word to describe her time on the mountain? *Kindness?* Still, too vague.

"Where *should* I go?" she replied.

Crowley furrowed his brow. He knew as well as she did that there was no escape. Her father, the demons, hell, they would soon torment everyone, everywhere, physically and psychically. She had to go.

Another explosion shook the room. Light fixtures burst in showering sparks. The screen froze on a close-up of Charles Delamour flashing his trademark roughish smile before it went black.

Crowley sighed fatalistically and pulled out his revolver. Although Eliza hated guns, she found the sight of Crowley loading bullets into his ridiculously large weapon comforting, not because it could save them—the thing had already proven useless against Aurora—but because it showed her that Crowley cared.

Caring? No.

If Eliza couldn't define her experience verbally, she would have to rely on an image. She recalled the sun setting over the sea, and her trepidation abated slightly.

Crowley opened the screening room door.

"You can't go out there!" screamed Ethan as he stumbled up to them. "That guy's huge, and he has horns, and he shoots lightning, and he's huge!"

Crowley put his hand on Ethan's shoulder. "Young man, to win a woman's heart, you must show courage."

"Aw, jeez!" moaned Ethan and turned to Eliza. "Are you really going out there?"

She nodded.

Ethan winced. "Will you like me if I go with you?"

"I won't like you less."

"Aw, jeez," he whined.

Eliza sighed the way girls do when they're about to boss a boy around. She brushed the hair off his face, untucked his filthy polo shirt, and gave him a hug.

"You did that just so I'd come with you, didn't you?"

"No," Eliza replied kindly.

Ethan's chest filled with air. He gritted his teeth and bravely whimpered, "Let's do this."

Crowley marched out of the screening room. Eliza, Ethan, Jaime, the homunculus, and the skeletons followed. Ryan intercepted them before they reached the back of the house.

"Eliza!" he gasped. "Are you all right? I was so worried about you. Have you seen what's going on out there? We've got to get out of here. Come on. I know a way."

"It's okay, Ryan."

"No, it's not. What are you talking about?" he asked, glancing from Jaime, to the zombies, to Crowley.

"Professor, this is Ryan."

"We've met," Crowley remarked evenly. Then he pulled out his revolver and shot Ryan in the face.

The young man disappeared in a puff of smoke. In his place, stood a grotesquely old, bipedal iguana in old-fashioned pajamas and a night cap.

The iguana let out a deafening squeal.

"Ow!" Eliza exclaimed, covering her ears, more disturbed by the gunshot than the revelation that she had dated a lizard.

"How did you know?" Iguana Ryan asked Crowley in a wheezy old voice.

"You saw the flying demon without looking up; ergo you have a third, parietal, eye atop your head, common to iguanas and other select reptilian species."

"Very observant, Professor. I applaud your—"

Crowley shot him again.

"AH!" Eliza and Ryan screamed simultaneously, for different reasons.

Crowley turned to Ethan. "This is your cue."

It took Ethan a second to catch on, but he did. "Tear him apart!" he yelled. His zombies hurled themselves at Ryan, who dropped on all fours and scurried away as fast as an arthritic iguana chased by two dozen rabid human skeletons could.

A few days ago, Eliza would have marveled at discovering that she had contemplated sleeping with a demon. Today, she found it mundane. She pushed past Crowley and stepped outside. Her father's well-manicured Bel Air backyard had turned into a hellish inferno worthy of a Bosch triptych. Flames rose from the earth, releasing a kaleidoscope of horrors into the night. Skeletal faces frozen in agony, wolves with human bodies, serpents with goat heads, rodents clutching severed human body parts, pig-men, lizard-bats, fish-birds, and a multitude of other creatures that some perverted creator had ripped apart and rearranged haphazardly surged into the air and through Eliza's mind, obliterating the boundary between thought and matter, reality and fantasy.

Naked, slack-jawed youths danced around dozens of bonfires, occasionally dropping to the ground and ranting in strange languages. Beyond the celebrants rose a massive dome made of stone. It had a tall, arched entrance, and within it burned a tremendous fire. Atop this giant oven, upon a black granite throne, sat Moloch, revered as Ba'al by the ancient Carthaginians, Kronos by the Phoenicians, King of the First Kingdom, God of the Half-Born, devourer of children. He had the head of a bull and the body of a man. A gold ring pierced his snout, and a pentagram branded his muscular chest. And, of course, he had horns.

Moloch held his arms out and bellowed, "My beloved children, tear down the system! Recruit the faithful! Bring the apostates that they may pass through my sacred fire!"

The students wailed their approval.

Beside Moloch, dwarfed by his size, but somehow more commanding, hovered Aurora. Her robe, now blood red, billowed around her. A fluorescent-green miasma oozed from her hands, curled down onto the ground and spread through the crowd. She had no face. The void beneath her hood consumed light and hope.

A wave of dread washed over Eliza, not for herself—she had sat on the mountain, gazing at the infinite sea. She did not fear death. She was afraid for her father. Eliza could feel the anxiety driving his ferocious rapture. She could see the insecure, plaintive man inside the beast. If only she could reach him.

Crowley sensed her concern. "Miss Horowitz?"

She looked at him, mute with grief.

"Don't worry. I'm here. I promise that I will—"

A massive swarm of flying wraiths crashed into Crowley and swept him off into the dark sky.

"Professor!" cried Eliza. She looked around. Jaime, Ethan, and the skeletons had disappeared as well.

"I am the god of hell on earth!"

Demons encircled Eliza. A cacophony of threats and insults rang through her brain. "Pitiful! Worthless! Despair and die!"

"Daddy!" she called out.

The demons stopped. An eerie silence followed, pierced by a shrill laugh that heralded disaster. The demons parted, creating an open passage between Eliza and Aurora.

"Eliza," Aurora intoned in her true, horrendous voice.

"Daddy!" she cried.

"I am Moloch! Come to me, my children!" the bull god shouted, shooting bolts of lightning from his hands aimlessly into the night.

He can't hear me.

"He can hear you," Aurora rasped, reading her thoughts. "He just doesn't care. He never has."

"Daddy?" pleaded Eliza.

"Why should he? You are pathetic."

The creature's words tore through Eliza's chest.

"You're worthless."

Aurora's taunts echoed through the depths of Eliza's soul. They were the very words she heard when she was alone, friendless, fatherless, when her mother would yell at her in the night. Once, the words had cast her down into a pit of despair, where she feared she would die, all alone. But she never did, because Eliza had never been alone. The little girl had always arrived at the right moment with a kind word, a smile, or a liberating shrug of indifference that had swept away Eliza's fears. The little girl had been with her, always, and she always would be.

"He bred you to slaughter like a pig," growled Aurora.

That is true, Eliza admitted with cool detachment.

"He never loved you."

Is that true? Eliza shut her eyes. Memories flashed through her mind—her head resting on her father's shoulder while they watched a Buster Keaton film, his beaming face when he picked her up at the airport, his laughter when they gobbled down chicken at The Ivy, the admiration in his eyes when she recited Shakespeare, his gratitude when she helped him pick out his clothes, his tears when he left her at the airport, and the letters he wrote condemning the world but praising her.

He did love me.

Aurora laughed derisively. Eliza looked past the malicious goddess to her father, who sat on his massive chair, screaming and laughing, reveling in his size and strength. His eyes darted about with frenzied elation. This was the culmination of his life's work, his great dream—to sit on a rock and rule the world, unassailable and safe. She recalled what he said before he took her life. He had grown up in a ghetto, menaced by neighbors, powerless to defend himself. He had watched his mother die. He couldn't save her. Shame must have haunted him his entire life. He lived in constant fear. He needed refuge. He needed power. To achieve this, he gave up everything, including his child, the only person in the world who loved him unconditionally. He sacrificed love to squelch the terror that tormented him, never realizing that only love can conquer fear, and there he sat, upon his ridiculous throne, the god of... what?

An overwhelming feeling of pity washed over Eliza.

"Oh, Daddy," she whispered. "I am so sorry."

The world stopped. Demons quieted. Students stood still. Aurora hissed.

Moloch finally looked at her. He snorted. He did not know Eliza, but she knew him. She saw through the madness in his grey eyes. She recognized the horrific monster for what he truly was and had always been. A scared little boy. Her heart went out to him.

Compassion.

That was the word. That was what she felt atop the mountain as she looked at her life and the life of all human beings, every one of them desperately searching for a little peace in their pitiful, beautiful lives.

"She's trying to destroy you!" screamed Aurora. "Kill her!"

Moloch's eyes turned bright red, just like in Eliza's dreams. He thrust his arms out and blasted Eliza with a tremendous bolt of lightning. The world exploded in blinding light that rocked the earth and obliterated the sky. On and on it came, burning brighter, thundering louder, reeking of smoke and ozone.

When the barrage finally ceased, Eliza stood, unharmed and unaffected. Moloch gaped at her, confused and frightened. It broke her heart.

"Daddy," she said. "I forgive you."

Moloch lurched back as if she had punched him in the chest. Aurora wailed. Students and demons froze. The ensuing silence lasted but a moment before Eliza felt her heart open, and with a tremendous shriek, the demons swirled through the air and swept straight into her chest. Eliza gasped. As the whirlpool of horrors passed through her, she saw the demons for what they really were: wretched manifestations of anger, loss, jealousy and fear—so much fear.

In that instant, Eliza understood her nightmare. When she had tried to enter the house, she always ended up back where she started. She could not move forward or backward. She was rooted to the spot like the door itself because... she *was* the door. *She* was the gate to hell. The wound through which demons entered the world was not a tear somewhere in the cosmos. It was inside her. It was her own personal injury, created by her father's abandonment, intentionally exacerbated by his dark arts. The wound was deep and terrible, but it was hers. Which meant, she could mend it.

Compassion. That was Bonnie's gift to Eliza. Years of spiritual companionship and gentle guidance led Eliza to that mountain and to the realization that she had the power to heal herself. She could forgive.

The more demons she took in, the calmer they grew, as if accepting their pain alleviated it. By the time the last demon disappeared inside her heart, all their power had gone.

Only her father remained. Moloch glared down at Eliza with terror in his eyes. Then with a sickening wheeze, he deflated like a balloon.

"No!" he screamed as he shriveled.

"Daddy, you can stop this!" Eliza shouted as he shrank. "It's not too late. You have a choice. Forgive your father. Forgive them all."

"I am Moloch!" he wailed as he grew smaller and smaller.

"You don't have to be alone. Stay with me!"

He withered until he was no more than an insect hovering before her eyes. "I am the god of hell," he squeaked. Then he vanished in an insignificant puff of smoke.

"And hell is a small place," Eliza whispered.

The world fell quiet. The naked students looked bewildered as if they'd just woken up from a dream, which they had. One girl screamed, covered herself, and ran. *Poor Tammy.* All trace of hell had vanished but for a solitary malevolence blotting the starry sky.

Aurora's red robe rippled like flames rising from a black hole. Eliza tried to step back, but Aurora held her in place. Eliza could only gape in horror as the apparition pulled her into the dark hole that should have held a face.

Chapter Sixty-Two

Eliza falls through nothingness, tumbling aimlessly, powerless and alone.

Now, she walks through a stone chamber so vast that its massive columns disappear into the distance as if reflected between mirrors. The floor is dirt, and the ceiling too distant to see. A dull green light weighs her down, making each step slow and cumbersome.

Not again, she thinks, not because she has been here before, she has not, not even in her nightmares, but because this place has always been a part of her. It is a primal place, immutable and timeless, made from the cold stone of reality that exposes the insignificance of all human endeavors and confirms the fundamental truth that all sentient beings try to deny: Life is nothing.

Eliza hears vague whispers but sees no one.

"Hello?" Her voice dies in her mouth as if sound has no air through which to travel. The whispers grow louder.

Two fountains of fire ignite before her, illuminating a staircase that rises to a craggy dais where a black figure, more shadow than substance, sits upon an ancient curule. The silhouette ripples as if it were breathing. Eliza doubts that it is. The apparition raises a long black arm, and light flares behind her. Eliza turns. Above her, suspended from a rusted hook, hangs the purple mottled corpse of a woman. Another hook dangles beside the body. It is empty.

For me, she realizes.

The shadow stands and a terrible voice rips through Eliza's head, "I am Ereshkegal. Daughter of Enki. Wife of Man. First Mother. Welcome."

Gaunt, ashen waifs, draped in rags, emerge from the darkness. Their plaintive eyes glimmer in the firelight as they converge upon Eliza, dirt dribbling from their mouths, moaning so desperately that Eliza's chest aches with sorrow. The pathetic children press their filthy bodies against her and paw at her face. Eliza recoils, but they overwhelm her, holding her arms and legs, smothering her. They lift her off her feet and pass her over their heads, one to another, up a pyramid of writhing children, higher and higher…

Toward the empty hook.

Eliza screams as they lower her onto the sharp iron. It pierces her upper back, and her mind explodes with white, blinding pain.

The dirt feels cold against her face. Eliza opens her eyes. She's lying on the floor of the immense chamber. The shadow and the children have gone. Only the corpse, rotting on the hook, remains.

The cadaver opens its eyes.

"The sacrifice was not made," the dead woman says, without moving her black rotted mouth, in a voice so comforting that Eliza's fear dissolves.

A strong hand grips Eliza's arm and lifts her up.

Chapter Sixty-Three

"Miss Horowitz? Can you hear me?"

Eliza blinked and saw Crowley standing before her. Jaime loomed behind him with the homunculus on his shoulder. Ethan sat on the grass several yards away, disheveled but alive. Students ran in haphazard clusters, fleeing her father's devastated backyard. She did not see Aurora.

"Her name is Ereshkegal," Eliza whispered.

Crowley winced in recognition.

"She was going to kill me, but then she didn't. A dead woman on a hook said the sacrifice hadn't been made. What did she mean?"

"You lived," replied Crowley pensively. "There was no sacrifice. Ereshkegal has no power over you."

"Who is Ereshkegal?"

"According to legend, she is Adam's first wife, expelled from the garden because she wouldn't submit to him."

"Submit?"

"Ereshkegal fancied herself Adam's equal—"

"Fancied?"

"So, the Creator banished her to the underworld and made her barren, according to Sumerian texts. Babylonians claimed she ate children. Hebrew mystics called her Lilith, a demonic seductress. Zoroastrians describe her as—"

"Wait," Eliza commanded, rubbing her temples. "First of all, this is *so* sexist. She wouldn't submit so now she's a child-eating whore? Plus, Adam and Eve aren't real. It's just a story."

"Everything is just a story, Miss Horowitz."

"So, my stupid stepmother was the very first woman *ever*?"

"According to the ancient tablets found in the ziggurat of An."

"And Adam rejected her because she thought she was his equal?"

"Yes."

"No wonder she's so angry."

"Hell hath no fury like a woman scorned."

"*That's* sexist, too!"

"It's Shakespeare."

"It's William Congreve, but that's not my point."

"And Congreve was sexist?"

"Of course, but he lived in the 1600s. He was a product of his time."

"As am I, Miss Horowitz."

Eliza frowned. Now she sympathized with the demon who wanted to kill her. She could hear Ereshkegal's voice in her head. *Welcome.* She wasn't gone. She waited in the shadows of Eliza's own rage, biding her time, searching for a breach to exploit, aching for vengeance against humanity. Eliza thought of the horror movie poster in her room and realized that she had finally become the Sentinel. *Be careful what you wish for.* Perhaps, everyone bore some responsibility for keeping demons at bay, but that did not mitigate Eliza's obligation. The gates were within her. She must keep them closed.

A police helicopter roared overhead, illuminating the fleeing students with its spotlight.

Eliza began to ask an unformed question, but Crowley interrupted her. "I could use a hearty meal, you?"

Eliza exhaled. "Yes."

Chapter Sixty-Four

Jaime hadn't used public transportation since he was a kid. He forgot how much he liked it. Every Sunday his grandfather would take him on the bus to the zoo or a museum. His grandfather always let him sit by the window. It was great, 'cause he could just kick back and talk and look around and not have to worry about driving or getting his car scratched up, or Angel telling him where to go. 'Course he didn't have to worry about that anymore, what with Angel being dead and all.

Yeah, Jaime really liked this train chugging along under the city. It had these old ads over the windows for soda and cigarettes and booze. It must have been fun to live back then with no one telling you to eat kale and recycle and shit. Jaime hated recycling. He did it 'cause, you know, you were supposed to, but it really pissed him off.

Best thing about this train was it was empty except for him and Little Cholo, who was swinging on the handholds like a monkey.

Little Cholo sure had a lot of energy. Not Jaime. He was real tired. Well, not so much tired as dead, which he figured was just being really, really tired. He didn't know what was going to happen next, and he didn't really care. He was in hell. *What's the worst that can happen?*

Jaime'd kinda hoped that when Eliza killed the devil, he'd get to go to heaven, but now he realized how stupid that was. He didn't belong in heaven. He'd never done anything good except when he *had* to, like recycling. He always did the easy thing. Guys like his grandfather, they'd done hard things like go to war and raise a family and shave every day. Jaime wished his grandfather hadn't died when he did, and that his mom hadn't married Vince, and that he'd listened to his teachers instead of his homeboys, and that he'd asked Sandy if she wanted to get some coffee or something. He'd messed up his life pretty bad, and now he had nothing to live for, which was funny 'cause he wasn't living. He was dead, but he could still think about things. Then Jaime realized that was his punishment. It wasn't devils and fire. It was thinking. He had to relive all his fuck-ups over and over again, and he couldn't do nothing about it. He couldn't change a pinche thing.

Hell is having no hope.

Jaime sat there like a lump of dirt, feeling really bad while the train cruised down the tunnel and Little Cholo ripped up the upholstery.

Then he felt this tiny spark in his chest. It wasn't much, just this little zing that kinda tickled. *What is that?* He concentrated on it, and it got bigger and buzzed down his arms and legs. It was a feeling, a good one, like something nice could happen—maybe, somewhere—but he couldn't figure out what. It had to have a name. He thought about it real hard, and a word popped into his head, and he knew its name. He wanted to say it out loud, so he pushed as hard as he could, straining and groaning until he heard the word come out of his mouth.

"Eliza."

Chapter Sixty-Five

When the match ended, and the sweaty cricket players ran to the pond, shedding their whites to frolic naked in the water alongside their delighted spaniels, Eliza thought, *Rule Britannia.*

She had made friends with a young British couple while hiking the West Highland Way in Scotland, and they'd invited her to their family's annual cricket match in Wiltshire. "It will be the most English day you will ever have," they'd promised.

The night before, Eliza had shopped furiously for a floral dress and a big white picture hat, which she claimed to have brought from home when the young man picked her up in his red roadster convertible, explaining with a casual shrug that "You never know."

They sat in loungers along the cricket pitch, beneath the spires of Fonthill Abbey, while the young man's father kept score in the same book the family had used since 1925. During the tea interval, they strolled over to a long table under the trees, arrayed with scones, clotted cream, meat pies, cold game pie, stewed tomatoes, and fairy cakes.

After watching the boys swim, they all retired to the family's estate where they sat on fabulous shabby sofas, drinking wine, surrounded by dogs, and talked until late in the evening.

It had indeed been the most English day of her life and one of the most magical.

Eliza had decided to take time off school after her ordeal. The surreal incident shocked the nation. Psychologists and law enforcement officials attributed the students' aberrant behavior to collective hysteria induced by drugs and peer pressure. Most people found that explanation hard to believe after watching hundreds of online videos of a giant bull shooting fire into the sky. Moloch's appearance dominated news cycles throughout the world. People couldn't get enough of demonic beasts and ogres. Students recounted their harrowing stories on social media. They started political movements such as Hell No, You Too? and No Lives Matter to protest Satan, Hollywood, Wall Street, processed foods, and many other bad things. Eliza's roommate, Tammy, started her own YouTube channel, "Children of the Night," which received millions of hits a week, turning her into a major influencer.

Ethan, whom hundreds of students had seen commanding an army of skeletal zombies, became quite popular on campus. He switched his major to Film and Television and made a series of short films about a demon-hunting lady's man, starring himself, that were so bad they became cult classics, landing him a development deal with Warner Brothers.

Eliza just wanted to get away. She knew that the police would not believe her story about her father's disappearance, but since a few thousand students corroborated her version of events, and they found no evidence of foul play, within a month, Eliza had cut her hair short and boarded a plane to Britain. By the time she saw the handsome cricket players jump into the pond, the twenty-four-hour news cycle had lost interest in demonic bacchanalias. Although, it spawned a slew of memoirs, movies, graphic novels, and television shows. "The Hollywood Hell House," as the event came to be called, much like "The Tinseltown Tragedy of 1925," became just another unexplained mystery to delight conspiracy theorists and their poorly educated believers.

After spending a couple of wonderful months in Britain, Eliza backpacked the continent as young people often do. She explored museums, cafés, and castles through France, Italy, and Greece. She socialized with other young travelers, and finally, she had sex.

He was an older man, of course. Eliza hadn't changed into a different person in a puff of smoke. He was in his midthirties, but he was very different from her father and Oliver Crowley. Gabriel was a gregarious, floppy-haired, Spanish artist that she met in Malaga. He barely spoke English, and she pretended not to understand Spanish, so they got along beautifully. She posed for him. He taught her to make paella and to appreciate a good sherry. They spent two glorious weeks wandering the sunny beaches of the Mediterranean, after which he returned to his wife in Madrid, and she came back to Los Angeles with several charcoal sketches that she would lock away until she met someone new.

She sat on the beach in Santa Monica watching the sunset. She had just registered for spring quarter after having taken almost a year off school. She was looking forward to her new classes. Her recent experiences had matured her. She felt centered, confident. From now on, she would love wisely and hate reluctantly.

Something's gained and something's lost.

She hadn't seen Oliver Crowley since that night.

After leaving her father's house, she had parted company with Ethan, who had earned her respect by facing a demonic god as bravely as any rational human being could. Jaime and the homunculus went back to the lab, and she allowed Crowley to take her to Musso and Frank's in Hollywood. Crowley paid the maître d' a substantial tip to secure the corner table where he ordered a gin martini and sighed wistfully as he scanned the wood-paneled dining room with its soft lighting, mahogany bar, and liveried waiters.

"This used to be my booth until Charlie Chaplin started joining me for lunch. Then it became his booth. Fame has its prerogatives."

Crowley sipped his martini, which he did not allow Eliza to taste because she was underage, and then he did something that took her by surprise. He talked about himself. He told her about his mother and father. He described the small farm, his father's love of Don Quixote, and his own tragic love for Dolores. He recounted his sudden rise to fame and the night that destroyed his life. She listened intently when he mentioned her father. Crowley did not malign him, but the truth came through. Jack Larson had been well on his way to becoming Moloch even back then. Eliza's presence may have softened him somewhat, but it had not changed him.

Eliza cried. Crowley waited patiently until, after quite a while, her sobs culminated in one long, heartrending sigh. She blew her nose into Crowley's handkerchief and handed it back to him. He folded it neatly and returned it to his pocket before talking about her grandfather, the rabbi. Crowley had grown to love the old man. He described how the rabbi and Rudolf Valentino's wife had tried to save Bonnie and helped get her to Russia where the rabbi taught him the great art.

Crowley spoke for two hours until Eliza had finished her second helping of chocolate pie and he had taken his last sip of espresso. Then, he laid a wad of cash on the table and stood. "I'll have the maître d' call you a cab," he announced and marched out of the restaurant. Eliza found him standing on the sidewalk shaking his head. "Hollywood is not what it used to be."

"It was nice back then?"

Crowley thought about it for a moment. "It was."

Eliza gazed at the lights of the old Egyptian Theater across the street. Her father's movies must have played there in the 1920s. She stifled a sob. She would relive this terrible night over and over for the rest of her life, but for now, she just felt grateful to be alive.

"What about Bonnie?" she asked.

Crowley did not respond. Eliza pressed him. "Will you try to bring her back?"

"I will give her the burial she deserves."

"May I come?"

"That is an ordeal I would prefer to face alone."

Eliza nodded. "What are you going to do after that?"

"I'll go to Union, Georgia."

"What's in Georgia?"

"The grandson of a very brave man."

"Will I see you again?"

"If you need me, go to Santa Monica beach at sunset."

"You'll be there?"

"Of course not, but a good sunset will make you feel better."

A taxi pulled up, and Crowley opened the door for her.

"What's the meaning of life?" she asked.

"Excuse me?"

"In class, you were about to tell us the secret of life, then you stopped. What is it?"

Crowley studied her for a moment then replied with a shrug. "Don't die."

Eliza scowled. She didn't like that answer.

"Good night—"

"Wait," she interrupted. "What did you and my grandfather do all those years? What about World War II and the holocaust? When did you come to America? Who was the dead woman hanging from a hook? What did—?"

Crowley held up his hand. "Those, Miss Horowitz, are tales for another day."

And with that, Eliza stepped into the cab.

☙ ❧

Oliver Crowley had been right. The sunset did make her feel better. She promised to treat herself to more of them. She lay back on the sand, closed her eyes and drifted off to sleep. She dreamt of the Scottish Highlands, cricket matches, and paella until her phone jolted her awake. It was a strange number. She would have let it go to voice mail if she had not recognized it as a European country code.

"Hello?"

"Miss Horowitz."

She inhaled sharply. He had never called her before. *How did he get my number?* It had taken her a considerable amount of time to come to terms with her father's death. She had worked hard on herself. She had met new people and seen new places. She had discovered that the world was a wondrous place full of possibilities that she could experience on her own terms. Crowley reminded her of her old self, the child she had outgrown. If she were to have a cordial relationship with him now, it could only be as equals. She took a deep, centering breath.

"Professor," she replied in a calm, steady tone.

"What do you know about vampires?"

Eliza gasped with excitement.

"Everything."

ACKNOWLEDGMENTS

It takes a village to write a novel. Many talented people helped this story come to life, but I'll mention only two because I'm lazy and forgetful. I would like to thank my longtime collaborator and friend, the superb storyteller Lana Griffin. I would never have attempted a novel without her help. And, I want to thank my wife, Carol Barbee, who inspires me every day with her great talent, courage, and kindness.

About the Author

Carlos Lacámara is a Cuban born actor and playwright. His plays, *Becoming Cuban, Havana Bourgeois, Exiles, Cuba Libre,* and *Nowhere on the Border,* have been produced in New York, Los Angeles, Miami, and Portland. *Eliza and the Alchemist* is his first novel, and he may or may not be doing research for a sequel. He lives in Santa Monica, California, with his loving wife, Carol Barbee, and their even more loving dog, Gracie.

Made in the USA
Monee, IL
12 April 2025